AMERICAN PSYCHO

Bret Easton Ellis is the author of six novels,
Less Than Zero, *The Rules of Attraction*, *American
Psycho*, *Glamorama*, *Lunar Park* and most recently
Imperial Bedrooms, which was a *Sunday Times* Top Ten
Bestseller, and a collection of stories, *The Informers*.
His work has been translated into twenty-seven
languages. He lives in Los Angeles.

D1342318

BRET EASTON ELLIS

AMERICAN PSYCHO

PICADOR

First published 1991 by Vintage Books, a division of Random House, Inc., New York

First published in Great Britain in paperback 1991 by Picador

This edition published 2011 by Picador
an imprint of Pan Macmillan, a division of Macmillan Publishers Limited
Pan Macmillan, 20 New Wharf Road, London N1 9RR
Basingstoke and Oxford
Associated companies throughout the world
www.panmacmillan.com

ISBN 978-0-330-53630-1

Typeset by SetSystems Ltd, Saffron Walden, Essex
Printed in the UK by CPI Mackays, Chatham ME5 8TD

Visit **www.picador.com** to read more about all our books
and to buy them. You will also find features, author interviews and
news of any author events, and you can sign up for e-newsletters
so that you're always first to hear about our new releases.

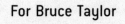

For Bruce Taylor

Both the author of these *Notes* and the *Notes* themselves are, of course, fictional. Nevertheless, such persons as the composer of these *Notes* not only exist in our society, but indeed must exist, considering the circumstances under which our society has generally been formed. I have wished to bring before the public, somewhat more distinctly than usual, one of the characters of our recent past. He represents a generation that is still living out its days among us. In the fragment entitled "Underground" this personage described himself and his views and attempts, as it were, to clarify the reasons why he appeared and was bound to appear in our midst. The subsequent fragment will consist of the actual "notes," concerning certain events in his life.

Fyodor Dostoevsky, *Notes from Underground*

One of the major mistakes people make is that they think manners are only the expression of happy ideas. There's a whole range of behavior that can be expressed in a mannerly way. That's what civilization is all about—doing it in a mannerly and not an antagonistic way. One of the places we went wrong was the naturalistic Rousseauean movement of the sixties in which people said, "Why can't you just say what's on your mind?" In civilization there have to be some restraints. If we followed every impulse, we'd be killing one another.

Miss Manners (Judith Martin)

And as things fell apart
Nobody paid much attention

Talking Heads

AMERICAN PSYCHO

APRIL FOOLS

Abandon all hope ye who enter here is scrawled in blood red
lettering on the side of the Chemical Bank near the corner of
Eleventh and First and is in print large enough to be seen from the
backseat of the cab as it lurches forward in the traffic leaving Wall
Street and just as Timothy Price notices the words a bus pulls up,
the advertisement for *Les Misérables* on its side blocking his view,
but Price who is with Pierce & Pierce and twenty-six doesn't seem
to care because he tells the driver he will give him five dollars to
turn up the radio, "Be My Baby" on WYNN, and the driver, black,
not American, does so.

"I'm resourceful," Price is saying. "I'm creative, I'm young,
unscrupulous, highly motivated, highly skilled. In essence what I'm
saying is that society can*not* afford to lose me. I'm an *asset*." Price
calms down, continues to stare out the cab's dirty window, probably
at the word FEAR sprayed in red graffiti on the side of a McDonald's
on Fourth and Seventh. "I mean the fact remains that no one gives
a shit about their work, everybody hates their job, *I* hate my job,
you've told me you hate yours. What do I do? Go back to Los
Angeles? *Not* an alternative. I didn't transfer from UCLA to Stan-
ford to put up with this. I mean am I *alone* in thinking we're not
making enough money?" Like in a movie another bus appears,
another poster for *Les Misérables* replaces the word—not the same
bus because someone has written the word DYKE over Eponine's
face. Tim blurts out, "I have a co-op here. I have a place in the
*Hamp*tons, for Christ sakes."

"Parents', guy. It's the parents'."

"I'm *buy*ing it from them. Will you fucking turn this *up*?" he
snaps but distractedly at the driver, the Crystals still blaring from
the radio.

"It don't go up no higher," maybe the driver says.

Timothy ignores him and irritably continues. "I could stay living in this city if they just installed Blaupunkts in the cabs. Maybe the ODM III or ORC II dynamic tuning systems?" His voice softens here. "Either one. Hip my friend, very hip."

He takes off the expensive-looking Walkman from around his neck, still complaining. "I hate to complain—I really do—about the trash, the garbage, the disease, about how filthy this city really is and *you* know and I know that it is a *sty* . . ." He continues talking as he opens his new Tumi calfskin attaché case he bought at D. F. Sanders. He places the Walkman in the case alongside a Panasonic wallet-size cordless portable folding Easa-phone (he used to own the NEC 9000 Porta portable) and pulls out today's newspaper. "In one issue—in *one* issue—let's see here . . . strangled models, babies thrown from tenement rooftops, kids killed in the subway, a Communist rally, Mafia boss wiped out, Nazis"—he flips through the pages excitedly—"baseball players with AIDS, more Mafia shit, gridlock, the homeless, various maniacs, faggots dropping like flies in the streets, surrogate mothers, the cancellation of a soap opera, kids who broke into a zoo and tortured and burned various animals alive, more Nazis . . . and the joke is, the punch line is, it's all in this city—nowhere else, just here, it sucks, whoa wait, more Nazis, gridlock, gridlock, baby-sellers, black-market babies, AIDS babies, baby junkies, building collapses on baby, maniac baby, gridlock, bridge collapses—" His voice stops, he takes in a breath and then quietly says, his eyes fixed on a beggar at the corner of Second and Fifth, "That's the twenty-fourth one I've seen today. I've kept count." Then asks without looking over, "Why aren't you wearing the worsted navy blue blazer with the gray pants?" Price is wearing a six-button wool and silk suit by Ermenegildo Zegna, a cotton shirt with French cuffs by Ike Behar, a Ralph Lauren silk tie and leather wing tips by Fratelli Rossetti. Pan down to the *Post*. There is a moderately interesting story concerning two people who disappeared at a party aboard the yacht of a semi-noted New York socialite while the boat was circling the island. A residue of spattered blood and three smashed champagne glasses are the only clues. Foul play is suspected and police think that perhaps a machete was the killer's weapon because of certain grooves and indentations found on the deck. No bodies have been found. There are no suspects. Price began his spiel today over lunch and then brought it up again during the squash game and continued ranting over drinks at Harry's where he had gone on, over three J&Bs and water, much more interestingly about the Fisher account that Paul Owen is handling. Price will not shut up.

"Diseases!" he exclaims, his face tense with pain. "There's this theory out now that if you can catch the AIDS virus through having *sex* with someone who *is* infected then you can also catch *any*thing, whether it's a virus per se or not—Alzheimer's, muscular dystrophy, hemophilia, leukemia, anorexia, diabetes, cancer, multiple sclerosis, cystic fibrosis, cerebral palsy, dyslexia, for Christ sakes—you can get dyslexia from *pussy*—"

"I'm not sure, guy, but I don't think dyslexia is a virus."

"Oh, who knows? *They* don't know that. Prove it."

Outside this cab, on the sidewalks, black and bloated pigeons fight over scraps of hot dogs in front of a Gray's Papaya while transvestites idly look on and a police car cruises silently the wrong way down a one-way street and the sky is low and gray and in a cab that's stopped in traffic across from this one, a guy who looks a lot like Luis Carruthers waves over at Timothy and when Timothy doesn't return the wave the guy—slicked-back hair, suspenders, horn-rimmed glasses—realizes it's not who he thought it was and looks back at his copy of *USA Today*. Panning down to the sidewalk there's an ugly old homeless bag lady holding a whip and she cracks it at the pigeons who ignore it as they continue to peck and fight hungrily over the remains of the hot dogs and the police car disappears into an underground parking lot.

"But then, when you've just come to the point when your reaction to the times is one of total and sheer acceptance, when your body has become some *tuned* into the insanity and you reach that point where it all makes sense, when it clicks, we get some crazy fucking homeless nigger who actually *wants*—listen to me, Bateman—*wants* to be out on the streets, this, *those* streets, see, *those*"—he points—"and we have a mayor who won't listen to her, a mayor who won't let the *bitch* have her way—Holy Christ—*let* the fucking bitch *freeze* to death, *put* her out of her own goddamn self-made misery, and look, you're back where you started, confused, fucked . . . Number twenty-four, nope, twenty-five . . . Who's going to be at Evelyn's? Wait, let me guess." He holds up a hand attached to an impeccable manicure. "Ashley, Courtney, Muldwyn,

Marina, Charles—am I right so far? Maybe one of Evelyn's 'artiste' friends from ohmygod the 'East' Village. You know the type—the ones who ask Evelyn if she has a nice dry *white* chardonnay—" He slaps a hand over his forehead and shuts his eyes and now he mutters, jaw clenched, "I'm leaving. I'm dumping Meredith. She's essentially *daring* me to like her. I'm gone. Why did it take me so long to realize that she has all the personality of a goddamn game-show host? . . . Twenty-six, twenty-seven . . . I mean I tell her I'm sensitive. I told her I was freaked out by the *Challenger* accident—what more does she want? I'm ethical, tolerant, I mean I'm extremely satisfied with my life, I'm optimistic about the future—I mean, aren't you?"

"Sure, but—"

"And all I get is *shit* from her . . . Twenty-eight, twenty-nine, holy shit it's a goddamn *cluster* of bums. I tell you—" He stops suddenly, as if exhausted, and turning away from another advertisement for *Les Misérables*, remembering something important, asks, "Did you read about the host from that game show on TV? He killed two teenage boys? Depraved faggot. Droll, really droll." Price waits for a reaction. There is none. Suddenly: Upper West Side.

He tells the driver to stop on the corner of Eighty-first and Riverside since the street doesn't go the right way.

"Don't bother going arou—" Price begins.

"Maybe I go other way around," the cabdriver says.

"Do not bother." Then barely an aside, teeth gritted, unsmiling: "Fucking nitwit."

The driver brings the cab to a stop. Two cabs behind this cab both blare their horns then move on.

"Should we bring flowers?"

"Nah. Hell, *you're* banging her, Bateman. Why should *we* get *Evelyn* flowers? You better have change for a fifty," he warns the driver, squinting at the red numbers on the meter. "Damnit. Steroids. Sorry I'm tense."

"Thought you were off them."

"I *was* getting acne on my legs and arms and the UVA bath wasn't fixing it, so I started going to a tanning salon instead and got rid of it. Jesus, Bateman, you should see how *ripped* my stomach is. The definition. Completely buffed out . . ." he says in a distant, odd way, while waiting for the driver to hand him the change. "Ripped."

He stiffs the driver on the tip but the driver is genuinely thankful anyway. "So long, Shlomo," Price winks.

"Damn, damn, damned," Price says as he opens the door. Coming out of the cab he eyes a beggar on the street—"Bingo: *thirty*"—wearing some sort of weird, tacky, filthy green jumpsuit, unshaven, dirty hair greased back, and jokingly Price holds the cab's door open for him. The bum, confused and mumbling, eyes locked shamefully on the pavement, holds an empty Styrofoam coffee cup out to us, clutched in a tentative hand.

"I suppose he doesn't want the cab," Price snickers, slamming the cab door. "Ask him if he takes American Express."

"Do you take Am Ex?"

The bum nods yes and moves away, shuffling slowly.

It's cold for April and Price walks briskly down the street toward Evelyn's brownstone, whistling "If I Were a Rich Man," the heat from his mouth creating smoky plumes of steam, and swinging his Tumi leather attaché case. A figure with slicked-back hair and horn-rimmed glasses approaches in the distance, wearing a beige double-breasted wool-gabardine Cerruti 1881 suit and carrying the same Tumi leather attaché case from D. F. Sanders that Price has, and Timothy wonders aloud, "Is it Victor Powell? It can't be."

The man passes under the fluorescent glare of a streetlamp with a troubled look on his face that momentarily curls his lips into a slight smile and he glances at Price almost as if they were acquainted but just as quickly he realizes that he doesn't know Price and just as quickly Price realizes it's not Victor Powell and the man moves on.

"Thank god," Price mutters as he nears Evelyn's.

"It looked a lot like him."

"Powell *and* dinner at Evelyn's? These two go together about as well as paisley and plaid." Price rethinks this. "White socks with gray trousers."

A slow dissolve and Price is bounding up the steps outside the brownstone Evelyn's father bought her, grumbling about how he forgot to return the tapes he rented last night to Video Haven. He rings the bell. At the brownstone next to Evelyn's, a woman—high heels, great ass—leaves without locking her door. Price follows her with his gaze and when he hears footsteps from inside coming down the hallway toward us he turns around and straightens his Versace tie ready to face whoever. Courtney opens the door and she's wearing a Krizia cream silk blouse, a Krizia rust tweed skirt and silk-satin d'Orsay pumps from Manolo Blahnik.

I shiver and hand her my black wool Giorgio Armani overcoat and she takes it from me, carefully airkissing my right cheek, then she performs the same exact movements on Price while taking his Armani overcoat. The new Talking Heads on CD plays softly in the living room.

"A bit late, aren't we, boys?" Courtney asks, smiling naughtily.

"Inept Haitian cabbie," Price mutters, airkissing Courtney back. "Do we have reservations somewhere and please don't tell me Pastels at nine."

Courtney smiles, hanging up both coats in the hall closet. "Eating in tonight, darlings. I'm sorry, I know, I know, I tried to talk Evelyn out of it but we're having . . . *su*shi."

Tim moves past her and down the foyer toward the kitchen. "Evelyn? Where *are* you, Evelyn?" he calls out in a singsong voice. "We have to *talk*."

"It's good to see you," I tell Courtney. "You look very pretty tonight. Your face has a . . . youthful glow."

"You really know how to charm the ladies, Bateman." There is no sarcasm in Courtney's voice. "Should I tell Evelyn you feel this way?" she asks flirtatiously.

"No," I say. "But I bet you'd like to."

"Come on," she says, taking my hands off her waist and placing her hands on my shoulders, steering me down the hall in the direction of the kitchen. "We have to save Evelyn. She's been rearranging the sushi for the past hour. She's trying to spell your initials—the *P* in yellowtail, the *B* in tuna—but she thinks the tuna looks too pale—"

"How romantic."

"—and she doesn't have enough yellowtail to finish the *B*"— Courtney breathes in—"and so I think she's going to spell Tim's initials instead. Do you mind?" she asks, only a bit worried. Courtney is Luis Carruthers' girlfriend.

"I'm terribly jealous and I think I better talk to Evelyn," I say, letting Courtney gently push me into the kitchen.

Evelyn stands by a blond wood counter wearing a Krizia cream silk blouse, a Krizia rust tweed skirt and the same pair of silk-satin d'Orsay pumps Courtney has on. Her long blond hair is pinned back into a rather severe-looking bun and she acknowledges me without looking up from the oval Wilton stainless-steel platter on which she has artfully arranged the sushi. "Oh honey, I'm sorry. I wanted to go to this darling little new Salvadorian bistro on the Lower East side—"

Price groans audibly.

"—but we couldn't get reservations. Timothy, *don't groan*." She picks up a piece of the yellowtail and places it cautiously near the top of the platter, completing what looks like a capital *T*. She stands back from the platter and inspects it. "I don't know. Oh, I'm so unsure."

"I told you to keep Fin*landia* in this place," Tim mutters, looking through the bottles—most of them magnums—at the bar. "She never has Fin*landia*," he says to no one, to all of us.

"Oh god, *Tim*othy. Can't handle *Absolut*?" Evelyn asks and then contemplatively to Courtney, "The California roll should circle the rim of the plate, no?"

"Bateman. Drink?" Price sighs.

"J&B rocks," I tell him, suddenly thinking it's strange that Meredith wasn't invited.

"Oh god. It's a *mess*," Evelyn gasps. "I swear I'm going to *cry*."

"The sushi looks *marvelous*," I tell her soothingly.

"Oh it's a *mess*," she wails. "It's a *mess*."

"No, no, the sushi looks *marvelous*," I tell her and in an attempt to be as consoling as possible I pick up a piece of the fluke and pop it in my mouth, groaning with inward pleasure, and hug Evelyn from behind; my mouth still full, I manage to say "Delicious."

She slaps at me in a playful way, obviously pleased with my reaction, and finally, carefully, airkisses my cheek and then turns back to Courtney. Price hands me a drink and walks toward the living room while trying to remove something invisible from his blazer. "Evelyn, do you have a lint brush?"

I would rather have watched the baseball game or gone to the gym and worked out or tried that Salvadorian restaurant that got a couple of pretty good reviews, one in *New York* magazine, the other in the *Times*, than have dinner here but there is one good thing about dinner at Evelyn's: it's close to my place.

"Is it okay if the soy sauce isn't exactly at room temperature?" Courtney is asking. "I think there's ice in one of the dishes."

Evelyn is placing strips of pale orange ginger delicately in a pile next to a small porcelain dish filled with soy sauce. "No, it's not okay. Now Patrick, could you be a dear and get the Kirin out of the refrigerator?" Then, seemingly harassed by the ginger, she throws the clump down on the platter. "Oh forget it. *I'll* do it."

I move toward the refrigerator anyway. Staring darkly, Price reenters the kitchen and says, "Who in the hell is in the living room?"

Evelyn feigns ignorance. "Oh who is that?"

Courtney warns, "Ev-el-yn. You *did* tell them, I hope."

"Who is it?" I ask, suddenly scared. "Victor Powell?"

"No, it's not Victor Powell, Patrick," Evelyn says casually. "It's an artist friend of mine, Stash. And Vanden, his girlfriend."

"Oh so that was a *girl* in there," Price says. "Go take a look, Bateman," he dares. "Let me guess. The East Village?"

"Oh Price," she says flirtatiously, opening beer bottles. "Why no. Vanden goes to Camden and Stash lives in SoHo, so there."

I move out of the kitchen, past the dining room, where the table has been set, the beeswax candles from Zona lit in their sterling silver candleholders from Fortunoff, and into the living room. I can't tell what Stash is wearing since it's all black. Vanden has green streaks in her hair. She stares at a heavy-metal video playing on MTV while smoking a cigarette.

"Ahem," I cough.

Vanden looks over warily, probably drugged to the eyeballs. Stash doesn't move.

"Hi. Pat Bateman," I say, offering my hand, noticing my reflection in a mirror hung on the wall—and smiling at how good I look.

She takes it, says nothing. Stash starts smelling his fingers.

Smash cut and I'm back in the kitchen.

"Just get her out of there." Price is seething. "She's doped up watching MTV and I want to watch the goddamn MacNeil/Leh*rer* report."

Evelyn is still opening large bottles of imported beer and absently mentions, "We've got to eat this stuff soon or else we're all going to be poisoned."

"She's got a green streak in her hair," I tell them. "*And* she's smoking."

"Bateman," Tim says, still glaring at Evelyn.

"Yes?" I say. "Timothy?"

"You're a dufus."

"Oh leave Patrick alone," Evelyn says. "He's the boy next door. That's Patrick. You're not a dufus, are you, honey?" Evelyn is on Mars and I move toward the bar to make myself another drink.

"Boy next door." Tim smirks and nods, then reverses his expression and hostilely asks Evelyn again if she has a lint brush.

Evelyn finishes opening the Japanese beer bottles and tells Courtney to fetch Stash and Vanden. "We have to eat this now or else we're going to be poisoned," she murmurs, slowly moving her head, taking in the kitchen, making sure she hasn't forgotten anything.

"If I can tear them away from the latest Megadeth video," Courtney says before exiting.

"I have to talk to you," Evelyn says.

"What about?" I come up to her.

"No," she says and then pointing at Tim, "to Price."

Tim still glares at her fiercely. I say nothing and stare at Tim's drink.

"Be a hon," she tells me, "and place the sushi on the table. Tempura is in the microwave and the sake is just about done boiling . . ." Her voice trails off as she leads Price out of the kitchen.

I am wondering where Evelyn got the sushi—the tuna, yellow-tail, mackerel, shrimp, eel, even *bonito*, all seem so fresh and there are piles of wasabi and clumps of ginger placed strategically around the Wilton platter—but I also like the idea that I *don't* know, will *never* know, will never *ask* where it came from and that the sushi will sit there in the middle of the glass table from Zona that Evelyn's father bought her like some mysterious apparition from the Orient and as I set the platter down I catch a glimpse of my reflection on the surface of the table. My skin seems darker because of the candlelight and I notice how good the haircut I got at Gio's last Wednesday looks. I make myself another drink. I worry about the sodium level in the soy sauce.

Four of us sit around the table waiting for Evelyn and Timothy to return from getting Price a lint brush. I sit at the head taking large swallows of J&B. Vanden sits at the other end reading disinterestedly from some East Village rag called *Deception*, its glaring headline THE DEATH OF DOWNTOWN. Stash has pushed a chopstick into a lone piece of yellowtail that lies on the middle of his plate like some shiny impaled insect and the chopstick stands straight up. Stash occasionally moves the piece of sushi around the plate with the chopstick but never looks up toward either myself or Vanden or Courtney, who sits next to me sipping plum wine from a champagne glass.

Evelyn and Timothy come back perhaps twenty minutes after we've seated ourselves and Evelyn looks only slightly flushed. Tim glares at me as he takes the seat next to mine, a fresh drink in hand, and he leans over toward me, about to say, to admit something, when suddenly Evelyn interrupts, "Not there, Timothy," then, barely a whisper, "Boy girl, boy girl." She gestures toward the empty chair next to Vanden. Timothy shifts his glare to Evelyn and hesitantly takes the seat next to Vanden, who yawns and turns a page of her magazine.

"Well, everybody," Evelyn says, smiling, pleased with the meal she has presented, "dig in," and then after noticing the piece of sushi that Stash has pinned—he's now bent low over the plate, whispering at it—her composure falters but she smiles bravely and chirps, "Plum wine anyone?"

No one says anything until Courtney, who is staring at Stash's plate, lifts her glass uncertainly and says, trying to smile, "It's . . . delicious, Evelyn."

Stash doesn't speak. Even though he is probably uncomfortable at the table with us since he looks nothing like the other men in the room—his hair isn't slicked back, no suspenders, no horn-rimmed glasses, the clothes black and ill-fitting, no urge to light and suck on a cigar, probably unable to secure a table at Camols, his net worth a pittance—still, his behaviour lacks warrant and he sits there as if hypnotized by the glistening piece of sushi and just as the table is about to finally ignore him, to look away and start eating, he sits up and loudly says, pointing an accusing finger at his plate, "It moved!"

Timothy glares at him with a contempt so total that I can't fully equal it but I muster enough energy to come clean. Vanden seems amused and so now, unfortunately, does Courtney, who I'm beginning to think finds this monkey attractive but I suppose if I were dating Luis Carruthers I might too. Evelyn laughs good-naturedly and says, "Oh Stash, you *are* a riot," and then asks worriedly, "Tempura?" Evelyn is an executive at a financial services company, FYI.

"I'll have some," I tell her and I lift a piece of eggplant off the platter, though I won't eat it because it's fried.

The table begins to serve themselves, successfully ignoring Stash. I stare at Courtney as she chews and swallows.

Evelyn, in an attempt to start a conversation, says, after what seems like a long, thoughtful silence, "Vanden goes to Camden."

"Oh really?" Timothy asks icily. "Where is that?"

"Vermont," Vanden answers without looking up from her paper.

I look over at Stash to see if he's pleased with Vanden's casually blatant lie but he acts as if he wasn't listening, as if he were in some other room or some *punk rock* club in the bowels of the city, but so does the rest of the table, which bothers me since I am fairly sure we all know it's located in New Hampshire.

"Where did *you* go?" Vanden sighs after it finally becomes clear to her that no one is interested in Camden.

"Well, I went to Le Ro*say*," Evelyn starts, "and then to business school in Switzerland."

"I also survived business school in Switzerland," Courtney says. "But I was in Geneva. Evelyn was in Lausanne."

Vanden tosses the copy of *Deception* next to Timothy and smirks in a wan, bitchy way and though I am pissed off a little that Evelyn doesn't take in Vanden's condescension and hurl it back at her, the J&B has relieved my stress to a point where I don't care enough to say anything. Evelyn probably thinks Vanden is sweet, lost, confused, an *artist*. Price isn't eating and neither is Evelyn; I suspect cocaine but it's doubtful. While taking a large gulp from his drink Timothy holds up the copy of *Deception* and chuckles to himself.

"The Death of Downtown," he says; then, pointing at each word in the headline, "Who-gives-a-rat's-ass?"

I automatically expect Stash to look up from his plate but he still stares at the lone piece of sushi, smiling to himself and nodding.

"Hey," Vanden says, as if she was insulted. "*That* affects us."

"Oh ho ho," Tim says warningly. "*That* affects us? What about the massacres in Sri Lanka, honey? Doesn't that affect us too? What about Sri Lanka?"

"Well, that's a cool club in the Village." Vanden shrugs. "Yeah, that affects us too."

Suddenly Stash speaks without looking up. "That's called The *Tonka*." He sounds pissed but his voice is even and low, his eyes still on the sushi. "It's called The Tonka, not Sri Lanka. Got it? The Tonka."

Vanden looks down, then meekly says, "Oh."

"I mean don't you know anything about Sri Lanka? About how the Sikhs are killing like tons of Israelis there?" Timothy goads her. "Doesn't *that* affect us?"

"Kappamaki roll anyone?" Evelyn cuts in cheerfully, holding up a plate.

"Oh come on, Price," I say. "There are more important problems than Sri Lanka to worry about. Sure our foreign policy is important, but there *are* more pressing problems at hand."

"Like what?" he asks without looking away from Vanden. "By the way, why is there an ice cube in my soy sauce?"

"No," I start, hesitantly. "Well, we have to end apartheid for one. And slow down the nuclear arms race, stop terrorism and world hunger. Ensure a strong national defense, prevent the spread of communism in Central America, work for a Middle East peace settlement, prevent U.S. military involvement overseas. We have to ensure that America is a respected world power. Now that's not to belittle our domestic problems, which are equally important, if not *more*. Better and more affordable long-term care for the elderly, control and find a cure for the AIDS epidemic, clean up environmental damage from toxic waste and pollution, improve the quality of primary and secondary education, strengthen laws to crack down on crime and illegal drugs. We also have to ensure that college education is affordable for the middle class and protect Social Security for senior citizens plus conserve natural resources and wilderness areas and reduce the influence of political action committees."

The table stares at me uncomfortably, even Stash, but I'm on a roll.

"But economically we're still a mess. We have to find a way to hold down the inflation rate and reduce the deficit. We also need to provide training and jobs for the unemployed as well as protect existing American jobs from unfair foreign imports. We have to make America the leader in new technology. At the same time we need to promote economic growth and business expansion *and* hold the line against federal income taxes and hold down interest rates while promoting opportunities for small businesses and controlling mergers and big corporate takeovers."

Price nearly spits up his Absolut after this comment but I try to make eye contact with each one of them, especially Vanden, who if she got rid of the green streak and the leather and got some color—maybe joined an aerobics class, slipped on a blouse, something by Laura Ashley—*might* be pretty. But why does she sleep with Stash? He's lumpy and pale and has a bad cropped haircut and is at least ten pounds overweight; there's no muscle tone beneath the black T-shirt.

"But we can't ignore our social needs either. We have to stop people from abusing the welfare system. We have to provide food and shelter for the homeless and oppose racial discrimination and promote civil rights while also promoting equal rights for women but change the abortion laws to protect the right to life yet still somehow maintain women's freedom of choice. We also have to control the influx of illegal immigrants. We have to encourage a return to traditional moral values and curb graphic sex and violence on TV, in movies, in popular music, everywhere. Most importantly we have to promote general social concern and less materialism in young people."

I finish my drink. The table sits facing me in total silence. Courtney's smiling and seems pleased. Timothy just shakes his head in bemused disbelief. Evelyn is completely mystified by the turn the conversation has taken and she stands, unsteadily, and asks if anyone would like dessert.

"I have . . . sor*bet*," she says as if in a daze. "Kiwi, carambola, cherimoys, cactus fruit and oh . . . what is that . . ." She stops her zombie monotone and tries to remember the last flavor. "Oh yes, Japanese pear."

Everyone stays silent. Tim quickly looks over at me. I glance at Courtney, then back at Tim, then at Evelyn. Evelyn meets my glance, then worriedly looks over at Tim. I also look over at Tim,

then at Courtney and then at Tim again, who looks at me once
more before answering slowly, unsurely, "Cactus pear."

"Cactus *fruit*," Evelyn corrects.

I look suspiciously over at Courtney and after she says "Cherimoya" I say "Kiwi" and then Vanden says "Kiwi" also and Stash says
quietly, but enunciating each syllable very clearly, "Chocolate chip."

The worry that flickers across Evelyn's face when she hears this
is instantaneously replaced by a smiling and remarkably good-natured
mask and she says, "Oh Stash, you know I don't have chocolate chip,
though admittedly that's pretty *exotic* for a *sorbet*. I told you I have
cherimoya, cactus *pear*, carambola, I *mean* cactus *fruit*—"

"I know. I heard you, I heard you," he says, waving her off.
"Surprise me."

"Okay," Evelyn says. "Courtney? Would you like to help?"

"Of course." Courtney gets up and I watch as her shoes click
away into the kitchen.

"No cigars, boys," Evelyn calls out.

"Wouldn't dream of it," Price says, putting a cigar back into his
coat pocket.

Stash is still staring at the sushi with an intensity that troubles
me and I have to ask him, hoping he will catch my sarcasm, "Did it,
uh, move again or something?"

Vanden has made a smiley face out of all the disks of California
roll she piled onto her plate and she holds it up for Stash's
inspection and asks, "Rex?"

"Cool," Stash grunts.

Evelyn comes back with the sorbet in Odean margarita glasses
and an unopened bottle of Glenfiddich, which remains unopened
while we eat the sorbet.

Courtney has to leave early to meet Luis at a company party at
Bedlam, a new club in midtown. Stash and Vanden depart soon
after to go "score" something somewhere in SoHo. I am the only
one who saw Stash take the piece of sushi from his plate and slip it
into the pocket of his olive green leather bomber jacket. When I
mention this to Evelyn, while she loads the dishwasher, she gives
me a look so hateful that it seems doubtful we will have sex later on
tonight. But I stick around anyway. So does Price. He is now lying
on a late-eighteenth-century Aubusson carpet drinking espresso

from a Ceralene coffee cup on the floor of Evelyn's room. I'm lying in Evelyn's bed holding a tapestry pillow from Jenny B. Goode, nursing a cranberry and Absolut. Evelyn sits at her dressing table brushing her hair, a Ralph Lauren green and white striped silk robe draped over a very nice body, and she is gazing at her reflection in the vanity mirror.

"Am I the only one who grasped the fact that Stash assumed his piece of sushi was"—I cough, then resume—"a pet?"

"Please stop inviting your 'artiste' friends over," Tim says tiredly. "I'm sick of being the only one at dinner who hasn't talked to an extraterrestrial."

"It was only that *once*," Evelyn says, inspecting a lip, lost in her own placid beauty.

"And at Odeon, no less," Price mutters.

I vaguely wonder why I wasn't invited to Odeon for the artists dinner. Had Evelyn picked up the tab? Probably. And I suddenly picture a smiling Evelyn, secretly morose, sitting at a whole table of Stash's friends—all of them constructing little log cabins with their french fries or pretending their grilled salmon was alive and moving the piece of fish around the table, the fish conversing with each other about the "art scene," new galleries; maybe even trying to fit the fish into the log cabin made of french fries . . .

"If you remember well enough, *I* hadn't seen one either," Evelyn says.

"No, but Bateman's your boyfriend, so that counted." Price guffaws and I toss the pillow at him. He catches it then throws it back at me.

"Leave Patrick alone. He's the boy next door," Evelyn says, rubbing some kind of cream into her face. "You're not an extra-terrestrial, are you honey?"

"Should I even dignify that question with an answer?" I sigh.

"Oh baby." She pouts into the mirror, looking at me in its reflection. "*I* know you're not an extraterrestrial."

"Relief," I mutter to myself.

"No, but Stash was there at Odeon that night," Price continues, and then, looking over at me, "At Odeon. Are you listening, Bateman?"

"No he *wasn't*," Evelyn says.

"Oh yes he *was*, but his name wasn't Stash last time. It was *Horseshoe* or *Magnet* or *Lego* or something *equally* adult," Price sneers. "I forget."

"Timothy, what *are* you going on about?" Evelyn asks tiredly. "I'm not even listening to you." She wets a cotton ball, wipes it across her forehead.

"No, we were at Odeon." Price sits up with some effort. "And don't ask me why, but I distinctly remember him ordering the tuna *cappuccino*."

"Car*paccio*," Evelyn corrects.

"No, Evelyn, dear, love of my life. I distinctly remember him ordering the tuna *cappuccino*," Price says, staring up at the ceiling.

"He said car*paccio*," she counters, running the cotton ball over her eyelids.

"*Cappuccino*," Price insists. "Until *you* corrected him."

"*You* didn't even recognize him earlier tonight," she says.

"Oh but I *do* remember him," Price says, turning to me. "Evelyn described him as 'the good-natured body builder.' That's how she introduced him. I swear."

"Oh shut up," she says, annoyed, but she looks over at Timothy in the mirror and smiles flirtatiously.

"I mean I doubt Stash makes the society pages of *W*, which I thought was your criterion for choosing friends," Price says, staring back, grinning at her in his wolfish, lewd way. I concentrate on the Absolut and cranberry I'm holding and it looks like a glassful of thin, watery blood with ice and a lemon wedge in it.

"What's going on with Courtney and Luis?" I ask, hoping to break their gaze.

"Oh god," Evelyn moans, turning back to the mirror. "The really *dreadful* thing about Courtney is *not* that she doesn't like Luis anymore. It's that—"

"They canceled her charge at Bergdorf's?" Price asks. I laugh. We slap each other high-five.

"No," Evelyn continues, also amused. "It's that she's *really* in love with her real estate *broker*. Some little *twerp* over at The Feathered *Nest*."

"Courtney might have her problems," Tim says, inspecting his recent manicure, "but my god, what is a . . . *Vanden*?"

"Oh don't *bring* this up," Evelyn whines and starts brushing her hair.

"Vanden is a cross between . . . The Limited and . . . used Benetton," Price says, holding up his hands, his eyes closed.

"No." I smile, trying to integrate myself into the conversation. "Used Fiorucci."

"Yeah," Tim says. "I guess." His eyes, now open, zone in on Evelyn.

"Timothy, lay *off*," Evelyn says. "She's a *Camden* girl. What do you *expect?*"

"Oh god," Timothy moans. "I am so sick of hearing *Camden*-girl problems. Oh my boyfriend, I love him but he loves someone else and oh how I *longed* for him and he ignored me and blahblah blahblahblah—god, how *bor*ing. College kids. It *matters*, you know? It's *sad*, right Bateman?"

"Yeah. Matters. Sad."

"See, Bateman agrees with me," Price says smugly.

"Oh he does *not*." With a Kleenex Evelyn wipes off whatever she rubbed on. "Patrick is *not* a cynic, Timothy. He's the boy next door, aren't you honey?"

"No I'm not," I whisper to myself. "I'm a fucking evil psychopath."

"Oh so what," Evelyn sighs. "She's not the brightest girl in the world."

"Hah! Understatement of the century!" Price cries out. "But Stash isn't the brightest guy either. Perfect couple. Did they meet on *Love Connection* or something?"

"Leave them *alone*," Evelyn says. "Stash *is* talented and I'm sure we're *under*estimating Vanden."

"This is a girl . . ." Price turns to me. "Listen, Bateman, this is a girl—Evelyn told me this—this is a girl who rented *High Noon* because she thought it was a movie about"—he gulps—"marijuana farmers."

"It just hit me," I say. "But have we deciphered what Stash—I assume he has a last name but don't tell me, I don't want to know, Evelyn—*does* for a living?"

"First of all he's *perfectly* decent and nice," Evelyn says in his defense.

"The man asked for *chocolate chip sorbet* for Christ sakes!" Timothy wails, disbelieving. "What are you *talking* about?"

Evelyn ignores this, pulls off her Tina Chow earrings. "He's a sculptor," she says tersely.

"Oh bullshit," Timothy says. "I remember talking to him at Odeon." He turns to me again. *"This* was when he ordered the tuna cappuccino and I'm sure if left unattended would have ordered the salmon *au lait*, and he told me he *did* parties, so that technically makes him—I don't know, correct me if I'm wrong, Evelyn—a *caterer*. He's a *caterer*!" Price cries out. "Not a fucking sculptor!"

"Oh gosh calm *down*," Evelyn says, rubbing more cream into her face.

"That's like saying you're a *poet*." Timothy is drunk and I'm beginning to wonder when he will vacate the premises.

"Well," Evelyn begins, "I've been known to—"

"You're a fucking word processor!" Tim blurts out. He walks over to Evelyn and bows next to her, checking out his reflection in the mirror.

"Have you been gaining weight, Tim?" Evelyn asks thoughtfully. She studies Tim's head in the mirror and says, "Your face looks . . . rounder."

Timothy, in retaliation, smells Evelyn's neck and says, "What is that fascinating . . . odor?"

"Obsession." Evelyn smiles flirtatiously, gently pushing Timothy away. "It's Ob*session*. Patrick, get your *friend* away from *me*."

"No, no, wait," Timothy says, sniffing loudly. "It's not Ob*session*. It's . . . it's . . ." and then, with a face twisted in mock horror, "It's . . . oh my god, it's *Q.T. Instatan!*"

Evelyn pauses and considers her options. She inspects Price's head one more time. "Are you losing your hair?"

"Evelyn," Tim says. "Don't change the subject but . . ." And then, genuinely worried, "Now that you mention it . . . too much gel?" Concerned, he runs a hand over it.

"Maybe," Evelyn says. "Now make yourself useful and do *sit down*."

"Well, at least it's not green and I haven't tried to cut it with a butter knife," Tim says, referring to Vanden's dye job and Stash's admittedly cheap, bad haircut. A haircut that's bad because it's cheap.

"Are you gaining weight?" Evelyn asks, more seriously this time.

"Jesus," Tim says, about to turn away, offended. "No, Evelyn."

"Your face definitely looks . . . rounder," Evelyn says. "Less . . . chiseled."

"I don't believe this." Tim again.

He looks deep into the mirror. She continues brushing her hair but the strokes are less definite because she's looking at Tim. He notices this and then smells her neck and I think he licks at it quickly and grins.

"Is that Q.T.?" he asks. "Come on, you can tell me. I smell it."

"No," Evelyn says, unsmiling. "*You* use that."

"No. As a matter of fact I don't. I go to a tanning salon. I'm quite honest about that," he says. "*You're* using Q.T."

"*You're* projecting," she says lamely.

"I told you," Tim says. "I go to a tanning salon. I mean I know it's expensive but . . ." Price blanches. "Still, *Q.T.*?"

"Oh how *brave* to admit you go to a tanning *salon*," she says.

"Q.T." He chuckles.

"I don't know what you're *talk*ing about," Evelyn says and resumes brushing her hair. "Patrick, escort your friend *out* of here."

Now Price is on his knees and he smells and sniffs at Evelyn's bare legs and she's laughing. I tense up.

"Oh god," she moans loudly. "Get *out* of here."

"You are *orange*." He laughs, on his knees, his head in her lap. "You look *orange*."

"I am *not*," she says, her voice a low prolonged growl of pain, ecstasy. "Jerk."

I lie on the bed watching the two of them. Timothy is in her lap trying to push his head under the Ralph Lauren robe. Evelyn's head is thrown back with pleasure and she is trying to push him away, but playfully, and hitting him only lightly on his back with her Jan Hové brush. I am fairly sure that Timothy and Evelyn are having an affair. Timothy is the only interesting person I know.

"You should go," she says finally, panting. She has stopped struggling with him.

He looks up at her, flashing a toothy, good-looking smile, and says, "Anything the lady requests."

"Thank you," she says in a voice that sounds to me tinged with disappointment.

He stands up. "Dinner? Tomorrow?"

"I'll have to ask my boyfriend," she says, smiling at me in the mirror.

"Will you wear that sexy black Anne Klein dress?" he asks, his hands on her shoulders, whispering this into her ear, as he smells it. "Bateman's not welcome."

I laugh good-naturedly while getting up from the bed, escorting him out of the room.

"Wait! My espresso!" he calls out.

Evelyn laughs, then claps as if delighted by Timothy's reluctance to vacate.

"Come on fella," I say as I push him roughly out of the bedroom. "Beddy-bye time."

He still manages to blow her a kiss before I get him out and away. He is completely silent as I walk him out of the brownstone.

After he leaves I pour myself a brandy and drink it from a checkered Italian tumbler and when I come back to the bedroom I find Evelyn lying in bed watching the Home Shopping Club. I lie down next to her and loosen my Armani tie. Finally I ask something without looking at her.

"Why don't you just go for Price?"

"Oh god, Patrick," she says, her eyes shut. "Why Price? *Price?*" And she says this in a way that makes me think she has had sex with him.

"He's rich," I say.

"*Everybody's* rich," she says, concentrating on the TV screen.

"He's good-looking," I tell her.

"*Everybody's* good-looking, Patrick," she says remotely.

"He has a great body," I say.

"*Everybody* has a great body now," she says.

I place the tumbler on the nightstand and roll over on top of her. While I kiss and lick her neck she stares passionlessly at the wide-screen Panasonic remote-control television set and lowers the volume. I pull my Armani shirt up and place her hand on my torso, wanting her to feel how rock-hard, how *halved* my stomach is, and I flex the muscles, grateful it's light in the room so she can see how bronzed and defined my abdomen has become.

"You know," she says clearly, "Stash tested positive for the AIDS virus. And . . ." She pauses, something on the screen catching

her interest; the volume goes slightly up and then is lowered. "And
. . . I think he will probably sleep with Vanden tonight."

"Good," I say, biting lightly at her neck, one of my hands on a
firm, cold breast.

"You're evil," she says, slightly excited, running her hands along
my broad, hard shoulder.

"No," I sigh. "Just your fiancé."

After attempting to have sex with her for around fifteen minutes, I decide not to continue trying.

She says, "You know, you can always be in better shape."

I reach for the tumbler of brandy. I finish it. Evelyn is addicted
to Parnate, an antidepressant. I lie there beside her watching the
Home Shopping Club—at glass dolls, embroidered throw pillows,
lamps shaped like footballs, Lady Zirconia—with the sound turned
off. Evelyn starts drifting.

"Are you using minoxidil?" she asks, after a long time.

"No. I'm not," I say. "Why should I?"

"Your hairline looks like it's receding," she murmurs.

"It's not," I find myself saying. It's hard to tell. My hair is very
thick and I can't tell if I'm losing it. I really doubt it.

I walk back to my place and say good night to a doorman I don't
recognize (he could be anybody) and then dissolve into my living
room high above the city, the sounds of the Tokens singing "The
Lion Sleeps Tonight" coming from the glow of the Wurlitzer 1015
jukebox (which is not as good as the hard-to-find Wurlitzer 850) that
stands in the corner of the living room. I masturbate, thinking about
first Evelyn, then Courtney, then Vanden and then Evelyn again, but
right before I come—a weak orgasm—about a near-naked model in
a halter top I saw today in a Calvin Klein advertisement.

MORNING

In the early light of a May dawn this is what the living room of
my apartment looks like: Over the white marble and granite gas-log
fireplace hangs an original David Onica. It's a six-foot-by-four-foot

portrait of a naked woman, mostly done in muted grays and olives, sitting on a chaise longue watching MTV, the backdrop a Martian landscape, a gleaming mauve desert scattered with dead, gutted fish, smashed plates rising like a sunburst above the woman's yellow head, and the whole thing is framed in black aluminum steel. The painting overlooks a long white down-filled sofa and a thirty-inch digital TV set from Toshiba; it's a high-contrast highly defined model plus it has a four-corner video stand with a high-tech tube combination from NEC with a picture-in-picture digital effects system (plus freeze-frame); the audio includes built-in MTS and a five-watt-per-channel on-board amp. A Toshiba VCR sits in a glass case beneath the TV set; it's a super-high-band Beta unit and has built-in editing function including a character generator with eight-page memory, a high-band record and playback, and three-week, eight-event timer. A hurricane halogen lamp is placed in each corner of the living room. Thin white venetian blinds cover all eight floor-to-ceiling windows. A glass-top coffee table with oak legs by Turchin sits in front of the sofa, with Steuben glass animals placed strategically around expensive crystal ashtrays from Fortunoff, though I don't smoke. Next to the Wurlitzer jukebox is a black ebony Baldwin concert grand piano. A polished white oak floor runs throughout the apartment. On the other side of the room, next to a desk and a magazine rack by Gio Ponti, is a complete stereo system (CD player, tape deck, tuner, amplifier) by Sansui with six-foot Duntech Sovereign 2001 speakers in Brazilian rosewood. A down-filled futon lies on an oakwood frame in the center of the bedroom. Against the wall is a Panasonic thirty-one-inch set with a direct-view screen and stereo and beneath it in a glass case is a Toshiba VCR. I'm not sure if the time on the Sony digital alarm clock is correct so I have to sit up then look down at the time flashing on and off on the VCR, then pick up the Ettore Sottsass push-button phone that rests on the steel and glass nightstand next to the bed and dial the time number. A cream leather, steel and wood chair designed by Eric Marcus is in one corner of the room, a molded plywood chair in the other. A black-dotted beige and white Maud Sienna carpet covers most of the floor. One wall is hidden by four chests of immense bleached mahogany drawers. In bed I'm wearing Ralph Lauren silk pajamas and when I get up I slip on a paisley ancient madder robe and walk to the bathroom. I urinate while trying to make out the puffiness of my reflection in the glass that encases a baseball poster hung over the toilet. After I change into Ralph Lauren mono-grammed boxer shorts and a Fair Isle sweater and slide into silk polka-dot Enrico Hidolin slippers I tie a plastic ice pack around my face and commence with the morning's stretching exercises. After-wards I stand in front of a chrome and acrylic Washmobile bath-room sink—with soap dish, cup holder, and railings that serve as towel bars, which I bought at Hastings Tile to use while the marble sinks I ordered from Finland are being sanded—and stare at my reflection with the ice pack still on. I pour some Plax anti-plaque formula into a stainless-steel tumbler and swish it around my mouth for thirty seconds. Then I squeeze Rembrandt onto a faux-tortoiseshell toothbrush and start brushing my teeth (too hung over to floss properly—but maybe I flossed before bed last night?) and rinse with Listerine. Then I inspect my hands and use a nail-brush. I take the ice-pack mask off and use a deep-pore cleanser lotion, then an herb-mint facial masque which I leave on for ten minutes while I check my toenails. Then I use the Probright tooth polisher and next the Interplak tooth polisher (this in addition to the toothbrush) which has a speed of 4200 rpm and reverses direction forty-six times per second; the larger tufts clean between teeth and massage the gums while the short ones scrub the tooth surfaces. I rinse again, with Cēpacol. I wash the facial massage off with a spearmint face scrub. The shower has a universal all-directional shower head that adjusts within a thirty-inch vertical range. It's made from Australian gold-black brass and covered with a white enamel finish. In the shower I use first a water-activated gel cleanser, then a honey-almond body scrub, and on the face an exfoliating gel scrub. Vidal Sassoon shampoo is especially good at getting rid of the coating of dried perspiration, salts, oils, airborne pollutants and dirt that can weigh down hair and flatten it to the scalp which can make you look older. The conditioner is also good—silicone technology permits conditioning benefits without weighing down the hair which can also make you look older. On weekends or before a date I prefer to use the Greune Natural Revitalizing Shampoo, the conditioner and the Nutrient Complex. These are formulas that contain D-panthenol, a vitamin B-complex factor; polysorbate 80, a cleansing agent for the scalp; and natural herbs. Over the weekend I plan to go to Bloomingdale's or Bergdorf's and on Evelyn's advice pick up

a Foltene European Supplement and Shampoo for thinning hair
which contains complex carbohydrates that penetrate the hair shafts
for improved strength and shine. Also the Vivagen Hair Enrichment
Treatment, a new Redken product that prevents mineral deposits
and prolongs the life cycle of hair. Luis Carruthers recommended
the Aramis Nutriplexx system, a nutrient complex that helps
increase circulation. Once out of the shower and toweled dry I put
the Ralph Lauren boxers back on and before applying the Mousse
A Raiser, a shaving cream by Pour Hommes, I press a hot towel
against my face for two minutes to soften abrasive beard hair. Then
I always slather on a moisturizer (to my taste, Clinique) and let it
soak in for a minute. You can rinse it off or keep it on and apply a
shaving cream over it—preferably with a brush, which softens the
beard as it lifts the whiskers—which I've found makes removing the
hair easier. It also helps prevent water from evaporating and reduces
friction between your skin and the blade. Always wet the razor with
warm water before shaving and shave in the direction the beard
grows, pressing gently on the skin. Leave the sideburns and chin for
last, since these whiskers are tougher and need more time to soften.
Rinse the razor and shake off any excess water before starting.
Afterwards splash cool water on the face to remove any trace of
lather. You should use an aftershave lotion with little or no alcohol.
Never use cologne on your face, since the high alcohol content dries
your face out and makes you look older. One should use an alcohol-
free antibacterial toner with a water-moistened cotton ball to nor-
malize the skin. Applying a moisturizer is the final step. Splash on
water before applying an emollient lotion to soften the skin and seal
in the moisture. Next apply Gel Appaisant, also made by Pour
Hommes, which is an excellent, soothing skin lotion. If the face
seems dry and flaky—which makes it look dull and older—use a
clarifying lotion that removes flakes and uncovers fine skin (it can
also make your tan look darker). Then apply an anti-aging eye balm
(Baume Des Yeux) followed by a final moisturizing "protective"
lotion. A scalp-programming lotion is used after I towel my hair dry.
I also lightly blow-dry the hair to give it body and control (but
without stickiness) and then add more of the lotion shaping it with
a Kent natural-bristle brush, and finally slick it back with a wide-
tooth comb. I pull the Fair Isle sweater back on and reslip my feet
into the polka-dot silk slippers, then head into the living room and

put the new Talking Heads in the CD player, but it starts to digitally skip so I take it out and put in a CD laser lens cleaner. The laser lens is very sensitive, and subject to interference from dust or dirt or smoke or pollutants or moisture, and a dirty one can inaccurately read CDs, making for false starts, inaudible passages, digital skipping, speed changes and general distortion; the lens cleaner has a cleaning brush that automatically aligns with the lens when the disc spins to remove residue and particles. When I put the Talking Heads CD back in it plays smoothly. I retrieve the copy of *USA Today* that lies in front of my door in the hallway and bring it with me into the kitchen where I take two Advil, a multivitamin and a potassium tablet, washing them down with a large bottle of Evian water since the maid, an elderly Chinese woman, forgot to turn the dishwasher on when she left yesterday, and then I have to pour the grapefruit-lemon juice into a St. Rémy wine-glass I got from Baccarat. I check the neon clock that hangs over the refrigerator to make sure I have enough time to eat breakfast unhurriedly. Standing at the island in the kitchen I eat kiwifruit and a sliced Japanese apple-pear (they cost four dollars each at Gristede's) out of aluminum storage boxes that were designed in West Germany. I take a bran muffin, a decaffeinated herbal tea bag and a box of oat-bran cereal from one of the large glass-front cabinets that make up most of an entire wall in the kitchen; complete with stainless-steel shelves and sandblasted wire glass, it is framed in a metallic dark gray-blue. I eat half of the bran muffin after it's been microwaved and lightly covered with a small helping of apple butter. A bowl of oat-bran cereal with wheat germ and soy milk follows; another bottle of Evian water and a small cup of decaf tea after that. Next to the Panasonic bread baker and the Salton Pop-Up coffee maker is the Cremina sterling silver espresso maker (which is, oddly, still warm) that I got at Hammacher Schlemmer (the thermal-insulated stainless-steel espresso cup and the saucer and spoon are sitting by the sink, stained) and the Sharp Model R-1810A Carousel II microwave oven with revolving turntable which I use when I heat up the other half of the bran muffin. Next to the Salton Sonata toaster and the Cuisinart Little Pro food processor and the Acme Supreme Juicerator and the Cordially Yours liqueur maker stands the heavy-gauge stainless-steel two-and-one-half-quart teakettle, which whistles "Tea for Two" when the water is boiling, and with it I make another small cup of the decaffeinated apple-cinnamon tea. For what seems like a long time I stare at the Black & Decker Handy Knife that lies on the counter next to the sink, plugged into the wall: it's a slicer/peeler with several attachments, a serrated blade, a scalloped blade and a rechargeable handle. The suit I wear today is from Alan Flusser. It's an eighties drape suit, which is an updated version of the thirties style. The favored version has extended natural shoulders, a full chest and a bladed back. The soft-rolled lapels should be about four inches wide with the peak finishing three quarters of the way across the shoulders. Properly used on double-breasted suits, peaked lapels are considered more elegant than notched ones. Low-slung pockets have a flapped double-besom design—above the flap there's a slit trimmed on either side with a flat narrow strip of cloth. Four buttons form a low-slung square; above it, about where the lapels cross, there are two more buttons. The trousers are deeply pleated and cut full in order to continue the flow of the wide jacket. An extended waist is cut slightly higher in the front. Tabs make the suspenders fit well at the center back. The tie is a dotted silk design by Valentino Couture. The shoes are crocodile loafers by A. Testoni. While I'm dressing the TV is kept on to *The Patty Winters Show*. Today's guests are women with multiple personalities. A nondescript overweight, older woman is on the screen and Patty's voice is heard asking, "Well, is it schizophrenia or what's the deal? *Tell us.*"

"No, oh no. Multiple personalities are *not* schizophrenics," the woman says, shaking her head. "We are *not* dangerous."

"Well," Patty starts, standing in the middle of the audience, microphone in hand. "Who were you last month?"

"Last month it seemed to be mostly Polly," the woman says.

A cut to the audience—a housewife's worried face; before she notices herself on the monitor, it cuts back to the multiple-personality woman.

"Well," Patty continues, "*now* who are you?"

"Well . . ." the women begins tiredly, as if she was sick of being asked this question, as if she had answered it over and over again and still no one believed it. "Well, this month I'm . . . Lambchop. Mostly . . . Lambchop."

A long pause. The camera cuts to a close-up of a stunned

housewife shaking her head, another housewife whispering something to her.

The shoes I'm wearing are crocodile loafers by A. Testoni.

Grabbing my raincoat out of the closet in the entranceway I find a Burberry scarf and matching coat with a whale embroidered on it (something a little kid might wear) and it's covered with what looks like dried chocolate syrup crisscrossed over the front, darkening the lapels. I take the elevator downstairs to the lobby, rewinding my Rolex by gently shaking my wrist. I say good morning to the doorman, step outside and hail a cab, heading downtown toward Wall Street.

HARRY'S

Price and I walk down Hanover Street in the darkest moments of twilight and as if guided by radar move silently toward Harry's. Timothy hasn't said anything since we left P & P. He doesn't even comment on the ugly bum that crouches beneath a Dumpster off Stone Street, though he does manage a grim wolf whistle toward a woman—big tits, blonde, great ass, high heels—heading toward Water Street. Price seems nervous and edgy and I have no desire to ask him what's wrong. He's wearing a linen suit by Canali Milano, a cotton shirt by Ike Behar, a silk tie by Bill Blass and cap-toed leather lace-ups from Brooks Brothers. I'm wearing a lightweight linen suit with pleated trousers, a cotton shirt, a dotted silk tie, all by Valentino Couture, and perforated cap-toe leather shoes by Allen-Edmonds. Once inside Harry's we spot David Van Patten and Craig McDermott at a table up front. Van Patten is wearing a double-breasted wool and silk sport coat, button-fly wool and silk trousers with inverted pleats by Mario Valentino, a cotton shirt by Gitman Brothers, a polka-dot silk tie by Bill Blass and leather shoes from Brooks Brothers. McDermott is wearing a woven-linen suit with pleated trousers, a button-down cotton and linen shirt by Basile, a silk tie by Joseph Abboud and ostrich loafers from Susan Bennis Warren Edwards.

The two are hunched over the table, writing on the backs of paper napkins, a Scotch and a martini placed respectively in front of them. They wave us over. Price throws his Tumi leather attaché case on an empty chair and heads toward the bar. I call out to him for a J&B on the rocks, then sit down with Van Patten and McDermott.

"Hey Bateman," Craig says in a voice that suggests this is not his first martini. "Is it proper to wear tasseled loafers with a business suit or not? Don't look at me like *I'm* insane."

"Oh shit, *don't* ask Bateman," Van Patten moans, waving a gold Cross pen in front of his face, absently sipping from the martini glass.

"Van Patten?" Craig says.

"Yeah?"

McDermott hesitates, then says "Shut up" in a flat voice.

"What are you screwballs up to?" I spot Luis Carruthers standing at the bar next to Price, who ignores him utterly. Carruthers is not dressed well: a four-button double-breasted wool suit, I think by Chaps, a striped cotton shirt and a silk bow tie plus horn-rimmed eyeglasses by Oliver Peoples.

"Bateman: we're sending these questions in to *GQ*," Van Patten begins.

Luis spots me, smiles weakly, then, if I'm not mistaken, blushes and turns back to the bar. Bartenders always ignore Luis for some reason.

"We have this bet to see which one of us will get in the Question and Answer column first, and so now I expect an answer. *What do you think?*" McDermott demands.

"About *what?*" I ask irritably.

"Tasseled loafers, jerk-*off*," he says.

"Well, guys . . ." I measure my words carefully. "The tasseled loafer is traditionally a casual shoe . . ." I glance back at Price, wanting the drink badly. He brushes past Luis, who offers his hand. Price smiles, says something, moves on, strides over to our table. Luis, once more, tries to catch the bartender's attention and once more fails.

"But it's become acceptable just be*cause* it's so popular, right?" Craig asks eagerly.

"Yeah." I nod. "As long as it's either black or cordovan it's okay."

"What about brown?" Van Patten asks suspiciously.

I think about this then say, "Too sporty for a business suit."

"What are you fags talking about?" Price asks. He hands me the drink then sits down, crossing his legs.

"Okay, okay, okay," Van Patten says. "This is *my* question. A two-parter . . ." He pauses dramatically. "Now are rounded collars too dressy or too casual? Part two, which tie knot looks best with them?"

A distracted Price, his voice still tense, answers quickly with an exact, clear enunciation that can be heard over the din in Harry's. "It's a very versatile look and it can go with both suits *and* sport coats. It should be starched for dressy occasions and a collar pin should be worn if it's particularly formal." He pauses, sighs; it looks as if he's spotted somebody. I turn around to see who it is. Price continues, "If it's worn with a blazer then the collar should look soft and it can be worn either pinned or unpinned. Since it's a traditional, preppy look it's best if balanced by a relatively small four-in-hand knot." He sips his martini, recrossing his legs. "Next question?"

"Buy the man a drink," McDermott says, obviously impressed.

"Price?" Van Patten says.

"Yes?" Price says, casing the room.

"You're priceless."

"Listen," I ask, "where are we having dinner?"

"I brought the trusty Mr. Zagat," Van Patten says, pulling the long crimson booklet out of his pocket and waving it at Timothy.

"Hoo-ray," Price says dryly.

"What do we want to eat?" Me.

"Something blond with big tits." Price.

"How about that Salvadorian bistro?" McDermott.

"Listen, we're stopping by Tunnel afterwards so somewhere near there." Van Patten.

"Oh shit," McDermott begins. "We're going to Tunnel? Last week I picked up this Vassar chick—"

"Oh god, not *again*," Van Patten groans.

"What's your *problem*?" McDermott snaps back.

"I was *there*. I don't need to hear this story *again*," Van Patten says.

"But I never told you what happened *afterwards*," McDermott says, arching his eyebrows.

"Hey, when were you guys there?" I ask. "Why wasn't *I* invited?"

"You were on that fucking *cruise* thing. Now shut up and listen. So okay I picked up this Vassar chick at Tunnel—hot number, big tits, great legs, this chick was a little hardbody—and so I buy her a couple of champagne kirs and she's in the city on spring break and she's practically blowing me in the Chandelier Room and so I take her back to my place—"

"Whoa, wait," I interrupt. "May I ask where *Pamela* is during all of this?"

Craig winces. "Oh *fuck* you. I want a blow-job, Bate*man*. I want a chick who's gonna let me—"

"I don't want to hear this," Van Patten says, clamping his hands over his ears. "He's going to say something disgusting."

"You prude," McDermott sneers. "Listen, we're not gonna invest in a co-*op* together or jet down to Saint Bart's. I just want some chick whose face I can sit on for thirty, forty minutes."

I throw my swizzle stick at him.

"Anyway, so we're back at my place and listen to this." He moves in closer to the table. "She's had enough champagne by now to get a fucking rhino tipsy, and get this—"

"She let you fuck her without a condom?" one of us asks.

McDermott rolls his eyes up. "This is a *Vassar* girl. She's not from *Queens*."

Price taps me on the shoulder. "What does *that* mean?"

"Anyway, listen," McDermott says. "She would . . . are you ready?" He pauses dramatically. "She would only give me a hand-job, and get this . . . she kept her *glove* on." He sits back in his chair and sips his drink in a smug, satisfied sort of way.

We all take this in solemnly. No one makes fun of McDermott's revelatory statement or of his inability to react more aggressively with this chick. No one says anything but we are all thinking the same thought: *Never* pick up a Vassar girl.

"What you need is a chick from *Camden*," Van Patten says, after recovering from McDermott's statement.

"Oh *great*," I say. "Some chick who thinks it's okay to fuck her brother."

"Yeah, but they think AIDS is a new band from England," Price points out.

"Where's dinner?" Van Patten asks, absently studying the question scrawled on his napkin. "Where the fuck are we going?"

"It's really funny that girls think guys are concerned with that, with diseases and stuff," Van Patten says, shaking his head.

"I'm not gonna wear a fucking condom," McDermott announces.

"I have read this article I've Xeroxed," Van Patten says, "and it says our chances of catching that are like zero zero zero zero point half a decimal percentage or something, and this no matter what kind of scumbag, slutbucket, horndog chick we end up boffing."

"Guys just can*not* get it."

"Well, not *white* guys."

"This girl was wearing a fucking glove?" Price asks, still shocked. "A *glove*? Jesus, why didn't *you* just jerk off instead?"

"Listen, the dick also rises," Van Patten says. "Faulkner."

"Where did you go to college?" Price asks. "Pine Manor?"

"Men," I announce: "Look who approaches."

"Who?" Price won't turn his head.

"Hint," I say. "Biggest weasel at Drexel Burnham Lambert."

"Connolly?" Price guesses.

"Hello, Preston," I say, shaking Preston's hand.

"Fellows," Preston says, standing over the table, nodding to everyone. "I'm sorry about not making dinner with you guys tonight." Preston is wearing a double-breasted wool suit by Alexander Julian, a cotton shirt and a silk Perry Ellis tie. He bends down, balancing himself by putting a hand on the back of my chair. "I feel really bad about canceling, but commitments, you know."

Price gives me an accusatory look and mouths "Was he invited?"

I shrug and finish what's left of the J&B.

"What did you do last night?" McDermott asks, and then, "Nice threads."

"*Who* did he do last night?" Van Patten corrects.

"No, no," Preston says. "Very respectable, decent evening. No babes, no blow, no brew. Went to The Russian Tea Room with Alexandra and her parents. She calls her father—get this—Billy.

But I'm so fucking tired and only *one* Stoli." He takes off his glasses
(Oliver Peoples, of course) and yawns, wiping them clean with an
Armani handkerchief. "I'm not sure, but I think our like weird
Orthodox waiter dropped some acid in the borscht. I'm so fucking
tired."

"What are you doing instead?" Price asks, clearly uninterested.

"Have to return these videos, Vietnamese with Alexandra, a
musical, Broadway, something British," Preston says, scanning the
room.

"Hey Preston," Van Patten says. "We're gonna send in the *GQ*
questions. You got one?"

"Oh yeah, I've got one," Preston says. "Okay, so when wearing
a tuxedo how do you keep the front of your shirt from riding up?"

Van Patten and McDermott sit silently for a minute before
Craig, concerned and his brow creased in thought, says, "That's a
good one."

"Hey Price," Preston says. "Do you have one?"

"Yeah," Price sighs. "If all of your friends are morons is it a
felony, a misdemeanor or an act of God if you blow their fucking
heads off with a thirty-eight magnum?"

"Not *GQ* material," McDermott says. "Try *Soldier of Fortune*."

"Or *Vanity Fair*." Van Patten.

"Who *is* that?" Price asks, staring over at the bar. "Is that *Reed
Robison*? And by the way, Preston, you simply have a tab with a
buttonhole sewn into the front of the shirt, which can then be
attached by a button to your trousers; and make sure that the stiff
pleated front of the shirt doesn't extend below the waistband of
your trousers or it will rise up when you sit down *now is that jerk
Reed Robison*? It looks a *hell*uva lot like him."

Stunned by Price's remarks, Preston slowly turns around, still
on his haunches, and after he puts his glasses back on, squints over
at the bar. "No, that's Nigel Morrison."

"Ah," Price exclaims. "One of those young British faggots
serving internship at . . .?"

"How do you know he's a faggot?" I ask him.

"They're all faggots," Price shrugs. "The British."

"How would *you* know, Timothy?" Van Patten grins.

"I saw him fuck Bateman up the ass in the men's room at
Morgan Stanley," Price says.

I sigh and ask Preston, "Where *is* Morrison interning?"

"I forget," Preston says, scratching his head. "Lazard?"

"Where?" McDermott presses. "First Boston? Goldman?"

"I'm not sure," Preston says. "Maybe Drexel? Listen, he's just an assistant corporate finance analyst and his ugly, black-tooth girlfriend is in some dinky *rat*hole doing leveraged *buy*-outs."

"Where are we *eat*ing?" I ask, my patience at an all-time low. "We need to make a reservation. I'm not standing at some fucking *bar*."

"What in the fuck is Morrison wearing?" Preston asks himself. "Is that really a glen-plaid suit with a *checkered* shirt?"

"That's *not* Morrison," Price says.

"Who is it then?" Preston asks, taking his glasses off again.

"That's Paul Owen," Price says.

"That's not Paul Owen," I say. "Paul Owen's on the other side of the bar. Over there."

Owen stands at the bar wearing a double-breasted wool suit.

"He's handling the Fisher account," someone says.

"Lucky bastard," someone else murmurs.

"Lucky *Jew* bastard," Preston says.

"Oh Jesus, Preston," I say. "What does *that* have to do with anything?"

"Listen, I've seen the bastard sitting in his office on the phone with CEOs, spinning a fucking menorah. The bastard brought a Hanukkah bush into the office last December," Preston says suddenly, peculiarly animated.

"You spin a dreidel, Preston," I say calmly, "not a menorah. You spin a dreidel."

"Oh my god, Bateman, do you want me to go over to the bar and ask Freddy to fry you up some fucking potato pancakes?" Preston asks, truly alarmed. "Some . . . *latkes*?"

"No," I say. "Just cool it with the anti-Semitic remarks."

"The voice of reason." Price leans forward to pat me on the back. "The boy next door."

"Yeah, a boy next door who according to you let a British corporate finance analyst intern sodomize him up the ass," I say ironically.

"I said you were the voice of reason," Price says. "I didn't say you *weren't* a homosexual."

"*Or* redundant," Preston adds.

"Yeah," I say, staring directly at Price. "Ask Meredith if I'm a homosexual. That is, if she'll take the time to pull my dick out of her mouth."

"Meredith's a *fag hag*," Price explains, unfazed, "that's why I'm dumping her."

"Oh wait, guys, listen, I got a joke." Preston rubs his hands together.

"Preston," Price says, "you *are* a joke. You do know you *weren't* invited to dinner. By the way, nice jacket; nonmatching but complementary."

"Price, you are a bastard, you are so fucking *mean* to me it hurts," Preston says, laughing. "Anyway, so JFK and Pearl Bailey meet at this party and they go back to the Oval Office to have sex and so they fuck and then JFK goes to sleep and . . ." Preston stops. "Oh gosh, now what happens . . . Oh yeah, so Pearl Bailey says Mr. President I wanna fuck you again and so he says I'm going to sleep now and in . . . thirty—no, wait . . ." Preston pauses again, confused. "Now . . . no, sixty minutes . . . no . . . okay, thirty minutes I'll wake up and we'll do it again but you've got to keep one hand on my cock and the other on my balls and she says okay but why do I have to keep one hand on your dick and one . . . one hand on your balls . . . and . . ." He notices that Van Patten is idly doodling something on the back of a napkin. "Hey Van Patten—are you listening to me?"

"I'm *list*ening," Van Patten says, irritated. "Go ahead. Finish it. One hand on my cock, one hand on my balls, go on."

Luis Carruthers is still standing at the bar waiting for a drink. Now it looks to me like his silk bow tie is by Agnes B. It's all unclear.

"*I'm* not," Price says.

"And he says because . . ." Again Preston falters. There's a long silence. Preston looks at me.

"Don't look at *me*," I say. "It's not *my* joke."

"And he says . . . My mind's a blank."

"Is that the punch line—My mind's a blank?" McDermott asks.

"He says, um, because . . ." Preston puts a hand over his eyes and thinks about it. "Oh gosh, I can't believe I forgot this . . ."

"Oh *great*, Preston," Price sighs. "You are one unfunny bastard."

"My mind's a blank?" Craig asks me. "I don't get it."

"Oh yeah, oh yeah, oh yeah," Preston says. "Listen, I remember. Because the last time I fucked a nigger she stole my wallet." He starts chuckling immediately. And after a short moment of silence the table cracks up too, except for me.

"That's it, that's the punch line," Preston says proudly, relieved. Van Patten gives him high-five. Even Price laughs.

"Oh Christ," I say. "That's awful."

"Why?" Preston says. "It's funny. It's *humor*."

"Yeah, Bateman," McDermott says. "Cheer up."

"Oh I forgot. Bateman's dating someone from the ACLU," Price says. "What bothers you about that?"

"It's not funny," I say. "It's *racist*."

"Bateman, you are some kind of morose bastard," Preston says. "You should stop reading all those Ted Bundy biographies." Preston stands up and checks his Rolex. "Listen men, I'm off. Will see you tomorrow."

"Yeah. Same Bat Time, same Bat Channel," Van Patten says, nudging me.

Preston leans forward before leaving. "Because the last time I fucked a nigger she stole my wallet."

"I get it. I get it," I say, pushing him away.

"Remember this, guys: Few things perform in life as well as a Kenwood." He exits.

"Yabba-dabba-do," Van Patten says.

"Hey, did anyone know cavemen got more fiber than we get?" McDermott asks.

PASTELS

I'm on the verge of tears by the time we arrive at Pastels since I'm positive we won't get seated but the table is good, and relief that is almost tidal in scope washes over me in an awesome wave. At Pastels McDermott knows the maître d' and though we made our reservations from a cab only minutes ago we're immediately led past the overcrowded bar into the pink brightly lit main dining room and seated at an excellent booth for four, up front. It's really impossible to get a reservation at Pastels and I think Van Patten, myself, even Price, are impressed by, maybe even envious of, McDermott's prowess in securing a table. After we piled into a cab on Water Street we realized that no one had made reservations anywhere and while debating the merits of a new California-Sicilian bistro on the Upper East Side—my panic so great I almost ripped Zagat in two—the consensus seemed to emerge. Price had the only dissenting voice but he finally shrugged and said, "I don't give a shit," and we used his portaphone to make the reservation. He slipped his Walkman on and turned the volume up so loud that the sound of Vivaldi was audible even with the windows halfway open and the noise of the uptown traffic blasting into the taxi. Van Patten and McDermott made rude jokes about the size of Tim's dick and I did too. Outside Pastels Tim grabbed the napkin with Van Patten's final version of his carefully phrased question for GQ on it and tossed it at a bum huddling outside the restaurant feebly holding up a sloppy cardboard sign: I AM HUNGRY AND HOMELESS PLEASE HELP ME.

Things seem to be going smoothly. The maître d' has sent over four complimentary Bellinis but we order drinks anyway. The Ronettes are singing "Then He Kissed Me," our waitress is a little hardbody and even Price seems relaxed though he hates the place. Plus there are four women at the table opposite ours, all great-looking—blond, big tits: one is wearing a chemise dress in double-faced wool by Calvin Klein, another is wearing a wool knit dress and jacket with silk faille bonding by Geoffrey Beene, another is wearing a symmetrical skirt of pleated tulle and an embroidered velvet bustier by, I think, Christian Lacroix plus high-heeled shoes by Sidonie Larizzi, and the last one is wearing a black strapless sequined gown under a wool crepe tailored jacket by Bill Blass. Now the Shirelles are coming out of the speakers, "Dancing in the Street," and the sound system plus the acoustics, because of the restaurant's high ceiling, are so loud that we have to practically scream out our order to the hardbody waitress—who is bearing a bicolored suit of wool grain with passementerie trim by Myrone de Prémonville and velvet ankle boots and who, I'm fairly sure, is flirting with me: laughs sexily when I order, as an appetizer, the monkfish and squid ceviche with golden caviar; gives me a stare so steamy, so penetrating when I order the gravlax potpie with green tomatillo sauce I have to look back at the pink Bellini in the tall champagne flute with a concerned, *deadly* serious expression so as not to let her think I'm *too* interested. Price orders the tapas and then the venison with yogurt sauce and fiddlehead ferns with mango slices. McDermott orders the sashimi with goat cheese and then the smoked duck with endive and maple syrup. Van Patten has the scallop sausage and the grilled salmon with raspberry vinegar and guacamole. The air-conditioning in the restaurant is on full blast and I'm beginning to feel bad that I'm not wearing the new Versace pullover I bought last week at Bergdorf's. It would look good with the suit I'm wearing.

"Could you *please* get rid of these things," Price tells the busboy as he gestures toward the Bellinis.

"Wait, Tim," Van Patten says. "*Cool* out. *I'll* drink them."

"*Euro*trash, David," Price explains. "*Euro*trash."

"You can have *mine*, Van Patten," I say.

"Wait," McDermott says, holding the busboy back. "I'm keeping mine too."

"Why?" Price asks. "Are you trying to entice that Armenian chick over by the bar?"

"What Armenian chick?" Van Patten is suddenly craning his neck, interested.

"Just take them all," Price says, practically seething.

The busboy humbly removes the glasses, nodding to no one as he walks away.

"Who made *you* boss?" McDermott whines.

"Look, guys. Look who just came in." Van Patten whistles. "Oh boy."

"Oh for Christ sakes, *not* fucking Preston," Price sighs.

"No. Oh no," Van Patten says ominously. "He hasn't spotted us yet."

"Victor Powell? Paul Owen?" I say, suddenly scared.

"He's twenty-four and worth, oh, let's say a *repulsive* amount of dough," Van Patten hints, grinning. He has obviously been spotted by the person and flashes a bright, toothy smile. "A veritable *shit*load."

I crane my neck but can't figure out who's doing anything.

"It's Scott Montgomery," Price says. "Isn't it? It's Scott Montgomery."

"Perhaps," Van Patten teases.

"It's that dwarf Scott Montgomery," says Price.

"Price," Van Patten says. "You're priceless."

"Watch me act thrilled," Price says, turning around. "Well, as thrilled as I can get meeting someone from Georgia."

"Whoa," McDermott says. "And he's dressed to im*press*."

"Hey," Price says. "I'm depressed, I mean impressed."

"Wow," I say, spotting Montgomery. "Elegant navies."

"Subtle plaids," Van Patten whispers.

"Lotsa beige," Price says. "You *know*."

"Here he comes," I say, bracing myself.

Scott Montgomery walks over to our booth wearing a double-breasted navy blue blazer with mock-tortoiseshell buttons, a pre-washed wrinkled-cotton striped dress shirt with red accent stitching, a red, white and blue fireworks-print silk tie by Hugo Boss and plum washed-wool trousers with a quadruple-pleated front and slashed pockets by Lazo. He's holding a glass of champagne and hands it to the girl he's with—definite model type, thin, okay tits, no ass, high heels—and she's wearing a wool-crepe skirt and a wool and cashmere velour jacket and draped over her arm is a wool and cashmere velour coat, all by Louis Dell'Olio. High-heeled shoes by Susan Bennis Warren Edwards. Sunglasses by Alain Mikli. Pressed-leather bag from Hermès.

"Hey fellas. How y'all doin'?" Montgomery speaks in a thick Georgia twang. "This is Nicki. Nicki, this is McDonald, Van Buren, Bateman—nice tan—and Mr. Price." He shakes only Timothy's hand and then takes the champagne glass from Nicki. Nicki smiles, politely, like a robot, probably doesn't speak English.

"Montgomery," Price says in a kindly, conversational tone, staring at Nicki. "How have things been?"

"Well, fellas," Montgomery says. "See y'all got the primo table. Get the check yet? Just kidding."

"Listen, Montgomery," Price says, staring at Nicki but still being unusually kind to someone I thought was a stranger. "Squash?"

"Call me," Montgomery says absently, looking over the room. "Is that Tyson? Here's my card."

"Great," Price says, pocketing it. "Thursday?"

"Can't. Going to Dallas tomorrow but . . ." Montgomery is already moving away from the table, hurrying toward someone else, snapping for Nicki. "Yeah, next week."

Nicki smiles at me, then looks at the floor—pink, blue, lime green tiles crisscrossing each other in triangular patterns—as if it had some kind of answer, held some sort of clue, offered a coherent reason as to why she was stuck with Montgomery. Idly I wonder if she's older than him, and then if she's flirting with me.

"Later," Price is saying.

"Later, fellas . . ." Montgomery is already about halfway across the room. Nicki slinks behind him. I was wrong: she *does* have an ass.

"Eight hundred million," McDermott whistles, shaking his head.

"College?" I ask.

"A joke," Price hints.

"Rollins?" I guess.

"Get this," McDermott says. "Hampden-Sydney."

"He's a parasite, a loser, a weasel," Van Patten concludes.

"But he's worth eight hundred *million*," McDermott repeats emphatically.

"Go over and give the dwarf *head*—will that shut you up?" Price says. "I mean how impressed can you *get*, McDermott?"

"Anyway," I mention, "nice babe."

"That girl *is* hot," McDermott agrees.

"Affirmative." Price nods, but grudgingly.

"Oh man," Van Patten says, distressed. "I *know* that chick."

"Oh bullshit," we all moan.

"Let me guess," I say. "Picked her up at Tunnel, right?"

"No," he says, then after sipping his drink, "She's a model. Anorexic, alcoholic, uptight bitch. *Totally* French."

"What a joke you are," I say, unsure if he's lying.

"Wanna bet?"

"So what?" McDermott shrugs. "I'd fuck her."

"She drinks a liter of Stoli a day then throws it up and *redrinks* it, McDermott," Van Patten explains. "Total alkie."

"Total *cheap* alkie," Price murmurs.

"I don't care," McDermott says bravely. "She is beautiful. I want to fuck her. I want to marry her. I want her to have my children."

"Oh Jesus," Van Patten says, practically gagging. "Who wants to marry a chick who's gonna give birth to a jug of vodka and cranberry juice?"

"He *has* a point," I say.

"Yeah. He also wants to shack up with the Armenian chick at the bar," Price sneers. "What'll she give birth to—a bottle of Kirbel and a pint of peach juice?"

"*What* Armenian chick?" McDermott asks, exasperated, craning his neck.

"Oh Jesus. Fuck off, you faggots." Van Patten sighs.

The maître d' stops by to say hello to McDermott, then notices we don't have our complimentary Bellinis, and runs off before any of us can stop him. I'm not sure how McDermott knows Alain so well—maybe Cecelia?—and it slightly pisses me off but I decide to even up the score a little bit by showing everyone my new business card. I pull it out of my gazelleskin wallet (Barney's, $850) and slap it on the table, waiting for reactions.

"What's that, a gram?" Price says, not apathetically.

"New card." I try to act casual about it but I'm smiling proudly. "What do you think?"

"Whoa," McDermott says, lifting it up, fingering the card, genuinely impressed. "Very nice. Take a look." He hands it to Van Patten.

"Picked them up from the printer's yesterday," I mention.

"Cool coloring," Van Patten says, studying the card closely.

"That's bone," I point out. "And the lettering is something called Silian Rail."

"Silian Rail?" McDermott asks.

"Yeah. Not bad, huh?"

"It *is* very cool, Bateman," Van Patten says guardedly, the jealous bastard, "but that's nothing . . ." He pulls out his wallet and slaps a card next to an ashtray. "Look at this."

We all lean over and inspect David's card and Price quietly says, "That's *really* nice." A brief spasm of jealousy courses through me when I notice the elegance of the color and the classy type. I clench my fist as Van Patten says, smugly, "Eggshell with Romalian type . . ." He turns to me. "What do you think?"

"Nice," I croak, but manage to nod, as the busboy brings four fresh Bellinis.

"Jesus," Price says, holding the card up to the light, ignoring the new drinks. "This is really super. How'd a nitwit like you get so tasteful?"

I'm looking at Van Patten's card and then at mine and cannot believe that Price actually likes Van Patten's better. Dizzy, I sip my drink then take a deep breath.

"But wait," Price says. "You ain't seen nothin' yet . . ." He pulls his out of an inside coat pocket and slowly, dramatically turns it over for our inspection and says, "*Mine.*"

Even I have to admit it's magnificent.

Suddenly the restaurant seems far away, hushed, the noise distant, a meaningless hum, compared to this card, and we all hear Price's words: "Raised lettering, pale nimbus white . . ."

"Holy shit," Van Patten exclaims. "I've never seen . . ."

"Nice, very nice," I have to admit. "But wait. Let's see Montgomery's."

Price pulls it out and though he's acting nonchalant, I don't see how he can ignore its subtle off-white coloring, its tasteful thickness. I am unexpectedly depressed that I started this.

"Pizza. Let's order a pizza," McDermott says. "Doesn't anyone want to split a pizza? Red snapper? Mmmmm. Bateman wants *that*," he says, rubbing his hands eagerly together.

I pick up Montgomery's card and actually finger it, for the sensation the card gives off to the pads of my fingers.

"Nice, huh?" Price's tone suggests he realizes I'm jealous.

"Yeah," I say offhandedly, giving Price the card like I don't give a shit, but I'm finding it hard to swallow.

"Red snapper pizza," McDermott reminds me. "I'm fucking starving."

"No pizza," I murmur, relieved when Montgomery's card is placed away, out of sight, back in Timothy's pocket.

"Come on," McDermott says, whining. "Let's order the red snapper pizza."

"Shut up, Craig," Van Patten says, eyeing a waitress taking a booth's order. "But call that hardbody over."

"But she's not ours," McDermott says, fidgeting with the menu he's yanked from a passing busboy.

"Call her over *any*way," Van Patten insists. "Ask her for water or a Corona or something."

"Why *her*?" I'm asking no one in particular. My card lies on the table, ignored next to an orchid in a blue glass vase. Gently I pick it up and slip it, folded, back into my wallet.

"She looks exactly like this girl who works in the Georgette Klinger section of Bloomingdale's," Van Patten says. "Call her over."

"Does anyone want the pizza or not?" McDermott's getting testy.

"How would *you* know?" I ask Van Patten.

"I buy Kate's perfume *there*," he answers.

Price's gestures gather the table's attention. "Did I forget to tell everyone that Montgomery's a dwarf?"

"Who's Kate?" I say.

"*Kate* is the chick who Van Patten's having the affair with," Price explains, staring back at Montgomery's table.

"What happened to Miss *Kitt*ridge?" I ask.

"Yeah," Price smiles. "What *about* Amanda?"

"Oh god, guys, *lighten* up. Fidelity? *Right*."

"Aren't you afraid of dis*eases*?" Price asks.

"From *who*, Amanda or Kate?" I ask.

"I thought we agreed that *we* can't get it." Van Patten's voice rises. "So-o-o-o . . . shithead. Shut up."

"Didn't I tell you—"

Four more Bellinis arrive. There are now eight Bellinis on the table.

"Oh my god," Price moans, trying to grab at the busboy before he scampers off.

"Red snapper pizza . . . red snapper pizza . . ." McDermott has found a mantra for the evening.

"We'll soon become targets for horny Iranian chicks," Price drones.

"It's like zero zero zero percentage whatever, you know—are you listening?" Van Patten asks.

". . . snapper pizza . . . red snapper pizza . . ." Then McDermott slams his hand on the table, rocking it. "Goddamnit, isn't anybody listening to me?"

I'm still tranced out on Montgomery's card—the classy coloring, the thickness, the lettering, the print—and I suddenly raise a fist as if to strike out at Craig and scream, my voice booming, "No one wants the fucking *red snapper pizza*! A pizza should be *yeasty* and slightly *bready* and have a *cheesy crust*! The crusts here are too fucking thin because the shithead chef who cooks here overbakes everything! The pizza is dried out and brittle!" Red-faced, I slam my Bellini down on the table and when I look up our appetizers have arrived. A hardbody waitress stands looking down at me with this strange, glazed expression. I wipe a hand over my face, genially smiling up at her. She stands there looking at me as if I were some kind of monster—she actually looks *scared*—and I glance over at Price—for what? guidance?—and he mouths "Cigars" and pats his coat pocket.

McDermott quietly says, "I don't think they're brittle."

"Honey," I say, ignoring McDermott, taking an arm and pulling her toward me. She flinches but I smile and she lets me pull her closer. "Now we're all going to eat a nice big meal here—" I start to explain.

"But this isn't what I ordered," Van Patten says, looking at his plate. "I wanted the *mussel* sausage."

"Shut up." I shoot him a glance then calmly turn toward the hardbody, grinning like an idiot, but a handsome idiot. "Now listen, we are good customers here and we're probably going to order some fine brandy, cognac, who knows, and we want to relax and bask in this"—I gesture with my arm—"atmosphere. Now"—with the other hand I pull out my gazelleskin wallet—"we would like to enjoy some *fine* Cuban cigars afterwards and we don't want to be bothered by some *lout*ish—"

"*Lout*ish." McDermott nods to Van Patten and Price.

"*Lout*ish and inconsiderate patrons or tourists who are inevitably going to complain about our innocuous little habit . . . So"—I press what I hope is fifty into a small-boned hand—"if you could make sure we aren't bothered while we do, we would *grate*fully appreciate it." I rub the hand, closing it into a fist over the bill. "And if anyone complains, well . . ." I pause, then warn menacingly, "Kick 'em out."

She nods mutely and backs away with this dazed, confused look on her face.

"And," Price adds, smiling, "if another round of Bellinis comes within a twenty-foot radius of this table we are going to set the maître d' on fire. So, you know, warn him."

After a long silence during which we contemplate our appetizers, Van Patten speaks up. "Bateman?"

"Yes?" I fork a piece of monkfish, push it into some of the golden caviar, then place the fork back down.

"You are pure prep perfection," he purrs.

Price spots another waitress approaching with a tray of four champagne flutes filled with pale pinkish liquid and says, "Oh for Christ sakes, this is getting *ridic*ulous . . ." She sets them down, however, at the table next to us, for the four babes.

"She is *hot*," Van Patten says, ignoring the scallop sausage.

"Hardbody." McDermott nods in agreement. "Definitely."

"I'm not impressed," Price sniffs. "Look at her knees."

While the hardbody stands there we check her out, and though her knees do support long, tan legs, I can't help noticing that one knee is, admittedly, bigger than the other one. The left knee is knobbier, almost imperceptibly thicker than the right knee and this unnoticeable flaw now seems overwhelming and we all lose interest. Van Patten is looking at his appetizer, stunned, and then he looks at McDermott and says, "That isn't what you ordered either. That's *sushi*, not sashimi."

"Jesus," McDermott sighs. "You don't come here for the food anyway."

Some guy who looks exactly like Christopher Lauder comes over to the table and says, patting me on the shoulder, "Hey Hamilton, nice tan," before walking into the men's room.

"Nice tan, Hamilton," Price mimics, tossing tapas onto my bread plate.

"Oh gosh," I say, "hope I'm not blushin'."

"Actually, where *do* you go, Bateman?" Van Patten asks. "For a tan."

"Yeah, Bateman. Where *do* you go?" McDermott seems genuinely intrigued.

"Read my lips," I say, "a tanning salon," then irritably, "like *everyone* else."

"I have," Van Patten says, pausing for maximum impact, "a

tanning bed at . . . home," and then he takes a large bite out of his scallop sausage.

"Oh bullshit," I say, cringing.

"It's *true*," McDermott confirms, his mouth full. "I've seen it."

"That is *fuck*ing outrageous," I say.

"Why the hell is it *fuck*ing outrageous?" Price asks, pushing tapas around his plate with a fork.

"Do you know how expensive a fucking tanning salon membership *is*?" Van Patten asks me. "A *member*ship for a *year*?"

"You're crazy," I mutter.

"Look, guys," Van Patten says. "Bateman's indignant."

Suddenly a busboy appears at our table and without asking if we're finished removes our mostly uneaten appetizers. None of us complain except for McDermott, who asks, "Did he just take our appetizers away?" and then laughs uncomprehendingly. But when he sees no one else laughing he stops.

"He took them away because the portions are so small he probably thought we were finished," Price says tiredly.

"I just think that's crazy about the tanning bed," I tell Van Patten, though secretly I think it would be a hip luxury except I really have no room for one in my apartment. There are things one could do with it besides getting a tan.

"Who is Paul Owen with?" I hear McDermott asking Price.

"Some weasel from Kicker Peabody," Price says distractedly. "*He* knew McCoy."

"Then why is he sitting with those dweebs from Drexel?" McDermott asks. "Isn't that Spencer Wynn?"

"Are you freebasing or *what*?" Price asks. "That's not Spencer Wynn."

I look over at Paul Owen, sitting in a booth with three other guys—one of whom could be Jeff Duvall, suspenders, slicked-back hair, horn-rimmed glasses, all of them drinking champagne—and I lazily wonder about how Owen got the Fisher account. It makes me not hungry but our meals arrive almost immediately after our appetizers are taken away and we begin to eat. McDermott undoes his suspenders. Price calls him a slob. I feel paralyzed but manage to turn away from Owen and stare at my plate (the potpie a yellow hexagon, strips of smoked salmon circling it, squiggles of pea-green tomatillo sauce artfully surrounding the dish) and then I gaze at the waiting crowd. They seem hostile, drunk on complimentary Bellinis perhaps, tired of waiting hours for shitty tables near the open kitchen even though they had reservations. Van Patten interrupts the silence at our table by slamming his fork down and pushing his chair back.

"What's wrong?" I say, looking up from my plate, a fork poised over it, but my hand will not move; it's as if it appreciated the plate's setup too much, as if my hand had a mind of its own and refused to break up its design. I sigh and put the fork down, hopeless.

"Shit. I have to *tape* this movie on cable for *Mandy*." He wipes his mouth with a napkin, stands up. "I'll be back."

"Have *her* do it, idiot," Price says. "What are you, demented?"

"She's in Boston, seeing her *den*tist." Van Patten shrugs, pussywhipped.

"What in the hell are *you* going to do?" My voice wavers. I'm still thinking about Van Patten's card. "Call up HBO?"

"No," he says. "I have a touch-tone phone hooked up to program a Videonics VCR programmer I bought at Hammacher Schlemmer." He walks away pulling his suspenders up.

"How hip," I say tonelessly.

"Hey, what do you want for dessert?" McDermott calls out.

"Something chocolate and flourless," he shouts back.

"Has Van Patten stopped working out?" I ask. "He looks puffy."

"It looks that way, doesn't it," Price says.

"Doesn't he have a membership at the Vertical Club?" I ask.

"I don't know," Price murmurs, studying his plate, then sitting up he pushes it away and motions to the waitress for another Finlandia on the rocks.

Another hardbody waitress approaches us tentatively, bringing over a bottle of champagne, Perrier-Jouët, nonvintage, and tells us it's complimentary from Scott Montgomery.

"Nonvintage, that weasel," Price hisses, craning his neck to find Montgomery's table. "Loser." He gives him a thumbs-up sign from across the room. "The fucker's so short I could barely see him. I think I gave thumbs-up to Conrad. I can't be sure."

"Where's Conrad?" I ask. "I should say hello to him."

"The dude who called you Hamilton," Price says.

"That wasn't Conrad," I say.

"Are you sure? It looked a helluva lot like him," he says but he's not really listening; he blatantly stares at the hardbody waitress, at exposed cleavage as she leans down to get a firmer grip on the bottle's cork.

"No. That wasn't *Con*rad," I say, surprised at Price's inability to recognize co-workers. "That guy had a better haircut."

We sit in silence while the hardbody pours the champagne. Once she leaves, McDermott asks if we liked the food. I tell him the potpie was fine but there was way too much tomatillo sauce. McDermott nods, says, "That's what I've heard."

Van Patten returns, mumbling, "They don't have a good bathroom to do coke in."

"Dessert?" McDermott suggests.

"Only if I can order the Bellini sorbet," Price says, yawning.

"How about just the check," Van Patten says.

"Time to go bird-dogging, gentlemen," I say.

The hardbody brings the check over. The total is $475, much less than we expected. We split it but I need the cash so I put it on my platinum AmEx and collect their bills, mostly fresh fifties. McDermott demands ten dollars back since his scallop sausage appetizer was only sixteen bucks. Montgomery's bottle of champagne is left at the table, undrunk. Outside Pastels a different bum sits in the street, with a sign that says something completely illegible. He gently asks us for some change and then, more hopefully, for some food.

"That dude needs a facial *real* bad," I say.

"Hey McDermott," Price cackles. "Throw him your tie."

"Oh shit. What's *that* gonna get him?" I ask, staring at the bum.

"Appetizers at Jams." Van Patten laughs. He gives me high-five.

"*Dude*," McDermott says, inspecting his tie, clearly offended.

"Oh, sorry . . . cab," Price says, waving down a cab. ". . . *and* a beverage."

"Off to Tunnel," McDermott tells the driver.

"Great, McDermott," Price says, getting in the front seat. "You sound really excited."

"So what if I'm not some burned-out decadent faggot like yourself," McDermott says, getting in ahead of me.

"Did anyone know cavemen got more fiber than we do?" Price asks the cabdriver.

"Hey, *I* heard that too," McDermott says.

"Van Patten," I say. "Did you see the comp bottle of champagne Montgomery sent over?"

"Really?" Van Patten asks, leaning over McDermott. "Let me guess. Perrier-Jouët?"

"*Bingo*," Price says. "Nonvintage."

"Fucking weasel," Van Patten says.

TUNNEL

All of the men outside Tunnel tonight are for some reason wearing tuxedos, except for a middle-aged homeless bum who sits by a Dumpster, only a few feet away from the ropes, holding out to anyone who pays attention a Styrofoam coffee cup, begging for change, and as Price leads us around the crowd up to the ropes, motioning to one of the doormen, Van Patten waves a crisp one-dollar bill in front of the homeless bum's face, which momentarily lights up, then Van Patten pockets it as we're whisked into the club, handed a dozen drink tickets and two VIP Basement passes. Once inside we're vaguely hassled by two more doormen—long wool coats, ponytails, probably German—who demand to know why we're not wearing tuxedos. Price handles this all suavely, somehow, either by tipping the dorks or by persuading them with his clout (probably the former). I stay uninvolved and with my back to him try to listen as McDermott complains to Van Patten about how crazy I am for putting down the pizzas made at Pastels, but it's hard to hear anything with Belinda Carlisle's version of "I Feel Free" blasting over the sound system. I have a knife with a serrated blade in the pocket of my Valentino jacket and I'm tempted to gut McDermott with it right here in the entranceway, maybe slice his face open, sever his spine; but Price finally waves us in and the temptation to kill McDermott is replaced by this strange anticipation to have a good time, drink some champagne, flirt with a hardbody, find some blow, maybe even dance to some oldies or that new Janet Jackson song I like.

It gets quieter as we move into the front hallway, heading toward the actual entrance, and we pass by three hardbodies. One is wearing a black side-buttoned notched-collar wool jacket, wool-crepe trousers and a fitted cashmere turtleneck, all by Oscar de la Renta; another is wearing a double-breasted coat of wool, mohair and nylon tweed, matching jeans-style pants and a man's cotton dress shirt, all by Stephen Sprouse; the best-looking one is wearing a checked wool jacket and high-waisted wool skirt, both from Barney's, and a silk blouse by Andra Gabrielle. They're definitely paying attention to the four of us and we repay the compliment, turning our heads—except for Price, who ignores them and says something rude.

"Jesus Christ, Price, lighten up," McDermott whines. "What's your problem? Those girls were *very* hot."

"Yeah, if you speak Farsi," Price says, handing McDermott a couple of drink tickets as if to placate him.

"What?" Van Patten says. "They didn't look Spanish to me."

"You know, Price, you're going to have to change your attitude if you want to get laid," McDermott says.

"*You're* telling *me* about getting laid?" Price asks Craig. "*You*, who scored with a hand-job the other night?"

"Your outlook *sucks*, Price," Craig says.

"Listen, you think I act like I do around you guys when I want some *pussy*?" Price challenges.

"Yeah, I *do*," McDermott and Van Patten say at the same time.

"You know," I say, "it's possible to act differently from how one actually feels to get sex, guys. I hope I'm not causing you to relose your innocence, McDermott." I start walking faster, trying to keep up with Tim.

"No, but that doesn't explain why Tim acts like such a *major* asshole," McDermott says, trying to catch up with me.

"Like these girls *care*," Price snorts. "When I tell them what my annual income is, believe me, my behaviour couldn't matter less."

"And how do you drop this little tidbit of info?" Van Patten asks. "Do you say, 'Here's a Corona and by the way I pull in a hundred eighty thou a year and what's your sign?'"

"One ninety," Price corrects him, and then, "Yeah, I do. Subtlety is not what these girls are after."

"And what are these girls after, O knowledgeable one?" McDermott asks, bowing slightly as he walks.

Van Patten laughs and still in motion they give each other high-five.

"Hey," I laugh, "you wouldn't ask if you *knew*."

"They want a hardbody who can take them to Le Cirque twice a week, get them into Nell's on a regular basis. Or maybe a close personal acquaintance of Donald Trump," Price says flatly.

We hand our tickets to an okay-looking girl wearing a wool-melton duffel coat and a silk scarf from Hermès. As she lets us in, Price winks at her and McDermott is saying, "I worry about disease just walking into this place. These are some skanky chicks. I can just *feel* it."

"I told you, dude," Van Patten says and then patiently restates his facts. "We can't get *that*. It's like zero zero zero point oh one percentage—"

Luckily, the long version of "New Sensation" by INXS drowns out his voice. The music is so loud that conversation is possible only by screaming. The club is fairly packed; the only real light coming in flashes off the dance floor. Everyone is wearing a tuxedo. Everyone is drinking champagne. Since we only have two VIP Basement passes Price shoves them at McDermott and Van Patten and they eagerly wave the cards at the guy guarding the top of the stairs. The guy who lets them pass is wearing a double-breasted wool tuxedo, a cotton wing-collar shirt by Cerruti 1881 and a black and white checkered silk bow tie from Martin Dingman Neckwear.

"Hey," I shout to Price. "Why didn't *we* use those?"

"Because," he screams over the music, grabbing me by the collar, "*we* need some Bolivian Marching Powder . . ."

I follow him as he rushes through the narrow corridor that runs parallel to the dance floor, then into the bar and finally into the Chandelier Room, which is jammed with guys from Drexel, from Lehman's, from Kidder Peabody, from First Boston, from Morgan Stanley, from Rothschild, from Goldman, even from *Citibank* for Christ sakes, all of them wearing tuxedos, holding champagne flutes, and effortlessly, almost as if it were the same song, "New Sensation" segues into "The Devil Inside" and Price spots Ted Madison leaning against the railing in the back of the room, wearing a double-breasted wool tuxedo, a wing-collar cotton shirt from Paul Smith, a bow tie and cummerbund from Rainbow Neckwear, diamond studs from Trianon, patent-leather and grosgrain pumps by Ferrangamo and an antique Hamilton watch from Saks; and past Madison, disappearing into darkness, are the twin train tracks which tonight are lit garishly in preppy greens and pinks and Price suddenly stops walking, stares past Ted, who smiles knowingly when he spots Timothy, and Price gazes longingly at the tracks as if they suggest some kind of freedom, embody an escape that Price has been searching for, but I shout out to him, "Hey, there's Teddy," and this breaks his gaze and he shakes his head as if to clear it, refocuses his gaze on Madison and shouts decisively, "No, that's not Madison for Christ sakes, that's *Turnball*," and the guy who I thought was Madison is greeted by two other guys in tuxedos and he turns his back to us and suddenly, behind Price, Ebersol wraps an arm around Timothy's neck and laughingly pretends to strangle him, then Price pushes the arm away, shakes Ebersol's hand and says, "Hey Madison."

Madison, who I thought was Ebersol, is wearing a splendid double-breasted white linen jacket by Hackett of London from Bergdorf Goodman. He has a cigar that hasn't been lit in one hand and a champagne glass, half full, in the other.

"Mr. Price," shouts Madison. "Very good to see you, sir."

"Madison," Price cries back. "We need your services."

"Looking for trouble?" Madison smiles.

"Something more immediate," Price shouts back.

"Of course," Madison shouts and then, coolly for some reason, nods at me, shouting, I think, "Bateman," and then, "Nice tan."

A guy standing behind Madison who looks a lot like Ted Dreyer is wearing a double-breasted shawl-collared tuxedo, a cotton shirt and a silk tartan bow tie, all of it, I'm fairly sure, from Polo by Ralph Lauren. Madison stands around, nodding to various people who pass by in the crush.

Finally Price loses his cool. "Listen. We need drugs," I think I hear him shout.

"Patience, Price, patience," Madison shouts. "I'll talk to Ricardo."

But he still stands there, nodding to people who push past us.

"Like what about *now*?" Price screams.

"Why aren't you wearing a tux?" Madison shouts.

"How much do we want?" Price asks me, looking desperate.

"A gram is fine," I shout. "I have to be at the office early tomorrow."

"Do you have cash?"

I can't lie, nod, hand him forty.

"A gram," Price shouts to Ted.

"Hey," Madison says, introducing his friend, "this is You."

"A gram." Price presses cash into Madison's hand. "*You?* What?"

This guy and Madison both smile and Ted shakes his head and shouts a name I can't hear.

"No," Madison shouts, "Hugh." I think.

"Yeah. Great to meet you, Hugh." Price holds up his wrist and taps the gold Rolex with his index finger.

"I'll be right back," Madison shouts. "Keep my friend company. Use your drink tickets." He disappears. You, Hugh, Who, fades into the crowd. I follow Price over to the railings.

I want to light my cigar but don't have any matches; yet just holding it, catching some of its aroma along with the knowledge that drugs are incoming, comforts me and I take two of the drink tickets from Price and try to get him a Finlandia on the rocks which they don't have, the hardbody behind the bar informs me bitchily, but she's got a rad body and is so hot-looking that I will leave her a big tip because of this. I settle on an Absolut for Price and order a J&B on the rocks for myself. As a joke I almost bring Tim a Bellini but he seems far too edgy tonight to appreciate this so I wade back through the crowd to where he stands and hand him the Absolut and he takes it thanklessly and finishes it with one gulp, looks at the glass and grimaces, giving me an accusatory look. I shrug helplessly. He resumes staring at the train tracks as if possessed. There are very few chicks in Tunnel tonight.

"Hey, I'm going out with Courtney tomorrow night."

"*Her?*" he shouts back, staring at the tracks. "Great." Even with the noise I catch the sarcasm.

"Well, why *not*? Carruthers is *out* of town."

"Might as well hire someone from an *escort* service," he shouts bitterly, almost without thinking.

"Why?" I shout.

"Because she's gonna cost you a *lot* more to get laid."

"No *way*," I scream.

"Listen, I put up with it too," Price shouts, lightly shaking his glass. Ice cubes clank loudly, surprising me. "Meredith's the same way. She expects to be paid. They *all* do."

"Price?" I take a large gulp of Scotch. "You're priceless . . ."

He points behind him. "Where do those tracks go?" Laser lights start flashing.

"I don't know," I say after a long time, I don't even know how long.

I get bored watching Price, who is neither moving nor speaking. The only reason he occasionally turns away from the train tracks is to look for Madison or Ricardo. No women anywhere, just an army of professionals from Wall Street in tuxedos. The one female spotted is dancing alone in a corner to some song I think is called "Love Triangle." She's wearing what looks like a sequined tank top by Ronaldus Shamask and I concentrate on that but I'm in an edgy pre-coke state and I start chewing nervously on a drink ticket and some Wall Street guy who looks like Boris Cunningham blocks my view of the girl. I'm about to head off to the bar when Madison comes back—it's been twenty minutes—and he sniffs loudly, a big plastered jittery grin on his face as he shakes hands with a sweaty stern-looking Price who moves away so quickly that when Ted tries to slap him in a friendly sort of way on his back he just hits air.

I follow Price back past the bar and the dance floor, past the basement, and upstairs, past the long line for the women's room which is strange since there seem to be no women at the club tonight, and then we're in the men's room, which is empty, and Price and I slip into one of the stalls together and he bolts the door.

"I'm shaking," Price says, handing me the small envelope. "You open it."

I take it from him, carefully unfolding the edges of the tiny white package, exposing the supposed gram—it looks like less—to the dim fluorescent light of the men's room.

"Jeez," Price whispers in a surprisingly gentle way. "That's not a helluva lot, is it?" He leans forward to inspect it.

"Maybe it's just the light," I mention.

"What the fuck is Ricardo's problem?" Price asks, gaping at the coke.

"Shhh," I whisper, taking out my platinum American Express card. "Let's just do it."

"Is he fucking selling it by the *milligram*?" Price asks. He sticks his own platinum American Express card into the powder, bringing it up to his nose to inhale it. He stands there silently for a moment, and then gasps "Oh my god" in a low, throaty voice.

"What?" I ask.

"It's a fucking milligram of . . . *Sweet'n Low*," he chokes.

I do some of it and come to the same conclusion. "It's definitely weak but I have a feeling if we do enough of it we'll be okay—" But Price is furious, red-faced and sweating; he screams at me as if this was my fault, as if buying the gram from Madison was *my* idea.

"I want to get high off this, Bateman," Price says slowly, his voice rising. "Not sprinkle it on my fucking All-Bran!"

"You can always put it in your café au lait," this prissy voice in the next stall cries out.

Price stares at me, eyes widening in disbelief, then flies into a rage and whirls around, pounding his fist against the side of the stall.

"Calm down," I tell him. "Let's do it anyway."

Price turns back to me and, after running a hand over his stiff, slicked-back hair, seems to relent. "I guess you're right," and then he raises his voice, "that is, if the faggot in the next stall thinks it's *okay*."

We wait for a sign and then the voice in the next stall finally lisps, "It's okay with me . . ."

"Fuck yourself!" Price roars.

"Fuck *your*self," the voice mimics.

"No, *fuck yourself*," Price screams back, trying to scramble over the aluminum divider, but I pull him down with one hand and in the next stall the toilet flushes and the unidentified person, obviously unnerved, scampers out of the men's room. Price leans against the door of our stall and stares at me in this hopeless way. He rubs a trembling hand over his still-crimson face and shuts his eyes tightly, lips white, slight residue of cocaine under one nostril—and then quietly he says, without opening his eyes, "Okay. Let's do it."

"*That's* the spirit," I say. We take turns digging our respective cards into the envelope until what we can't get with the cards we press our fingers into and snort or lick off the tips then rub into our gums. I'm not anywhere near high but another J&B might give the body a false enough impression to kick in some kind of rush no matter how weak.

Stepping out of the stall we wash our hands, inspecting our reflections in the mirror, and, once satisfied, head back to the Chandelier Room. I'm beginning to wish I'd checked my overcoat (Armani) but no matter what Price says I feel kind of high and minutes later as I wait at the bar trying to get this hardbody's attention it starts not to matter. I finally have to lay a twenty on the counter to get her attention, even though I have plenty of drink tickets left. It works. Taking advantage of the drink tickets, I order two double Stolis on the rocks. She pours the drinks in front of me.

I'm feeling good and I shout out to her, "Hey, don't you go to NYU?"

She shakes her head, unsmiling.

"Hunter?" I shout.

She shakes her head again. Not Hunter.

"Columbia?" I shout—though that's a joke.

She continues to concentrate on the bottle of Stoli. I decide not to continue the conversation and just slap the drink tickets on the bar as she places the two glasses in front of me. But she shakes her head and shouts, "It's after eleven. Those aren't good anymore. It's a cash bar. That'll be twenty-five dollars," and without complaining, playing it totally cool, I pull out my gazelleskin wallet and hand her a fifty which she eyes, I swear, contemptuously and, sighing, turns to the cash register and finds my change and I say, staring at her, quite clearly but muffled by "Pump Up the Volume" and the crowd, "You are a fucking ugly bitch I want to stab to death and play around with your blood," but I'm smiling. I leave the cunt no tip and find Price who is standing again, morosely, by the railings, his hands gripping the steel bars. Paul Owen, who is handling the Fisher account, is wearing a six-button double-breasted wool tuxedo and he stands next to Price screaming something like "Ran five hundred iterations of discounted cash flow minus on an ICM PC took company cab to Smith and Wollensky."

I hand the drink to Price, while nodding to Paul. Price says nothing, not even thanks. He just holds the drink and mournfully stares at the tracks and then he squints and bends his head down to the glass and when the strobe lights start flashing, he stands up straight and murmurs something to himself.

"Aren't you high?" I ask him.

"How are you?" Owen shouts.

"Very happy," I say.

The music is one long, unending song that overlaps with other, separate songs connnected only by a dull thumping beat and it obliterates all conversation which, while I'm talking to a weasel like Owen, is perfectly okay with me. There seem to be more girls in the Chandelier Room now and I try to make eye contact with one of them—model type with big tits. Price nudges me and I lean in to ask if we should perhaps get another gram.

"Why aren't you wearing a tuxedo?" Owen asks, behind me.

"I'm leaving," Price shouts. "I'm getting out."

"Leaving what?" I shout back, confused.

"*This*," he shouts, referring to, I'm not sure but I think, his double Stoli.

"Don't," I tell him. "I'll drink it."

"Listen to me, Patrick," he screams. "I'm *leaving*."

"Where to?" I really am confused. "You want me to find Ricardo?"

"I'm leaving," he screams. "I . . . am . . . *leaving!*"

I start laughing, not knowing what he means. "Well, *where* are you going to go?"

"*Away!*" he shouts.

"Don't tell me," I shout back at him. "Merchant banking?"

"*No*, Bateman. I'm serious, you dumb son-of-a-bitch. *Leaving*. Disappearing."

"Where to?" I'm still laughing, still confused, still shouting. "Morgan Stanley? Rehab? What?"

He looks away from me, doesn't answer, just keeps staring past the railings, trying to find the point where the tracks come to an end, find what lies behind the blackness. He's becoming a drag but Owen seems worse and I've already accidentally made eye contact with the weasel.

"Tell him don't worry, be happy," Owen shouts.

"Are you still handling the Fisher account?" What else can I say to him?

"What?" Owen asks. "Wait. Is that Conrad?"

He points at some guy wearing a shawl-collar, single-breasted wool tuxedo, a cotton shirt with a bow tie, all by Pierre Cardin, who stands near the bar, directly beneath the chandelier, holding a glass of champagne, inspecting his nails. Owen pulls out a cigar, then asks for a light. I'm bored so I go for the bar without excusing myself to ask the hardbody I want to cut up for some matches. The Chandelier Room is packed and everyone looks familiar, everyone looks the same. Cigar smoke hangs heavy, floating in midair, and the music, INXS again, is louder than ever, but building toward what? I touch my brow by mistake and my fingers come back wet. At the bar I pick up some matches. On my way back through the crowd I bump into McDermott and Van Patten, who start begging me for more drink tickets. I hand them the rest of the tickets knowing that they are no longer valid, but we're crushed together in the middle of the room and the drink tickets don't offer enough incentive for them to make the trek to the bar.

"Skanky chicks," Van Patten says. "Beware. No hardbodies."

"Basement sucks," McDermott shouts.

"Did you find drugs?" Van Patten shouts. "We saw Ricardo."

"No," I shout. "Negative. Madison couldn't find any."

"Service, damnit, service," the guy behind me shouts.

"It's useless," I shout. "I can't hear anything."

"*What?*" Van Patten shouts. "I can't hear anything."

Suddenly McDermott grabs my arm. "What the fuck is Price doing? Look."

As in a movie, I turn around with some difficulty, standing on my toes to see Price perched on the rails, trying to balance himself, and someone has handed him a champagne glass and drunk or wired he holds both arms out and closes his eyes, as if blessing the crowd. Behind him the strobe light continues to flash off and on and off and on and the smoke machine is going like crazy, gray mist billowing up, enveloping him. He's shouting something but I can't hear what—the room is jammed to overcapacity, the sound level an earsplitting combination of Eddie Murphy's "Party All the Time" and the constant din of businessmen—so I push my way forward, my eyes glued on Price, and manage to pass Madison and Hugh and Turnball and Cunningham and a few others. But the crowd is too densely packed and it's futile to even keep trying. Only a few of the faces are fixated on Tim, still balancing on the railing, eyes half closed, shouting something. Embarrassed, I'm suddenly glad I'm stuck in the crowd, unable to reach him, to save him from almost certain humiliation, and during a perfectly timed byte of silence I can hear Price shout, "Goodbye!" and then, the crowd finally paying attention, "Fuckheads!" Gracefully he twists his body around and hops over the railing and leaps onto the tracks and starts running, the champagne flute bobbing as he holds it out to his side. He stumbles once, twice, with the strobe light flashing, in what looks like slow motion, but he regains his composure before disappearing into blackness. A security guard sits idly by the railing as Price recedes into the tunnel. He just shakes his head, I think.

"Price! Come back!" I yell but the crowd is actually applauding his performance. "Price!" I yell once more, over the clapping. But he's gone and it's doubtful that if he *did* hear me he would do anything about it. Madison is standing nearby and sticks his hand out as if to congratulate me for something. "That guy's a *riot*."

McDermott appears behind me and pulls at my shoulder. "Does Price know about a VIP room that we don't?" He looks worried.

Outside Tunnel now, I'm high but really tired and my mouth tastes surprisingly like NutraSweet, even after drinking two more Stolis and half a J&B. Twelve-thirty and we watch limousines try to make left turns onto the West Side Highway. The three of us, Van Patten, McDermott and myself, discuss the possibilities of finding this new club called Nekenieh. I'm not really high, just sort of drunk.

"Lunch?" I ask them, yawning. "Tomorrow?"

"Can't," McDermott says. "Haircut at the Pierre."

"What about breakfast?" I suggest.

"Nope," Van Patten says. "Gio's. Manicure."

"That reminds me," I say, inspecting a hand. "I need one too."

"How about dinner?" McDermott asks me.

"I've got a date," I say. "Shit."

"What about you?" McDermott asks Van Patten.

"No can do," Van Patten says. "I've got to go to Sunmakers. Then private workout."

OFFICE

In the elevator Frederick Dibble tells me about an item on Page Six, or some other gossip column, about Ivana Trump and then about this new Italian-Thai place on the Upper East Side that he went to last night with Emily Hamilton and starts raving about this great fusilli shiitake dish. I have taken out a gold Cross pen to write down the name of the restaurant in my address book. Dibble is wearing a subtly striped double-breasted wool suit by Canali Milano, a cotton shirt by Bill Blass, a mini-glen-plaid woven silk tie by Bill Blass Signature and he's holding a Missoni Uomo raincoat. He has a good-looking, expensive haircut and I stare at it, admiringly, while he starts humming along to the Muzak station—a version of what could be "Sympathy for the Devil"—that plays throughout all the elevators in the building our offices are in. I'm about to ask Dibble if he watched *The Patty Winters Show* this morning—the topic was Autism—but he gets out on the floor before mine and repeats the name of the restaurant, "Thaidialano," and then "See you, Marcus" and steps out of the elevator. The doors shut. I am wearing a mini-houndstooth-check wool suit with pleated trousers by Hugo Boss, a silk tie, also by Hugo Boss, a cotton broadcloth shirt by Joseph Abboud and shoes from Brooks Brothers. I flossed too hard this morning and I can still taste the coppery residue of swallowed blood in the back of my throat. I used Listerine afterwards and my mouth feels like it's on fire but I manage a smile to no one as I step out of the elevator, brushing past a hung-over Wittenborn, swinging my new black leather attaché case from Bottega Veneta.

My secretary, Jean, who is in love with me and who I will probably end up marrying, sits at her desk and this morning, to get my attention as usual, is wearing something improbably expensive and completely inappropriate: a Chanel cashmere cardigan, a cashmere crewneck and a cashmere scarf, faux-pearl earrings, wool-crepe pants from Barney's. I pull my Walkman off from around my neck as I approach her desk. She looks up and smiles shyly.

"Late?" she asks.

"Aerobics class." I play it cool. "Sorry. Any messages?"

"Ricky Hendricks has to cancel today," she says. "He didn't say what it was he is canceling or why."

"I occasionally box with Ricky at the Harvard Club," I explain. "Anyone else?"

"And . . . Spencer wants to meet you for a drink at Fluties Pier 17," she says, smiling.

"When?" I ask.

"After six."

"Negative," I tell her as I walk into my office. "Cancel it."

She gets up from behind her desk and follows me in. "Oh? And what should I say?" she asks, amused.

"Just . . . say . . . no," I tell her, taking my Armani overcoat off and hanging it on the Alex Loeb coatrack I bought at Bloomingdale's.

"Just . . . say . . . no?" she repeats.

"Did you see *The Patty Winters Show* this morning?" I ask. "On Autism?"

"No." She smiles as if somehow charmed by my addiction to *The Patty Winters Show*. "How was it?"

I pick up this morning's *Wall Street Journal* and scan the front page—all of it one ink-stained senseless typeset blur. "I think I was hallucinating while watching it. I don't know. I can't be sure. I don't remember," I murmur, placing the *Journal* back down and then, picking up today's *Financial Times*, "I really don't know." She just stands there waiting for instructions. I sigh and place my hands together, sitting down at the Palazzetti glass-top desk, the halogen lamps on both sides already burning. "Okay, Jean," I start. "I need reservations for three at Camols at twelve-thirty and if not there, try Crayons. All right?"

"Yes sir," she says in a joky tone and then turns to leave.

"Oh wait," I say, remembering something. "And I need reservations for two at Arcadia at eight tonight."

She turns around, her face falling slightly but still smiling. "Oh, something . . . romantic?"

"No, silly. Forget it," I tell her. "I'll make them. Thanks."

"I'll do it," she says.

"No. No," I say, waving her off. "Be a doll and just get me a Perrier, okay?"

"You look nice today," she says before leaving.

She's right, but I'm not saying anything—just staring across the office at the George Stubbs painting that hangs on the wall, wondering if I should move it, thinking maybe it's too close to the Aiwa AM/FM stereo receiver and the dual cassette recorder and the semiautomatic belt-drive turntable, the graphic equalizer, the matching bookshelf speakers, all in twilight blue to match the color scheme of the office. The Stubbs painting should probably go over the life-size Doberman that's in the corner ($700 at Beauty and the Beast in Trump Tower) or maybe it would look better over the Pacrizinni antique table that sits next to the Doberman. I get up and move all these sporting magazines from the forties—they cost me thirty bucks *apiece*—that I bought at Funchies, Bunkers, Gaks and Gleeks, and then I lift the Stubbs painting off the wall and balance it on the table then sit back at my desk and fiddle with the pencils I keep in a vintage German beer stein I got from Mantiques. The Stubbs looks good in either place. A reproduction Black Forest umbrella stand ($675 at Hubert des Forges) sits in another corner without, I'm just noticing, any umbrellas in it.

I put a Paul Butterfield tape in the cassette player, sit back at the desk and flip through last week's *Sports Illustrated*, but can't concentrate. I keep thinking about that damn tanning bed Van Patten has and I'm moved to pick up the phone and buzz Jean.

"Yes?" she answers.

"Jean. Listen, keep your eyes open for a tanning bed, okay?"

"What?" she asks—increduously, I'm sure, but she's still probably smiling.

"You know. A tanning bed," I repeat casually. "For a . . . tan."

"Okay . . ." she says hesitantly. "Anything else?"

"And, oh shit, yeah. Remind me to return the videotapes I rented last night back to the store." I start to open and close the sterling silver cigar holder that sits by the phone.

"Anything else?" she asks, and then, flirtatiously, "How about that Perrier?"

"Yeah. That sounds good. And Jean?"

"Yes," she says, and I'm relieved by her patience.

"You don't think I'm crazy?" I ask. "I mean for wanting a tanning bed?"

There's a pause and then, "Well, it *is* a little unusual," she admits, and I can tell she is choosing her words *very* carefully. "But no, of course not. I mean how else are you going to keep up that devilishly handsome skin tone?"

"Good girl," I say before hanging up. I have a great secretary.

She comes into the office five minutes later with the Perrier, a wedge of lime and the Ransom file, which she did not need to bring, and I am vaguely touched by her almost total devotion to me. I can't help but be flattered.

"You have a table at Camols at twelve-thirty," she announces as she pours the Perrier into a glass tumbler. "Non-smoking section."

"Don't wear that outfit again," I say, looking her over quickly. "Thanks for the Ransom file."

"Um . . ." She stalls, about to hand me the Perrier, and asks, "What? I didn't hear you," before setting the drink on my desk.

"I said," and I repeat myself calmly, grinning, "do not wear that outfit again. Wear a dress. A skirt or something."

She stands there only a little stunned, and after she looks down at herself, she smiles like some kind of cretin. "You don't like this, I take it," she says humbly.

"Come on," I say, sipping my Perrier. "You're prettier than that."

"Thanks Patrick," she says sarcastically, though I bet tomorrow she'll be wearing a dress. The phone on her desk rings. I tell her I'm not here. She turns to leave.

"And high heels," I mention. "I like high heels."

She shakes her head good-naturedly as she exits, shutting my door behind her. I take out a Panasonic pocket watch with a three-inch diagonal color TV and an AM/FM radio and try to find something to watch, hopefully *Jeopardy!*, before turning to my computer terminal.

HEALTH CLUB

The health club I belong to, Xclusive, is private and located four blocks from my apartment on the Upper West Side. In the two years since I signed up as a member, it has been remodeled three times and though they carry the latest weight machines (Nautilus, Universal, Keiser) they have a vast array of free weights which I like to use also. The club has ten courts for tennis and racquetball, aerobics classes, four aerobic dance studios, two swimming pools, Lifecycles, a Gravitron machine, rowing machines, treadmills, cross-country skiing machines, one-on-one training, cardiovascular evaluations, personalized programs, massage, sauna and steam rooms, a sun deck, tanning booths and a café with a juice bar, all of it designed by J. J. Vogel, who designed the new Norman Prager club, Petty's. Membership runs five thousand dollars annually.

It was cool this morning but seems warmer after I leave the office, and I'm wearing a six-button double-breasted chalk-striped suit by Ralph Lauren with a spread-collar pencil-striped Sea Island cotton shirt with French cuffs, also by Polo, and I remove the clothes, gratefully, in the air-conditioned locker room, then slip into a pair of crow-black cotton and Lycra shorts with a white waistband and side stripes and a cotton and Lycra tank top, both by Wilkes, which can be folded so tightly that I can actually carry them in my briefcase. After getting dressed and putting my Walkman on, clipping its body to the Lycra shorts and placing the phones over my ears, a Stephen Bishop/Christopher Cross compilation tape Todd Hunter made for me, I check myself in the mirror before entering the gym and, dissatisfied, go back to my briefcase for some mousse to slick my hair back and then I use a moisturizer and, for a small blemish I notice under my lower lip, a dab of Clinique Touch-Stick. Satisfied, I turn the Walkman on, the volume up, and leave the locker room.

Cheryl, this dumpy chick who is in love with me, sits at her desk up front signing people in, reading one of the gossip columns in the *Post*, and she brightens up noticeably when she sees me

approaching. She says hello but I move past her quickly, barely
registering her presence since there's no line at the Stairmaster, for
which usually one has to wait twenty minutes. With the Stairmaster
you work the body's largest muscle group (between the pelvis and
knees) and you can end up burning more calories per minute than
by doing any other aerobic activity, except maybe Nordic skiing.

I should probably be stretching first but if I do that I'll have to
wait in line—already some faggot is behind me, probably checking
out my back, ass, leg muscles. No hardbodies at the gym today.
Only faggots from the West Side, probably unemployed actors,
waiters by night, and Muldwyn Butner of Sachs, who I went to
Exeter with, over at the biceps curl machine. Butner is wearing a
pair of knee-length nylon and Lycra shorts with checkerboard
inserts and a cotton and Lycra tank top and leather Reeboks. I
finish twenty minutes on the Stairmaster and let the overmuscled,
bleached-blond, middle-aged faggot behind me use it and I commence with stretching exercises. While I stretch, *The Patty Winters
Show* I watched this morning comes back to me. The topic was Big
Breasts and there was a woman on it who had a breast *reduction*
since she thought her tits were too big—the dumb bitch. I immediately called McDermott who was also watching it and we both
ridiculed the woman through the rest of the segment. I do about
fifteen minutes of stretching before heading off to the Nautilus
machines.

I used to have a personal trainer whom Luis Carruthers had
recommended but he came on to me last fall and I decided to
develop my own fitness program which incorporates both aerobic
exercises and training. With weights I alternate between free
weights and weight machines that use hydraulic, pneumatic or
electromechanical resistance. Most of the machines are very
efficient since computerized keypads allow one to make adjustments
in weight resistance without getting up. The positive aspects of the
machines include minimizing muscle soreness and reducing any
chance of injury. But I also like the versatility and freedom that free
weights offer and the many variations in lifting that I can't get on
the machines.

On the leg machines I do five sets of ten repetitions. For the
back I also do five sets of ten repetitions. On the stomach crunch
machine I've gotten so I can do six sets of fifteen and on the biceps

curl machine I do seven sets of ten. Before moving to the free weights I spend twenty minutes on the exercise bike while reading the new issue of *Money* magazine. Over at the free weights I do three sets of fifteen repetitions of leg extensions, leg curls and leg presses, then three sets and twenty repetitions of barbell curls, then three sets and twenty repetitions of bent-over lateral raises for the rear deltoids and three sets and twenty repetitions of latissimus pulldowns, pulley rows, dead lifts and bent-over barbell rows. For the chest I do three sets and twenty reps of incline-bench presses. For the front deltoids I also do three sets of lateral raises and seated dumbbell presses. Finally, for the triceps I do three sets and twenty reps of cable pushdowns and close-grip bench presses. After more stretching exercises to cool down I take a quick hot shower and then head to the video store where I return two tapes I rented on Monday, *She-Male Reformatory* and *Body Double*, but I rerent *Body Double* because I want to watch it again tonight even though I know I won't have enough time to masturbate over the scene where the woman is getting drilled to death by a power drill since I have a date with Courtney at seven-thirty at Café Luxembourg.

DATE

Heading home from working out at Xclusive, and after an intense shiatsu massage, I stop at a newsstand near my building, scanning the Adults Only rack with my Walkman still on, the soothing strains of Pachelbel's Canon somehow complementing the harshly lit, laminated photographs in the magazines I flip through. I buy *Lesbian Vibrator Bitches* and *Cunt on Cunt* along with the current *Sports Illustrated* and the new issue of *Esquire*, even though I subscribe to them and both have already arrived in the mail. I wait until the stand is empty to make my purchase. The vendor says something, motions toward his hook nose, while handing me the magazines along with my change. I lower the volume and lift one of the Walkman's earphones up and ask, "What?" He touches his nose again and in a thick, nearly impenetrable accent says, I think, "Nose

uise bleding." I put my Bottega Veneta briefcase down and lift a
finger up to my face. It comes away red, wet with blood. I reach
into my Hugo Boss overcoat and bring out a Polo handkerchief and
wipe the blood away, nod my thanks, slip my Wayfarer aviator
sunglasses back on and leave. Fucking Iranian.

In the lobby of my building I stop at the front desk and try to
get the attention of a black Hispanic doorman I don't recognize.
He's on the phone to his wife or his dealer or some crack addict
and stares at me as he nods, the phone cradled in the premature
folds of his neck. When it dawns on him that I want to ask
something, he sighs, rolls his eyes up and tells whoever is on the
line to hold on. "Yeah whatchooneed?" he mumbles.

"Yes," I begin, my tone as gentle and polite as I can possibly
muster. "Could you please tell the superintendent that I have a
crack in my ceiling and . . ." I stop.

He's looking at me as if I have overstepped some kind of
unspoken boundary and I'm beginning to wonder what word confused him: certainly not *crack*, so what was it? *Superintendent?*
Ceiling? Maybe even *please?*

"Whatchoomean?" He sighs thickly, slumped back, still staring
at me.

I look down at the marble floor and also sigh and tell him,
"Look. I don't know. Just tell the superintendent it's Bateman . . .
in Ten I." When I bring my head back up to see if any of this has
registered I'm greeted by the expressionless mask of the doorman's
heavy, stupid face. I am a ghost to this man, I'm thinking. I am
something unreal, something not quite tangible, yet still an obstacle
of sorts and he nods, gets back on the phone, resumes speaking in
a dialect totally alien to me.

I collect my mail—Polo catalog, American Express bill, June
Playboy, invitation to an office party at a new club called Bedlam—
then walk to the elevator, step in while inspecting the Ralph Lauren
brochure and press the button for my floor and then the Close
Door button, but someone gets in right before the doors shut and
instinctively I turn to say hello. It's the actor Tom Cruise, who lives
in the penthouse, and as a courtesy, without asking him, I press the
PH button and he nods thank you and keeps his eyes fixed on the
numbers lighting up above the door in rapid succession. He is much
shorter in person and he's wearing the same pair of black Wayfarers

I have on. He's dressed in blue jeans, a white T-shirt, an Armani jacket.

To break the noticeably uncomfortable silence, I clear my throat and say, "I thought you were very fine in *Bartender*. I thought it was quite a good movie, and *Top Gun* too. I really thought that was good."

He looks away from the numbers and then straight at me. "It was called *Cocktail*," he says softly.

"Pardon?" I say, confused.

He clears his throat and says, "*Cocktail*. Not *Bartender*. The film was called *Cocktail*."

A long pause follows; just the sound of cables moving the elevator up higher into the building competes with the silence, obvious and heavy between us.

"Oh yeah . . . Right," I say, as if the title just dawned on me. "*Cocktail*. Oh yeah, that's right," I say. "Great, Bateman, what are you thinking about?" I shake my head as if to clear it and then, to patch things up, hold out my hand. "Hi. Pat Bateman."

Cruise tentatively shakes it.

"So," I go. "You like living in this building?"

He waits a long time before answering, "I guess."

"It's great," I say. "Isn't it?"

He nods, not looking at me, and I press the button for my floor again, an almost involuntary reaction. We stand there in silence.

"So . . . *Cocktail*," I say, after a while. "That's the name."

He doesn't say anything, doesn't even nod, but now he's looking at me strangely and he lowers his sunglasses and says, with a slight grimace, "Uh . . . your nose is bleeding."

I stand there rock still for a moment, before understanding that I have to do something about this, so I pretend to be suitably embarrassed, quizzically touch my nose then bring out my Polo handkerchief—already spotted brown—and wipe the blood away from my nostrils, overall handling it sort of well. "Must be the altitude." I laugh. "We're up so high."

He nods, says nothing, looks up at the numbers.

The elevator stops at my floor and when the doors open I tell Tom, "I'm a big fan. It's really good to finally meet you."

"Oh yeah, right." Cruise smiles that famous grin and jabs at the Close Door button.

The girl I'm going out with tonight, Patricia Worrell—blond, model, dropped out of Sweet Briar recently after only one semester —has left two messages on the answering machine, letting me know how incredibly important it is that I call her. While loosening my Matisse-inspired blue silk tie from Bill Robinson I dial her number and walk across the apartment, cordless phone in hand, to flip on the air-conditioning.

She answers on the third ring. "Hello?"

"Patricia. Hi. It's Pat Bateman."

"Oh hi," she says. "Listen, I'm on the other line. Can I call you back?"

"Well . . ." I say.

"Look, it's my health club," she says. "They've screwed up my account. I'll call you back in a sec."

"Yeah," I say and hang up.

I go into the bedroom and take off what I was wearing today: a herringbone wool suit with pleated trousers by Giorgio Correggiari, a cotton oxford shirt by Ralph Lauren, a knit tie from Paul Stuart and suede shoes from Cole-Haan. I slip on a pair of sixty-dollar boxer shorts I bought at Barney's and do some stretching exercises, holding the phone, waiting for Patricia to call back. After ten minutes of stretching, the phone rings and I wait six rings to answer it.

"Hi," she says. "It's me, Patricia."

"Could you hold on? I've got another call."

"Oh sure," she says.

I put her on hold for two minutes, then get back on the line. "Hi," I say. "Sorry."

"That's okay."

"So. Dinner," I say. "Stop by my place around eight?"

"Well, that's what I wanted to talk to you about," she says slowly.

"Oh no," I moan. "What is it?"

"Well, see, it's like this," she begins. "There's this concert at Radio City and—"

"No, no, no," I tell her adamantly. "No music."

"But my ex-boyfriend, this keyboardist from Sarah Lawrence, he's in the backup band and—" She stops, as if she has already decided to protest my decision.

"No. Uh-uh, Patricia," I tell her firmly, thinking to myself: Damnit, why *this* problem, why *tonight*?

"Oh Patrick," she whines into the phone. "It'll be so much fun."

I am now fairly sure that the odds of having sex with Patricia this evening are quite good, but not if we attend a concert in which an ex-boyfriend (there is no such thing with Patricia) is in the backup band.

"I don't like concerts," I tell her, walking into the kitchen. I open the refrigerator and take out a liter of Evian. "I don't like concerts," I say again. "I don't like 'live' music."

"But this one isn't like the *others*." She lamely adds, "We *have* good seats."

"Listen. There's no need to argue," I say. "If you want to go, *go*."

"But I thought we were going to be to*geth*er," she says, straining for emotion. "I thought we were going to have din*ner*," and then, almost definitely an afterthought, "Be tog*ether*. The *two* of us."

"I know, I know," I say. "Listen, we should all be allowed to do exactly what we *want* to do. *I* want you to do what *you* want to do."

She pauses and tries a new angle. "This music is so beautiful, so . . . I know it sounds corny, but it's . . . gl*orious*. The band is one of the best you'll ever see. They're funny and wonderful and the music is so great and, oh, gosh, I just want you to see them so badly. We'll have a great time, I guarantee it," she says with dripping earnestness.

"No, no, you go," I say. "You have a good time."

"Pat*rick*," she says. "I have *two* tickets."

"No. I don't like concerts," I say. "Live music *bugs* me."

"Well," she says and her voice sounds genuinely tinged with maybe real disappointment, "I'll feel bad that you're not there with me."

"I say go and have a good time." I unscrew the cap off the Evian bottle, timing my next move. "Don't worry. I'll just go to Dorsia alone then. It's okay."

There is a very long pause that I am able to translate into: Uh-huh, right, now see if you want to go to that lousy fucking concert. I take a large gulp of Evian, waiting for her to tell me what time she'll be over.

"Dorsia?" she asks and then, suspiciously, "You have reservations there? I mean for us?"

"Yes," I say. "Eight-thirty."

"Well . . ." She emits a little laugh and then, faltering, "It was . . . well, what I mean is, *I've* seen them. I just wanted *you* to see them."

"Listen. What are you doing?" I ask. "If you're not coming I have to call someone else. Do you have Emily Hamilton's number?"

"Oh now now, Patrick, don't be . . . *rash*." She giggles nervously. "They *are* playing two more nights so I *can* see them tomorrow. Listen, calm down, okay?"

"Okay," I say. "I'm calm."

"Now what time should I be over?" Restaurant Whore asks.

"I said eight," I tell her, disgusted.

"That's fine," she says and then in a seductive whisper, "See you at eight." She lingers on the phone as if she expects me to say something else, as if maybe I should congratulate her for making the correct decision, but I hardly have time to deal with this so I abruptly hang up.

The instant after I hang up on Patricia I dash across the room and grab the Zagat guide and flip through it until I find Dorsia. With trembling fingers I dial the number. Busy. Panicked, I put the phone on Constant Redial and for the next five minutes nothing but a busy signal, faithful and ominous, repeats itself across the line. Finally a ring and in the seconds before there's an answer I experience that rarest of occurrences—an adrenaline rush.

"Dorsia," someone answers, sex not easily identifiable, made androgynous by the wall-of-sound noise in the background. "Please hold."

It sounds slightly less noisy than a packed football stadium and it takes every ounce of courage I can muster to stay on the line and not hang up. I'm on hold for five minutes, my palm sweaty, sore from clenching the cordless phone so tightly, a fraction of me realizing the futility of this effort, another part hopeful, another fraction pissed off that I didn't make the reservations earlier or get Jean to. The voice comes back on the line and says gruffly, "Dorsia."

I clear my throat. "Um, yes, I know it's a little late but is it possible to reserve a table for two at eight-thirty or nine perhaps?" I'm asking this with both eyes shut tight.

There is a pause—the crowd in the background a surging, deafening mass—and with real hope coursing through me I open my eyes, realizing that the maître d', god love him, is probably looking through the reservation book for a cancellation—but then he starts giggling, low at first but it builds to a high-pitched crescendo of laughter which is abruptly cut off when he slams down the receiver.

Stunned, feverish, feeling empty, I contemplate the next move, the only sound the dial tone buzzing noisily from the receiver. Gather my bearings, count to six, reopen the Zagat guide and steadily regain my concentration against the almost overwhelming panic about securing an eight-thirty reservation somewhere if not as trendy as Dorsia then at least in the next-best league. I eventually get a reservation at Barcadia for two at nine, and that *only* because of a cancellation, and though Patricia will probably be disappointed she might actually *like* Barcadia—the tables are well spaced, the lighting is dim and flattering, the food Nouvelle Southwestern—and if she doesn't, what is the bitch going to do, *sue me*?

I worked out heavily at the gym after leaving the office today but the tension has returned, so I do ninety abdominal crunches, a hundred and fifty push-ups, and then I run in place for twenty minutes while listening to the new Huey Lewis CD. I take a hot shower and afterwards use a new facial scrub by Caswell-Massey and a body wash by Greune, then a body moisturizer by Lubriderm and a Neutrogena facial cream. I debate between two outfits. One is a wool-crepe suit by Bill Robinson I bought at Saks with this cotton jacquard shirt from Charivari and an Armani tie. Or a wool and cashmere sport coat with blue plaid, a cotton shirt and pleated wool trousers by Alexander Julian, with a polka-dot silk tie by Bill Blass. The Julian might be a little too warm for May but if Patricia's wearing this outfit by Karl Lagerfeld that I *think* she's going to, then maybe I *will* go with the Julian, because it would go well with *her* suit. The shoes are crocodile loafers by A. Testoni.

A bottle of Scharffenberger is on ice in a Spiros spun-aluminum bowl which is in a Christine Van der Hurd etched-glass champagne cooler which sits on a Cristofle silver-plated bar tray. The Scharffenberger isn't bad—it's not Cristal, but why waste Cristal on this bimbo? She probably wouldn't be able to tell the difference anyway. I have a glass of it while waiting for her, occasionally rearranging the Steuben animals on the glass-top coffee table by Turchin, or sometimes I flip through the last hardcover book I bought, something by Garrison Keillor. Patricia is late.

While waiting on the couch in the living room, the Wurlitzer jukebox playing "Cherish" by the Lovin' Spoonful, I come to the conclusion that Patricia *is* safe tonight, that I am not going to unexpectedly pull a knife out and use it on her just for the sake of doing so, that I am not going to get any pleasure watching her bleed from slits I've made by cutting her throat or slicing her neck open or gouging her eyes out. She's lucky, even though there is no real reasoning behind the luck. It could be that she's safe because her wealth, her *family's* wealth, protects her tonight, or it could be that it's simply *my* choice. Maybe the glass of Scharffenberger has deadened my impulse or maybe it's simply that I don't want to ruin this particular Alexander Julian suit by having the bitch spray her blood all over it. Whatever happens, the useless fact remains: Patricia will stay alive, and this victory requires no skill, no leaps of the imagination, no ingenuity on anyone's part. This is simply how the world, *my* world, moves.

She arrives thirty minutes late and I tell the doorman to let her up even though I meet her outside my door while I'm locking it. She isn't wearing the Karl Lagerfeld suit I expected, but she looks pretty decent anyway: a silk gazar blouse with rhinestone cuff links by Louis Dell'Olio and a pair of embroidered velvet pants from Saks, crystal earrings by Wendy Gell for Anne Klein and gold slingback pumps. I wait until we're in the cab heading midtown to tell her about not going to Dorsia and then I apologize profusely, mention something about disconnected phone lines, a fire, a vengeful maître d'. She gives a little gasp when I drop the news, ignores the apologies and turns away from me to glare out the window. I try to placate her by describing how trendy, how *luxurious* the restaurant we're going to is, explaining its pasta with fennel and banana, its *sorbets*, but she only shakes her head and then I'm reduced to telling her, oh Christ, about how Barcadia has gotten much more expensive even than Dorsia, but she is relentless. Her eyes, I swear, intermittently tear.

She doesn't say anything until we're seated at a mediocre table near the back section of the main dining room and that's only to order a Bellini. For dinner I order the shad-roe ravioli with apple compote as an appetizer and the meat loaf with chèvre and quail-stock sauce for an entrée. She orders the red snapper with violets and pine nuts and for an appetizer a peanut butter soup with smoked duck and mashed squash which sounds strange but is actually quite good. *New York* magazine called it a "playful but mysterious little dish" and I repeat this to Patricia, who lights a cigarette while ignoring my lit match, sulkily slumped in her seat, exhaling smoke directly into my face, occasionally shooting furious looks at me which I politely ignore, being the gentleman that I can be. Once our plates arrive I just stare at my dinner—the meat loaf dark red triangles topped by chèvre which has been tinted pink by pomegranate juice, squiggles of thick tan quail stock circling the beef, and mango slices dotting the rim of the wide black plate—for a long time, a little confused, before deciding to eat it, hesitantly picking up my fork.

Even though dinner lasts only ninety minutes it feels as if we have been sitting in Barcadia for a week, and though I have no desire to visit Tunnel afterwards it seems appropriate punishment for Patricia's behavior. The bill comes to $320—less than I expected, actually—and I put it on my platinum AmEx. In the cab heading downtown, my eyes locked on the meter, our driver tries to make conversation with Patricia who completely ignores him while checking her makeup in a Gucci compact, adding lipstick to an already heavily colored mouth. There was a baseball game on tonight that I think I forgot to videotape so I won't be able to watch it when I get home but I remember that I bought two magazines after work today and I can always spend an hour or so poring over those. I check my Rolex and realize that if we have one drink, maybe two, I'll get home in time for *Late Night with David Letterman*. Though physically Patricia is appealing and I wouldn't mind having sex with her body, the idea of treating her gently, of being a kind date, of apologizing for this evening, for not being able to get into Dorsia (even though Barcadia is *twice* as expensive for Christ sakes), rubs me the wrong way. The bitch is probably pissed we don't have a limo.

The cab stops outside Tunnel. I pay the fare and leave the driver a decent tip and hold the door open for Patricia who ignores my hand when I try to help her step out of the cab. No one stands outside the ropes tonight. In fact the only person on Twenty-fourth

Street is a bum who sits by a Dumpster, writhing in pain, moaning for change or food, and we pass quickly by him as one of the three doormen who stand behind the ropes lets us in, another one patting me on the back saying, "How are you, Mr. McCullough?" I nod, opening the door for Patricia, and before following her in say, "Fine, uh, Jim," and I shake his hand.

Once inside, after paying fifty dollars for the two of us, I head immediately to the bar without really caring if Patricia follows. I order a J&B on the rocks. She wants a Perrier, no lime, and orders this herself. After I down half the drink, leaning against the bar and checking the hardbody waitress out, something suddenly seems out of place; it's not the lighting or INXS singing "New Sensation" or the hardbody behind the bar. It's something else. When I slowly turn around to take in the rest of the club I'm confronted by space that is completely deserted. Patricia and myself are the only two customers in the entire club. We are, except for the occasional hardbody, literally the *only two people in Tunnel*. "New Sensation" becomes "The Devil Inside" and the music is full blast but it feels less loud because there isn't a crowd reacting to it, and the dance floor looks vast when empty.

I move away from the bar and decide to check out the club's other areas, expecting Patricia to follow but she doesn't. No one guards the stairs that lead to the basement and as I step down them the music from upstairs changes, melds itself into Belinda Carlisle singing "I Feel Free." The basement has one couple in it who look like Sam and Ilene Sanford but it's darker down here, *warmer*, and I could be wrong. I move past them as they stand by the bar drinking champagne and head over toward this extremely well-dressed Mexican-looking guy sitting on a couch. He's wearing a double-breasted wool jacket and matching trousers by Mario Valentino, a cotton T-shirt by Agnes B. and leather slip-ons (no socks) by Susan Bennis Warren Edwards, and he's with a good-looking muscular Eurotrash chick—dirty blond, big tits, tan, no makeup, smoking Merit Ultra Lights—who has on a cotton gown with a zebra print by Patrick Kelly and silk and rhinestone high-heeled pumps.

I ask the guy if his name is Ricardo.

He nods. "Sure."

I ask for a gram, tell him Madison sent me. I pull my wallet out and hand over a fifty and two twenties. He asks the Eurotrash chick for her purse. She hands him a velvet bag by Anne Moore. Ricardo reaches in and hands me a tiny folded envelope. Before I leave, the Eurotrash girl tells me she likes my gazelleskin wallet. I tell her I would like to tit-fuck her and then maybe cut her arms off, but the music, George Michael singing "Faith," is too loud and she can't hear me.

Back upstairs I find Patricia where I left her, alone at the bar, nursing a Perrier.

"Listen, Patrick," she says, her attitude relenting. "I just want you to know that I'm—"

"A bitch? Listen, do you want to do some coke?" I shout, cutting her line off.

"Uh, yeah . . . Sure." She's wildly confused.

"Come on," I yell, taking her hand.

She puts her drink down on the bar and follows me through the deserted club, up the stairs toward the rest rooms. There's really no reason why we couldn't do it downstairs but that seems tacky and so we do most of it in one of the men's room stalls. Back outside the men's room I sit on a couch and smoke one of her cigarettes while she goes downstairs to get us drinks.

She comes back apologizing for her behavior earlier this evening. "I mean I loved Barcadia, the food was outstanding and that mango sorbet, ohmygod I was in heaven. Listen, it's okay that we didn't go to Dorsia. We can always go some other night and I know that you probably tried to get us in but it's just so hot right now. But, oh yeah, I really loved the food at Barcadia. How long has it been open? I think it's been three, four months. I read a great review in *New York* or maybe it was *Gourmet* . . . But anyway, do you want to come with me to this band tomorrow night, or maybe we can go to Dorsia and then see Wallace's band or maybe go to Dorsia after, but maybe it's not even open that late. Patrick, I'm serious: you should really see them. Avatar is such a great lead singer and I actually thought I was in love with him once—well, actually I was in lust, not love. I really liked Wallace then but he was into this whole investment banking thing and he couldn't handle the routine and he broke down, it was the acid not the cocaine that did it. I mean I *know* but so when that all fell apart I knew that it would be, like, best to just hang out and not deal with

J&B I am thinking. Glass of J&B in my right hand I am thinking. Hand I am thinking. Charivari. Shirt from Charivari. Fusilli I am thinking. Jami Gertz I am thinking. I would like to fuck Jami Gertz I am thinking. Porsche 911. A sharpei I am thinking. I would like to own a sharpei. I am twenty-six years old I am thinking. I will be twenty-seven next year. A Valium. I would like a Valium. No, *two* Valium I am thinking. Cellular phone I am thinking.

DRY CLEANERS

The Chinese dry cleaners I usually send my bloody clothes to delivered back to me yesterday a Soprani jacket, two white Brooks Brothers shirts and a tie from Agnes B. still covered with flecks of someone's blood. I have a lunch appointment at noon—in forty minutes—and beforehand I decide to stop by the cleaners and complain. In addition to the Soprani jacket, the shirts and tie, I bring along a bag of bloodstained sheets that also need cleaning. The Chinese dry cleaners is located twenty blocks up from my apartment on the West Side, almost by Columbia, and since I've never actually been there before the distance shocks me (previously my clothes were always picked up after a phone call from my apartment and then were delivered back within twenty-four hours). Because of this excursion I have no time for a morning workout, and since I overslept, owing to a late-night-predawn coke binge with Charles Griffin and Hilton Ashbury that started innocently enough at a magazine party none of us were invited to at M.K. and ended at my automated teller sometime around five, I've missed *The Patty Winters Show* which actually was a repeat of an interview with the President, so it doesn't really matter, I guess.

I'm tense, my hair is slicked back, Wayfarers on, my skull is aching, I have a cigar—unlit—clenched between my teeth, am wearing a black Armani suit, a white cotton Armani shirt and a silk tie, also by Armani. I look sharp but my stomach is doing flip-flops, my brain is churning. On my way into the Chinese cleaners I brush past a crying bum, an old man, forty or fifty, fat and grizzled, and just as I'm opening the door I notice, to top it off, that he's also *blind* and I step on his foot, which is actually a stump, causing him to drop his cup, scattering change all over the sidewalk. Did I do this on purpose? What do you think? Or did I do this accidentally?

Then for ten minutes I point out the stains to the tiny old Chinese woman who, I'm supposing, runs the cleaners and she's even brought her husband out from the back of the shop since I can't understand a word she's saying. But the husband remains utterly mute and doesn't bother to translate. The old woman keeps jabbering in what I guess is Chinese and finally I have to interrupt.

"Listen, wait . . ." I hold up a hand with the cigar in it, the Soprani jacket draped over my other arm. "You're not . . . shhh, wait . . . shhh, you are *not* giving me *valid* reasons."

The Chinese woman keeps squealing something, grabbing at the arms of the jacket with a tiny fist. I brush her hand away and, leaning in, speak very slowly. "What are *you* trying to say to *me*?"

She keeps yipping, wild-eyed. The husband holds the two sheets he's taken out of the bag in front of him, both splattered with dried blood, and stares at them dumbly.

"Bleach-ee?" I ask her. "Are you trying to say *bleach-ee*?" I shake my head, disbelieving. "Bleach-ee? Oh my god."

She keeps pointing at the sleeves on the Soprani jacket and when she turns to the two sheets behind her, the yipping voice rises another octave.

"Two things," I say, talking over her. "One. You can't bleach a Soprani. Out of the question. Two"—and then louder, still over her—"*two*, I can only get these sheets in Santa Fe. These are very expensive sheets and I *really* need them clean . . ." But she's still talking and I'm nodding as if I understand her gibberish, then I break into a smile and lean right into her face. "If-you-don't-shut-your-fucking-mouth-I-will-kill-you-are-you-understanding-me?"

The Chinese woman's panicked jabbering speeds up incoherently, her eyes still wide. Her face overall, maybe because of the wrinkles, seems oddly expressionless. Pathetically I point at the stains again, but then realize this is useless and lower my hand, straining to understand what she's saying. Then, casually, I cut her off, talking over her again.

"Now listen, I have a very important lunch meeting"—I check my Rolex—"at Hubert's in thirty minutes"—then looking back at the woman's flat, slanty-eyed face—"and I need those . . . no, wait, *twenty* minutes. I have a lunch meeting at Hubert's in twenty minutes with Ronald Harrison and I need those sheets cleaned by this after*noon*."

But she's not listening; she keeps blabbering something in the same spastic, foreign tongue. I have never firebombed anything and I start wondering how one goes about it—what materials are involved, gasoline, matches . . . or would it be lighter fluid?

"Listen." I snap out of it, and sincerely, in singsong, leaning into her face—her mouth moving chaotically, she turns to her husband, who nods during a rare, brief pause—I tell her, "I *cannot* understand you."

I'm laughing, appalled at how ridiculous this situation is, and slapping a hand on the counter look around the shop for someone else to talk to, but it's empty, and I mutter, "This is crazy." I sigh, rubbing a hand over my face, and then abruptly stop laughing, suddenly furious. I snarl at her, "You're a *fool*. I *can't* cope with this."

She jabbers something back at me.

"What?" I ask spitefully. "You didn't hear me? You want some ham? Is that what you just said? You want . . . some *ham*?"

She grabs at the arm of the Soprani jacket again. Her husband stands behind the counter, sullen and detached.

"*You . . . are . . . a . . . fool!*" I bellow.

She jabbers back, undaunted, pointing relentlessly at the stains on the sheets.

"Stupid bitch-ee? Understand?" I shout, red-faced, on the verge of tears. I'm shaking and I yank the jacket away from her, muttering "Oh Christ."

Behind me the door opens and a bell chimes and I compose myself. Close my eyes, breathe in deeply, remind myself about stopping in at the tanning salon after lunch, maybe Hermès or—

"Patrick?"

Jolted by the sound of a real voice, I turn around and it's someone I recognize from my building, someone I've seen a number of times lingering in the lobby, staring admiringly at me whenever I run into her. She's older than me, late twenties, okay-looking, a little overweight, wearing a jogging suit—from where, Bloomingdale's? I have no idea—and she's . . . *beaming*. Taking off her sunglasses she offers a wide smile. "Hi Patrick, I thought it was you."

Having no idea what her name is I sigh a muted "Hello" then very quickly mumble something that resembles a woman's name and then I just stare at her, stumped, drained, trying to control my viciousness, the Chinese woman still screeching behind me. Finally I clap my hands together and say, "Well."

She stands there, confused, until nervously moving toward the counter, ticket in hand. "Isn't it ridiculous? Coming *all* the way up *here*, but you know they really *are* the best."

"Then why can't they get *these* stains out?" I ask patiently, still smiling, both eyes closed until the Chinese woman has finally shut up and then I open them. "I mean can you talk to these people or *some*thing?" I delicately propose. "I'm not getting *any*where."

She moves towards the sheet the old man holds up. "Oh my, I see," she murmurs. The moment she tentatively touches the sheet the old lady starts jabbering away, and ignoring her, the girl asks me, "What *are* those?" She looks at the stains again and says, "Oh my."

"Um, well . . ." I look over at the sheets, which are really quite a mess. "It's, um, cranberry juice, cranapple juice."

She looks at me and nods, as if unsure, then timidly ventures, "It doesn't look like cranberry, I mean cranapple, to me."

I stare at the sheets for a long time before stammering, "Well, I mean, um, it's really . . . *Bosco*. You know, like . . ." I pause. "Like a Dove Bar. It's a Dove Bar . . . Hershey's Syrup?"

"Oh yeah." She nods, understanding, maybe a hint of skepticism. "Oh my."

"Listen, if you could talk to them"—I reach over, yanking the sheet out of the old man's hand—"I would *really* appreciate it." I fold the sheet and lay it gently on the counter, then, checking my Rolex again, explain, "I'm really late. I have a lunch appointment at Hubert's in fifteen minutes." I move toward the door of the dry cleaners and the Chinese woman starts yapping again, desperately, shaking a finger at me. I glare at her, forcing myself not to mimic the hand gestures.

"Hubert's? Oh *really*?" the girl asks, impressed. "It moved uptown, right?"

"Yeah, well, oh boy, listen, I've got to go." I pretend to spot an oncoming cab across the street through the glass door and, faking gratitude, tell her, "Thank you, uh . . . Samantha."

"It's Victoria."

"Oh right, Victoria." I pause. "Didn't I say that?"

"No. You said Samantha."

"Well, I'm sorry." I smile. "I'm having problems."

"Maybe we could have lunch one day next week?" she suggests hopefully, moving toward me while I'm backing out of the store. "You know, I'm downtown near Wall Street quite often."

"Oh, I don't know, Victoria." I force an apologetic grin, avert my gaze from her thighs. "I'm at work all the time."

"Well, what about, oh, you know, maybe a Saturday?" Victoria asks, afraid she'll offend.

"Next Saturday?" I ask, checking my Rolex again.

"Yeah." She shrugs timidly.

"Oh. Can't, I'm afraid. Matinee of *Les Misérables*," I lie. "Listen. I've *really* got to go. I'll . . ." I run a hand over my hair and mutter "Oh Christ" before forcing myself to add, "I'll call you."

"Okay." She smiles, relieved. "Do."

I glare at the Chinese woman once more and rush the hell out of there, dashing after a nonexistent cab, and then I slow down a block or two up past the cleaners and—

suddenly I find myself eyeing a very pretty homeless girl sitting on the steps of a brownstone on Amsterdam, a Styrofoam coffee cup resting on the step below her feet, and as if guided by radar I move toward her, smiling, fishing around in my pocket for change. Her face seems too young and fresh and tan for a homeless person's; it makes her plight all the more heartbreaking. I examine her carefully in the seconds it takes to move from the edge of the sidewalk to the steps leading up to the brownstone where she sits, her head bowed down, staring dumbly into her empty lap. She looks up, unsmiling, after she notices me standing over her. My nastiness vanishes and, wanting to offer something kind, something simple, I lean in, still staring, eyes radiating sympathy into her blank, grave face, and dropping a dollar into the Styrofoam cup I say, "Good luck."

Her expression changes and because of this I notice the book— Sartre—in her lap and then the Columbia book bag by her side and finally the tan-colored coffee in the cup and my dollar bill floating in it and though this all happens in a matter of seconds it's played out in slow motion and she looks at me, then at the cup, and shouts, "Hey, what's your goddamn problem?" and frozen, hunched over the cup, cringing, I stutter, "I didn't . . . I didn't know it was . . . full," and shaken, I walk away, hailing a taxi, and heading toward Hubert's in it I hallucinate the buildings into mountains, into volcanoes, the streets become jungles, the sky freezes into a back-drop, and before stepping out of the cab I have to cross my eyes in order to clear my vision. Lunch at Hubert's becomes a permanent hallucination in which I find myself dreaming while still awake.

HARRY'S

"You should match the socks with the trousers," Todd Hamlin tells Reeves, who is listening intently, stirring his Beefeater on the rocks with a swizzle stick.

"Who says?" George asks.

"Now listen," Hamlin patiently explains. "If you wear *gray* trousers, you wear *gray* socks. It's as simple as that."

"But wait," I interrupt. "What if the shoes are *black*?"

"That's okay," Hamlin says, sipping his martini. "But then the belt has to *match* the shoes."

"So what you're saying is that with a *gray* suit you can either wear gray or *black* socks," I ask.

"Er . . . yeah," Hamlin says, confused. "I guess. Did I say that?"

"See, Hamlin," I say, "I disagree about the belt since the shoes are so far away from the actual *belt* line. I think you should concentrate on wearing a belt that coordinates with the *trousers*."

"He *has* a point," Reeves says.

The three of us, Todd Hamlin and George Reeves and myself, are sitting in Harry's and it's a little after six. Hamlin is wearing a suit by Lubiam, a great-looking striped spread-collar cotton shirt from Burberry, a silk tie by Resikeio and a belt from Ralph Lauren. Reeves is wearing a six-button double-breasted suit by Christian Dior, a cotton shirt, a patterned silk tie by Claiborne, perforated cap-toe leather lace-ups by Allen-Edmonds, a cotton handkerchief in his pocket, probably from Brooks Brothers; sunglasses by Lafont Paris lie on a napkin by his drink and a fairly nice attaché case from T. Anthony rests on an empty chair by our table. I'm wearing a two-button single-breasted chalk-striped wool-flannel suit, a multi-colored candy-striped cotton shirt and a silk pocket square, all by Patrick Aubert, a polka-dot silk tie by Bill Blass and clear prescription eyeglasses with frames by Lafont Paris. One of our CD Walkman headsets lies in the middle of the table surrounded by drinks and a calculator. Reeves and Hamlin left the office early today for facials somewhere and they both look good, faces pink but tan, hair short and slicked back. *The Patty Winters Show* this morning was about Real-Life Rambos.

"But what about vests?" Reeves asks Todd. "Aren't they . . . *out*?"

"No, George," Hamlin says. "Of *course* not."

"No," I agree. "Vests have *never* been out of fashion."

"Well, the question really *is*—how should they be worn?" Hamlin inquires.

"They should fit—" Reeves and I start simultaneously.

"Oh sorry," Reeves says. "Go ahead."

"No, it's okay," I say. "You go ahead."

"I insist," George says.

"Well, they should fit trimly around the body and cover the waistline," I say. "It should peek just above the waist button of the suit jacket. Now if too much of the vest appears, it'll give the suit a tight, constricted look that you don't want."

"Uh-huh," Reeves says, nearly mute, looking confused. "Right. I knew that."

"I need another J&B," I say, getting up. "Guys?"

"Beefeater on rocks with a twist." Reeves, pointing at me.

Hamlin. "Martini."

"Sure thing." I walk over toward the bar and while waiting for Freddy to pour the drinks I hear some guy, I think it's this Greek William Theodocropopolis, from First Boston, who's wearing a sort of tacky wool jacket in a houndstooth check and an okay-looking shirt, but he also has on a super-looking cashmere tie from Paul Stuart that makes the suit look better than it deserves to, and he's telling some guy, another Greek, drinking a Diet Coke, "So listen, Sting was at Chernoble—you know that place the guys who opened Tunnel opened—and so this was on Page Six and someone drives up in a Porsche 911 and in the car was Whitney and—"

Back at our table Reeves is telling Hamlin about how he taunts the homeless in the streets, about how he hands a dollar to them as he approaches and then yanks it away and pockets it right when he passes the bums.

"Listen, it *works*," he insists. "They're so shocked they shut *up*."

"Just . . . say . . . no," I tell him, setting the drinks on the table. "That's *all* you have to say."

"Just say no?" Hamlin smiles. "It works?"

"Well, actually only with pregnant homeless women," I admit.

"I take it you haven't tried the just-say-no approach with the seven-foot gorilla on Chambers Street?" Reeves asks. "The one with the crack pipe?"

"Listen, has *any*one heard of this club called Nekenieh?" Reeves asks.

From my POV Paul Owen sits at a table across the room with someone who looks a lot like Trent Moore, or Roger Daley, and some other guy who looks like Frederick Connell. Moore's grandfather owns the company he works at. Trent is wearing a mini-houndstooth-check worsted wool suit with multicolored overplaid.

"Nekenieh?" Hamlin asks. "What's Nekenieh?"

"Guys, guys," I say. "Who's sitting with Paul Owen over there? Is that Trent Moore?"

"Where?" Reeves.

"They're getting up. That table," I say. "Those guys."

"Isn't that Madison? No, it's Dibble," Reeves says. He puts on his clear prescription eyeglasses just to make sure.

"No," Hamlin says. "It's Trent Moore."

"Are you sure?" Reeves asks.

Paul Owen stops by our table on his way out. He's wearing sunglasses by Persol and he's carrying a briefcase by Coach Leatherware.

"Hello, men," Owen says and he introduces the two guys he's with, Trent Moore and someone named Paul Denton.

Reeves and Hamlin and I shake their hands without standing

up. George and Todd start talking to Trent, who is from Los Angeles and knows where Nekenieh is located. Owen turns his attention my way, which makes me slightly nervous.

"How have you been?" Owen asks.

"I've been great," I say. "And you?"

"Oh terrific," he says. "How's the Hawkins account going?"

"It's . . ." I stall and then continue, faltering momentarily, "It's . . . all right."

"Really?" he asks, vaguely concerned. "That's interesting," he says, smiling, hands clasped together behind his back. "Not *great*?"

"Oh well," I say. "You . . . know."

"And how's Marcia?" he asks, still smiling, looking over the room, not really listening to me. "She's a *great* girl."

"Oh yes," I say, shaken. "I'm . . . lucky."

Owen has mistaken me for Marcus Halberstam (even though Marcus is dating Cecelia Wagner) but for some reason it really doesn't matter and it seems a logical faux pas since Marcus works at P & P also, in fact does the same exact thing I do, and he also has a penchant for Valentino suits and clear prescription glasses and we share the same barber at the same place, the Pierre Hotel, so it seems understandable; it doesn't irk me. But Paul Denton keeps staring at me, or trying not to, as if he knows something, as if he's not quite sure if he recognizes me or not, and it makes me wonder if maybe he was on that cruise a long time ago, one night last March. If that's the case, I'm thinking, I should get his telephone number or, better yet, his address.

"Well, we should have drinks," I tell Owen.

"*Great*," he says. "Let's. Here's my card."

"Thanks," I say, looking at it closely, relieved by its crudeness, before slipping it into my jacket. "Maybe I'll bring . . ." I pause, then carefully say, "Marcia?"

"That would be *great*," he says. "Hey, have you been to that Salvadorian bistro on Eighty-third?" he asks. "We're eating there tonight."

"Yeah. I mean no," I say. "But I've heard it's quite good." I smile weakly and take a sip of my drink.

"Yes, so have I." He checks his Rolex. "Trent? Denton? Let's split. Reservation's in fifteen minutes."

Goodbyes are said and on their way out of Harry's they stop by the table Dibble and Hamilton are sitting at, or at least I *think* it's Dibble and Hamilton. Before they leave, Denton looks over at our table, at me, one last time, and he seems panicked, convinced of something by my presence, as if he recognized me from somewhere, and this, in turn, freaks *me* out.

"The Fisher account," Reeves says.

"Oh shit," I say. "Don't remind us."

"Lucky bastard," Hamlin says.

"Has anyone seen his girlfriend?" Reeves asks. "Laurie Kennedy? Total hardbody."

"I know her," I say, admit, "I knew her."

"Why do you say it like that?" Hamlin asks, intrigued. "Why *does* he says it like that, Reeves?"

"Because he *dated* her," Reeves says casually.

"How did you know that?" I ask, smiling.

"Girls dig Bateman." Reeves sounds a little drunk. "He's *GQ*. You're *total GQ*, Bateman."

"Thanks guy, but . . ." I can't tell if he's being sarcastic but it makes me feel proud in a way and I try to downplay my good looks by saying, "She's got a *lousy* personality."

"Oh Christ, Bateman," Hamlin groans. "What does *that* mean?"

"What?" I say. "*She does.*"

"So what? It's all *looks*. Laurie Kennedy is a *babe*," Hamlin says, emphatically. "Don't even pretend you were interested for *any* other reason."

"If they have a good personality then . . . something is very wrong," Reeves says, somehow confused by his own statement.

"If they have a good personality and they are *not* great-looking" —Reeves holds his hands up, signifying something—"who fucking *cares?*"

"Well, let's just say hypo*thet*ically, okay? What *if* they have a good personality?" I ask, knowing full well what a hopeless, asinine question it is.

"Fine. *Hypo*thetically even better but—" Hamlin says.

"I know, I know." I smile.

"There *are* no girls with good personalities," we all say in unison, laughing, giving each other high-five.

"A good personality," Reeves begins, "consists of a chick who has a little hardbody and who will satisfy all sexual demands without being too slutty about things and who will essentially keep her dumb fucking mouth *shut*."

"Listen," Hamlin says, nodding in agreement. "The only girls with good personalities who are smart or maybe funny or halfway intelligent or even talented—though god knows what the fuck *that* means—are *ugly* chicks."

"*Absolutely*." Reeves nods.

"And this is because they have to make up for how fucking *unattractive* they are," Hamlin says, sitting back in his chair.

"Well, my theory's always been," I start, "men are only here to procreate, to carry on the species, you know?"

They both nod.

"And so the only way to do that," I continue, choosing words carefully, "is . . . to get turned on by a little hardbody, but sometimes *money* or *fame*—"

"No *buts*," Hamlin says, interrupting. "Bateman, are you telling me that you're gonna make it with Oprah Winfrey—hey, she's rich, she's powerful—or go down on Nell Carter—hey, she's got a show on Broadway, a great voice, residuals pouring in?"

"Wait," Reeves says. "*Who* is Nell Carter?"

"I don't know," I say, confused by the name. "She owns Nell's, I guess."

"Listen to me, Bateman," Hamlin says. "The only reason chicks exist is to get us turned on, like you said. Survival of the species, right? It's as simple"—he lifts an olive out of his drink and pops it into his mouth—"as that."

After a deliberate pause I say, "Do you know what Ed Gein said about women?"

"*Ed Gein?*" one of them asks. "Maître d' at Canal Bar?"

"No," I say. "Serial killer, Wisconsin in the fifties. He was an interesting guy."

"You've always been interested in stuff like that, Bateman," Reeves says, and then to Hamlin, "Bateman reads these biographies all the time: Ted Bundy and Son of Sam and *Fatal Vision* and Charlie Manson. All of them."

"So what did Ed say?" Hamlin asks, interested.

"He said," I begin, "'When I see a pretty girl walking down the street I think two things. One part of me wants to take her out and talk to her and be real nice and sweet and treat her right.'" I stop, finish my J&B in one swallow.

"What does the other part of him think?" Hamlin asks tentatively.

"What her head would look like on a stick," I say.

Hamlin and Reeves look at each other and then back at me before I start laughing, and then the two of them uneasily join in.

"Listen, what about dinner?" I say, casually changing subjects.

"How about that Indian-Californian place on the Upper West Side?" Hamlin suggests.

"Fine with me," I say.

"Sounds good," Reeves says.

"Who'll make the rez?" Hamlin asks.

DECK CHAIRS

Courtney Lawrence invites me out to dinner on Monday night and the invitation seems vaguely sexual so I accept, but part of the catch is that we have to endure dinner with two Camden graduates, Scott and Anne Smiley, at a new restaurant they chose on Columbus called Deck Chairs, a place I had my secretary research so thoroughly that she presented me with three alternative menus of what I should order before I left the office today. The things that Courtney told me about Scott and Anne—he works at an advertising agency, she opens restaurants with her father's money, most recently 1968 on the Upper East Side—on the interminable cab ride uptown was only slightly less interesting than hearing about Courtney's day: facial at Elizabeth Arden, buying kitchen utensils at the Pottery Barn (all of this, by the way, on lithium) before coming down to Harry's where we had drinks with Charles Murphy and Rusty Webster, and where Courtney forgot the bag of Pottery Barn utensils she'd put underneath our table. The only detail of Scott and Anne's life that seems even remotely suggestive to me is that they adopted a Korean boy of thirteen the year after they married, named him Scott Jr. and sent him to Exeter, where Scott had gone to school four years before I attended.

"They better have reservations," I warn Courtney in the cab.

"Just don't smoke a cigar, Patrick," she says slowly.

"Is that Donald Trump's car?" I ask, looking over at the limousine stuck next to us in gridlock.

"Oh god, Patrick. Shut up," she says, her voice thick and drugged.

"You know, Courtney, I have a Walkman in my Bottega Veneta briefcase I could easily put on," I say. "You should take some more lithium. Or have a Diet Coke. Some caffeine might get you out of this slump."

"I just want to have a child," she says softly, staring out the window, to no one. "Just . . . two . . . perfect . . . children."

"Are you talking to me or Shlomo here?" I sigh, but loudly enough for the Israeli driver to hear me, and predictably Courtney doesn't say anything.

The Patty Winters Show this morning was about Perfumes and Lipsticks and Makeups. Luis Carruthers, Courtney's boyfriend, is out of town in Phoenix and will not be back in Manhattan until late Thursday. Courtney is wearing a wool jacket and vest, a wool jersey T-shirt and wool gabardine pants by Bill Blass, crystal, enamel and gold-plated earrings by Gerard E. Yosca and silk-satin d'Orsay pumps from Manolo Blahnik. I am wearing a custom-made tweed jacket, pants and a cotton shirt from the Alan Flusser shop and a silk tie by Paul Stuart. There was a twenty-minute wait at the Stairmaster machine at my health club this morning. I wave to a beggar on the corner of Forty-ninth and Eighth, then give him the finger.

Tonight the talk centers around Elmore Leonard's new book— which I haven't read; certain restaurant critics—who I have; the British soundtrack from *Les Misérables* versus the American cast recording; that new Salvadorian bistro on Second and Eighty-third; and which gossip columns are better written—the *Post*'s or the *News*'s. It seems that Anne Smiley and I share a mutual acquaintance, a waitress from Abetone's in Aspen who I raped with a can of hairspray last Christmas when I was skiing there over the holidays. Deck Chairs is crowded, earsplitting, the acoustics lousy because of the high ceilings, and if I'm not mistaken, accompanying the din is a New Age version of "White Rabbit" blaring from speakers mounted in the ceiling corners. Someone who looks like Forrest Atwater—slicked-back blond hair, nonprescription redwood-framed glasses, Armani suit with suspenders—is sitting with Caroline Baker, an investment banker at Drexel, maybe, and she doesn't look too good. She needs more makeup, the Ralph Lauren tweed outfit is too severe. They're at a mediocre table up front by the bar.

"It's called California *classic* cuisine," Anne tells me, leaning in close, after we ordered. The statement deserves a reaction, I suppose, and since Scott and Courtney are discussing the merits of the *Post*'s gossip column, it's up to me to reply.

"You mean compared to, say, Cali*fornia* cuisine?" I ask carefully, measuring each word, then lamely add, "Or *post*-California cuisine?"

"I mean I know it sounds so trendy but there *is* a world of difference. It's *sub*tle," she says, "but it's *there*."

"I've heard of post-California cuisine," I say, acutely aware of the design of the restaurant: the exposed pipe and the columns and the open pizza kitchen and the . . . deck chairs. "In fact I've even eaten it. No baby vegetables? Scallops in burritos? Wasabi crackers? Am I on the right track? And by the way, did anyone ever tell you that you look exactly like Garfield but run over and skinned and then someone threw an ugly Ferragamo sweater over you before they rushed you to the vet? Fusilli? Olive oil on Brie?"

"Exactly," Anne says, impressed. "Oh Courtney, where *did* you find Patrick? He's so knowledgeable about things. I mean Luis's idea of California cuisine is half an orange and some *gelati*," she gushes, then laughs, encouraging me to laugh with her, which I do, hesitantly.

For an appetizer I ordered radicchio with some kind of free-range squid. Anne and Scott both had the monkfish ragout with violets. Courtney almost fell asleep when she had to exert the energy to read the menu, but before she slid off her chair I grabbed both shoulders, propping her up, and Anne ordered for her, something simple and light like Cajun popcorn perhaps, which wasn't on the menu but since Anne knows Noj, the chef, he made up a special little batch . . . *just for Courtney!* Scott and Anne insisted that we all order some kind of blackened medium-rare redfish, a Deck

Chairs specialty which was, luckily for them, an entrée on one of the mock menus that Jean made up for me. If it hadn't, and if they nevertheless insisted on my ordering it, the odds were pretty good that after dinner tonight I would have broken into Scott and Anne's studio at around two this morning—after *Late Night with David Letterman*—and with an ax chopped them to pieces, first making Anne watch Scott bleed to death from gaping chest wounds, and then I would have found a way to get to Exeter where I would pour a bottle of acid all over their son's slanty-eyed zipperhead face. Our waitress is a little hardbody who is wearing gold faux-pearl tasseled lizard sling-back pumps. I forgot to return my videotapes to the store tonight and I curse myself silently while Scott orders two large bottles of San Pellegrino.

"It's called California *classic* cuisine," Scott is telling me.

"Why don't we all go to Zeus Bar next week?" Anne suggests to Scott. "You think we'd have a problem getting a table on Friday?" Scott is wearing a red and purple and black striped cashmere intarsia sweater from Paul Stuart, baggy Ralph Lauren corduroys and Cole-Haan leather moccasins.

"Well . . . maybe," he says.

"That's a *good* idea. I *like* it a lot," Anne says, picking up a small violet off her plate and sniffing the flower before placing it carefully on her tongue. She's wearing a red, purple and black hand-knitted mohair and wool sweater from Koos Van Den Akker Couture and slacks from Anne Klein, with suede open-toe pumps.

A waiter, though not the hardbody, strides over to take another drink order.

"J&B. Straight," I say before anyone else orders.

Courtney orders a champagne on the rocks, which secretly appalls me. "Oh," she says as if reminded by something, "can I have that with a twist?"

"A twist of *what*?" I ask irritably, unable to stop myself. "Let me guess. *Melon*?" And I'm thinking oh my god why didn't you return those goddamn videos Bateman you dumb son-of-a-bitch.

"You mean *lemon*, miss," the waiter says, giving *me* an icy stare.

"Yes, of course. Lemon." Courtney nods, seeming lost in some kind of dream—but enjoying it, oblivious to it.

"I'll have a glass of the . . . oh gosh, I guess the Acacia," Scott says and then addresses the table: "Do I want a white? Do I really want a chardonnay? We can eat the redfish with a cabernet."

"Go for it," Anne says cheerily.

"Okay, I'll have the . . . oh jeez, the sauvignon blanc," Scott says.

The waiter smiles, confused.

"*Scottie*," Anne shrieks. "The sauvignon *blanc*?"

"Just teasing," he snickers. "I'll have the chardonnay. The Acacia."

"You complete *jerk*." Anne smiles, relieved. "You're *fun*ny."

"I'm having the chardonnay," Scott tells the waiter.

"That's nice," Courtney says, patting Scott's hand.

"I'll just have . . ." Anne stalls, deliberating. "Oh, I'll just have a Diet Coke."

Scott looks up from a piece of corn bread he was dipping into a small tin of olive oil. "You're not drinking tonight?"

"No," Anne says, smiling naughtily. Who knows why? And who fucking cares? "I'm not in the mood."

"Not even for a glass of the chardonnay?" Scott asks. "How about a sauvignon blanc?"

"I have this aerobics class at nine," she says, slipping, losing control. "I really shouldn't."

"Well then, I don't want anything," Scott says, disappointed. "I mean I have one at eight at Xclusive."

"Does anyone want to guess where I *won't* be tomorrow morning at eight?" I ask.

"No, honey. I know how much you like the Acacia." Anne reaches out and squeezes Scott's hand.

"No, babe. I'll stick to the Pellegrino," Scott says, pointing.

I'm tapping my fingers very loudly on the tabletop, whispering "shit, shit, shit, shit" to myself. Courtney's eyes are half closed and she's breathing deeply.

"Listen. I'll be *daring*," Anne says finally. "I'll have a Diet Coke with *rum*."

Scott sighs, then smiles, beaming really. "Good."

"That's a *caffeine-free* Diet Coke, right?" Anne asks the waiter.

"You know," I interrupt, "you should have it with Diet Pepsi. It's much better."

"Really?" Anne asks. "What do you mean?"

"You should have the Diet Pepsi instead of the Diet Coke," I say. "It's much better. It's fizzier. It has a cleaner taste. It mixes better with rum and has a lower sodium content."

The waiter, Scott, Anne, and even Courtney—they all stare at me as if I've offered some kind of diabolical, apocalyptic observation, as if I were shattering a myth highly held, or destroying an oath that was solemnly regarded, and it suddenly seems almost hushed in Deck Chairs. Last night I rented a movie called *Inside Lydia's Ass* and while on two Halcion and in fact sipping a Diet Pepsi, I watched as Lydia—a totally tan bleached-blond hardbody with a perfect ass and great full tits—while on all fours gave head to this guy with a huge cock while another gorgeous blond little hardbody with a perfectly trimmed blond pussy knelt behind Lydia and after eating her ass out and sucking on her cunt, started to push a long, greased silver vibrator into Lydia's ass and fucked her with it while she continued to eat her pussy and the guy with the huge cock came all over Lydia's face as she sucked his balls and then Lydia bucked to an authentic-looking, fairly strong orgasm and then the girl behind Lydia crawled around and licked the come from Lydia's face and then made Lydia suck on the vibrator. The new Stephen Bishop came out last Tuesday and at Tower Records yesterday I bought the compact disc, the cassette and the album because I wanted to own all three formats.

"Listen," I say, my voice trembling with emotion, "have whatever you want but I'm telling you I recommend the Diet Pepsi." I look down at my lap, at the blue cloth napkin, the words Deck Chairs sewn into the napkin's edge, and for a moment think I'm going to cry; my chin trembles and I can't swallow.

Courtney reaches over and touches my wrist gently, stroking my Rolex. "It's okay Patrick. It really is . . ."

A sharp pain near my liver overcomes the surge of emotion and I sit up in my chair, startled, confused, and the waiter leaves and then Anne asks if we've seen the recent David Onica exhibit and I'm feeling calmer.

It turns out we haven't seen the show but I don't want to be tacky enough to bring up the fact I own one, so I lightly kick Courtney under the table. This raises her out of the lithium-induced stupor and she says robotically, "Patrick owns an Onica. He really does."

I smile, pleased; sip my J&B.

"Oh that's fan*tas*tic, Patrick," Anne says.

"Really? An Onica?" Scott asks. "Isn't he *quite* expensive?"

"Well, let's just say . . ." I sip my drink, suddenly confused: say . . . say what? "Nothing."

Courtney sighs, anticipating another kick. "Patrick's cost twenty thousand dollars." She seems bored out of her mind, picking at a flat, warm piece of corn bread.

I give her a sharp look and try not to hiss. "Uh, no Courtney, it was really *fifty*."

She slowly looks up from the corn bread she's mashing between her fingers and even in her lithium haze manages a stare so malicious that it automatically humbles me, but not enough to tell Scott and Anne the truth: that the Onica cost only twelve grand. But Courtney's frightening gaze—though I might be overreacting; she might be staring disapprovingly at the patterns on the columns, the venetian blinds on the skylight, the Montigo vases full of purple tulips lining the bar—scares me enough to not elaborate on the procedure of purchasing an Onica. It's a stare that I can interpret fairly easily. It warns: Kick me again and no pussy, do you understand?

"That seems . . ." Anne starts.

I hold my breath, my face tight with tension.

". . . *low*," she murmurs.

I exhale. "It *is*. But I got a fabulous deal," I say, gulping.

"But *fifty* thousand?" Scott asks suspiciously.

"Well, I think his work . . . it has a kind of . . . wonderfully proportioned, purposefully mock-superficial quality." I pause, then, trying to remember a line from a review I saw in *New York* magazine: "Purposefully mock . . ."

"Doesn't Luis own one, Courtney?" Anne asks, and then tapping Courtney's arm. "Courtney?"

"Luis . . . owns . . . what?" Courtney shakes her head as if to clear it, widening her eyes to make sure they don't close on her.

"Who's Luis?" Scott asks, waving to the waitress to have the butter the busboy recently placed on the table removed—what a *party animal*.

Anne answers for Courtney. "Her *boyfriend*," she says after seeing Courtney, confused, actually looking at me for help.

"Where's he at?" Scott asks.

"Texas," I say quickly. "He's out of town in Phoenix, I mean."

"No," Scott says. "I mean what *house*."

"L. F. Rothschild," Anne says, about to look at Courtney for confirmation, but then at me. "Right?"

"No. He's at P & P," I say. "We work together, sort of."

"Wasn't he dating Samantha Stevens at one point?" Anne asks.

"No," Courtney says. "That was just a photo someone took of them that was in *W*."

I down my drink as soon as it arrives and wave almost immediately for another and I'm thinking Courtney *is* a babe but no sex is worth this dinner. The conversation violently shifts while I'm staring across the room at a great-looking woman—blond, big tits, tight dress, satin pumps with gold cones—when Scott starts telling me about his new compact disc player while Anne unwittingly prattles on to a stoned and completely oblivious Courtney about new kinds of low-sodium wheat-rice cake, fresh fruit and New Age music, particularly Manhattan Steamroller.

"It's Aiwa," Scott's saying. "You've *got* to hear it. The sound"—he pauses, closes his eyes in ecstasy, chewing on corn bread—"is fan*tastic*."

"Well, you know, Scottie, the Aiwa *is* okay." Oh holy shit, *dream on, Scot-tie*, I'm thinking. "But Sansui is really *top* of the line." I pause, then add, "I should know. I own one."

"But I thought *Aiwa* was top of the line." Scott looks worried but not yet upset enough to please me.

"No way, Scott," I say. "Does Aiwa have digital remote control?"

"Yeah," he says.

"Computer controls?"

"Uh-huh." What a complete and total *dufus*.

"Does the system come with a turntable that has a metacrylate and brass platter?"

"Yes," the bastard lies!

"Does your system have an . . . Accophase T-106 tuner?" I ask him.

"Sure," he says, shrugging.

"Are you sure?" I say. "Think carefully."

"Yeah. I think so," he says, but his hand shakes as it reaches for more of the corn bread.

"What kind of speakers?"

"Well, Duntech wood," he answers too quickly.

"*So solly* dude. You've got to have the Infinity IRS V speakers," I say. "Or—"

"Wait a minute," he interrupts. "V speakers? I've never heard of V speakers."

"See, that's what I mean," I say. "If you don't have the V's, you might as well be listening to a goddamn Walkman."

"What's the bass response on those speakers?" he asks suspiciously.

"An ultralow fifteen hertz," I purr, enunciating each word.

That shuts him up for a minute. Anne drones on about nonfat frozen yogurt and chow chows. I sit back, satisfied at having stumped Scott, but too quickly he regains his composure and says, "Anyway"—trying to act blissfully uncaring that he owns a cheap, shitty stereo—"we bought the new Phil Collins today. You should hear how great 'Groovy Kind of Love' sounds on it."

"Yeah, I think it's by the far best song he's written," I say, blah blah blah, and though it's finally something Scott and I can agree on, the plates of blackened redfish appear and they look bizarre and Courtney excuses herself to the ladies' room and, after thirty minutes, when she hasn't reappeared I wander into the back of the restaurant and find her asleep in the coatcheck room.

But at her apartment she lies naked on her back, her legs—tan and aerobicized and muscular and worked out—are spread and I'm on my knees giving her head while jerking myself off and in the time since I've started licking and sucking on her pussy she's already come twice and her cunt is tight and hot and wet and I keep it spread open, fingering it with one hand, keeping myself hard with the other. I lift her ass up, wanting to push my tongue into her, but she doesn't want me to and so I raise up my head and reach over to the Portian antique nightstand for the condom that sits in the ashtray from Palio next to the halogen Tensor lamp and the D'Oro pottery urn and I tear the package open with two shiny slick fingers and my teeth, then slip it, easily, onto my cock.

"I want you to fuck *me*," Courtney moans, pulling her legs back, spreading her vagina even wider, fingering herself, making me suck her fingers, the nails on her hand long and red, and the juice from her cunt, glistening in the light coming from the street-lamps through the Stuart Hall venetian blinds, tastes pink and sweet and she rubs it over my mouth and lips and tongue before it cools.

"Yeah," I say, moving on top of her, sliding my dick gracefully into her cunt, kissing her on the mouth hard, pushing into her with long fast strokes, my cock, my hips crazed, moving on their own desirous momentum, already my orgasm builds from the base of my balls, my asshole, coming up through my cock so stiff that it aches—but then in mid-kiss I lift my head up, leaving her tongue hanging out of her mouth starting to lick her own red swollen lips, and while still humping but lightly now I realize there . . . is . . . a . . . problem of sorts but I cannot think of what it is right now . . . but then it hits me while I'm staring at the half-empty bottle of Evian water on the nightstand and I gasp "Oh shit" and pull out.

"What?" Courtney moans. "Did you forget something?"

Without answering I get up from the futon and stumble into her bathroom trying to pull off the condom but it gets stuck halfway and while easing it off I accidentally trip over the Genold scale while also trying to flip on the light switch and in the process stubbing my big toe, then, cursing, I manage to open the medicine cabinet.

"Patrick, what are you *doing*?" she calls from the bedroom.

"I'm looking for the water-soluble spermicidal lubricant," I call back. "What do you think I'm doing? Looking for an *Advil*?"

"Oh my god," she cries out. "You didn't have *any on*?"

"Courtney," I call back, noticing a small razor nick above my lip. "Where *is* it?"

"I *can*not hear you, Patrick," she calls out.

"Luis has terrible taste in cologne," I mutter, picking up a bottle of Paco Rabanne, sniffing it.

"What *are* you saying?" she cries out.

"The water-soluble spermicidal lubricant," I shout back, staring into the mirror, searching her counter for a Clinique Touch-Stick to put over the razor nick.

"What do you mean—*where is it?*" she calls out. "Didn't you have it *with* you?"

"Where is the goddamn *water-soluble spermicidal lubricant*?" I scream. "Water! Soluble! Spermicidal! Lubricant!" I'm shouting this while using some of her Clinique cover-up over the blemish, then combing my hair back.

"Top shelf," she says, "I think."

While looking through the medicine cabinet I glance over at her tub, noticing how plain it is, which moves me to say, "You know, Courtney, you should really get your act together and get your tub marbleized or maybe add some jacuzzi jets." I call out, "Can you hear me? Courtney?"

After a long while she says, "Yes . . . Patrick. I hear you."

I finally find the tube behind a huge bottle—a *jar*—of Xanax on the top shelf of the medicine cabinet and before my dick totally softens place a small dab of it inside the tip of the condom, slather it on the latex sheath and then walk back into the bedroom, jumping onto the futon, causing her to snap, "Patrick, this is *not* a fucking *trampoline*." Ignoring her I kneel over her body, sliding my cock up into Courtney and immediately she's pushing her hips up to meet my thrusts, then she licks her thumb and starts rubbing her clit. I watch as my cock moves in then out then into her vagina with long fast strokes.

"Wait," she gasps.

"What?" I moan, puzzled but almost there.

"Luis is a despicable twit," she gasps, trying to push me out of her.

"Yes," I say, leaning on top of her, tonguing her ear. "Luis *is* a despicable twit. I hate him too," and now, spurred on by her disgust for her wimp boyfriend, I start moving faster, my climax approaching.

"No, you idiot," she groans. "I said *Is it a receptacle tip?* Not 'Is Luis a despicable twit.' Is it a *receptacle tip*? Get off me."

"Is what a *what*?" I moan.

"Pull out," she groans, struggling.

"I'm ignoring you," I say, moving my mouth down on her small perfect nipples, both of them stiff, sitting on hard, big tits.

"Pull out, goddamnit!" she screams.

"What do you want, Courtney?" I grunt, slowing my thrusts down until I finally straighten up and then I'm just kneeling over her, my cock still half inside. She hunches back against the headboard and my dick slides out.

"It's a plain end," I point. "I think."

"Turn the light on," she says, trying to sit up.

"Oh Jesus," I say. "I'm going home."

"Patrick," she warns. "Turn *on* the light."

I reach over and flip on the halogen Tensor.

"It's a plain end, *see*?" I say. "So?"

"Take it off," she says curtly.

"Why?" I ask.

"Because you have to leave half an inch at the tip," she says, covering her breasts with the Hermès comforter, her voice rising, her patience shot, "to catch the force *of the ejaculate!*"

"I'm getting out of here," I threaten, but don't move. "Where's your lithium?"

She throws a pillow over her head and mumbles something, retreating into a fetal position. I think she's starting to cry.

"Where is your lithium, Courtney?" I calmly ask again. "You *must* take some."

Something indecipherable is mumbled again and she shakes her head—no, no, no—beneath the pillow.

"What? *What* did you say?" I ask with forced politeness, jerking myself feebly back to an erection. "*Where?*" Sobs beneath the pillow, barely audible.

"You are crying now and though it sounds clearer to me I still *cannot* hear a word you're saying." I try to grab the pillow off her head. "Now *speak up!*"

Again she mumbles, again it doesn't make any sense.

"Courtney," I warn, getting furious, "if you just said what I think you said: that your lithium is in a carton in the freezer next to the Frusen Glädjé and is a *sorbet*"—I'm screaming this—"if this is really what you said then I will *kill* you. Is it a *sorbet*? Is your lithium really a *sorbet*?" I scream, finally pulling the pillow from her head and slapping her hard once, across the face.

"Do you think you're turning me on by having *unsafe sex*?" she screams back.

"Oh Christ, this really isn't worth it," I mutter, pulling the condom down so there is half an inch to spare—a little less actually. "And see, Courtney, it's there for what? Huh? Tell us." I slap her again, this time lightly. "Why is it pulled down half an inch? So it can catch the *force of the ejaculate!*"

"Well, it's *not* a turn-on *for me*." She's hysterical, racked with tears, choking. "I have a promotion coming to me. I'm going to Barbados in August and I don't want a case of Kaposi's sarcoma to fuck it up." She chokes, coughing. "Oh god I want to wear a bikini," she wails. "A Norma Kamali I just bought at Bergdorf's."

I grab her head and force her to look at the placement of the condom. "See? Happy? You dumb bitch? Are you happy, you dumb bitch?"

Without looking at my dick she sobs, "Oh god just get it over with," and falls back down on the bed.

Roughly I push my cock back into her and bring myself to an orgasm so weak as to be almost nonexistent and my groan of a massive but somewhat expected disappointment is mistaken by Courtney for pleasure and momentarily spurs her on as she lies sobbing beneath me on the bed, sniffling, to reach down and touch herself but I start getting soft almost instantly—actually *during* the moment I came—but if I don't withdraw from her while still erect she'll freak out so I hold on to the base of the condom as I literally *wilt* out of her. After lying there on separate sides of the bed for what might be twenty minutes with Courtney whimpering about Luis and antique cutting boards and the sterling silver cheese grater and muffin tin she left at Harry's, she then tries to give me head. "I want to fuck you again," I tell her, "but I don't want to wear a condom because I don't feel anything," and she says calmly, taking her mouth off my limp shrunken dick, glaring at me, "If you don't use one you're not going to feel anything anyway."

BUSINESS MEETING

Jean, my secretary who is in love with me, walks into my office without buzzing, announcing that I have a very important company meeting to attend at eleven. I'm sitting at the Palazzetti glass-top desk, staring into my monitor with my Ray-Bans on, chewing Nuprin, hung over from a coke binge that started innocently enough last night at Shout! with Charles Hamilton, Andrew Spencer and Chris Stafford and then moved on to the Princeton Club, progressed to Barcadia and ended at Nell's around three-thirty, and though earlier this morning, while soaking in a bath, sipping a Stoli Bloody Mary after maybe four hours of sweaty, dreamless sleep, I realized that there *was* a meeting, I seemed to have forgotten about it on the cab ride downtown. Jean is wearing a red stretch-silk jacket, a crocheted rayon-ribbon skirt, red suede pumps with satin bows by Susan Bennis Warren Edwards and gold-plated earrings by Robert Lee Morris. She stands there, in front of me, oblivious to my pain, a file in her hand.

After pretending to ignore her for close to a minute, I finally lower my sunglasses and clear my throat. "Yes? Something *else*? Jean?"

"Mr. Grouchy today." She smiles, placing the file timidly on my desk, and stands there expecting me to . . . what, amuse her with vignettes from last night?

"Yes, you *simpleton*. I am Mr. Grouchy today," I hiss, grabbing the file and shoving it in the top desk drawer.

She stares at me, uncomprehending, then, actually looking crestfallen, says, "Ted Madison called and so did James Baker. They want to meet you at Fluties at six."

I sigh, glaring at her. "Well, what should you do?"

She laughs nervously, standing there, her eyes wide. "I'm not sure."

"Jean." I stand up to lead her out of the office. "What . . . do . . . you . . . say?"

It takes her a little while but finally, frightened, she guesses, "Just . . . say . . . no?"

"Just . . . say . . . no." I nod, pushing her out and slamming the door.

Before leaving my office for the meeting I take two Valium, wash them down with a Perrier and then use a scuffing cleanser on my face with premoistened cotton balls, afterwards applying a moisturizer. I'm wearing a wool tweed suit and a striped cotton shirt, both by Yves Saint Laurent, and a silk tie by Armani and new black cap-toed shoes by Ferragamo. I Plax then brush my teeth and when I blow my nose, thick, ropy strings of blood and snot stain a forty-five-dollar handkerchief from Hermès that, unfortunately, wasn't a gift. But I've been drinking close to twenty liters of Evian water a day and going to the tanning salon regularly and one night of binging hasn't affected my skin's smoothness or color tone. My complexion is still excellent. Three drops of Visine clear the eyes. An ice pack tightens the skin. All it comes down to is: I feel like shit but look great.

I'm also the first to make it to the boardroom. Luis Carruthers follows like a puppy dog at my heels, a close second, and takes the seat next to mine which means I'm supposed to take off my Walkman. He's wearing a wool plaid sports jacket, wool slacks, a Hugo Boss cotton shirt and paisley tie—slacks, I'm guessing, from Brooks Brothers. He starts rattling on about a restaurant in Phoenix, Propheteers, that I'm actually interested in hearing about but not from Luis Carruthers, yet I'm on ten milligrams of Valium and for that reason I can manage. On *The Patty Winters Show* this morning were descendants of members of the Donner Party.

"The clients were *total* hicks, pre*dict*ably," Luis is saying. "They wanted to take me to a local production of *Les Miz*, which I already *saw* in *Lon*don, but—"

"Did you have any trouble getting reservations at Propheteers?" I ask, cutting him off.

"No. None at all," he says. "We ate late."

"What did you order?" I ask.

"I had the poached oysters, the lotte and the walnut tart."

"I hear the lotte is good there," I murmur, lost in thought.

"The client had the boudin blanc, the roasted chicken and the cheesecake," he says.

"Cheesecake?" I say, confused by this plain, alien-sounding list. "What sauce or fruits were on the roasted chicken? What shapes was it cut into?"

"None, Patrick," he says, also confused. "It was . . . roasted."

"And the cheesecake, what flavour? Was it heated?" I say. "Ricotta cheesecake? Goat cheese? Were there flowers or cilantro in it?"

"It was just . . . regular," he says, and then, "Patrick, you're sweating."

"What did she have?" I ask, ignoring him. "The client's bimbo."

"Well, she had the country salad, the scallops and the lemon tart," Luis says.

"The scallops were grilled? Were they sashimi scallops? In a ceviche of sorts?" I'm asking. "Or were they *gratinized*?"

"No, Patrick," Luis says. "They were . . . broiled."

It's silent in the boardroom as I contemplate this, thinking it through before asking, finally, "What's 'broiled', Luis?"

"I'm not sure," he says. "I think it involves . . . a pan."

"Wine?" I ask.

"An '85 sauvignon blanc," he says. "Jordan. Two bottles."

"Car?" I ask. "Did you rent while in Phoenix?"

"BMW." He smiles. "Little black beamer."

"Hip," I murmur, remembering last night, how I lost it completely in a stall at Nell's—my mouth foaming, all I could think about were insects, lots of insects, and running at pigeons, foaming at the mouth and running at pigeons. "Phoenix. Janet Leigh was from Phoenix . . ." I stall, then continue. "She got stabbed in the shower. Disappointing scene." I pause. "Blood looked fake."

"Listen, Patrick," Luis says, pressing his handkerchief into my hand, my fingers clenched into a fist that relaxes at Luis's touch. "Dibble and I are having lunch next week at the Yale Club. Would you like to join us?"

"Sure." I think about Courtney's legs, spread and wrapped around my face, and when I look over at Luis in one brief flashing moment his head looks like a talking vagina and it scares the bejesus out of me, moves me to say something while mopping the sweat off my brow. "That's a nice . . . suit, Luis." The farthest thing from my mind.

He looks down as if stunned, and then blushing, embarrassed, he touches his own lapel. "Thanks, Pat. You look great too . . . as usual." And when he reaches out to touch my tie, I catch his hand before his fingers make it, telling him, "Your compliment was sufficient."

Reed Thompson walks in wearing a wool plaid four-button double-breasted suit and a striped cotton shirt and a silk tie, all Armani, plus slightly tacky blue cotton socks by Interwoven and black Ferragamo cap-toe shoes that look exactly like mine, with a copy of the *Wall Street Journal* held in a nicely manicured fist and a Bill Kaiserman tweed balmacaan overcoat draped casually across the other arm. He nods and sits across from us at the table. Soon after, Todd Broderick walks in wearing a wool chalk-striped, six-button, double-breasted suit and a striped broadcloth shirt and silk tie, all by Polo, plus an affected linen pocket square that I'm fairly sure is also by Polo. McDermott walks in next, carrying a copy of this week's *New York* magazine and this morning's *Financial Times*, wearing new nonprescription Oliver Peoples redwood-framed glasses, black and white wool houndstooth-check single-breasted suit with notch lapels, a striped cotton dress shirt with spread collar and a silk paisley tie, all of it designed and tailored by John Reyle.

I smile, raising my eyebrows at McDermott, who sullenly takes the seat next to mine. He sighs and opens the newspaper, silently reading. Since he hasn't offered a "hello" or "good morning" I can tell that he's pissed off and I suspect that it has something to do with me. Finally, sensing that Luis is about to ask something, I turn to McDermott.

"So, McDermott, what's wrong?" I smirk. "Long line at the Stairmaster this morning?"

"Who said anything's wrong?" he asks, sniffing, turning pages in the *Financial Times*.

"Listen," I tell him, leaning in, "I already apologized about yelling at you because of the pizza at Pastels the other night."

"Who said it was about that?" he asks tensely.

"I thought we already cleared this up," I whisper, gripping the arm of his chair, smiling over at Thompson. "I'm sorry I insulted the pizzas at Pastels. Happy?"

"Who said it's about that?" he asks again.

"Then *what* is it, McDermott?" I whisper, noticing movement behind me. I count to three then whirl around, catching Luis leaning toward me trying to eavesdrop. He knows he's been caught and he sinks slowly back into his chair, guilty.

"McDermott, this is ri*dic*ulous," I whisper. "You can't stay angry at me because I think the pizza at Pastels is . . . *crusty*."

"*Brittle*," he says, shooting me a glance. "The word you used was *brittle*."

"I apologize," I say. "But I'm right. It *is*. You read the review in the *Times*, right?"

"Here." He reaches into his pocket and hands me a Xeroxed article. "I just wanted to prove you wrong. Read *this*."

"What is it?" I ask, opening the folded page.

"It's an article on your hero, Donald Trump." McDermott grins.

"It sure is," I say apprehensively. "Why didn't I ever see this, I wonder."

"And . . ." McDermott scans the article and points an accusatory finger at the bottom paragraph, which he's highlighted in red ink. "Where does Donald Trump think the best pizza in Manhattan is served?"

"Let *me* read this," I sigh, waving him away. "You might be wrong. What a lousy photo."

"Bateman. *Look*. I circled it," he says.

I pretend to read the fucking article but I'm getting very angry and I have to hand the article back to McDermott and ask, thoroughly annoyed, "So *what*? What does it mean? What are *you*, McDermott, trying to tell *me*?"

"What do you think of the pizza at Pastels *now*, Bateman?" he asks smugly.

"Well," I say, choosing my words carefully. "I think I have to go back and *re*taste the pizza . . ." I'm saying this through gritted teeth. "I'm just suggesting that the last time I was there the pizza was . . ."

"Brittle?" McDermott offers.

"Yeah." I shrug. "Brittle."

"Uh-huh." McDermott smiles, triumphant.

"Listen, if the pizza at Pastels is okay with Donny," I start, hating to admit this to McDermott, then sighing, almost unintelligibly, "it's okay with me."

McDermott cackles gleefully, a victor.

I count three silk-crepe ties, one Versace silk-satin woven tie, two silk foulard ties, one silk Kenzo, two silk jacquard ties. The fragrances of Xeryus and Tuscany and Armani and Obsession and Polo and Grey Flannel and even Antaeus mingle, wafting into each other, rising from the suits and into the air, forming their own mixture: a cold, sickening perfume.

"But I'm not apologizing," I warn McDermott.

"You already have, Bateman," he says.

Paul Owen walks in wearing a cashmere one-button sports jacket, tropical wool flannel slacks, a button-down tab-collared shirt by Ronaldus Shamask, but it's really the tie—blue and black and red and yellow bold stripes from Andrew Fezza by Zanzarra—that impresses me. Carruthers gets excited too, and he leans into my chair and asks, if I'm listening correctly, "Do you think he has a power *jock* strap to go along with that thing?" When I don't answer he retreats, opens one of the *Sports Illustrated*s that sit in the middle of the table and, humming to himself, starts to read an article on Olympic divers.

"Hello, Halberstam," Owen says, walking by.

"Hello, Owen," I say, admiring the way he's styled and slicked back his hair, with a part so even and sharp it . . . devastates me and I make a mental note to ask him where he purchases his hair-care products, which kind of mousse he uses, my final guess after mulling over the possibilities being Ten-X.

Greg McBride walks in and stops by my chair. "Did you watch the *Winters Show* this morning? Riot. Total riot," and we give each other high-five before he takes a seat between Dibble and Lloyd. God knows where they came from.

Kevin Forrest, who walks in with Charles Murphy, is saying, "My call waiting is busted. Felicia screwed it up somehow." I'm not even paying attention to what they're wearing. But I find myself staring at Murphy's vintage owl cuff links with blue crystal eyes.

VIDEO STORE THEN D'AGOSTINO'S

I'm wandering around VideoVisions, the video rental store near my apartment on the Upper West Side, sipping from a can of Diet Pepsi, the new Christopher Cross tape blaring from the earphones of my Sony Walkman. After the office I played racquetball with Montgomery, then had a shiatsu massage and met Jesse Lloyd, Jamie Conway and Kevin Forrest for drinks at Rusty's on Seventy-third Street. Tonight I'm wearing a new wool topcoat by Ungaro Uomo Paris and carrying a Bottega Veneta briefcase and an umbrella by Georges Gaspar.

The video store is more crowded than usual. There are too many couples in line for me to rent *She-Male Reformatory* or *Ginger's Cunt* without some sense of awkwardness or discomfort, plus I've already bumped into Robert Ailes from First Boston in the Horror aisle, or at least I think it was Robert Ailes. He mumbled "Hello, McDonald" as he passed me by, holding *Friday the 13th: Part 7* and a documentary on abortions in what I noticed were nicely manicured hands marred only by what looked to me like an imitation-gold Rolex.

Since pornography seems out of the question I browse through Light Comedy and, feeling ripped off, settle for a Woody Allen movie but I'm still not satisfied. I *want* something *else*. I pass through the Rock Musical section—nothing—then find myself in Horror Comedy—ditto—and suddenly I'm seized by a minor anxiety attack. *There are too many fucking movies to choose from.* I duck behind a promotional cardboard display for the new Dan Aykroyd comedy and take two five-milligram Valiums, washing them down with the Diet Pepsi. Then, almost by rote, as if I've been programmed, I reach for *Body Double*—a movie I have rented thirty-seven times—and walk up to the counter where I wait for twenty minutes to be checked out by a dumpy girl (five pounds overweight, dry frizzy hair). She's actually wearing a baggy, nondescript sweater—definitely *not* designer—probably to hide the fact that she has *no* tits, and even though she *has* nice eyes: *so fucking what*? Finally it's my turn. I hand her the empty boxes.

"Is this it?" she asks, taking my membership card from me. I'm wearing Mario Valentino Persian-black gloves. My VideoVisions membership costs only two hundred and fifty dollars annually.

"Do you have any Jami Gertz movies?" I ask her, trying to make direct eye contact.

"What?" she asks, distracted.

"Any movies that Jami *Gertz* is in?"

"*Who?*" She enters something into the computer and then says without looking at me, "How many nights?"

"Three," I say. "Don't you know who Jami Gertz *is*?"

"I don't think so." She actually sighs.

"Jami *Gertz*," I say. "She's an *actress*."

"I don't think I know who you mean," she says in a tone that suggests I'm harassing her, but hey, she works in a video rental store and since it's such a demanding high-powered profession her bitchy behavior is completely reasonable, *right*? The things I could do to this girl's body with a hammer, the words I could carve into her with an ice pick. She hands the guy behind her my boxes—and I pretend to ignore his horrified reaction as he recognizes me after he looks at the *Body Double* box—but he dutifully walks into some kind of vault in the back of the store to get the movies.

"Yeah. Sure you do," I say good-naturedly. "She's in those Diet Coke commercials. You know the ones."

"I really don't think so," she says in a monotone that almost cuts me off. She types the names of the movies and then my membership into the computer.

"I like the part in *Body Double* where the woman . . . gets drilled by the . . . power driller in the movie . . . the best," I say almost gasping. It seems very hot in the video store right now all of a sudden and after murmuring "oh my god" under my breath I place a gloved hand on the counter to settle it from shaking. "And the blood starts pouring out of the ceiling." I take a deep breath and while I'm saying this my head starts nodding of its own accord and I keep swallowing, thinking *I have to see her shoes*, and so as inconspicuously as possible I try to peer over the counter to check out what kind of shoes she's wearing, but maddeningly they're only sneakers—*not* K-Swiss, *not* Tretorn, *not* Adidas, *not* Reebok, just cheap ones.

"Sign here." She hands me the tapes without even looking at me, refusing to recognize who I am; and breathing in hard and exhaling, she motions for the next in line, a couple with a baby.

On the way back to my apartment I stop at D'Agostino's, where for dinner I buy two large bottles of Perrier, a six-pack of Coke Classic, a head of arugula, five medium-sized kiwis, a bottle of tarragon balsamic vinegar, a tin of crème fraîche, a carton of microwave tapas, a box of tofu and a white-chocolate candy bar I pick up at the checkout counter.

Once inside, ignoring the bum lounging below the *Les Misérables* poster and holding a sign that reads: I'VE LOST MY JOB I AM HUNGRY I HAVE NO MONEY PLEASE HELP, whose eyes tear after I pull the tease-the-bum-with-a-dollar trick and tell him, "Jesus, will you get a fucking shave, *please*," my eyes almost like they were guided by radar, focus in on a red Lamborghini Countach parked at the curb, gleaming beneath the streetlamps, and I have to stop moving, the Valium shockingly, unexpectedly kicking in, everything else becomes obliterated: the crying bum, the black kids on crack rapping along to the blaring beatbox, the clouds of pigeons flying overhead looking for space to roost, the ambulance sirens, the honking taxis, the decent-looking babe in the Betsey Johnson dress, all of that fades and in what seems like time-lapse photography—

but in slow motion, like a movie—the sun goes down, the city gets darker and all I can see is the red Lamborghini and all I can hear is my own even, steady panting. I'm still standing, drooling, in front of the store, staring, minutes later (I don't know how many).

FACIAL

I leave the office at four-thirty, head up to Xclusive where I work out with free weights for an hour, then taxi across the park to Gio's in the Pierre Hotel for a facial, a manicure and, if time permits, a pedicure. I'm lying on the elevated table in one of the private rooms waiting for Helga, the skin technician, to facialize me. My Brooks Brothers shirt and Garrick Anderson suit hang in the closet, my A. Testoni loafers sit on the floor, thirty-dollar socks from Barney's balled up in them, sixty-dollar boxer shorts from Comme des Garçons are the only article of clothing I'm still wearing. The smock I'm supposed to have on is crumpled next to the shower stall since I want Helga to check my body out, notice my chest, see how fucking *buff* my abdominals have gotten since the last time I was here, even though she's much older than I am—maybe thirty or thirty-five—and there's no way I'd ever fuck her. I'm sipping a Diet Pepsi that Mario, the valet, brought me, with crushed ice in a glass on the side that I asked for but don't want.

I pick up today's *Post* that hangs from a Smithly Watson glass magazine rack and scan the gossip columns, then my eye catches a story about recent sightings of these creatures that seem to be part bird, part rodent—essentially pigeons with the heads and tails of rats—found deep in the center of Harlem and now making their way steadily toward midtown. A grainy photograph of one of these things accompanies the article, but experts, the *Post* assures us, are fairly certain this new breed is a hoax. As usual this fails to soothe my fear, and it fills me with a nameless dread that someone out there has wasted the energy and time to think this up: to fake a photograph (and do a half-assed job at that, the thing looks like a fucking Big Mac) and send the photograph in to the *Post*, then for the *Post* to decide to run the story (meetings, debates, last-minute temptations to cancel the whole thing?), to print the photograph, to have someone write about the photo and interview the experts, finally to run this story on page three in today's edition and have it discussed over hundreds of thousands of lunches in the city this afternoon. I close the paper and lie back, exhausted.

The door to the private room opens and a girl I haven't seen before walks in and through half-closed eyes I can see that she's young, Italian, okay-looking. She smiles, sitting in a chair at my feet, and begins the pedicure. She switches off the ceiling light and except for strategically placed halogen bulbs shining down on my feet, hands and face, the room darkens, making it impossible to tell what kind of body she has, only that she's wearing gray suede and black leather buttoned ankle boots by Maud Frizon. *The Patty Winters Show* this morning was about UFOs That Kill. Helga arrives.

"Ah, Mr. Bateman," Helga says. "How are you?"

"Very good, Helga," I say, flexing the muscles in my stomach and chest. My eyes are closed so it looks casual, as if the muscles are acting on their own accord and I can't help it. But Helga drapes the smock gently across my heaving chest and buttons it up, pretending to ignore the undulations beneath the tan, clean skin.

"You're back so soon," she says.

"I was only here two days ago," I say, confused.

"I know, but . . ." She stalls, washing her hands in the sink. "Never mind."

"Helga?" I ask.

"Yes, Mr. Bateman?"

"Walking in here I spotted a pair of men's gold-tasseled loafers from Bergdorf Goodman, waiting to be shined, outside the door of the next room. Who do they belong to?" I ask.

"That's Mr. Erlanger," she says.

"Mr. Erlanger from Lehman's?"

"No. Mr. Erlanger from Salomon Brothers," she says.

"Did I ever tell you that I want to wear a big yellow smiley-face mask and then put on the CD version of Bobby McFerrin's 'Don't Worry, Be Happy' and then take a girl and a dog—a collie, a chow, a sharpei, it doesn't really matter—and then hook up this transfusion pump, this IV set, and switch their blood, you know, pump the dog's blood into the hardbody and vice versa, did I ever tell you this?" While I'm speaking I can hear the girl working on my feet humming one of the songs from *Les Misérables* to herself, and then Helga runs a moistened cotton ball across my nose, leaning close to the face, inspecting the pores. I laugh maniacally, then take a deep breath and touch my chest—expecting a heart to be thumping quickly, impatiently, but there's nothing there, not even a beat.

"Shhh, Mr. Bateman," Helga says, running a warm loofah sponge over my face, which stings then cools the skin. "Relax."

"Okay," I say. "I'm relaxing."

"Oh Mr. Bateman," Helga croons, "you have such a nice complexion. How old are you? May I ask?"

"I'm twenty-six."

"Ah, that's why. It's so clean. So smooth." She sighs. "Just relax."

I drift, my eyes rolling back into my head, the Muzak version of "Don't Worry, Baby" drowning out all bad thoughts, and I start thinking only positive things—the reservations I have tonight with Marcus Halberstam's girlfriend, Cecelia Wagner, the mashed turnips at Union Square Café, skiing down Buttermilk Mountain in Aspen last Christmas, the new Huey Lewis and the News compact disc, dress shirts by Ike Behar, by Joseph Abboud, by Ralph Lauren, beautiful oiled hardbodies eating each other's pussies and assholes under harsh video lights, truckloads of arugula and cilantro, my tan line, the way the muscles in my back look when the lights in my bathroom fall on them at the right angle, Helga's hands caressing the smooth skin on my face, lathering and spreading cream and lotions and tonics into it admiringly, whispering, "Oh Mr. Bateman, your face is so clean and smooth, so clean," the fact that I don't live in a trailer park or work in a bowling alley or attend hockey games or eat barbecued ribs, the look of the AT&T building at midnight, only at midnight. Jeannie comes in and starts the manicure, first clipping and filing the nails, then brushing them with a sandpaper disk to smooth out the remaining edges.

"Next time I'd prefer them a bit longer, Jeannie," I warn her.

Silently she soaks them in warm lanolin cream, then dries both hands off and uses a cuticle moisturizer, then removes all the cuticles while cleaning under the nails with a cotton-on-wood stick.

A heat vibrator massages the hand and forearm. The nails are buffed first with chamois and then with buffing lotion.

DATE WITH EVELYN

Evelyn comes in on the call waiting of my third line and I wasn't going to take it, but since I'm holding on the second line to find out if Bullock, the maître d' at the new Davis François restaurant on Central Park South, has any cancellations for tonight so Courtney (holding on the first line) and I might have dinner, I pick it up in the hope that it's my dry cleaners. But *no*, it's Evelyn and though it really isn't fair to Courtney, I take her call. I tell Evelyn I'm on the other line with my private trainer. I then tell Courtney I have to take Paul Owen's call and that I'll see her at Turtles at eight and then I cut myself off from Bullock, the maître d'. Evelyn's staying at the Carlyle since the woman who lives in the brownstone next to hers was found murdered last night, decapitated, and this is why Evelyn's all shook up. She couldn't deal with the office today so she spent the afternoon calming herself with facials at Elizabeth Arden. She demands that we have dinner tonight, and then says, before I can make up a plausible lie, an acceptable excuse, "Where *were* you last night, *Patrick*?"

I pause. "Why? Where were *you*?" I ask, while guzzling from a liter of Evian, still slightly sweaty from this afternoon's workout.

"Arguing with the concierge at the Carlyle," she says, sounding *rather* pissed off. "Now tell me, Patrick, where *were* you?"

"Why were you arging with him?" I ask.

"Patrick," she says—a declarative statement.

"I'm here," I say after a minute.

"Patrick. It doesn't matter. The phone in my room didn't have two lines and there was *no* call waiting," she says. "*Where* were you?"

"I was . . . fooling around renting videotapes," I say, pleased, giving myself high-five, the cordless phone cradled in my neck.

"I wanted to come over," she says in a whiny, little-girl tone. "I was scared. I still am. Can't you hear it in my voice?"

"Actually, you sound like anything but."

"No, Patrick, seriously. I'm quite terrified," she says. "I'm shaking. Just like a leaf I'm shaking. Ask Mia, my facialist. *She* said I was tense."

"Well," I say, "you couldn't have come over anyway."

"Honey, why not?" she whines, and then addresses someone who just entered her suite. "Oh wheel it over there near the window . . . no, *that* window . . . and can you tell me where that damn masseuse is?"

"Because your neighbor's head was in my freezer." I yawn, stretching. "Listen. Dinner? Where? Can you hear me?"

At eight-thirty, the two of us are sitting across from each other in Barcadia. Evelyn's wearing an Anne Klein rayon jacket, a wool-crepe skirt, a silk blouse from Bonwit's, antique gold and agate earrings from James Robinson that cost, roughly, four thousand dollars; and I'm wearing a double-breasted suit, a silk shirt with woven stripes, a patterned silk tie and leather slip-ons, all by Gianni Versace. I neither canceled the reservation at Turtles nor told Courtney not to meet me there, so she'll probably show up around eight-fifteen, completely confused, and if she hasn't taken any Elavil today she'll probably be furious and it's this fact—not the bottle of Cristal that Evelyn insists on ordering and then adds cassis to—that I laugh out loud about.

I spent most of the afternoon buying myself early Christmas presents—a large pair of scissors at a drugstore near City Hall, a letter opener from Hammacher Schlemmer, a cheese knife from Bloomingdale's to go along with the cheese board that Jean, my secretary who's in love with me, left on my desk before she went to lunch while I was in a meeting. *The Patty Winters Show* this morning was about the possibility of nuclear war, and according to the panel of experts the odds are pretty good it will happen sometime within the next month. Evelyn's face seems chalky to me right now, her mouth lined with a purple lipstick that gives off an almost startling effect, and I realize that she's belatedly taken Tim Price's advice to stop using her tanning lotion. Instead of mentioning this and have her bore me silly with inane denials, I ask about Tim's girlfriend, Meredith, whom Evelyn despises for reasons never made quite clear to me. And because of rumors about Courtney and myself, Courtney's also on Evelyn's shit list, for reasons that are a little clearer. I place a hand over the top of the champagne flute when the apprehensive waitress, at Evelyn's request, attempts to add some blueberry cassis into my Cristal.

"No thank you," I tell her. "Maybe later. In a separate glass."

"Party pooper." Evelyn giggles, then takes a sharp breath. "But you smell nice. What are you wearing—Obsession? You party pooper, is it Obsession?"

"No," I say grimly. "Paul Sebastian."

"Of course." She smiles, downs her second glass. She seems in a much better mood, boisterous almost, more than you'd expect of someone whose neighbor's head was sliced off in a matter of seconds while she was still conscious by an electric mini-chain saw. Evelyn's eyes momentarily glitter in the candlelight, then revert to their normal pallid gray.

"How *is* Meredith?" I ask, trying to mask my void of disinterest.

"Oh god. She's dating Richard Cunningham." Evelyn moans. "He's at First Boston. If you can *believe* it."

"You know," I mention, "Tim was going to break it off with her. Call it quits."

"*Why*, for god's sake?" Evelyn asks, surprised, intrigued. "They had that *fabulous* place in the Hamptons."

"I remember him telling me that he was sick to death of watching her do nothing but her nails all weekend."

"Oh my god," Evelyn says, and then, genuinely confused, "You mean . . . wait, she didn't have someone do them for her?"

"Tim said, and he reiterated this fact quite often, that she had all the personality of a game-show host," I say dryly, sipping from the flute.

She smiles to herself, secretly. "Tim is a rascal."

Idly, I wonder if Evelyn would sleep with another woman if I brought one over to her brownstone and, if I insisted, whether they'd let me watch the two of them get it on. If they'd let me direct, tell them what to do, position them under hot halogen lamps. Probably not; the odds don't look good. But what if I forced her at *gunpoint*? Threatened to cut them both up, maybe, if they didn't comply? The thought doesn't seem unappealing and I can imagine the whole scenario quite clearly. I start counting the banquettes that encircle the room, then I start counting the people sitting in the banquettes.

She's asking me about Tim. "Where do you think *that* rascal has been? Rumor is he's at *Sachs*," she says ominously.

"Rumor is," I say, "he's in rehab. This champagne isn't cold enough." I'm distracted. "Doesn't he send you postcards?"

"Has he been sick?" she asks, with the slightest trepidation.

"Yes, I think so," I say. "I think that's what it is. You know, if you order a bottle of Cristal it should at least be, you know, *cold*."

"Oh my god," Evelyn says. "You think he might be *sick*?"

"Yes. He's in a hospital. In Arizona," I add. The word *Arizona* has a mysterious tinge to it and I say it again. "Arizona. I think."

"Oh my *god*," Evelyn exclaims, now truly alarmed, and she gulps down what little Cristal is left in her glass.

"Who knows?" I manage the slightest of shrugs.

"You don't think . . ." She breathes in and puts her glass down. "You don't think it's"—and now she looks around the restaurant before leaning in, whispering—"AIDS?"

"Oh no, nothing like that," I say, though immediately I wish I had paused long enough before answering to scare her. "Just . . . general . . . brain"—I bite the tip off an herbed breadstick and shrug—"injuries."

Evelyn sighs, relieved, and then says, "Is it warm in here?"

"All I can think about is this poster I saw in the subway station the other night before I killed those two black kids—a photo of a baby calf, its head turned toward the camera, its eyes caught wide and staring by the flash, and its body seemed like it was boxed into some kind of crate, and in big, black letters below the photo it read, 'Question: Why Can't This Veal Calf Walk?' Then, 'Answer: Because It Only Has Two Legs.' But then I saw another one, the same exact photo, the same exact calf, yet beneath it, this one read, 'Stay Out of Publishing.'" I pause, still fingering the breadstick, then ask, "Is any of this registering with you or would I get more of a response from, oh, an ice bucket?" I say all of this staring straight at Evelyn, enunciating precisely, trying to explain myself, and she opens her mouth and I finally expect her to acknowledge my character. And for the first time since I've known her she is straining to say something interesting and I pay very close attention and she asks, "Is that . . ."

"Yes?" This is the only moment of the evening where I feel any genuine interest toward what she has to say, and I urge her to go on. "Yes? Is that . . .?"

"Is that . . . Ivana Trump?" she asks, peering over my shoulder. I whirl around. "Where? Where's Ivana?"

"In the booth near the front, second in from"—Evelyn pauses—"Brooke Astor. See?"

I squint, put on my Oliver Peoples nonprescription glasses and realize that Evelyn, her vision clouded by the cassis-riddled Cristal, not only has mistaken Norris Powell for Ivana Trump but has mistaken Steve Rubell for Brooke Astor, and I can't help it, I almost explode.

"No, oh my *god*, oh my *god*, Evelyn," I moan, crushed, disappointed, my adrenaline rush turning sour, my head in my hands. "How could you mistake that *wench* for Ivana?"

"Sorry," I hear her chirp. "Girlish mistake?"

"That is in*furiat*ing," I hiss, both eyes clenched tight.

Our hardbody waitress, who has on satin high-backed pumps, sets down two new champagne flutes for the second bottle of Cristal Evelyn orders. The waitress pouts her lips at me when I reach for another breadstick and I lift my head toward her and pout mine back, then press my head again into the palms of my hands, and this happens again when she brings our appetizers. Dried peppers in a spicy pumpkin soup for me; dried corn and jalapeño pudding for Evelyn. I've kept my hands over both ears trying to block out Evelyn's voice during this whole interim between her mistaking Norris Powell for Ivana Trump and the arrival of our appetizers but now I'm hungry so I tentatively remove my right hand from my ear. Immediately the whine seems deafening.

". . . Tandoori chicken and foie gras, and lots of jazz, and he adored the Savoy, but shad roe, the colors were gorgeous, aloe, shell, citrus, Morgan Stanley . . ."

I clasp my hands back where they were, pressing even tighter. Once again hunger overtakes me and so humming loudly to myself I reach again for the spoon, but it's hopeless: Evelyn's voice is at a particular pitch that cannot be ignored.

"Gregory's graduating from Saint Paul soon and will be attending Columbia in September," Evelyn is saying, carefully blowing on her pudding, which, by the way, is served cold. "And I've *got* to get him a graduation present and I'm at a total loss. Suggestions, hon?"

"A poster from *Les Misérables*?" I sigh, only half joking.

"*Per*fect," she says, blowing on the pudding again, then after a sip of Cristal she makes a face.

"Yes, dear?" I ask, spitting a pumpkin seed that arches through the air before gracefully hitting the dead center of the ashtray instead of Evelyn's dress, my original target. "Hmmm?"

"We need more cassis," she says. "Will you get our waitress?"

"Of course we do," I say good-naturedly and, still smiling, "I have no idea who Gregory is. You do know that, right?"

Evelyn put her spoon down delicately next to the plate of pudding and looks into my eyes. "Mr. Bateman, I really like you. I *adore* your sense of humor." She gives my hand a soft squeeze and laughs, actually *says*, "Ha-ha-ha . . ." but she's serious, not joking. Evelyn really *is* paying me a compliment. She *does* admire my sense of humor. Our appetizers are removed and at the same time our entrées arrive, so Evelyn has to take her hand off mine to make room for the plates. She ordered quail stuffed into blue corn tortillas garnished with oysters in potato skins. I have the free-range rabbit with Oregon morels and herbed french fries.

". . . He went to Deerfield then Harvard. She went to Hotchkiss then Radcliffe . . ."

Evelyn is talking but I'm not listening. Her dialogue overlaps her own dialogue. Her mouth is moving but I'm not hearing anything and I can't listen, I can't really concentrate, since my rabbit has been cut to look . . . just . . . like . . . a . . . star! Shoestring french fries surround it and chunky red salsa has been smeared across the top of the plate—which is white and porcelain and two feet wide—to give the appearance of a sunset but it looks like one big gunshot wound to me and shaking my head slowly in disbelief I press a finger into the meat, leaving the indentation of one finger, then another, and then I look for a napkin, not my own, to wipe my hand with. Evelyn hasn't broken her monologue—she talks and chews exquisitely—and smiling seductively at her I reach under the table and grab her thigh, wiping my hand off, and still talking she smiles naughtily at me and sips more champagne. I keep studying her face, bored by how beautiful it is, flawless really, and I think to myself how strange it is that Evelyn has pulled me through so much;

how she's always been there when I needed her most. I look back at the plate, thoroughly unhungry, pick up my fork, study the plate hard for a minute or two, whimper to myself before sighing and putting the fork down. I pick up my champagne glass instead.

". . . Groton, Lawrenceville, Milton, Exeter, Kent, Saint Paul's, Hotchkiss, Andover, Milton, Choate . . . oops, already said Milton."

"If I'm not eating this tonight, and I'm not, I want some cocaine," I announce. But I haven't interrupted Evelyn—she's unstoppable, a machine—and she continues talking.

"Jayne Simpson's wedding was so beautiful," she sighs. "And the reception afterwards was wild. Club Chernoble, covered by Page Six. Billy covered it. *WWD* did a layout."

"I heard there was a two-drink minimum," I say warily, signaling for a nearby busboy to remove my plate.

"Weddings are *so* romantic. She had a diamond engagement ring. You *know*, Patrick, I *won't* settle for less," she says coyly. "It *has* to be diamond." Her eyes glaze over and she tries to recount the wedding in mind-numbing detail. "It was a sit-down dinner for five hundred . . . no, excuse me, seven hundred and fifty, followed by a sixteen-foot tiered Ben and Jerry's ice cream cake. The gown was by Ralph and it was white lace and low-cut and sleeveless. It was darling. Oh Patrick, what would *you* wear?" she sighs.

"I would demand to wear Ray-Ban sunglasses. Expensive Ray-Bans," I say carefully. "In fact I would demand that everyone would have to wear Ray-Ban sunglasses."

"I'd want a zydeco band, Patrick. That's what I'd want. A zydeco band," she gushes breathlessly. "Or mariachi. Or reggae. Something ethnic to shock Daddy. Oh I *can't* decide."

"I'd want to bring a Harrison AK-47 assault rifle to the ceremony," I say, bored, in a rush, "with a thirty-round magazine so after thoroughly blowing your fat mother's head off with it I could use it on that fag brother of yours. And though personally I don't like to use anything the Soviets designed, I don't know, the Harrison somehow reminds me of . . ." Stopping, confused, inspecting yesterday's manicure, I look back at Evelyn. "Stoli?"

"Oh, and lots of chocolate truffles. *Godiva*. And oysters. Oysters on the half shell. Marzipan. Pink *tents*. Hundreds, *thousands* of roses. Photographers. Annie Leibovitz. We'll get *Annie Leibovitz*," she says excitedly. "*And* we'll hire someone to *videotape* it!"

"Or an AR-15. You'd like it, Evelyn: it's the most expensive of guns, but worth every penny." I wink at her. But she's still talking; she doesn't hear a word; nothing registers. She does not fully grasp a *word* I'm saying. My essence is eluding her. She stops her onslaught and breathes in and looks at me in a way that can only be described as dewy-eyed. Touching my hand, my Rolex, she breathes in once more, this time expectantly, and says, "We should do it."

I'm trying to catch a glimpse of our hardbody waitress; she's bending over to pick up a dropped napkin. Without looking back at Evelyn, I ask, "Do . . . what?"

"Get married," she says, blinking. "Have a wedding."

"Evelyn?"

"Yes, darling?"

"Is your kir . . . spiked?" I ask.

"We should do it," she says softly. "Patrick . . ."

"Are you proposing *to me*?" I laugh, trying to fathom this reasoning. I take the champagne glass away from her and sniff its rim.

"*Pat*rick?" she asks, waiting for my answer.

"Jeez, Evelyn," I say, stuck. "I don't know."

"Why *not*?" she asks petulantly. "Give me *one* good reason we shouldn't."

"Because trying to fuck you is like trying to French-kiss a very . . . small and . . . lively gerbil?" I tell her. "I don't know."

"Yes?" she says. "And?"

"With braces?" I finish, shrugging.

"What are you going to do?" she asks. "Wait three years until you're thirty?"

"*Four* years," I say, glaring. "It's *four* years until I'm thirty."

"Four years. Three years. Three *months*. Oh god, what's the difference? You'll still be an old man." She takes her hand away from mine. "You know, you wouldn't be saying this if you'd been to Jayne Simpson's wedding. You'd take one look at it and want to marry me immediately."

"But I *was* at Jayne Simpson's wedding, Evelyn, love of my life," I say. "I was seated next to Sukhreet Gabel. Believe me, I was *there*."

"You're im*poss*ible," she whines. "You're a party pooper."

"Or maybe I didn't," I wonder aloud. "Maybe I . . . was it covered by MTV?"

"And their honeymoon was *so* romantic. Two hours later they were on the Concorde. To London. Oh, Claridge's." Evelyn sighs, her hand clasped under her chin, eyes tearing.

Ignoring her, I reach into my pocket for a cigar, pull it out and tap it against the table. Evelyn orders three flavors of sorbet: peanut, licorice and doughnut. I order a decaffeinated espresso. Evelyn sulks. I light a match.

"Patrick," she warns, staring at the flame.

"What?" I ask, my hand frozen in midair, about to light the tip of the cigar.

"You didn't ask permission," she says, unsmiling.

"Did I tell you I'm wearing sixty-dollar boxer shorts?" I ask, trying to appease her.

TUESDAY

There's a black-tie party at the Puck Building tonight for a new brand of computerized professional rowing machine, and after playing squash with Frederick Dibble I have drinks at Harry's with Jamie Conway, Kevin Wynn and Jason Gladwin, and we hop into the limousine Kevin rented for the night and take it uptown. I'm wearing a wing-collar jacquard waistcoat by Kilgour, French & Stanbury from Barney's, a silk bow tie from Saks, patent-leather slip-ons by Baker-Benjes, antique diamond studs from Kentshire Galleries and a gray wool silk-lined coat with drop sleeves and a button-down collar by Luciano Soprani. An ostrich wallet from Bosca carries four hundred dollars cash in the back pocket of my black wool trousers. Instead of my Rolex I'm wearing a fourteen-karat gold watch from H. Stern.

I wander aimlessly around the Puck Building's first-floor ballroom, bored, sipping bad champagne (could it be nonvintage Bollinger?) from plastic flutes, chewing on kiwi slices, each topped with a dollop of chèvre, vaguely looking around to score some cocaine. Instead of finding anyone who knows a dealer I bump into Courtney by the stairs. Wearing a silk and cotton stretch-tulle bodywrap with jeweled lace pants, she seems tense and warns me to stay away from Luis. She mentions that he suspects something. A cover band plays lame versions of old Motown hits from the sixties.

"Like what?" I ask, scanning the room. "That two plus two equals four? That you're secretly Nancy Reagan?"

"Don't have lunch with him next week at the Yale Club," she says, smiling for a photographer, the flash blinding us momentarily.

"You look . . . voluptuous tonight," I say, touching her neck, running a finger up over her chin until it reaches the bottom lip.

"I'm not joking, Patrick." Smiling, she waves to Luis, who is dancing clumsily with Jennifer Morgan. He's wearing a cream-colored wool dinner jacket, wool trousers, a cotton shirt, and a silk glen-plaid cummerbund, all from Hugo Boss, a bow tie from Saks and a pocket square from Paul Stuart. He waves back. I give him thumbs-up.

"What a dork," Courtney whispers sadly to herself.

"Listen, I'm leaving," I say, finishing the champagne. "Why don't you go dance with the . . . receptacle tip?"

"Where *are* you going?" she asks, gripping my arm.

"Courtney, I don't want to experience another one of your . . . emotional outbursts," I tell her. "Besides, the canapés are shitty."

"Where *are* you going?" she asks again. "Details, Mr. Bateman."

"Why are *you* so concerned?"

"Because I'd like to know," she says. "You're not going to Evelyn's, are you?"

"Maybe," I lie.

"Patrick," she says. "Don't leave me here. I don't *want* you to go."

"I *have* to return some videos," I lie again, handing her my empty champagne glass, just as another camera flashes somewhere. I walk away.

The band segues into a rousing version of "Life in the Fast Lane" and I start looking around for hardbodies. Charles Simpson—or someone who looks remarkably like him, slicked-back hair, suspenders, Oliver Peoples glasses—shakes my hand, shouts "Hey, Williams" and tells me to meet a group of people with Alexandra

Craig at Nell's around midnight. I give him a reassuring squeeze on the shoulder and tell him I'll be there.

Outside, smoking a cigar, contemplating the sky, I spot Reed Thompson, who emerges from the Puck Building with his entourage —Jamie Conway, Kevin Wynn, Marcus Halberstam, no babes—and invites me along to dinner; and though I suspect they have drugs, I have misgivings about spending the evening with them and decide not to trek up to that Salvadorian bistro, especially since they don't have reservations and aren't guaranteed a table. I wave them off, then cross Houston, dodging other limos leaving the party, and start moving uptown. Walking along Broadway I stop at an automated teller where just for the hell of it I take out another hundred dollars, feeling better having an even five hundred in my wallet.

I find myself walking through the antique district below Fourteenth Street. My watch has stopped so I'm not sure what time it is, but probably ten-thirty or so. Black guys pass by offering crack or hustling tickets to a party at the Palladium. I walk by a newsstand, a dry cleaners, a church, a diner. The streets are empty; the only noise breaking up the silence is an occasional taxi cruising toward Union Square. A couple of skinny faggots walk by while I'm at a phone booth checking my messages, staring at my reflection in an antique store's window. One of them whistles at me, the other laughs: a high, fey, horrible sound. A torn playbill from *Les Misérables* tumbles down the cracked, urine-stained sidewalk. A streetlamp burns out. Someone in a Jean-Paul Gaultier topcoat takes a piss in an alleyway. Steam rises from below the streets, billowing up in tendrils, evaporating. Bags of frozen garbage line the curbs. The moon, pale and low, hangs just above the tip of the Chrysler Building. Somewhere from over in the West Village the siren from an ambulance screams, the wind picks it up, it echoes then fades.

The bum, a black man, lies in the doorway of an abandoned antique store on Twelfth Street on top of an open grate, surrounded by bags of garbage and a shopping cart from Gristede's loaded with what I suppose are personal belongings: newspapers, bottles, aluminum cans. A handpainted cardboard sign attached to the front of the cart reads I AM HUNGRY AND HOMELESS PLEASE HELP ME. A dog, a small mutt, short-haired and rail thin, lies next to him, its makeshift leash tied to the handle of the grocery cart. I don't notice the dog the first time I pass by. It's only after I circle the block and come back that I see it lying on a pile of newspapers, guarding the bum, a collar around its neck with an oversize nameplate that reads GIZMO. The dog looks up at me wagging its skinny, pathetic excuse for a tail and when I hold out a gloved hand it licks at it hungrily. The stench of some kind of cheap alcohol mixed with excrement hangs here like a heavy, invisible cloud, and I have to hold my breath, before adjusting to the stink. The bum wakes up, opens his eyes, yawning, exposing remarkably stained teeth between cracked purple lips.

He's fortyish, heavyset, and when he attempts to sit up I can make out his features more clearly in the glare of the streetlamp: a few days' growth of beard, triple chin, a ruddy nose lined with thick brown veins. He's dressed in some kind of tacky-looking lime green polyester pantsuit with washed-out Sergio Valente jeans worn *over* it (this season's homeless person's fashion statement) along with a ripped orange and brown V-neck sweater stained with what looks like burgundy wine. It seems he's very drunk—either that or he's crazy or stupid. His eyes can't even focus when I stand over him, blocking out the light from a streetlamp, covering him in shadow. I kneel down.

"Hello," I say, offering my hand, the one the dog licked. "Pat Bateman."

The bum stares at me, panting with the exertion it takes to sit up. He doesn't shake my hand.

"You want some money?" I ask gently. "Some . . . food?"

The bum nods and starts to cry, thankfully.

I reach into my pocket and pull out a ten-dollar bill, then change my mind and hold out a five instead. "Is this what you need?"

The bum nods again and looks away, shamefully, his nose running, and after clearing his throat says quietly, "I'm so hungry."

"It's cold out, too," I say. "Isn't it?"

"I'm so hungry." He convulses once, twice, a third time, then looks away, embarrassed.

"Why don't you get a job?" I ask, the bill still held in my hand but not within the bum's reach. "If you're so hungry, why don't you get a job?"

He breathes in, shivering, and between sobs admits, "I lost my job . . ."

"Why?" I ask, genuinely interested. "Were you drinking? Is that why you lost it? Insider trading? Just joking. No, really—were you drinking on the job?"

He hugs himself, between sobs, chokes, "I was fired. I was laid off."

I take this in, nodding. "Gee, uh, that's too bad."

"I'm so hungry," he says, then starts crying hard, still holding himself. His dog, the thing called Gizmo, starts whimpering.

"Why don't you get another one?" I ask. "Why don't you get another job?"

"I'm not . . ." He coughs, holding himself, shaking miserably, violently, unable to finish the sentence.

"You're not what?" I ask softly. "Qualified for anything else?"

"I'm hungry," he whispers.

"I know that, I know that," I say. "Jeez, you're like a broken record. I'm trying to help you . . ." My impatience rises.

"I'm hungry," he repeats.

"Listen. Do you think it's fair to take money from people who *do* have jobs? Who *do* work?"

His face crumples and he gasps, his voice raspy, "What am I gonna do?"

"Listen," I say. "What's your name?"

"Al," he says.

"Speak up," I tell him. "Come on."

"Al," he says, a little louder.

"Get a goddamn job, Al," I say earnestly. "You've got a negative attitude. That's what's stopping you. You've got to get your act together. I'll help you."

"You're so kind, mister. You're kind. You're a kind man," he blubbers. "I can tell."

"Shhh," I whisper. "It's okay." I start petting the dog.

"Please," he says, grabbing for my wrist. "I don't know what to do. I'm so cold."

"Do you know how bad you smell?" I whisper this soothingly, stroking his face. "The *stench*, my god . . ."

"I can't . . ." He chokes, then swallows. "I can't find a shelter."

"You *reek*," I tell him. "You *reek* of . . . *shit*." I'm still petting the dog, its eyes wide and wet and grateful. "Do you know that? Goddamnit, Al—look at me and stop crying like some kind of *faggot,*" I shout. My rage builds, subsides, and I close my eyes, bringing my hand up to squeeze the bridge of my nose, then I sigh. "Al ... I'm sorry. It's just that ... I don't know. I don't have anything in common with you."

The bum's not listening. He's crying so hard he's incapable of a coherent answer. I put the bill slowly back into the pocket of my Luciano Soprani jacket and with the other hand stop petting the dog and reach into the other pocket. The bum stops sobbing abruptly and sits up, looking for the fiver or, I presume, his bottle of Thunderbird. I reach out and touch his face gently once more with compassion and whisper, "Do you know what a fucking loser you are?" He starts nodding helplessly and I pull out a long, thin knife with a serrated edge and, being very careful not to kill him, push maybe half an inch of the blade into his right eye, flicking the handle up, instantly popping the retina.

The bum is too surprised to say anything. He only opens his mouth in shock and moves a grubby, mittened hand slowly up to his face. I yank his pants down and in the passing headlights of a taxi can make out his flabby black thighs, rashed because of his constantly urinating in the pantsuit. The stench of shit rises quickly into my face and breathing through my mouth, down on my haunches, I start stabbing him in the stomach, lightly, above the dense matted patch of pubic hair. This sobers him up somewhat and instinctively he tries to cover himself with his hands and the dog starts yipping, really furiously, but it doesn't attack, and I keep stabbing at the bum now between his fingers, stabbing the backs of his hands. His eye, burst open, hangs out of its socket and runs down his face and he keeps blinking which causes what's left of it inside the wound to pour out like red, veiny egg yolk. I grab his head with one hand and push it back and then with my thumb and forefinger hold the other eye open and bring the knife up and push the tip of it into the socket, first breaking its protective film so the socket fills with blood, then slitting the eyeball open sideways, and he finally starts screaming once I slit his nose in two, lightly spraying me and the dog with blood, Gizmo blinking to get the blood out of his eyes. I quickly wipe the blade clean across the bum's face, breaking open the muscle above his cheek. Still kneeling, I throw a quarter in his face, which is slick and shiny with blood, both sockets hollowed out and filled with gore, what's left of his eyes literally oozing over his screaming lips in thick, webby strands. Calmly, I whisper, "There's a quarter. Go buy some *gum*, you crazy fucking *nigger*." Then I turn to the barking dog and when I get up, stomp on its front legs while it's crouched down ready to jump at me, its fangs bared, immediately shattering the bones in both its legs, and it falls on its side squealing in pain, front paws sticking up in the air at an obscene, satisfying angle. I can't help but start laughing and I linger at the scene, amused by this tableau. When I spot an approaching taxi, I slowly walk away.

Afterwards, two blocks west, I feel heady, ravenous, pumped up, as if I'd just worked out and endorphins are flooding my nervous system, or just embraced that first line of cocaine, inhaled the first puff of a fine cigar, sipped that first glass of Cristal. I'm starving and need something to eat, but I don't want to stop by Nell's, though I'm within walking distance and Indochine seems an unlikely place for a celebratory drink. So I decide to go somewhere Al would go, the McDonald's in Union Square. Standing in the line, I order a vanilla milk shake ("*Extra*-thick," I warn the guy, who just shakes his head and flips on a machine) and take it to a table up front, where Al would probably sit, my jacket, and its sleeves, lightly spattered with flecks of his blood. Two waitresses from the Cat Club walk in after me and sit in the booth across from mine, both smiling flirtatiously. I play it cool and ignore them. An old, crazy woman, wrinkled, chain-smoking, sits near us, nodding at no one. A police car passes by, and after two more milk shakes my high slowly dissolves, its intensity diminishing. I grow bored, tired; the evening seems horribly anticlimactic and I start cursing myself for not going to that Salvadorian bistro with Reed Thompson and the guys. The two girls linger, still interested. I check my watch. One of the Mexicans working behind the counter stares at me while smoking a cigarette and he studies the stains on the Soprani jacket in a way that suggests he's going to say something about it, but a customer comes in, one of the black guys who tried to sell me crack earlier, and he has to take the black guy's order. So the Mexican puts out his cigarette and that's what he does.

GENESIS

I've been a big Genesis fan ever since the release of their 1980 album, *Duke*. Before that I didn't really understand any of their work, though on their last album of the 1970s, the concept-laden *And Then There Were Three* (a reference to band member Peter Gabriel, who left the group to start a lame solo career), I *did* enjoy the lovely "Follow You, Follow Me." Otherwise all the albums before *Duke* seemed too artsy, too intellectual. It was *Duke* (Atlantic; 1980), where Phil Collins' presence became more apparent, and the music got more modern, the drum machine became more prevalent and the lyrics started getting less mystical and more specific (maybe because of Peter Gabriel's departure), and complex, ambiguous studies of loss became, instead, smashing first-rate pop songs that I gratefully embraced. The songs themselves seemed arranged more around Collins' drumming than Mike Rutherford's bass lines or Tony Banks' keyboard riffs. A classic example of this is "Misunderstanding," which not only was the group's first big hit of the eighties but also seemed to set the tone for the rest of their albums as the decade progressed. The other standout on *Duke* is "Turn It On Again," which is about the negative effects of television. On the other hand, "Heathaze" is a song I just don't understand, while "Please Don't Ask" is a touching love song written to a separated wife who regains custody of the couple's child. Has the negative aspect of divorce ever been rendered in more intimate terms by a rock 'n' roll group? I don't think so. "Duke Travels" and "Dukes End" might mean something but since the lyrics aren't printed it's hard to tell what Collins is singing about, though there *is* complex, gorgeous piano work by Tony Banks on the latter track. The only bummer about *Duke* is "Alone Tonight," which is way too reminiscent of "Tonight Tonight Tonight" from the group's later masterpiece *Invisible Touch* and the only example, really, of where Collins has plagiarized himself.

Abacab (Atlantic; 1981) was released almost immediately after *Duke* and it benefits from a new producer, Hugh Padgham, who gives the band a more eighties sound and though the songs seem fairly generic, there are still great bits throughout: the extended jam in the middle of the title track and the horns by some group called Earth, Wind and Fire on "No Reply at All" are just two examples. Again the songs reflect dark emotions and are about people who feel lost or who are in conflict, but the production and sound are gleaming and upbeat (even if the titles aren't: "No Reply at All," "Keep It Dark," "Who Dunnit?" "Like It or Not"). Mike Rutherford's bass is obscured somewhat in the mix but otherwise the band sounds tight and is once again propelled by Collins' truly amazing drumming. Even at its most despairing (like the song "Dodo," about extinction), *Abacab* musically is poppy and lighthearted.

My favorite track is "Man on the Corner," which is the only song credited solely to Collins, a moving ballad with a pretty synthesized melody plus a riveting drum machine in the background. Though it could easily come off any of Phil's solo albums, because the themes of loneliness, paranoia and alienation are overly familiar to Genesis it evokes the band's hopeful humanism. "Man on the Corner" profoundly equates a relationship with a solitary figure (a bum, perhaps a poor homeless person?), "that lonely man on the corner" who just stands around. "Who Dunnit?" profoundly expresses the theme of confusion against a funky groove, and what makes this song so exciting is that it ends with its narrator never finding anything out at all.

Hugh Padgham produced next an even less conceptual effort, simply called *Genesis* (Atlantic; 1983), and though it's a fine album a lot of it now seems too derivative for my tastes. "That's All" sounds like "Misunderstanding," "Taking It All Too Hard" reminds me of "Throwing It All Away." It also seems less jazzy than its predecessors and more of an eighties pop album, more rock 'n' roll. Padgham does a brilliant job of producing, but the material is weaker than usual and you can sense the strain. It opens with the autobiographical "Mama," that's both strange and touching, though I couldn't tell if the singer was talking about his actual mother or to a girl he likes to call "Mama." "That's All" is a lover's lament about being ignored and beaten down by an unreceptive partner; despite the despairing tone it's got a bright sing-along melody that makes the song less depressing than it probably needed to be. "That's All" is the best tune on the album, but Phil's voice is strongest on "House by the

Sea," whose lyrics are, however, too stream-of-consciousness to make much sense. It might be about growing up and accepting adulthood but it's unclear; at any rate, its second instrumental part puts the song more in focus for me and Mike Banks gets to show off his virtuosic guitar skills while Tom Rutherland washes the tracks over with dreamy synthesizers, and when Phil repeats the song's third verse at the end it can give you chills.

"Illegal Alien" is the most explicitly political song the group has yet recorded and their funniest. The subject is supposed to be sad —a wetback trying to get across the border into the United States— but the details are highly comical: the bottle of tequila the Mexican holds, the new pair of shoes he's wearing (probably stolen); and it all seems totally accurate. Phil sings it in a brash, whiny pseudo-Mexican voice that makes it even funnier, and the rhyme of "*fun*" with "*illegal alien*" is inspired. "Just a Job to Do" is the album's funkiest song, with a killer bass line by Banks, and though it seems to be about a detective chasing a criminal, I think it could also be about a jealous lover tracking someone down. "Silver Rainbow" is the album's most lyrical song. The words are intense, complex and gorgeous. The album ends on a positive, upbeat note with "It's Gonna Get Better." Even if the lyrics seem a tiny bit generic to some, Phil's voice is so confident (heavily influenced by Peter Gabriel, who never made an album this polished and heartfelt himself) that he makes us believe in glorious possibilities.

Invisible Touch (Atlantic; 1986) is the group's undisputed masterpiece. It's an epic meditation on intangibility, at the same time it deepens and enriches the meaning of the preceding three albums. It has a resonance that keeps coming back at the listener, and the music is so beautiful that it's almost impossible to shake off because every song makes some connection about the unknown or the spaces between people ("Invisible Touch"), questioning authoritative control whether by domineering lovers or by government ("Land of Confusion") or by meaningless repetition ("Tonight Tonight Tonight"). All in all it ranks with the finest rock 'n' roll achievements of the decade and the mastermind behind this album, along of course with the brilliant ensemble playing of Banks, Collins and Rutherford, is Hugh Padgham, who has never found as clear and crisp and modern a sound as this. You can practically hear every nuance of every instrument.

In terms of lyrical craftsmanship and sheer songwriting skills this album hits a new peak of professionalism. Take the lyrics to "Land of Confusion," in which a singer addresses the problem of abusive political authority. This is laid down with a groove funkier and blacker than anything Prince or Michael Jackson—or any other black artist of recent years, for that matter—has come up with. Yet as danceable as the album is, it also has a stripped-down urgency that not even the overrated Bruce Springsteen can equal. As an observer of love's failings Collins beats out the Boss again and again, reaching new heights of emotional honesty on "In Too Deep"; yet it also showcases Collins' clowny, prankish, unpredictable side. It's the most moving pop song of the 1980s about monogamy and commitment. "Anything She Does" (which echoes the J. Geils Band's "Centerfold" but is more spirited and energetic) starts off side two and after that the album reaches its peak with "Domino," a two-part song. Part one, "In the Heat of the Night," is full of sharp, finely drawn images of despair and it's paired with "The Last Domino," which fights it with an expression of hope. This song is extremely uplifting. The lyrics are as positive and affirmative as anything I've heard in rock.

Phil Collins' solo efforts seem to be more commercial and therefore more satisfying in a narrower way, especially *No Jacket Required* and songs like "In the Air Tonight" and "Against All Odds" (though that song was overshadowed by the masterful movie from which it came) and "Take Me Home" and "Sussudio" (great, great song; a personal favorite) and his remake of "You Can't Hurry Love," which I'm not alone in thinking is better than the Supremes' original. But I also think that Phil Collins works better within the confines of the group than as a solo artist—and I stress the word *artist*. In fact it applies to all three of the guys, because Genesis is still the best, most exciting band to come out of England in the 1980s.

LUNCH

I'm sitting in DuPlex, the new Tony McManus restaurant in Tribeca, with Christopher Armstrong, who also works at P & P. We went to Exeter together, then he went to the University of Pennsylvania and Wharton, before moving to Manhattan. We, inexplicably, could not get reservations at Subjects, so Armstrong suggested this place. Armstrong is wearing a four-button double-breasted chalk-striped spread-collar cotton shirt by Christian Dior and a large paisley-patterned silk tie by Givenchy Gentleman. His leather agenda and leather envelope, both by Bottega Veneta, lie on the third chair at our table, a good one, up front by the window. I'm wearing a nailhead-patterned worsted wool suit with overplaid from DeRigueur by Schoeneman, a cotton broadcloth shirt by Bill Blass, a Macclesfield silk tie by Savoy and a cotton handkerchief by Ashear Bros. A Muzak rendition of the score from *Les Misérables* plays lightly throughout the restaurant. Armstrong's girlfriend is Jody Stafford, who used to date Todd Hamlin, and this fact plus the TV monitors hanging from the ceilings with closed-circuit video of chefs working in the kitchen fills me with nameless dread. Armstrong just got back from the islands and has a very deep, very even tan, but so do I.

"So how were the Bahamas?" I ask after we order. "You just got back, right?"

"Well, Taylor," Armstrong begins, staring at a point somewhere behind me and slightly above my head—on the column that has been terra-cotta-ized or perhaps on the exposed pipe that runs the length of the ceiling. "Travelers looking for that perfect vacation this summer may do well to look south, as far south as the Bahamas and the Caribbean islands. There are at least five smart reasons for visiting the Caribbean including the weather and the festivals and events, the less crowded hotels and attractions, the price and the unique cultures. While many vacationers leave the cities in search of cooler climates during the summer months, few have realized that the Caribbean has a year-round climate of seventy-five to eighty-five degrees and that the islands are constantly cooled by the trade winds. It is frequently hotter north in . . ."

On *The Patty Winters Show* this morning the topic was Toddler-Murderers. In the studio audience were parents of children who'd been kidnapped, tortured and murdered, while on stage a panel of psychiatrists and pediatricians were trying to help them *cope*—somewhat futilely I might add, and much to my delight— with their confusion and anger. But what really cracked me up was—via satellite on a lone TV monitor—three convicted Toddler-Murderers on death row who due to fairly complicated legal loopholes were now seeking parole and would probably get it. But something kept distracting me while I watched the huge Sony TV over a breakfast of sliced kiwi and Japanese apple-pear, Evian water, oat-bran muffins, soy milk and cinnamon granola, ruining my enjoyment of the grieving mothers, and it wasn't until the show was almost over that I figured out what it was: the crack above my David Onica that I had asked the doorman to tell the superintendent to fix. On my way out this morning I stopped at the front desk, about to complain to the doorman, when I was confronted with a *new* doorman, my age but balding and homely and *fat*. Three glazed jelly doughnuts *and* two steaming mugs of extra-dark *hot chocolate* lay on the desk in front of him beside a copy of the *Post* opened to the comics and it struck me that I was infinitely better-looking, more successful and richer than this poor bastard would ever be and so with a passing rush of sympathy I smiled and nodded a curt though not impolite good morning without lodging a complaint. "Oh really?" I find myself saying loudly, completely uninterested, to Armstrong.

"Like the United States it celebrates the summer months with festivals and special events including music concerts, art exhibits, street fairs and sporting tournaments, and because of the vast number of people traveling elsewhere, the islands are less crowded, allowing for better service and no lines when waiting to use that sailboat or dine in that restaurant. I mean I think most people go to sample the culture, the food, the history . . ."

On the way to Wall Street this morning, due to gridlock I had to get out of the company car and was walking down Fifth Avenue to find a subway station when I passed what I thought was a Halloween parade, which was disorienting since I was fairly sure this was May. When I stopped on the corner of Sixteenth Street and made a closer inspection it turned out to be something called a "Gay Pride Parade," which made my stomach turn. Homosexuals proudly marched down Fifth Avenue, pink triangles emblazoned on pastel-colored windbreakers, some even holding hands, most singing "Somewhere" out of key and in unison. I stood in front of Paul Smith and watched with a certain traumatized fascination, my mind reeling with the concept that a human being, a *man*, could feel pride over sodomizing another man, but when I began to receive fey cat-calls from aging, overmuscled beachboys with walruslike mustaches in between the lines *"There's a place for us, Somewhere a place for us,"* I sprinted over to Sixth Avenue, decided to be late for the office and took a cab back to my apartment where I put on a new suit (by Cerruti 1881), gave myself a pedicure and tortured to death a small dog I had bought earlier this week in a pet store on Lexington. Armstrong drones on.

"Water sports are of course the leading attraction. But golf courses and tennis courts are in excellent condition and the pros at many of the resorts are made more available during the summer. Many of the courts are lit for night playing as well . . ."

Fuck . . . yourself . . . Armstrong, I'm thinking while staring out the window at the gridlock and pacing bums on Church Street. Appetizers arrive: sun-dried-tomato brioche for Armstrong. Poblano chilies with an oniony orange-purple marmalade on the side for me. I hope Armstrong doesn't want to pay because I need to show the dim-witted bastard that I in fact *do* own a platinum American Express card. I feel very sad at this moment for some reason, listening to Armstrong, and a lump forms in my throat but I swallow and take a sip from my Corona and the emotion passes and during a pause while he's chewing, I ask, "The food? How's the food?" almost involuntarily, thinking about anything but.

"Good question. As for dining out, the Caribbean has become more attractive as the island cuisine has mixed well with the European culture. Many of the restaurants are owned and managed by Americans, British, French, Italian, even Dutch expatriates . . ." Mercifully, he pauses, taking a bite out of his brioche, which looks like a sponge drenched in blood—*his brioche looks like a big bloody sponge*—and he washes it down with a sip from his Corona. My turn.

"How about sightseeing?" I ask disinterestedly, concentrating on the blackened chilies, the yellowish marmalade circling the plate in an artful octagon, cilantro leaves circling the marmalade, chili seeds circling the cilantro leaves.

"Sightseeing is highlighted by the European culture which established many of the islands as regional fortresses in the seventeen hundreds. Visitors can see the various spots where Columbus landed and as we near the three hundredth anniversary of his first sailing in 1590 there is a heightened awareness in the islands as to the history and culture that is an integral part of island life . . ."

Armstrong: you are an . . . *asshole*. "Uh-huh." I nod. "Well . . ." Paisley ties, plaid suits, my aerobics class, returning videotapes, spices to pick up from Zabar's, beggars, white-chocolate truffles . . . The sickening scent of Drakkar Noir, which is what Christopher is wearing, floats over near my face, mingling with the scent of the marmalade and cilantro, the onions and the blackened chilies. "Uh-huh," I say, repeat.

"And for the active vacationer there is mountain climbing, cave exploring, sailing, horseback riding and white-water river rafting, and for the gamblers there are casinos on many of the islands . . ."

Fleetingly I imagine pulling out my knife, slicing a wrist, one of mine, aiming the spurting vein at Armstrong's head or better yet his suit, wondering if he would still continue to talk. I consider getting up without excusing myself, taking a cab to another restaurant, somewhere in SoHo, maybe farther uptown, having a drink, using the rest room, maybe even making a phone call to Evelyn, coming back to DuPlex, and every molecule that makes up my body tells me that Armstrong would still be talking about not only his vacation but what seems like the *world's* vacation in the fucking Bahamas. Somewhere along the line the waiter removes half-eaten appetizers, brings fresh Coronas, free-range chicken with raspberry vinegar and guacamole, calf's liver with shad roe and leeks, and though I'm not sure who ordered what it doesn't really matter since both plates look exactly the same. I end up with the free-range chicken with extra tomatillo sauce, I think.

"Visitors to the Caribbean don't need a passport—just proof of U.S. citizenship—and even better, Taylor, is that *language* is no barrier. English is spoken *everywhere*, even on those islands where the local language is French or Spanish. Most of the islands are former British . . ."

"My life is a living hell," I mention off the cuff, while casually moving leeks around on my plate, which by the way is a porcelain triangle. "And there are many more people I, uh, want to . . . want to, well, I guess *murder*." I say this emphasizing the last word, staring straight into Armstrong's face.

"Service has improved to the islands as both American Airlines and Eastern Airlines have created hubs in San Juan where they have set up connecting flights to those islands they don't serve with direct flights. With additional service from BWIA, Pan Am, ALM, Air Jamaica, Bahamas Air and Cayman Airways, most islands are easy to reach. There are additional connections within the islands from LIAT and BWIA, which provides a series of scheduled island-hopping flights . . ."

Someone who I think is Charles Fletcher walks over while Armstrong keeps talking and he pats me on the shoulder and says "Hey Simpson" and "See you at Fluties" and then at the door meets up with a very attractive woman—big tits, blond, tight dress, not his secretary, not his wife—and they leave DuPlex together in a black limousine. Armstrong is still eating, cutting into the perfectly square slices of calf's liver, and he keeps talking while I become increasingly mournful.

"Vacationers who can't take a full week away will find the Caribbean an ideal spot for the alternative weekend escape. Eastern Airlines has created its Weekender Club which includes many Caribbean destinations and enables members to visit many places at sharply reduced prices which I know doesn't matter but I still think people are going

CONCERT

Everyone is very uptight at the concert Carruthers drags us to in New Jersey this evening, an Irish band called U2 who were on the cover of *Time* magazine last week. The tickets were originally for a group of Japanese clients who canceled their trip to New York at the last minute, making it virtually impossible for Carruthers (or so he says) to sell these front-row seats. So it's Carruthers and Courtney, Paul Owen and Ashley Cromwell, and Evelyn and myself. Earlier, when I found out that Paul Owen was coming, I tried to call Cecelia Wagner, Marcus Halberstam's girlfriend, since Paul Owen seems fairly sure that I'm Marcus, and though she was flattered by my invitation (I always suspected I was one of her crushes) she had to attend a black-tie party for the opening of the new British musical *Maggie!* But she did mention something about lunch next week and I told her I would give her a call on Thursday. I was supposed to have dinner with Evelyn tonight, but the thought of sitting alone with her during a two-hour meal fills me with a nameless dread and so I call and reluctantly explain the schedule changes and she asks if Tim Price is coming and when I tell her no, there is the briefest hesitation before she accepts and then I cancel the reservation Jean made for us at H_2O, the new Clive Powell restaurant in Chelsea, and leave the office early for a quick aerobics class before the concert.

None of the girls are particularly excited about seeing the band and all have confided in me, separately, that they don't want to be here, and in the limousine heading toward somewhere called the Meadowlands, Carruthers keeps trying to placate everyone by telling us that Donald Trump is a big U2 fan and then, even more desperately, that John Gutfreund also buys their records. A bottle of Cristal is opened, then another. The TV is tuned to a press conference Reagan's giving but there's a lot of static and no one pays attention, except for me. *The Patty Winters Show* this morning was about Shark Attack Victims. Paul Owen has called me Marcus four times and Evelyn, much to my relief, Cecelia twice, but Evelyn doesn't notice since she's been glaring at Courtney the entire time we've been in the limousine. Anyway, no one has corrected Owen and it's unlikely that anyone will. I even called her Cecelia a couple of times myself when I was sure she wasn't listening, while she was staring hatefully at Courtney. Carruthers keeps telling me how nice I look and complimenting my suit.

Evelyn and I are by far the best-dressed couple. I'm wearing a lamb's wool topcoat, a wool jacket with wool flannel trousers, a cotton shirt, a cashmere V-neck sweater and a silk tie, all from

Armani. Evelyn's wearing a cotton blouse by Dolce & Gabbana, suede shoes by Yves Saint Laurent, a stenciled calf skirt by Adrienne Landau with a suede belt by Jill Stuart, Calvin Klein tights, Venetian-glass earrings by Frances Patiky Stein, and clasped in her hand is a single white rose that I bought at a Korean deli before Carruthers' limousine picked me up. Carruthers is wearing a lamb's wool sport coat, a cashmere/vicuña cardigan sweater, cavalry twill trousers, a cotton shirt and a silk tie, all from Hermès. ("How tacky," Evelyn whispered to me; I silently agreed.) Courtney is wearing a triple-layered silk organdy top and a long velvet skirt with a fishtail hem, velvet-ribbon and enamel earrings by José and Maria Barrera, gloves by Portolano and shoes from Gucci. Paul and Ashley are, I think, a bit *over*dressed, and she has sunglasses on even though the windows in the limo are tinted and it's already dusk. She holds a small bouquet of flowers, daisies, Carruthers gave her, which failed to make Courtney jealous since she seems intent upon clawing Evelyn's face open, which right now, though it's the better-looking face, seems not a bad idea and one I wouldn't mind watching Courtney carry out. Courtney has a *slightly* better body, Evelyn nicer tits.

The concert has been dragging on now for maybe twenty minutes. I *hate* live music but everyone around us is standing, their screams of approval competing with the racket coming from the towering walls of speakers stacked over us. The only real pleasure I get from being here is seeing Scott and Anne Smiley ten rows behind us, in shittier though probably not less expensive seats. Carruthers changes seats with Evelyn to discuss business with me, but I can't hear a word so I change seats with Evelyn to talk to Courtney.

"Luis is a *weasel*," I shout. "He suspects *nothing*."

"The Edge is wearing Armani," she shouts, pointing at the bassist.

"That's *not* Armani," I shout back. "It's Em*po*rio."

"No," she shouts. "Ar*mani*."

"The grays are too muted and so are the taupes and navies. Definite winged lapels, subtle plaids, polka dots and stripes are Armani. *Not* Emporio," I shout, extremely irritated that she doesn't know this, can't differentiate, both my hands covering both ears. "There's a difference. Which one's The Ledge?"

"The drummer might be The Ledge," she shouts. "I think. I'm not sure. I need a cigarette. Where were you the other night? If you tell me with Evelyn I'm going to hit you."

"The drummer is not wearing anything by Armani," I scream. "Or Emporio for that matter. Nowhere."

"I don't know which one the drummer is," she shouts.

"Ask Ashley," I suggest, screaming.

"Ashley?" she screams, reaching over across Paul and tapping Ashley's leg. "Which one's The Ledge?" Ashley shouts something at her that I can't hear and then Courtney turns back to me, shrugging. "She said she can't believe she's in New Jersey."

Carruthers motions for Courtney to change seats with him. She waves the little twit away and grips my thigh, which I flex rock-hard, and her hand lingers admiringly. But Luis persists and she gets up, and screams at me, "I think we need drugs tonight!" I nod. The lead singer, Bono, is screeching out what sounds like "Where the Beat Sounds the Same." Evelyn and Ashley leave to buy cigarettes, use the ladies' room, find refreshments. Luis sits next to me.

"The girls are bored," Luis screams at me.

"Courtney wants us to find her some cocaine tonight," I shout.

"Oh, *great*." Luis looks sulky.

"Do we have reservations anywhere?"

"*Brussels*," he shouts, checking his Rolex. "But it's *doubt*ful if we'll make it."

"If we *don't* make it," I warn him, "I'm not going *any*where else. You can drop me at my apartment."

"We'll *make* it," he shouts.

"If we *don't*, what about Japanese?" I suggest, relenting. "There's a really top sushi bar on the Upper West Side. Blades. Chef used to be at Isoito. It got a *great* rating in Zagat."

"Bateman, I *hate* the Japanese," Carruthers screams at me, one hand placed over an ear. "Little slanty-eyed bastards."

"What," I scream, "in the hell are you talking about?"

"Oh I know, I know," he screams, eyes bulging. "They save more than we do and they don't innovate much, but they sure in the fuck know how to take, *steal*, our innovations, improve on them, then ram them down our fucking throats!"

I stare at him, disbelieving for a moment, then look at the stage, at the guitarist running around in circles, Bono's arms outstretched as he runs back and forth across the length of its edge, and then back at Luis whose face is still crimson with fury and he's still staring at me, wide-eyed, spittle on his lips, not saying anything.

"What in the *hell* does that have to do with *Blades*?" I ask finally, genuinely confused. "Wipe your mouth."

"That's why I *hate* Japanese food," he screams back. "Sashimi. California roll. Oh *Jesus*." He makes a gagging motion, with one finger going down his throat.

"Carruthers . . ." I stop, still looking at him, studying his face closely, slightly freaked out, unable to remember what I wanted to say.

"*What*, Bateman?" Carruthers asks, leaning in.

"Listen, I can't believe this shit," I scream. "I can't believe you didn't make the reservations for *later*. We're going to have to *wait*."

"What?" he screams, cupping his ear, as if it makes a difference.

"We are going to have to *wait*!" I scream louder.

"This is not a problem," he shouts.

The lead singer reaches out to us from the stage, his hand outstretched, and I wave him away. "It's okay? It's *okay*? No, Luis. You're *wrong*. It's not *okay*." I look over at Paul Owen, who seems equally bored, his hands clamped over both ears, but still managing to confer with Courtney about something.

"We won't have to wait," Luis screams. "I promise."

"Promise *nothing*, you geek," I scream, then, "Is Paul Owen still handling the Fisher account?"

"I don't want you to be mad at me, Patrick," Luis screams desperately. "It'll be *all* right."

"Oh Jesus, forget it," I scream. "Now listen to me: is Paul Owen still handling the Fisher account?"

Carruthers looks over at him and then back at me. "Yeah, I guess. I heard Ashley has chlamydia."

"I'm going to talk to him," I shout, getting up, taking the empty seat next to Owen.

But when I sit down something strange on the stage catches my eye. Bono has now moved across the stage, following me to my seat, and he's staring into my eyes, kneeling at the edge of the stage, wearing black jeans (maybe Gitano), sandals, a leather vest with no shirt beneath it. His body is white, covered with sweat, and it's not worked out enough, there's no muscle tone and what definition there might be is covered beneath a paltry amount of chest hair. He has a cowboy hat on and his hair is pulled back into a ponytail and he's moaning some dirge—I catch the lyric "A hero is an insect in this world"—and he has a faint, barely noticeable but nonetheless intense smirk on his face and it grows, spreading across it confidently, and while his eyes blaze, the backdrop of the stage turns red and suddenly I get this tremendous surge of feeling, this rush of knowledge and my own heart beats faster because of this and it's not impossible to believe that an invisible cord attached to Bono has now encircled me and now the audience disappears and the music slows down, gets softer, and it's just Bono onstage—the stadium's deserted, the band fades away . . .

And then everyone, the audience, the band, reappears and the music slowly swells up and Bono turns away and I'm left tingling, my face flushed, an aching erection pulsing against my thigh, my hands clenched in fists of tension. But suddenly everything stops, as if a switch has been turned off, the backdrop flashes back to white. Bono is on the other side of the stage now and everything, the feeling in my heart, the sensation combing my brain, vanishes and now more than ever I need to know about the Fisher account that Owen is handling and this information seems vital, more pertinent than the bond I feel I have with Bono, who is now dissolving and remote. I turn to Paul Owen.

"Hey," I shout. "How's it going?"

"Those guys over there . . ." He motions toward a group of stagehands standing by the edge of the far side of the front row, peering into the crowd, conferring with one another. "They were pointing over here at Evelyn and Courtney and Ashley."

"Who are they?" I shout. "Are they from Oppenheimer?"

"No," Owen shouts back. "I think they're roadies who look for chicks to go backstage and have sex with the band."

"Oh," I scream. "I thought maybe they worked at Barney's."

"No," he shouts. "They're called *trim* coordinators."

"How do you know *that*?"

"I have a cousin who manages All We Need of Hell," he shouts.

"It's irritating that you know this," I say.

"What?" he shouts.

"Are you still handling the Fisher account?" I shout back.

"Yeah," he screams. "Lucked out, huh, Marcus?"

"You sure did," I scream. "How did you get it?"

"Well, I had the Ransom account and things just fell into place." He shrugs helplessly, the smooth bastard. "You know?"

"Wow," I shout.

"Yeah," he shouts back, then turns around in his seat and shouts at two dumb-looking fat girls from New Jersey passing an oversize joint between them, one of the cows wrapped in what I'm guessing is the Irish flag. "Will you please put your *skunk-weed* away—it *reeks*."

"I want it," I shout, staring at his perfect, even part; even his scalp is tan.

"You want *what*?" he shouts back. "Marijuana?"

"No. Nothing," I scream, my throat raw, and I slump back into my seat, stare emptily at the stage, biting my thumbnail, ruining yesterday's manicure.

We leave after Evelyn and Ashley return and later, in the limousine racing back toward Manhattan to make the reservations at Brussels, another bottle of Cristal is opened, Reagan still on the television set, Evelyn and Ashley tell us that two bouncers accosted them near the ladies' room and demanded they come backstage. I explain who they were and what purpose they serve.

"My *god*," Evelyn gasps. "Are you telling me I've been . . . *trim-coordinated*?"

"I bet Bono has a small dick," Owen says, staring out the tinted window. "Irish, you know."

"Do you think they had an automated teller back there?" Luis asks.

"Ashley," Evelyn shouts. "Did you hear that? We've been *trim-coordinated*!"

"How does my hair look?" I ask.

"More Cristal?" Courtney asks Luis.

A GLIMPSE OF A THURSDAY AFTERNOON

and it's midafternoon and I find myself standing at a phone booth on a corner somewhere downtown, I don't know where, but I'm sweaty and a pounding migraine thumps dully in my head and I'm experiencing a major-league anxiety attack, searching my pockets for Valium, Xanax, a leftover Halcion, anything, and all I find are three faded Nuprin in a Gucci pillbox, so I pop all three into my mouth and swallow them down with a Diet Pepsi and I couldn't tell you where it came from if my life depended on it. I've forgotten who I had lunch with earlier and, even more important, *where*. Was it Robert Ailes at Beats? Or was it Todd Hendricks at Ursula's, the new Philip Duncan Holmes bistro in Tribeca? Or was it Ricky Worrall and were we at December's? Or would it have been Kevin Weber at Contra in SoHo? Did I order the partridge sandwich on brioche with green tomatoes, or a big plate of endive with clam sauce? "Oh god, *I can't remember*," I moan, my clothes—a linen and silk sport coat, a cotton shirt, pleated linen khaki trousers, all by Matsuda, a silk tie with a Matsuda insignia, with a belt from Coach Leatherware—drenched with sweat, and I take off the jacket and wipe my face with it. The phone keeps ringing but I don't know who I've called and I just stand on the corner, Ray-Bans balanced on my forehead at what feels like an odd, crooked angle, and then I hear a faint familiar sound coming through the wires—Jean's soft voice competing with the endless gridlock stuck on Broadway. *The Patty Winters Show* this morning was Aspirin: Can It Save Your Life? "Jean?" I cry out. "Hello? *Jean?*" "Patrick? Is that you?" she calls back. "*Hello?*" "*Jean*, I need *help*," I shout. "Patrick?" "What?" "Jessie Forrest called," Jean says. "He has a reservation at Melrose tonight at eight, and Ted Madison and Jamie Conway want to meet you for drinks at Harry's. Patrick?" Jean asks. "Where are you?" "Jean?" I sigh, wiping my nose. "I'm not—" "Oh, and Todd Lauder called," Jean says, "no, I mean Chris—oh no, it was Todd Lauder. Yeah, Todd Lauder." "Oh god," I moan, loosening my tie, the August sun beating down on me, "what do you say, you dumb bitch?" "Not *Bice*, Patrick. The reservation is at *Melrose*. Not Bice." "What am I *doing*?" I cry out. "Where are you?" and then, "Patrick? What's wrong?" "I'm not going to make it, Jean," I say, then choke out, "to the office this afternoon." "Why?" She sounds depressed or maybe it's just simple confusion. "Just . . . say . . . no . . ." I scream. "What is it, Patrick? Are you all right?" she asks. "Stop sounding so fucking . . . sad. *Jesus*," I shout. "Patrick. I'm sorry. I mean I meant to say 'Just say no,' but—" I hang up on her and lunge away from the phone booth and the Walkman around my neck suddenly feels like a boulder strapped around my throat (and the sounds blaring from it—early Dizzy Gillespie—deeply irritate) and I have to throw the Walkman, a cheap one, into the nearest trash can I stumble into and then I hang on to the rim of the can, breathing heavily, the chap Matsuda jacket tied around my waist, staring at the still-functioning Walkman, the sun melting the mousse on my head and it mingles with the sweat pouring down my face and I can taste it when I lick my lips and it starts tasting good and I'm suddenly ravenous and I run my hand through my hair and lick greedily at the palm while moving up Broadway, ignoring the old ladies passing out fliers, past jeans stores, music blasting from inside, pouring out onto the streets, people's movements matching the beat of the song, a Madonna single, Madonna crying out, *"life is a mystery, everyone must stand alone . . ."* bike messengers whiz by and I'm standing on a corner scowling at them, but people pass, oblivious, no one pays attention, they don't even pretend to *not* pay attention, and this fact sobers me up long enough that I walk toward a nearby Connan's to buy a teapot, but just when I assume my normalcy has returned and I'm all straightened out, my stomach tightens and the cramps are so intense that I hobble into the nearest doorway and clutch my waist, doubling over with pain, and as suddenly as it appears it fades long enough for me to stand up straight and rush into the next hardware store I come across, and once inside I buy a set of butcher knives, an ax, a bottle of hydrochloric acid, and then, at the pet store down the block, a Habitrail and two white rats that I plan to torture with the knives and acid, but somewhere, later in the afternoon, I leave the package with the rats in it at the Pottery Barn while shopping for candles or did I finally buy the teapot? Now I'm lunging up Lafayette, sweating and moaning and pushing people out of my way, foam pouring out of my mouth, stomach contracting with horrendous abdominal cramps—they might be caused by the steroids but that's doubtful—and I calm myself down enough to walk into a Gristede's, rush up and down the aisles and shoplift a canned ham that I calmly walk out of the store with, hidden under the Matsuda jacket, and down the block, where I try to hide in the lobby of the American Felt Building, breaking the tin open with my keys, ignoring the doorman, who at first seems to recognize me, then, after I start shuffling handfuls of the ham into my mouth, scooping the lukewarm pink meat out of the can, getting it stuck beneath my nails, threatens to call the police. I'm outta there, outside, throwing up all the ham, leaning against a poster for *Les Misérables* at a bus stop and I kiss the drawing of Eponine's lovely face, her lips, leaving brown streaks of bile smeared across her soft, unassuming face and the word DYKE scrawled beneath it. Loosening my suspenders, ignoring beggars, beggars ignoring me, sweat-drenched, delirious, I find myself back downtown in Tower Records and I compose myself, muttering over and over to no one, "I've gotta return my videotapes, I've gotta return my videotapes," and I buy two copies of my favorite compact disc, Bruce Willis, *The Return of Bruno*, and then I'm stuck in the revolving door for five full spins and I trip out onto the street, bumping into Charles Murphy from Kidder Peabody or it could be Bruce Barker from Morgan Stanley, *whoever*, and he says "Hey, Kinsley" and I belch into his face, my eyes rolling back into my head, greenish bile dripping in strings from my bared fangs, and he suggests, unfazed, "See you at Fluties, okay? Severt too?" I screech and while backing away I bump into a fruit stand at a Korean deli, collapsing stacks of apples and oranges and lemons, that go rolling onto the sidewalk, over the curb and into the street where they're splattered by cabs and cars and buses and trucks and I'm apologizing, delirious, offering a screaming Korean my platinum AmEx accidentally, then a twenty, which he immediately takes, but still he grabs me by the lapels of the stained, wrinkled jacket I've forced myself back into and when I look up into his slanty-eyed round face he suddenly bursts into the chorus of Lou Christie's "Lightnin' Strikes." I pull away, horrified, stumbling uptown, toward home, but people, places, stores keep interrupting me, a drug dealer on Thirteenth Street who offers me crack and blindly I wave a fifty at him and he says "Oh, man" gratefully and shakes my hand, pressing five vials into my palm which I proceed to *eat whole* and the crack dealer stares at me, trying to mask his deep disturbance with an amused glare, and I grab him by the neck and croak out, my breath reeking, "*The best engine is in the BMW 750iL*," and then I move on to a phone booth, where I babble gibberish at the operator until I finally spit out my credit card number and then I'm speaking to the front office of Xclusive, where I cancel a massage appointment that I never made. I'm able to compose myself by simply staring at my feet, actually at the A. Testoni loafers, kicking pigeons aside, and without even noticing, I enter a shabby delicatessen on Second Avenue and I'm still confused, mixed up, sweaty, and I walk over to a short, fat Jewish woman, old and hideously dressed. "Listen," I say. "I have a reservation. Bateman. Where's the maître d'? I know Jackie Mason," and she sighs, "I can seat you. Don't need a reservation," as she reaches for a menu. She leads me to a horrible table in back near the rest rooms and I grab the menu away from her and rush to a booth up front and I'm appalled by the cheapness of the food—"Is this a goddamn joke?"—and sensing a waitress is near I order without looking up. "A cheeseburger. I'd like a cheeseburger and I'd like it medium rare." "I'm sorry, sir," the waitress says. "No cheese. Kosher," and I have no idea what the fuck she's talking about and I say, "Fine. A *kosher*burger but *with cheese*, Monterey Jack perhaps, and—oh god," I moan, sensing more cramps coming on. "No cheese, sir," she says. "*Kosher* . . ." "Oh god, is this a *nightmare*, you fucking *Jew*?" I mutter, and then, "*Cottage cheese*? Just *bring it*?" "I'll get the manager," she says. "Whatever. But bring me a beverage in the meanwhile," I hiss. "Yes?" she asks. "A . . . vanilla . . . milk shake . . ." "No milk shakes. *Kosher*," she says, then, "I'll get the manager." "No, *wait*." "Mister, I'll get the manager." "What in the fuck is going on?" I ask, seething, my platinum AmEx already slapped on the greasy table. "No milk shake. *Kosher*," she says, thick-lipped, just one of billions of people who have passed over this planet. "Then bring me a fucking . . . vanilla . . . *malted*!" I roar, spraying spit all over my open menu. She just stares. "*Extra thick!*" I add. She walks away to get the manager and when I see him approaching, a bald carbon copy of the waitress, I get up and scream, "Fuck yourself you retarded cocksucking kike," and I run out of the delicatessen and onto the street where this

YALE CLUB

"What are the rules for a sweater vest?" Van Patten asks the table.

"What do you mean?" McDermott furrows his brow, takes a sip of Absolut.

"Yes," I say. "*Clar*ify."

"Well, is it strictly in*for*mal—"

"Or can it be worn with a *suit*?" I interrupt, finishing his sentence.

"Exactly." He smiles.

"Well, according to Bruce Boyer—" I begin.

"Wait." Van Patten stops me. "Is he with Morgan Stanley?"

"No." I smile. "He's not with Morgan Stanley."

"Wasn't he a serial killer?" McDermott asks suspiciously, then moans. "Don't tell me he was another serial killer, Bateman. *Not* another serial killer."

"No, Mc*Dufus*, he wasn't a *serial* killer," I say, turning back to Van Patten, but before continuing turn back to McDermott. "That really pisses me off."

"But you *always* bring them up," McDermott complains. "And always in this casual, educational sort of way. I mean, I don't want to know anything about Son of Sam or the fucking Hillside Strangler or Ted Bundy or Featherhead, for god sake."

"Featherhead?" Van Patten asks. "Who's Featherhead? He sounds exceptionally dangerous."

"He means Leatherface," I say, teeth slightly clenched. "Leatherface. He was part of the Texas Chainsaw Massacre."

"Oh." Van Patten smiles politely. "Of course."

"And he *was* exceptionally dangerous," I say.

"And now okay, go on. Bruce Boyer, what did *he* do?" McDermott demands, releasing a sigh, rolling his eyes up. "Let's see—

skin them alive? Starve them to death? Run them over? Feed them to dogs? What?"

"You guys," I say, shaking my head, then teasingly admit, "He did something *far* worse."

"Like what—take them to dinner at McManus's new restaurant?" McDermott asks.

"That would do it," Van Patten agrees. "Did you go? It was grubby, wasn't it?"

"Did you have the meat loaf?" McDermott asks.

"The meat loaf?" Van Patten's in shock. "What about the *interior*. What about the fucking *tablecloths*?"

"But did you *have* the meat loaf?" McDermott presses.

"Of course I had the meat loaf, *and* the squab, *and* the marlin," Van Patten says.

"Oh god, I forgot about the marlin," McDermott groans. "The marlin chili."

"After reading Miller's review in the *Times*, who in their right mind *wouldn't* order the meat loaf, or the marlin for that matter?"

"But Miller got it wrong," McDermott says. "It was just grubby. The quesadilla with papaya? Usually a good dish, but *there*, Jesus." He whistles, shaking his head.

"And *cheap*," Van Patten adds.

"So cheap." McDermott is in total agreement. "And the watermelon-brittle tart—"

"Gentlemen." I cough. "Ahem. I hate to interrupt, but . . ."

"Okay, okay, go on," McDermott says. "Tell us more about Charles Moyer."

"Bruce Boyer," I correct him. "He was the author of *Elegance: A Guide to Quality in Menswear*." Then as an aside, "And no, Craig, he wasn't a serial killer in his spare time."

"What did Brucie baby have to say?" McDermott asks, chewing on ice.

"You're a clod. It's an excellent book. His theory remains we shouldn't feel restricted from wearing a sweater vest with a suit," I say. "Did you hear me call you a clod?"

"Yeah."

"But doesn't he point out that a vest shouldn't overpower the suit?" Van Patten offers tentatively.

"Yes . . ." I'm mildly irritated that Van Patten has done his homework but asks for advice nonetheless. I calmly continue. "With discreet pinstripes you should wear a subdued blue or charcoal gray vest. A plaid suit would call for a bolder vest."

"And remember," McDermott adds, "with a regular vest the last button should be left undone."

I glance sharply at McDermott. He smiles, sips his drink and then smacks his lips, satisfied.

"Why?" Van Patten wants to know.

"It's traditional," I say, still glaring at McDermott. "But it's also more comfortable."

"Will wearing suspenders help the vest sit better?" I hear Van Patten ask.

"Why?" I ask, turning to face him.

"Well, since you avoid the . . ." He stops, stuck, looking for the right word.

"Encumbrance of—?" I begin.

"The belt buckle?" McDermott finishes.

"Sure," Van Patten says.

"You have to remember—" Again I'm interrupted by McDermott.

"Remember that while the vest should be in keeping with the color and the style of the suit, completely avoid matching the vest's pattern with your socks or tie," McDermott says, smiling at me, at Van Patten.

"I thought you hadn't read this . . . this book," I stammer angrily. "You just told me you couldn't tell the difference between Bruce Boyer and . . . and John Wayne Gacy."

"It came back to me." He shrugs.

"Listen." I turn back to Van Patten, finding McDermott's one-upmanship totally cheap. "Wearing argyle socks with an argyle vest will look too studied."

"You think so?" he asks.

"You'll look like you consciously worked for this look," I say, then, suddenly upset, turn back to McDermott. "*Featherhead?* How in the hell did you get Featherhead from Leatherface?"

"Ah, cheer up, Bateman," he says, slapping me on the back, then massaging my neck. "What's the matter? No shiatsu this morning?"

"Keep touching me like this," I say, eyes shut tight, entire body

wired and ticking, coiled up ready, *wanting* to spring, "and you'll
draw back a stump."

"Whoa, hold on there, little buddy," McDermott says, backing
off in mock fear. The two of them giggle like idiots and give each
other high-five, completely unaware that I'd cut his hands off, and
much more, with pleasure.

The three of us, David Van Patten, Craig McDermott and
myself, are sitting in the dining room of the Yale Club at lunch. Van
Patten is wearing a glen-plaid wool-crepe suit from Krizia Uomo, a
Brooks Brothers shirt, a tie from Adirondack and shoes by Cole-
Haan. McDermott is wearing a lamb's wool and cashmere blazer,
worsted wool flannel trousers by Ralph Lauren, a shirt and tie *also*
by Ralph Lauren and shoes from Brooks Brothers. I'm wearing a
tick-weave wool suit with a windowpane overplaid, a cotton shirt by
Luciano Barbera, a tie by Luciano Barbera, shoes from Cole-Haan
and nonprescription glasses by Bausch & Lomb. *The Patty Winters
Show* this morning was about Nazis and, inexplicably, I got a real
charge out of watching it. Though I wasn't exactly charmed by their
deeds, I didn't find them unsympathetic either, nor I might add did
most of the members of the audience. One of the Nazis, in a rare
display of humor, even juggled grapefruits and, delighted, I sat up
in bed and clapped.

Luis Carruthers sits five tables away from this one, dressed as if
he'd had some kind of frog attack this morning—he's wearing an
unidentifable suit from some French tailor; and if I'm not mistaken
the bowler hat on the floor beneath his chair also belongs to him—
it has Luis written all over it. He smiles but I pretend not to have
noticed. I worked out at Xclusive for two hours this morning and
since the three of us have taken the rest of the afternoon off, we're
all getting massages. We haven't ordered yet, in fact we haven't
even seen menus. We've just been drinking. A bottle of champagne
is what Craig originally wanted, but David shook his head vehe-
mently and said "Out, out, *out*" when this was suggested and so we
ordered drinks instead. I keep watching Luis and whenever he looks
over at our table I tip my head back and laugh even if what Van
Patten or McDermott's saying isn't particularly funny, which is
practically always. I've perfected my fake response to a degree
where it's so natural-sounding that no one notices. Luis stands up,

wipes his mouth with a napkin and glances over here again before exiting the dining area and, I'm supposing, goes to the men's room.

"But there's a limit," Van Patten is saying. "The point is, I mean, I don't want to spend the evening with the Cookie Monster."

"But you're still dating Meredith so, uh, what's the difference?" I ask. Naturally he doesn't hear.

"But ditsy is cute," McDermott says. "Ditsy is very cute."

"Bateman?" Van Patten asks. "Any style opinions on ditsiness?"

"What?" I ask, getting up.

"Ditsy? No?" McDermott this time. "Ditsy's desirable, *comprende*?"

"Listen," I say, pushing my chair in. "I just want everyone to know that I'm pro-family and anti-drug. Excuse me."

As I walk away Van Patten grabs a passing waiter and says, his voice fading, "Is this tap water? I don't drink tap water. Bring me an Evian or something, okay?"

Would Courtney like me less if Luis was dead? This is the question I have to face, with no clear answer burning back across my mind, as I make my way slowly through the dining room, waving to someone who looks like Vincent Morrison, someone else who I'm fairly sure is someone who looks like Tom Newman. Would Courtney spend more time with me—the time she now spends with Luis—if he was out of the picture, no longer an alternative, if he was perhaps . . . *dead*? If Luis were killed would Courtney be upset? Could I genuinely be of comfort without laughing in her face, my own spite doubling back on me, giving everything away? Is the fact that she dates me behind his back what excites her, my body or the size of my dick? Why, for that matter, do I want to please Courtney? If she likes me only for my muscles, the heft of my cock, then she's a shallow bitch. *But* a physically superior, near-perfect-looking shallow bitch, and *that* can override anything, except maybe bad breath or yellow teeth, either of which is a real deal-breaker. Would I ruin things by strangling Luis? If I married Evelyn would she make me buy her Lacroix gowns until we finalized our divorce? Have the South African colonial forces and the Soviet-backed black guerrillas found peace yet in Namibia? Or would the world be a safer, kinder place if Luis was hacked to bits? *My* world might, so why not? There really is no . . . *other hand*. It's really even too late to be asking these questions since now I'm in the men's room, staring at myself in the mirror—tan and haircut perfect—checking out my teeth which are completely straight and white and gleaming. Winking at my reflection I breathe in, sliding on a pair of leather Armani gloves, and then make my way toward the stall Luis occupies. The men's room is deserted. All the stalls are empty except for the one at the end, the door not locked, left slightly ajar, the sound of Luis whistling something from *Les Misérables* getting almost oppressively louder as I approach.

He's standing in the stall, his back to me, wearing a cashmere blazer, pleated wool trousers, a cotton-silk white shirt, pissing into the toilet. I can tell he senses movement in the stall because he stiffens noticeably and the sound of his urine hitting water stops abruptly in midstream. In slow motion, my own heavy breathing blocking out all other sounds, my vision blurring slightly around the edges, my hands move up over the collar of his cashmere blazer and cotton-flannel shirt, circling his neck until my thumbs meet at the nape and my index fingers touch each other just above Luis's Adam's apple. I start to squeeze, tightening my grip, but it's loose enough to let Luis turn around—still in slow motion—so he can stand facing me, one hand over his wool and silk Polo sweater, the other hand reaching up. His eyelids flutter for an instant, then widen, which is exactly what I want. I want to see Luis's face contort and turn purple and I want him to know who it is who is killing him. I want to be the last face, the last *thing*, that Luis sees before he dies and I want to cry out, "I'm fucking Courtney. Do you hear me? *I'm* fucking Courtney. Ha-ha-ha," and have these be the last words, the last *sounds* he hears until his own gurglings, accompanied by the crunching of his trachea, drown everything else out. Luis stares at me and I tense the muscles in my arms, preparing myself for a struggle that, disappointingly, never comes.

Instead he looks down at my wrists and for a moment wavers, as if he's undecided about something, and then he lowers his head and . . . *kisses* my left wrist, and when he looks back up at me, shyly, it's with an expression that's . . . loving and only part awkward. His right hand reaches up and tenderly touches the side of my face. I stand there, frozen, my arms still stretched out in front of me, fingers still circled around Luis's throat.

"God, Patrick," he whispers. "Why *here*?"

His hand is playing with my hair now. I look over at the side of the stall, where someone has scratched into the paint *Edwin gives marvelous head*, and I'm still paralyzed in this position and gazing at the words, confused, studying the frame surrounding the words as if that contained an answer, a truth. Edwin? Edwin who? I shake my head to clear it and look back at Luis, who has this horrible, love-struck grin plastered on his face, and I try to squeeze harder, my face twisted with exertion, but I *can't* do it, my hands *won't* tighten, and my arms, still stretched out, look ludicrous and useless in their fixed position.

"I've seen you looking at me," he says, panting. "I've noticed your"—he gulps—"hot body."

He tries to kiss me on the lips but I back away, into the stall door, accidentally closing it. I drop my hands from Luis's neck and he takes them and immediately places them back. I drop them once again and stand there contemplating my next move, but I'm immobile.

"Don't be . . . shy," he says.

I take a deep breath, close my eyes, count to ten, open them and make a helpless attempt to lift my arms back up to strangle Luis, but they feel weighed down and lifting them becomes an impossible task.

"You don't know how long I've wanted it . . ." He's sighing, rubbing my shoulders, trembling. "Ever since that Christmas party at Arizona 206. You know the one, you were wearing that red striped paisley Armani tie."

For the first time I notice his pants are still unzipped and calmly and without difficulty I turn out of the stall and move over to a sink to wash my hands, but my gloves are still on and I don't want to take them off. The bathroom at the Yale Club suddenly seems to me to be the coldest room in the universe and I shudder involuntarily. Luis trails behind, touching my jacket, leaning next to me at the sink.

"I *want* you," he says in a low, faggoty whisper and when I slowly turn my head to glare at him, while hunched over the sink, seething, my eye contact radiating revulsion, he adds, *"too."*

I storm out of the men's room, bumping into Brewster Whipple, I think. I smile at the maître d' and after shaking *his* hand I make a run for the closing elevator but I'm too late and I cry out, pounding a fist against the doors, cursing. Composing myself, I notice the maître d' conferring with a waiter, the two of them looking my way questioningly, and so I straighten up, smile shyly and wave at them. Luis strides over calmly, still grinning, *flushed*, and I just stand there and let him walk up to me. He says nothing.

"What . . . is . . . it?" I finally hiss.

"Where are you going?" he whispers, bewildered.

"I . . . I've gotta . . ." Stumped, I look around the crowded dining room, then back at Luis's quivering, yearning face. "I've gotta return some videotapes," I say, jabbing at the elevator button, then, my patience shot, I start to walk away and head back toward my table.

"Patrick," he calls out.

I whirl round. "*What?*"

He mouths "I'll call you" with this expression on his face that lets me know, that *assures* me, my "secret" is safe with him. "Oh my god," I practically gag, and shaking visibly I sit back at our table, completely defeated, my gloves still on, and gulp down the rest of a watery J&B on the rocks. As soon as I've seated myself Van Patten asks, "Hey Bateman, what's the right way to wear a tie bar or clasp?"

"While a tie holder is by no means required businesswear, it adds to a clean, neat overall appearance. But the accesssory shouldn't dominate the tie. Choose a simple gold bar or a small clip and place it at the lower end of the tie at a downward forty-five-degree angle."

KILLING DOG

Courtney calls, too wasted on Elavil to meet me for a coherent dinner at Cranes, the new Kitty Oates Sanders restaurant in Gramercy Park where Jean, my secretary, made reservations for us last week, and I'm nonplussed. Even though it got excellent reviews (one in *New York* magazine; the other in *The Nation*) I don't complain or persuade Courtney to change her mind since I have

two files I should go over and *The Patty Winters Show* I taped this
morning hasn't been watched yet. It's sixty minutes about women
who've had mastectomies, which at seven-thirty, over breakfast,
before the office, I couldn't bear to sit through, but after today—
hanging out at the office, where the air-conditioning broke down, a
tedious lunch with Cunningham at Odeon, my fucking Chinese
cleaners unable to get bloodstains out of another Soprani jacket,
four videotapes overdue that ended up costing me a fortune, a
twenty-minute wait at the Stairmaster—I've adapted; these events
have toughened me and I'm prepared to deal with this particular
topic.

Two thousand abdominal crunches and thirty minutes of rope-
jumping in the living room, the Wurlitzer jukebox blasting "The
Lion Sleeps Tonight" over and over, even though I worked out in
the gym today for close to two hours. After this I get dressed to
pick up groceries at D'Agostino's: blue jeans by Armani, a white
Polo shirt, an Armani sport coat, no tie, hair slicked back with
Thompson mousse; since it's drizzling, a pair of black waterproof
lace-ups by Manolo Blahnik; three knives and two guns carried in a
black Epi leather attaché case ($3,200) by Louis Vuitton; because
it's cold and I don't want to fuck up my manicure, a pair of Armani
deerskin gloves. Finally, a belted trench coat in black leather by
Gianfranco Ferré that cost four thousand dollars. Though it's only a
short walk to D'Agostino's I put on a CD Walkman anyway, with
the long version of Bon Jovi's "Wanted Dead or Alive" already in it.
I grab an Etro wood-handled paisley umbrella from Bergdorf
Goodman, three hundred dollars on sale, off a newly installed
umbrella rack in the closet near the entranceway and I'm out the
door.

After the office I worked out at Xclusive and once home made
obscene phone calls to young Dalton girls, the numbers I chose
coming from the register I stole a copy of from the administration
office when I broke in last Thursday night. "I'm a corporate raider,"
I whispered lasciviously into the cordless phone. "I orchestrate
hostile takeovers. What do you think of that?" and I would pause
before making sucking noises, freakish piglike grunt, and then ask,
"Huh, *bitch*?" Most of the time I could tell they were frightened
and this pleased me greatly, enabled me to maintain a strong,
pulsing erection for the duration of the phone calls, until one of the

girls, Hilary Wallace, asked, unfazed, "Dad, is that you?" and whatever enthusiasm I'd built up plummeted. Vaguely disappointed, I made a few more calls, but only halfheartedly, opening today's mail while doing so, and I finally hung up in midsentence when I came across a personalized reminder from Clifford, the guy who helps me at Armani, that there was a private sale at the boutique on Madison . . . *two weeks ago!* and though I figured out that one of the doormen probably withheld the card to piss me off, it still doesn't erase the fact that I *missed the fucking sale*, and dwelling over this loss while wandering down Central Park West somewhere around Seventy-sixth, Seventy-fifth, it strikes me profoundly that the world is more often than not a bad and cruel place.

Someone who looks almost exactly like Jason Taylor—black hair slicked back, navy double-breasted cashmere coat with a beaver collar, black leather boots, Morgan Stanley—passes beneath a streetlamp and nods as I turn down the volume on the Walkman to hear him say "Hello, Kevin" and I catch a whiff of Grey Flannel and, still walking, I look back at the person who resembles Taylor, who *could* be Taylor, wondering if he's still dating Shelby Phillips, when I almost stumble over a beggar lying on the street, sprawled in the doorway of an abandoned restaurant—a place Tony McManus opened two summers ago called Amnesia—and she's black and out-of-her-mind crazy, repeating the words "Money please help mister money please help mister" like some kind of Buddhist chant. I try to lecture her on the merits of getting a job somewhere—perhaps at Cineplex Odeon, I suggested not impolitely—silently debating whether or not to open the briefcase, pull out the knife or the gun. But it strikes me that she's too easy a target to be truly satisfying, so I tell her to go to hell and turn up the Walkman just as Bon Jovi cries *"It's all the same, only the names have changed . . ."* and move on, stopping at an automated teller to take three hundred dollars out for no particular reason, all the bills crisp, freshly printed twenties, and I delicately place them in my gazelleskin wallet so as not to wrinkle them. At Columbus Circle, a juggler wearing a trench coat and top hat, who is usually at this location afternoons and who calls himself Stretch Man, performs in front of a small, uninterested crowd; though I smell prey, and he seems fully worthy of my wrath, I move on in search of a less dorky target. Though if he'd been a mime, odds are he'd already be dead.

Faded posters of Donald Trump on the cover of *Time* magazine
cover the windows of another abandoned restaurant, what used to
be Palaze, and this fills me with a newfound confidence. I've arrived
at D'Agostino's, standing directly in front of it, gazing into it, and I
have an almost overwhelming urge to walk in and browse through
each aisle, filling my basket with bottles of balsamic vinegar and sea
salt, roam through the vegetable and produce stands inspecting the
color tones of red peppers and yellow peppers and green peppers
and purple peppers, deciding what flavor, what *shape* of gingerbread
cookie to buy, but I'm still longing for something deeper, something
undefined to do beforehand, and I start to stalk the dark, cold
streets off Central Park West and I catch sight of my face reflected
in the tinted windows of a limousine that's parked in front of Café
des Artistes and my mouth is moving involuntarily, my tongue
wetter than usual, and my eyes are blinking uncontrollably of their
own accord. In the streetlamp's glare, my shadow is vividly cast on
the wet pavement and I can see my gloved hands moving, alternately
clutching themselves into fist, fingers stretching, wriggling, and I
have to stop in the middle of Sixty-seventh Street to calm myself
down, whisper soothing thoughts, anticipating D'Agostino's, a reservation at Dorsia, the new Mike and the Mechanics CD, and it
takes an awesome amount of strength to fight down the urge to
start slapping myself in the face.

Coming slowly up the street is an old queer wearing a cashmere
turtleneck, a paisley wool ascot and a felt hat, walking a brown and
white sharpie, its bunched-up face sniffing low to the ground. The
two of them get closer, passing beneath one streetlamp, then
another, and I've composed myself sufficiently to slowly take off the
Walkman and inconspicuously unlock the briefcase. I'm standing in
the middle of the thin strip of sidewalk next to a white BMW 320i
and the queer with the sharpei is now within feet of me and I get a
good look at him: late fifties, pudgy, with obscenely healthy-looking
pink skin, no wrinkles, all of this topped off with a ridiculous
mustache that accentuates his feminine features. He gives me the
once-over with a quizzical smile, while the sharpei sniffs a tree, then
a garbage bag sitting next to the BMW.

"Nice dog," I smile, leaning down.

The sharpei eyes me warily, then growls.

"*Richard*." The man glares at the dog, then looks back up at me, apologetic, and I can sense he's flattered, not only that I've noticed his dog but that I've actually stopped to talk to him about it, and I swear the old bastard is positively flushed, creaming in his tacky loose corduroys from, I'm guessing, Ralph Lauren.

"It's okay," I tell him and pet the dog gently, laying the briefcase on the ground. "It's a sharpei, right?"

"No. Shar-*pei*," he says, lisping, a way I've never heard it pronounced before.

"Shar-pei?" I try to say it the same way he does, still stroking the velvet bumpiness of the dog's neck and back.

"No." He laughs flirtatiously. "Shar*pei*. Accent on the last syllable." Akthent on thee latht thyllable.

"Well, whatever," I say, standing up and grinning boyishly. "It's a beautiful animal."

"Oh thank you," he says, then, exathperated, "It cost a fortune."

"Really? Why?" I ask, leaning down again and stroking the dog. "Hiya Richard. Hiya little fella."

"You wouldn't *believe* it," he says. "You see, the bags around its eyes have to be lifted surgically *every two years*, so we have to go all the way down to Key West—which has the only vet I really trust in this world—and a little snip, a little tuck, and Richard can see splendidly once again, can't you, baby?" He nods approvingly as I continue to run my hand seductively across the dog's back.

"Well," I say. "He looks great."

There's a pause in which I watch the dog. The owner keeps eyeing me and then he just can't help it, he has to break the silence.

"Listen," he says. "I really hate to ask this."

"Go ahead," I urge.

"Oh gosh, this is so silly," he admits, chuckling.

I start laughing. "Why?"

"Are you a model?" he asks, not laughing anymore. "I could swear I've seen you in a magazine or somewhere."

"No, I'm not," I say, deciding not to lie. "But I'm flattered."

"Well, you look just like a movie star." He waves a limp wrist, then, "I don't know," and finally he lisps the following—I swear to God—to himself: "Oh stop it, silly, you're embarrassing yourself."

I lean down, giving the appearance of picking up the briefcase, but because of the shadows I'm leaning into he doesn't see me pull out the knife, the sharpest one, with the serrated edge, and I'm asking him what he paid for Richard, naturally but also very deliberately, without even looking up to check to see if other people are walking down the street. In one swift movement I pick the dog up quickly by the neck and hold it with my left arm, pushing it back against the streetlamp while it nips at me, trying to bite my gloves, its jaws snapping, but since I've got such a tight grip on its throat it can't bark and I can actually *hear* my hand crush its trachea. I push the serrated blade into its stomach and quickly slice open its hairless belly in a squirt of brown blood, its legs kicking and clawing at me, then blue and red intestines bulge out and I drop the dog onto the sidewalk, the queer just standing there, still gripping the leash, and this has all happened so fast he's in shock and he just stares in horror saying "oh my god oh my god" as the sharpei drags itself around in a circle, its tail wagging, squealing, and it starts licking and sniffing the pile of its own intestines, spilled out in a mound on the sidewalk, some still connected to its stomach, and as it goes into its death throes still attached to its leash I whirl around on its owner and I push him back, hard, with a bloodied glove and start randomly stabbing him in the face and head, finally slashing his throat open in two brief chopping motions; an arc of red-brown blood splatters the white BMW 320i parked at the curb, setting off its car alarm, four fountainlike bursts coming from below his chin. The spraylike sound of the blood. He falls to the sidewalk, shaking like mad, blood still pumping, as I wipe the knife clean on the front of his jacket and toss it back in the briefcase and begin to walk away, but to make sure the old queer is really dead and not faking it (they sometimes do) I shoot him with a silencer twice in the face and then I leave, almost slipping in the puddle of blood that has formed by the side of his head, and I'm down the street and out of darkness and like in a movie I appear in front of the D'Agostino's, sales clerks beckoning for me to enter, and I'm using an expired coupon for a box of oat-bran cereal and the girl at the checkout counter—black, dumb, slow—doesn't get it, doesn't notice the expiration date has passed even though it's the only thing I buy, and I get a small but incendiary thrill when I walk out of the store, opening the box, stuffing handfuls of the cereal into my mouth, trying to whistle "Hip to Be Square" at the same time, and then I've opened my umbrella and I'm running down Broadway, then up Broadway, then down again, screaming like a banshee, my coat open, flying out behind me like some kind of cape.

GIRLS

Tonight an infuriating dinner at Raw Space with a vaguely ditzed-out Courtney who keeps asking me questions about spa menus and George Bush and Tofutti that belong only in someone's nightmare. I utterly ignore her, to no avail, and while she's in midsentence—Page Six, Jackie O—I resort to waving our waiter over and ordering the cold corn chowder lemon bisque with peanuts and dill, an arugula Caesar salad and swordfish meat loaf with kiwi mustard, even though I already ordered this and he tells me so. I look up at him, not even trying to feign surprise, and smile grimly. "Yes, I did, didn't I?" The Floridian cuisine looks impressive but the portions are small and costly, especially in a place with a dish of crayons on each table. (Courtney draws a Laura Ashley print on her paper place mat and I draw the insides of Monica Lustgarden's stomach and chest on mine and when Courtney, charmed by what I'm drawing, inquires as to what it is, I tell her, "Uh, a . . . watermelon.") The bill, which I pay for with my platinum American Express card, comes to over three hundred dollars. Courtney looks okay in a Donna Karan wool jacket, silk blouse and cashmere wool skirt. I'm wearing a tuxedo for no apparent reason. *The Patty Winters Show* this morning was about a new sport called Dwarf Tossing.

In the limousine, dropping her off at Nell's, where we're supposed to have drinks with Meredith Taylor, Louise Samuelson and Pierce Towers, I tell Courtney that I need to score some drugs and I promise that I'll be back before midnight. "Oh, and tell Nell I say hi," I add casually.

"Just buy some down*stairs* if you have to, for *god*'s sake," she whines.

"But I promised someone I'd stop by *their* place. Paranoia. Understand?" I whine back.

"Who's paranoid?" she asks, eyes squinting. "I don't get it."

"Honey, the drugs downstairs are usually a notch below Nutra-Sweet in terms of potency," I tell her. "*You* know."

"Don't implicate *me*, Patrick," she warns.

"Just go inside and order me a Foster's, *okay*?"

"Where are you really going?" she asks after a beat, now suspicious.

"I'm going to . . . Noj's," I say. "I'm buying coke from Noj."

"But Noj is the chef at Deck Chairs," she says, as I'm pushing her out of the limousine. "Noj isn't a drug dealer. He's a *chef*!"

"Don't have a hissy fit, Courtney," I sigh, my hands on her back.

"But don't lie to me about Noj," she whines, struggling to stay in the car. "Noj is the chef at Deck Chairs. Did you hear me?"

I stare at her, dumbfounded, caught in the harsh lights hung above the ropes outside Nell's.

"I mean Fiddler," I finally admit, weakly. "I'm going to Fiddler's to score."

"You're impossible," she mutters, walking away from the limo. "There is something seriously wrong with you."

"I'll be back," I call out after her, slamming the limo's door shut, then I cackle gleefully to myself while relighting a cigar. "Don't you *bet* on it."

I tell the chauffeur to head over to the meat-packing district just west of Nell's, near the bistro Florent, to look for prostitutes and after heavily scanning the area twice—actually, I've spent *months* prowling this section of town for the appropriate babe—I find her on the corner of Washington and Thirteenth. She's blond and slim and young, trashy but not an escort bimbo, and most important, she's *white*, which is a rarity in these parts. She's wearing tight cutoff shorts, a white T-shirt and a cheap leather jacket, and except for a bruise over her left knee her skin is pale all over, including the face, though her thickly lipsticked mouth is done up in pink. Behind her, in four-foot-tall red block letters painted on the side of an abandoned brick warehouse, is the word M E A T and the way the letters are spaced awakens something in me and above the building like a backdrop is a moonless sky, which earlier, in the afternoon, was hung with clouds but tonight isn't.

The limousine cruises up alongside the girl. Through its tinted windows, closer up, she's paler, the blond hair now seems bleached and her facial features indicate someone even younger than I first imagined, and because she's the only white girl I've seen tonight in this section of town, she seems—whether she is or not—especially clean; you could easily mistake her for one of the NYU girls walking home from Mars, a girl who has been drinking Seabreezes all night while moving across a dance floor to the new Madonna songs, a girl who perhaps afterwards had a fight with her boyfriend, someone named Angus or Nick or . . . Pokey, a girl on her way to Florent to gossip with friends, to order another Seabreeze perhaps or maybe a cappuccino or a glass of Evian water—and unlike most of the whores around here, she barely registers the limousine as it pulls up next to her and stops, idling. Instead she lingers casually, pretending to be unaware of what the limousine actually signifies.

When the window opens, she smiles but looks away. The following exchange takes place in less than a minute.

"I haven't seen you around here," I say.

"You just haven't been looking," she says, really cool.

"Would you like to see my apartment?" I ask, flipping the light on inside the back of the limo so she can see my face, the tuxedo I'm wearing. She looks at the limousine, then at me, then back at the limo. I reach into my gazelleskin wallet.

"I'm not supposed to," she says, looking off into a pocket of darkness between two buildings across the street, but when her eyes fall back on me she notices the hundred-dollar bill I'm holding out to her and without asking what I'm doing, without asking what it is I really want of her, without even asking if I'm a cop, she takes the bill and then I'm allowed to rephrase my question. "Do you want to come up to my apartment or not?" I ask this grinning.

"I'm not supposed to," she says again, but after another glance at the black, long car and at the bill she's now putting into her hip pocket and at the bum, shuffling toward the limousine, a cup jangling with coins held in a scabby outstretched arm, she manages to answer, "But I can make an exception."

"Do you take American Express?" I ask, switching the light off. She's still gazing out into that wall of darkness, as if looking for a sign from someone invisible. She shifts her stare to meet mine and when I repeat "Do you take American Express?" she looks at me like I'm crazy, but I smile pointlessly anyway while holding the door open and tell her, "I'm joking. Come on, get in." She nods to someone across the street and I guide this girl into the back of the darkened limousine, slamming the door, then locking it.

Back in my apartment, while Christie takes a bath (I don't know her real name, I haven't asked, but I told her to respond *only* when I call her Christie) I dial the number for Cabana Bi Escort Service and, using my gold American Express card, order a woman, a blond, who services couples. I give the address twice and afterwards, again, stress *blond*. The guy on the other end of the line, some old dago, assures me that someone blond will be at my door within the hour.

After flossing and changing into a pair of silk Polo boxer shorts and a cotton Bill Blass sleeveless T-shirt, I walk into the bathroom, where Christie lies on her back in the tub, sipping white wine from a thin-stemmed Steuben wineglass. I sit on the tub's marble edge and pour Monique Van Frere herb-scented bath oil into it while inspecting the body lying in the milky water. For a long time my mind races, becomes flooded with impurities—her head is within my reach, is mine to crush; at this very moment my urge to strike out, to insult and punish her, rises then subsides, and afterwards I'm able to point out, "That's a very fine chardonnay you're drinking."

After a long pause, my hand squeezing a small, childlike breast, I say, "I want you to clean your vagina."

She stares up at me with this seventeen-year-old's gaze, then looks down at the length of her body soaking in the tub. With the mildest of shrugs she places the glass on the tub's edge and moves a hand down to the sparse hair, also blond, below her flat porcelain-smooth stomach, and then she spreads her legs slightly.

"No," I say quietly. "From behind. Get on your knees."

She shrugs again.

"I want to watch," I explain. "You have a very nice body," I say, urging her on.

She rolls over, kneeling on all fours, her ass raised up above the water, and I move to the other edge of the tub to get a better view of her cunt, which she fingers with a soapy hand. I move my hand above her moving wrist to her asshole, which I spread and with a dab of the bath oil finger lightly. It contracts, she sighs. I remove the finger, then slide it into her cunt, which hangs below it, both our fingers moving in, then out, then back into her. She's wet inside and using this wetness I move my index finger back up to her asshole and slide it in easily, up to the knuckle. She gasps twice and pushes herself back onto it, while still fingering her cunt. This goes on for a while until the doorman rings, announcing that Sabrina has arrived. I tell Christie to get out of the tub and dry off, to choose a robe—but not the Bijan—from the closet and meet me and our guest in the living room for drinks. I move back to the kitchen, where I pour a glass of wine for Sabrina.

Sabrina, however, is *not* a blond. And standing in the doorway after my initial shock subsides, I finally let her in. Her hair is *brownish* blond, not *real* blond, and though this infuriates me I don't say anything because she's also very pretty; not as young as Christie but not too used up either. In short, she looks like she'll be worth whatever it is I'm paying her by the hour. I calm down enough to become totally unangry when she takes off her coat and reveals a hardbody dressed in tight black peg pants and a flower-print halter top, with black pointy-toed high-heeled shoes. Relieved, I lead her into the living room and position her on the white down-filled sofa and, without asking if she wants anything to drink, bring her a glass of white wine and a coaster to place it on from the Mauna Kea Hotel in Hawaii. The Broadway cast recording of *Les Misérables* is playing on CD from the stereo. When Christie comes in from the bathroom to join us, wearing a Ralph Lauren terry-cloth robe, her blond hair slicked back, looking white now because of the bath, I place her on the couch next to Sabrina—they nod hello—and then I take a seat in the Nordian chrome and teakwood chair across from the couch. I decide it's probably best if we get to know each other before we adjourn to the bedroom and so I break a long, not unpleasant silence by clearing my throat and asking a few questions.

"So," I start, crossing my legs. "Don't you want to know what I do?"

The two of them stare at me for a long time. Fixed smiles locked on their faces, they glance at each other before Christie, unsure, shrugs and quietly answers, "No."

Sabrina smiles, takes this as a cue and agrees. "No, not really."

I stare at the two of them for a minute before recrossing my legs and sighing, very irritated. "Well, I work on Wall Street. At Pierce & Pierce."

A long pause.

"Have you heard of it?" I ask.

Another long pause. Finally Sabrina breaks the silence. "Is it connected with Mays . . . or Macy's?"

I pause before asking, "Mays?"

She thinks about it for a minute then says, "Yeah. A shoe outlet? Isn't P & P a shoe store?"

I stare at her, hard.

Christie stands up, surprising me, and moves over to admire the stereo. "You have a really nice place here . . . Paul," and then, looking through the compact discs, hundreds upon hundreds of them, stacked and lined up in a large white-oak shelf, all of them alphabetically listed, "How much did you pay for it?"

I'm standing up to pour myself another glass of the Acacia. "Actually, none of your business, Christie, but I can assure you it certainly *wasn't* cheap."

From the kitchen I notice Sabrina has taken a pack of cigarettes out of her handbag and I walk back into the living room, shaking my head before she can light one.

"No, no smoking," I tell her. "Not in here."

She smiles, pauses slightly and with a little nod slips the cigarette back into its box. I'm carrying a tray of chocolates with me and I offer one to Christie.

"Varda truffle?"

She stares blankly at the plate then politely shakes her head. I move over to Sabrina, who smiles and takes one, and then, concerned, I notice her wineglass, which is still full.

"I don't want you to get drunk," I tell her. "But that's a very fine chardonnay you're not drinking."

I place the tray of truffles on the glass-top Palazzetti coffee table and sit back in the armchair, motioning for Christie to get back on the couch, which she does. We sit here silently, listening to the *Les Misérables* CD. Sabrina chews on the truffle thoughtfully and takes another.

I have to break the silence again myself. "So have either of you been abroad?" It hits me almost immediately what the sentence sounds like, how it could be misinterpreted. "I mean to Europe?"

Both of them are looking at each other as if some secret signal is passing between them, before Sabrina shakes her head and then Christie follows with the same head movement.

The next question I ask, after another long silence, is, "Did either of you go to college, and if so, where?"

The response to this question consists of a barely contained glare from each of them, and so I decide to take this as an opportunity to lead them into the bedroom, where I make Sabrina dance a little before taking off her clothes in front of Christie and me while every halogen bulb in the bedroom burns. I have her put on a Christian Dior lace and charmeuse teddy and then I take off all my clothes—except for a pair of Nike all-sport sneakers—and Christie eventually takes off the Ralph Lauren robe and is buck naked except for an Angela Cummings silk and latex scarf, which I knot carefully around her neck, and suede gloves by Gloria Jose from Bergdorf Goodman that I bought on sale.

Now the three of us are on the futon. Christie is on all fours facing the headboard, her ass raised high in the air, and I'm straddling her back as if I was riding a dog or something, but backward, my knees resting on the mattress, my dick half hard, and I'm facing Sabrina, who is staring into Christie's spread-open ass with a determined expression. Her smile seems tortured and she's wetting her own lips by fingering herself and tracing her glistening index finger across them, like she's applying lip gloss. With both my hands I keep Christie's ass and cunt spread open and I urge Sabrina to move in closer and sniff them. Sabrina is now face level at Christie's ass and cunt, both of which I'm fingering lightly. I motion for Sabrina to move her face in even closer until she can smell my fingers which I push into her mouth and which she sucks on hungrily. With my other hand I keep massaging Christie's tight, wet pussy, which hangs heavy, soaked below her spread, dilated asshole.

"Smell it," I tell Sabrina and she moves in closer until she's two inches, an inch, away from Christie's asshole. My dick is standing straight up now and I keep jerking myself off to keep it that way.

"Lick her cunt first," I tell Sabrina and with her own fingers she spreads it open and starts lapping at it like a dog while massaging the clit and then she moves up to Christie's asshole which she laps at in the same way. Christie's moans are urgent and uncontrolled and she starts pushing her ass harder into Sabrina's face, onto

Sabrina's tongue, which Sabrina pushes slowly in and out of Christie's asshole. While she does this I watch, transfixed, and start rubbing Christie's clit quickly until she's humping onto Sabrina's face and shouts "I'm coming" and while pulling on her own nipples has a long, sustained orgasm. And though she could be faking it I like the way it looks so I don't slap her or anything.

Tired of balancing myself, I fall off Christie and lie on my back, positioning Sabrina's face over my stiff, huge cock which I guide into her mouth with my hand, jerking it off while she sucks on the head. I pull Christie toward me and while taking her gloves off start kissing her hard on the mouth, licking inside it, pushing my tongue against hers, past hers, as far down her throat as it will go. She fingers her cunt, which is so wet that her upper thighs look like someone's slathered something slick and oily all over them. I push Christie down past my waist to help Sabrina suck my cock off and after the two of them take turns licking the head and the shaft, Christie moves to my balls which are aching and swollen, as large as two small plums, and she laps at them before placing her mouth over the entire sac, alternately massaging and lightly sucking the balls, separating them with her tongue. Christie moves her mouth back to the cock Sabrina's still sucking on and they start kissing each other, hard, on the mouth, right above the head of my dick, drooling saliva onto it and jacking it off. Christie keeps masturbating herself this entire time, working three fingers in her vagina, wetting her clit with her juices, moaning. This turns me on enough to grab her by the waist and swivel her around and position her cunt over my face, which she gladly sits on. Clean and pink and wet and spread, her clit swollen, engorged with blood, her cunt hangs over my head and I push my face into it, tonguing it, craving its flavor, while fingering her asshole. Sabrina is still working on my cock, jacking off the base of it, the rest of it filling her mouth, and now she moves on top of me, her knees resting on either side of my chest, and I tear off her teddy so that her ass and cunt are facing Christie, whose head I force down and order to "lick them, suck on that clit" and she does.

It's an awkward position for all of us, so this only goes on for maybe two or three minutes, but during this short period Sabrina comes in Christie's face, while Christie, grinding her cunt hard against my mouth, comes all over mine and I have to steady her thighs and grip them firmly so she won't break my nose with her humping. I still haven't come and Sabrina's doing nothing special to my cock so I pull it out of her mouth and have her sit on it. My cock slides in almost too easily—her cunt is too wet, drenched with her own cunt juice and Christie's saliva, and there's no friction—so I take the scarf from around Christie's neck and pull my cock out of Sabrina's cunt and, spreading her open, wipe her cunt and my cock off and then try to resume fucking her while I continue to eat out Christie, who I bring to yet another climax within a matter of minutes. The two girls are facing each other—Sabrina's fucking my cock, Christie's sitting on my face—and Sabrina leans in to suck and finger Christie's small, firm, full tits. Then Christie starts French-kissing Sabrina hard on the mouth as I continue to eat her out, my mouth and chin and jaw covered with her juices, which momentarily dry, then are replaced by others.

I push Sabrina off my cock and lay her on her back, her head at the foot of the futon. Then I lay Christie over her, placing the two in a sixty-nine position, with Christie's ass raised up in the air, and with a surprisingly small amount of Vaseline, after slipping on a condom, finger her tight ass until it relaxes and loosens enough so I can ease my dick into it while Sabrina eats Christie's cunt out, fingering it, sucking on her swollen clit, sometimes holding on to my balls and squeezing them lightly, teasing my asshole with a moistened finger, and then Christie is leaning into Sabrina's cunt and she's roughly spread her legs open as wide as possible and starts digging her tongue into Sabrina's cunt, but not for long because she's interrupted by yet another orgasm and she lifts her head up and looks back at me, her face slick with cunt juice, and she cries out "Fuck me I'm coming oh god eat me I'm coming" and this spurs me on to start fucking her ass very hard while Sabrina keeps eating the cunt that hangs over her face, which is covered with Christie's pussy juice. I pull my cock out of Christie's ass and force Sabrina to suck on it before I push it back into Christie's spread cunt and after a couple of minutes of fucking it I start coming and at the same time Sabrina lifts her mouth off my balls and just before I explode into Christie's cunt, she spreads my ass cheeks open and forces her tongue up into my asshole which spasms around it and because of this my orgasm prolongs itself and then Sabrina removes her tongue and starts moaning that she's coming too because after Christie finishes coming she resumes eating Sabrina's cunt and I watch, hunched over Christie, panting, as Sabrina lifts her hips repeatedly into Christie's face and then I have to lie back, spent but still hard, my cock, glistening, still aching from the force of my ejaculation, and I close my eyes, my knees weak and shaking.

I awaken only when one of them touches my wrist accidentally. My eyes open and I warn them not to touch the Rolex, which I've kept on during this entire time. They lie quietly on either side of me, sometimes touching my chest, once in a while running their hands over the muscles in my abdomen. A half hour later I'm hard again. I stand up and walk over to the armoire, where, next to the nail gun, rests a sharpened coat hanger, a rusty butter knife, matches from the Gotham Bar and Grill and a half-smoked cigar; and turning around, naked, my erection jutting out in front of me, I hold these items out and explain in a hoarse whisper, "We're not through yet . . ." An hour later I will impatiently lead them to the door, both of them dressed and sobbing, bleeding but well paid. Tomorrow Sabrina will have a limp. Christie will probably have a terrible black eye and deep scratches across her buttocks caused by the coat hanger. Bloodstained Kleenex will lie crumpled by the side of the bed along with an empty carton of Italian seasoning salt I picked up at Dean & Deluca.

SHOPPING

The colleagues I have to buy presents for include Victor Powell, Paul Owen, David Van Patten, Craig McDermott, Luis Carruthers, Preston Nichols, Connolly O'Brien, Reed Robison, Scott Montgomery, Ted Madison, Jeff Duvall, Boris Cunningham, Jamie Conway, Hugh Turnball, Frederick Dibble, Todd Hamlin, Muldwyn Butner, Ricky Hendricks and George Carpenter, and though I could have sent Jean to make these purchases today, instead I asked her to sign, stamp and mail three hundred designer Christmas cards with a Mark Kostabi print on them and then I wanted her to find out as much as she could about the Fisher account that Paul Owen is handling. Right now I'm moving down Madison Avenue, after spending close to an hour standing in a daze near the bottom of the staircase at the Ralph Lauren store on Seventy-second, staring at cashmere sweater vests, confused, hungry, and when I finally took hold of my bearings, after failing to get the address of the blond hardbody who worked behind the counter and who was coming on to me, I left the store yelling "*Come* all ye faithful!" Now I scowl at a bum huddled in the doorway of a store called EarKarma and he's clutching a sign that reads HUNGRY AND HOMELESS . . . PLEASE HELP ME, GOD BLESS and then I find myself moving down Fifth toward Saks, trying to remember if I switched the tapes in my VCR, and suddenly I'm worried that I might be taping *thirtysomething* over *Pamela's Tight Fuckhole*. A Xanax fails to ward off the panic. Saks intensifies it.

. . . pens and photo albums, pairs of bookends and lightweight luggage, electric shoe polishers and heated towel stands and silver-plated insulated carafes and portable palm-sized color TVs with earphones, birdhouses and candleholders, place mats, picnic hampers and ice buckets, lace-trimmed oversize linen napkins and umbrellas and sterling silver monogrammed golf tees and charcoal-filter smoke trappers and desk lamps and perfume bottles, jewelry boxes and sweaters and baskets to hold magazines in and storage boxes, office tote bags, desk accessories, scarves, file holders, address books, agendas for handbags . . .

My priorities before Christmas include the following: (1) to get an eight o'clock reservation on a Friday night at Dorsia with Courtney, (2) to get myself invited to the Trump Christmas party aboard their yacht, (3) to find out as much as humanly possible about Paul Owen's mysterious Fisher account, (4) to saw a hardbody's head off and Federal Express it to Robin Barker—the dumb bastard—over at Salomon Brothers and (5) to apologize to Evelyn without making it look like an apology. *The Patty Winters Show* this morning was about women who married homosexuals and I almost called Courtney up to warn her—as a joke—but then decided against it, deriving a certain amount of satisfaction from imagining Luis Carruthers proposing to her, Courtney shyly accepting, their nightmarish honeymoon. Scowling at another beggar shivering in the misty drizzle at Fifty-seventh and Fifth, I walk up and squeeze his cheek affectionately, then laugh out loud. "His eyes how they tinkled! His dimples how merry!" The Salvation Army choir harmonizes badly on "Joy to the World." I wave to someone who looks exactly like Duncan McDonald, then duck into Bergdorf's.

. . . paisley ties and crystal water pitchers, tumbler sets and office clocks that measure temperature and humidity and barometric pressure, electric calling card address books and margarita glasses, valet stands and sets of dessert plates, correspondence cards and mirrors and shower clocks and aprons and sweaters and gym bags and bottles of champagne and porcelain cachepots and monogrammed bath sheets and foreign-currency-exchange minicalculators and silver-plated address books and paperweights with fish and boxes of fine stationery and bottle openers and compact discs and customized tennis balls and pedometers and coffee mugs . . .

I check my Rolex while I'm buying scruffing lotion at the Clinique counter, still in Bergdorf's, to make sure I have enough time to shop some more before I have to meet Tim Severt for drinks at the Princeton Club at seven. I worked out this morning for two hours before the office and though I could have used this time for a massage (since my muscles are sore from the exhausting exercise regimen I'm now on) or a facial, even though I had one yesterday, there are just too many cocktail parties in the upcoming weeks that I *have* to attend and my presence at them will put a crimp in my shopping schedule so it's best if I get the shopping out of the way now. I run into Bradley Simpson from P & P outside F.A.O. Schwarz and he's wearing a glen-plaid worsted wool suit with notched lapels by Perry Ellis, a cotton broadcloth shirt by Gitman Brothers, a silk tie by Savoy, a chronograph with a crocodile-skin band by Breil, a cotton raincoat by Paul Smith and a fur felt hat by Paul Stuart. After he says, "Hey Davis," I inexplicably start listing the names of all eight reindeer, alphabetically, and when I've finished, he smiles and says, "Listen, there's a Christmas party at Nekenieh on the twentieth, see you there?" I smile and assure him I'll be at Nekenieh on the twentieth and as I walk off, nodding to no one, I call back to him, "Hey asshole, I wanna watch you *die*, mother-*fuck-aaahhh*," and then I start screaming like a banshee, moving across Fifty-eighth, banging my Bottega Veneta briefcase against a wall. Another choir, on Lexington, sings "Hark the Herald Angels" and I tap-dance, moaning, in front of them before I move like a zombie toward Bloomingdale's, where I rush over to the first tie rack I see and murmur to the young faggot working behind the counter, "Too, too fabulous," while fondling a silk ascot. He flirts and asks if I'm a model. "I'll see you in hell," I tell him, and move on.

. . . vases and felt fedoras with feather headbands and alligator toiletry cases with gilt-silver bottles and brushes and shoehorns that cost two hundred dollars and candlesticks and pillow covers and gloves and slippers and powder puffs and handknitted cotton snowflake sweaters and leather skates and Porsche-design ski goggles and antique apothecary bottles and diamond earrings and silk ties and boots and perfume bottles and diamond earrings and boots and vodka glasses and card cases and cameras and mahogany servers and scarves and aftershaves and photo albums and salt and pepper shakers and ceramic-toaster cookie jars and two-hundred-dollar shoehorns and backpacks and aluminum lunch pails and pillow covers . . .

Some kind of existential chasm opens before me while I'm browsing in Bloomingdale's and causes me to first locate a phone and check my messages, then, near tears, after taking three Halcion (since my body has mutated and adapted to the drug it no longer causes sleep—it just seems to ward off total madness), I head toward the Clinique counter where with my platinum American Express card I buy six tubes of shaving cream while flirting nervously with the girls who work there and I decide this emptiness has, at least in part, some connection with the way I treated Evelyn at Barcadia the other night, though there is always the possibility it could just as easily have something to do with the tracking device on my VCR, and while I make a mental note to put in an appearance at Evelyn's Christmas party—I'm even tempted to ask one of the Clinique girls to escort me—I also remind myself to look through my VCR handbook and deal with the tracking device problem. I see a ten-year-old girl standing by her mother, who is buying a scarf, some jewelry, and I'm thinking: Not bad. I'm wearing a cashmere topcoat, a double-breasted plaid wool and alpaca sport coat, pleated wool trousers, patterned silk tie, all by Valentino Couture, and leather lace-ups by Allen-Edmonds.

CHRISTMAS PARTY

I'm having drinks with Charles Murphy at Rusty's to fortify myself before making an appearance at Evelyn's Christmas party. I'm wearing a four-button double-breasted wool and silk suit, a cotton shirt with a button-down collar by Valentino Couture, a patterned silk tie by Armani and cap-toed leather slip-ons by Allen-Edmonds. Murphy is wearing a six-button double-breasted wool gabardine suit by Courrèges, a striped cotton shirt with a tab collar and a foulard-patterned silk-crepe tie, both by Hugo Boss. He's on a tirade about the Japanese—"They've bought the Empire State Building and Nell's. *Nell's*, can you believe it, Bateman?" he exclaims over his second Absolut on the rocks—and it moves something in me, it sets something off, and after leaving Rusty's, while wandering around the Upper West Side, I find myself crouched in the doorway of what used to be Carly Simon's, a very hot J. Akail restaurant that closed last fall, and leaping out at a passing Japanese delivery boy, I knock him off his bicycle and drag him into the doorway, his legs tangled somehow in the Schwinn he was riding which works to my advantage since when I slit his throat—easily, effortlessly—the spasmodic kicking that usually accompanies this routine is blocked by the bike, which he still manages to lift five, six times while he's choking on his own hot blood. I open the cartons of Japanese food and dump their contents over him, but to my surprise instead of sushi and teriyaki and hand rolls and soba noodles, chicken with cashew nuts falls all over his gasping bloodied face and beef chew mein and shrimp fried rice and moo shu pork splatter onto his heaving chest, and this irritating setback—accidentally killing the wrong type of Asian—moves me to check where this order was going—Sally Rubinstein—and with my Mont Blanc pen to write *I'm gonna get you too . . . bitch* on the back of it, then place the order over the dead kid's face and shrug apologetically, mumbling "Uh, sorry" and recall that *The Patty Winters Show* this morning was about Teenage Girls Who Trade Sex for Crack. I spent two hours at the gym today and can now complete two hundred abdominal crunches in less than three minutes. Near Evelyn's brownstone I hand a freezing bum one of the fortune cookies I took from the delivery boy and he stuffs it, fortune and all, into his mouth, nodding thanks. "Fucking slob," I mutter loud enough for him to hear. As I turn the corner and head for Evelyn's, I notice the police lines are *still* up around the brownstone where her neighbor Victoria Bell was decapitated. Four limousines are parked in front, one still running.

I'm late. The living room and dining room are already crowded with people I don't really want to talk to. Tall, full blue spruces covered with white twinkling lights stand on either side of the fireplace. Old Christmas songs from the sixties sung by the Ronettes are on the CD player. A bartender in a tuxedo pours champagne and eggnog, mixes Manhattans and martinis, opens bottles of Calera Jensen pinot noir and a Chappellet chardonnay. Twenty-year-old ports line a makeshift bar between vases of poinsettias. A long folding table has been covered with a red tablecloth and is jammed with pans and plates and bowls of roasted hazelnuts and lobster and oyster bisques and celery root soup with apples and Beluga caviar on toast points and creamed onions and roast goose with chestnut stuffing and caviar in puff pastry and vegetable tarts with tapenade, roast duck and roast rack of veal with shallots and gnocchi gratin and vegetable strudel and Waldorf salad and scallops and bruschetta with mascarpone and white truffles and green chili soufflé and roast partridge with sage, potatoes and onion and cranberry sauce, mincemeat pies and chocolate truffles and lemon soufflé tarts and pecan tarte Tatin. Candles have been lit everywhere, all of them in sterling silver Tiffany candleholders. And though I cannot be positive that I'm not hallucinating, there seem to be midgets dressed in green and red elf suits and felt hats walking around with trays of appetizers. I pretend not to have noticed and head straight for the bar where I gulp down a glass of not-bad champagne then move over to Donald Petersen, and as with most of the men here, someone has tied paper antlers to his head. On the other side of the room Maria and Darwin Hutton's five-year-old daughter, Cassandra, is wearing a seven-hundred-dollar velvet dress and petticoat by Nancy Halser. After finishing a second glass of champagne I move to martinis—Absolut doubles—and after I've calmed down sufficiently I take a closer look around the room, *but the midgets are still there.*

"Too much red," I mutter to myself, trancing out. "It's makin' me nervous."

"Hey McCloy," Petersen says. "What do you say?"

I snap out of it and automatically ask, "Is this the British cast recording of *Les Misérables* or not?"

"Hey, have a holly jolly Christmas." He points a finger at me, drunk.

"So what *is* this music?" I ask, thoroughly annoyed. "And by the way, sir, deck the halls with boughs of holly."

"Bill Septor," he says, shrugging. "I think Septor or Skeptor."

"Why doesn't she put on some Talking Heads for Christ *sakes*," I complain bitterly.

Courtney is standing on the other side of the room, holding a champagne glass and ignoring me completely.

"Or *Les Miz*," he suggests.

"American or British cast recording?" My eyes narrowing, I'm testing him.

"Er, British," he says as a dwarf hands us each a plate of Waldorf salad.

"Definitely," I murmur, staring at the dwarf as he waddles away.

Suddenly Evelyn rushes up to us wearing a sable jacket and velvet pants by Ralph Lauren and in one hand she's holding a piece of mistletoe, which she places above my head, and in the other a candy cane.

"Mistletoe alert!" she shrieks, kissing me dryly on the cheek. "Merry Xmas, Patrick. Merry Xmas, Jimmy."

"Merry . . . Xmas," I say, unable to push her away since I've got a martini in one hand and a Waldorf salad in the other.

"You're late, honey," she says.

"I'm not late," I say, barely protesting.

"Oh yes you are," she says in singsong.

"I've been here the entire time," I say, dismissing her. "You just didn't see me."

"Oh, stop scowling. You're such a Grinch." She turns to Petersen. "Did you know Patrick's the Grinch?"

"Bah humbug," I sigh, staring over at Courtney.

"Hell, we all know McCloy's the Grinch," Petersen bellows drunkenly. "How ya doin', Mr. Grinch?"

"And what does Mr. Grinch want for Christmas?" Evelyn asks in a baby's voice. "Has Mr. Grinchie been a good boy this year?"

I sigh. "The Grinch wants a Burberry raincoat, a Ralph Lauren cashmere sweater, a new Rolex, a car stereo—"

Evelyn stops sucking on the candy cane to interrupt. "But you don't *have* a *car*, honey."

"I want one anyway." I sigh again. "The Grinch wants a car stereo anyway."

"How's the Waldorf salad?" Evelyn asks worriedly. "Do you think it tastes all right?"

"Delicious," I murmur, craning my neck, spotting someone, suddenly impressed. "Hey, you didn't tell me Laurence Tisch was invited to this party."

She turns around. "What are you talking about?"

"Why," I ask, "is Laurence Tisch passing around a tray of canapes?"

"Oh god, Patrick, that's *not* Laurence Tisch," she says. "That's one of the Christmas elves."

"One of the *what*? You mean the midgets."

"They're *elves*," she stresses. "Santa's helpers. God, what a sourpuss. Look at them. They're adorable. That one over there is Ruldoph, the one passing out candy canes is Blitzen. The other one is Donner—"

"Wait a minute, Evelyn, wait," I say, closing my eyes, holding up the hand with the Waldorf salad in it. I'm sweating, déjà vu, but why? Have I met these elves somewhere? Forget about it. "I . . . those are the names of reindeer. Not elves. Blitzen was a *reindeer*."

"The only Jewish one," Petersen reminds us.

"Oh . . ." Evelyn seems bewildered by this information and she looks over at Petersen to confirm this. "Is this true?"

He shrugs, thinks about it and looks confused. "Hey, baby— reindeer, elves, Grinches, brokers . . . Hell, what's the difference long as the Cristal flows, hey?" He chuckles, nudging me in the ribs. "Ain't that right, Mr. Grinch?"

"Don't you think it's Christmasy?" she ask hopefully.

"Oh yes, Evelyn," I tell her. "It's very Christmasy and I'm truthful, not lying."

"But Mr. Sourpuss was late," she pouts, shaking that damn

piece of mistletoe at me accusingly. "And not a word about the Waldorf salad."

"You know, Evelyn, there are a lot of other *Xmas* parties in this metropolis that I could have attended tonight yet I chose yours. Why? you might ask. Why? I asked myself. I didn't come up with a feasible answer, yet I'm here, so be, you know, grateful, babe," I say.

"Oh, so *this* is my Christmas present?" she asks, sarcastic. "How sweet, Patrick, how thoughtful."

"No, *this* is." I give her a noodle I just noticed was stuck on my shirt cuff. "Here."

"Oh Patrick, I'm going to cry," she says, dangling the noodle up to candlelight. "It's gorgeous. Can I put it on now?"

"No. Feed it to one of the elves. That one over there looks pretty hungry. Excuse me but I need another drink."

I hand Evelyn the plate of Waldorf salad and tweak one of Petersen's antlers and head toward the bar humming "Silent Night," vaguely depressed by what most of the women are wearing— pullover cashmere sweaters, blazers, long wool skirts, corduroy dresses, turtlenecks. Cold weather. No hardbodies.

Paul Owen is standing near the bar holding a champagne flute, studying his antique silver pocket watch (from Hammacher Schlemmer, no doubt), and I'm about to walk over and mention something about that damned Fisher account when Humphrey Rhinebeck bumps into me trying to avoid stepping on one of the elves and he's still wearing a cashmere chesterfield overcoat by Crombie from Lord & Taylor, a peak-lapeled double-breasted wool tuxedo, a cotton shirt by Perry Ellis, a bow tie from Hugo Boss and paper antlers in a way that suggests he's completely unaware, and as if by rote the twerp says, "Hey Bateman, last week I brought a new herringbone tweed jacket to my tailor for alterations."

"Well, uh, congratulations seem in order," I say, shaking his hand. "That's . . . *nifty.*"

"Thanks." He blushes, looking down. "Anyway, he noticed that the retailer had removed the original label and replaced it with one of his own. Now what I want to know is, is this *legal*?"

"It's confusing, I know," I say, still moving through the crowd. "Once a line of clothing has been purchased from its manufacturer, it's perfectly legal for the retailer to replace the original label with his own. However, it's *not* legal to replace it with *another* retailer's label."

"But wait, why *is* that?" he asks, trying to sip from his martini glass while attempting to follow me.

"Because details regarding fiber content and country of origin or the manufacturer's registration number must remain *intact*. Label tampering is very hard to detect and rarely reported," I shout over my shoulder. Courtney is kissing Paul Owen on the cheek, their hands already firmly clasped. I stiffen up and stop walking. Rhinebeck bumps into me. But she moves on, waving to someone across the room.

"So what's the best solution?" Rhinebeck calls out behind me.

"Shop for familiar labels from retailers you know and take those fucking antlers off your head, Rhinebeck. You look like a retard. Excuse me." I walk off but not before Humphrey reaches up and feels the headpiece. "Oh my *god*."

"Owen!" I exclaim, merrily holding out a hand, the other hand grabbing a martini off a passing elf tray.

"Marcus! Merry Christmas," Owen says, shaking my hand. "How've you been? Workaholic, I suppose."

"Haven't seen you in a while," I say, then wink. "Workaholic, huh?"

"Well, we just got back from the Knickerbocker Club," he says and then greets someone who bumps into him—"Hey Kinsley"—then back to me. "We're going to Nell's. Limo's out front."

"We should have lunch," I say, trying to figure out a way to bring up the Fisher account without being tacky about it.

"Yes, that would be great," he says. "Maybe you could bring . . ."

"*Cecelia?*" I guess.

"Yes. Cecelia," he says.

"Oh, *Cecelia* would . . . adore it," I say.

"Well, let's do it." He smiles.

"Yes. We could go to . . . Le Bernardin," I say, then after pausing, "for some . . . *seafood* perhaps? Hmmm?"

"Le Bernardin is in Zagat's top ten this year." He nods. "You know that?"

"We could have some . . ." I pause again, staring at him, then more deliberately, "*fish* there. No?"

"Sea urchins," Owen says, scanning the room. "Meredith loves the sea urchins there."

"Oh does she?" I ask, nodding.

"Meredith," he calls out, motioning for someone behind me. "Come here."

"She's *here*?" I ask.

"She's talking to Cecelia over there," he says. "Meredith," he calls out, waving. I turn around. Meredith and Evelyn make their way over to us.

I whirl around back to Owen.

Meredith walks over with Evelyn. Meredith is wearing a beaded wool gabardine dress and bolero by Geoffrey Beene from Barney's, diamond and gold earrings by James Savitt ($13,000), gloves by Geoffrey Beene for Portolano Products, and she says, "Yes boys? What are you two talking about? Making up Christmas lists?"

"The sea urchins at Le Bernardin, darling," Owen says.

"My *fav*orite topic." Meredith drapes an arm over my shoulder, while she confides to me as an aside, "They're fabulous."

"Delectable." I cough nervously.

"What does everyone think of the Waldorf salad?" Evelyn asks. "Did you like it?"

"Cecelia, darling, I haven't tried it yet," Owen says, recognizing someone across the room. "But I'd like to know why Laurence Tisch is serving the eggnog."

"That's *not* Laurence Tisch," Evelyn whines, genuinely upset. "That's a Christmas elf. *Patrick*, what did you tell him?"

"Nothing," I say. "*Cecelia!*"

"Besides, Patrick, you're the *Grinch*."

At the mention of my name I immediately start blabbering, hoping that Owen didn't notice. "Well, *Cecelia*, I told him I thought it was a, you know, a mixture of the two, like a . . ." I stop, briefly look at them before lamely spitting out, "a Christmas *Tisch*." Then, nervously, I lift a sprig of parsley off a slice of pheasant pâté that a passing elf is carrying, and hold it over Evelyn's head before she can say anything. "Mistletoe alert!" I shout, and people around us are suddenly ducking, and then I kiss her on the lips while looking at Owen and Meredith, both of them staring at me strangely, and out of the corner of my eye I catch Courtney, who is talking to Rhinebeck, gazing at me hatefully, outraged.

"Oh Patrick—" Evelyn starts.

"*Cecelia!* Come here at once." I pull her arm, then tell Owen and Meredith, "Excuse us. We have to talk to that elf and get this all straightened out."

"I'm so sorry," she says to the two of them, shrugging helplessly as I drag her away. "*Patrick*, what *is* going on?"

I maneuver her into the kitchen.

"Patrick?" she asks. "What are we doing in the *kitchen*?"

"Listen," I tell her, grabbing her shoulders, facing her. "Let's get out of here."

"Oh Patrick," she sighs. "I can't just leave. Aren't you having a good time?"

"*Why* can't you leave?" I ask. "Is it *so* unreasonable? You've been here long enough."

"Pat*rick*, this is *my* Christmas party," she says. "Besides, the elves are going to sing 'O Tannenbaum' any minute now."

"Come on, Evelyn. Let's just get out of here." I'm on the verge of hysteria, panicked that Paul Owen or, worse, Marcus Halberstam is going to walk into the kitchen. "I want to take you away from all this."

"From all *what*?" she asks, then her eyes narrow. "You didn't like the Waldorf salad, did you?"

"I want to take you away from *this*," I say, motioning around the kitchen, spastic. "From sushi and elves and . . . *stuff*."

An elf walks into the kitchen, setting down a tray of dirty plates, and past him, *over* him, I can see Paul Owen leaning into Meredith, who's shouting something into his ear over the din of Christmas music, and he scans the room looking for someone, nodding, then Courtney walks into view and I grab Evelyn, bringing her even closer to me.

"Sushi? Elves? Patrick, you're con*fusing* me," Evelyn says. "And I *don't* appreciate it."

"Let's *go*." I'm squeezing her roughly, pulling her toward the back door. "Let's be daring for once. For just once in your life, Evelyn, be daring."

She stops, refusing to be pulled along, and then she starts smiling, considering my offer but only slightly won over.

"Come on . . ." I start whining. "Let this be *my* Christmas present."

"Oh no, I was already at Brooks Brothers and—" she starts.

"Stop it. Come on, I want this," I say and then in a last, desperate attempt I smile flirtatiously, kissing her lightly on the lips, and add, "*Mrs*. Bateman?"

"Oh Patrick," she sighs, melting. "But what about cleanup?"

"The midgets'll do it," I assure her.

"But someone has to oversee it, honey."

"So choose an elf. Make that one over there the elf over-seer," I say. "But let's go, *now*." I start pulling her toward the back door of the brownstone, her shoes squeaking as they slide across the Muscoli marble tile.

And then we're out the door, rushing down the alley adjacent to the brownstone, and I stop and peer around the corner to see if anyone we know is leaving or entering the party. We make a run for a limousine I think is Owen's, but I don't want to make Evelyn suspicious so I simply walk up to the closest one, open the door and push her in.

"*Pat*rick," she squeals, pleased. "This is so naughty. *And* a limo—" I close the door on her and walk around the car and knock on the driver's window. The driver unrolls it.

"Hi," I say, holding out a hand. "Pat Bateman."

The driver just stares, an unlit cigar clenched in his mouth, first at my outstretched hand, then at my face, then at the top of my head.

"Pat Bateman," I repeat. "What, ah, what is it?"

He keeps looking at me. Tentatively I touch my hair to see if it's messed up or out of place and to my shock and surprise I feel two pairs of paper antlers. There are *four* antlers on my *fucking head*. I mutter, "Oh Jesus, whoa!" and tear them off, staring at them crumpled in my hands, horrified. I throw them on the ground, then turn back to the driver.

"So. Pat Bateman," I say, smoothing my hair back into place.

"Uh, yeah? Sid." He shrugs.

"Listen, Sid. Mr. Owen says we can take this car, so . . ." I stop, my breath steaming in the frozen air.

"Who's Mr. Owen?" Sid asks.

"Paul *Owen*. You know," I say. "Your customer."

"No. This is Mr. Baker's limo," he says. "Nice antlers though."

"Shit," I say, running around the limo to get Evelyn out of

there before something bad happens, but it's too late. The second I open the door, Evelyn sticks her head out and squeals, "Patrick, darling, I *love* it. *Champagne*"—she holds up a bottle of Cristal in one hand and a gold box in the other—"and *truffles* too."

I grab her arm and yank her out, mumbling by way of an explanation, under my breath, "Wrong limo, take the truffles," and we head over to the next limousine. I open the door and guide Evelyn in, then move around to the front and knock on the driver's window. He unrolls it. He looks exactly like the other driver.

"Hi. Pat Bateman," I say, holding out my hand.

"Yeah? Hi. Donald Trump. My wife Ivana's in the back," he says sarcastically, taking it.

"Hey, watch it," I warn. "Listen, Mr. Owen says we can take his car. I'm . . . oh damn. I mean I'm Marcus."

"You just said your name was Pat."

"No. I was wrong," I say sternly, staring directly at him. "I was wrong about my name being Pat. My name is Marcus. Marcus Halberstam."

"Now you're sure of this, right?" he asks.

"Listen, Mr. Owen said I can take his car for the night so . . ." I stop. "You know, let's just get on with it."

"I think I should talk to Mr. Owen first," the driver says, amused, toying with me.

"No, wait!" I say, then calming down, "Listen, I'm . . . it's fine, really." I start chuckling to myself. "Mr. Owen is in a very, *very* bad mood."

"I'm not supposed to do this," the driver says without looking up at me. "It's totally illegal. No way. Give it up."

"Oh come on, man," I say.

"It's totally against company regulations," he says.

"Fuck company regulations," I bark out at him.

"Fuck company regulations?" he asks, nodding, smiling.

"Mr. Owen says it's *okay*," I say. "Maybe you're not listening."

"Nope. No can do." He shakes his head.

I pause, stand up straight, run a hand over my face, breathe in and then lean back down. "Listen to me . . ." I breathe in again. "They've got midgets in there." I point with a thumb back at the brownstone. "Midgets who are about to sing 'O Tannenbaum' . . ." I look at him imploringly, begging for sympathy, at the same time looking appropriately frightened. "Do you know how scary *that* is? Elves"—I gulp—"*harmonizing*?" I pause, then quickly ask, "Think about it."

"Listen, mister—"

"Marcus," I remind him.

"Marcus. Whatever. I'm not gonna break the rules. I can't do anything about it. It's company rules. I'm not gonna break 'em."

We both lapse into silence. I sigh, look around, considering dragging Evelyn to the third limo, or maybe back to Barker's limo— he's a real asshole—but *no, goddamnit*, I want *Owen's*. Meanwhile the driver sighs to himself, "If the midgets want to sing, let them sing."

"Shit," I curse, taking out my gazelleskin wallet. "Here's a hundred." I hand him two fifties.

"Two hundred," he says.

"This city sucks," I mutter, handing the money over.

"Where do you want to go?" he asks, taking the bills with a sigh, as he starts the limousine.

"Club Chernoble," I say, rushing to the back and opening the door.

"Yes *sir*," he shouts.

I hop in, shutting the door just as the driver peels away from Evelyn's brownstone toward Riverside Drive. Evelyn's sitting next to me while I'm catching my breath, wiping cold sweat off my brow with an Armani handkerchief. When I look over at her, she's on the verge of tears, her lips trembling, silent for once.

"You're startling me. What happened?" I *am* alarmed. "What . . . what did I do? The Waldorf salad was good. What else?"

"Oh Patrick," she sighs. "It's . . . lovely. I don't know what to say."

"Well . . ." I pause carefully. "I don't . . . either."

"This," she says, presenting me with a diamond necklace from Tiffany's, Meredith's present from Owen. "Well, help me put it on, darling. You're not the Grinch, honey."

"Uh, Evelyn," I say, then curse under my breath as she turns her back toward me so I can clasp it around her neck. The limousine lurches forward and she falls against me, laughing, then kisses my cheek. "It's lovely, oh I love it . . . Oops, must have truffle breath. Sorry, honey. Find me some champagne and pour me a glass."

"But . . ." I stare helplessly at the glittering necklace. "That's not it."

"What?" Evelyn asks, looking around the limo. "Are there glasses in here? What's not it, honey?"

"That's not it." I'm speaking in monotone.

"Oh, honey." She smiles. "You have something *else* for me?"

"No, I mean—"

"Come on, you devil," she says, playfully grabbing at my coat pocket. "Come on, what is it?"

"What is *what*?" I ask calmly, annoyed.

"You've got something else. Let me guess. A ring to match?" she guesses. "A matching bracelet? A *brooch*? So that's it!" She claps her hands. "It's a matching brooch."

While I'm trying to push her away from me, holding one of her arms back, the other snakes behind me and grabs something out of my pocket—another fortune cookie I lifted from the dead Chinese boy. She stares at it, puzzled for a moment, and says, "Patrick, you're so . . . romantic," and then, studying the fortune cookie and with less enthusiasm, "so . . . original."

I'm also staring at the fortune cookie. It's got a lot of blood on it and I shrug and say, as jovially as I can, "Oh, you know me."

"But what's on it?" She holds it up close to her face, peering at it. "What's this . . . red stuff?"

"That's . . ." I peer also, pretending to be intrigued by the stains, then I grimace. "That's sweet 'n' sour sauce."

She cracks it openly excitedly, then studies the fortune, confused.

"What does it say?" I sigh, fooling around with the radio then scanning the limo for Owen's briefcase, wondering where the champagne could possibly be, the open box from Tiffany's, empty, empty on the floor, suddenly, overwhelmingly, depressing me.

"It says . . ." She pauses then squints at it closely, rereading it. "It says, *The fresh grilled foie gras at Le Cirque is excellent but the lobster salad is only so-so.*"

"That's nice," I murmur, looking for champagne glasses, tapes, anything.

"It really says this, Patrick." She hands me the fortune, a slight smile creeping up on her face that I can make out even in the darkness of the limo. "What could it possibly mean?" she asks slyly.

I take it from her, read it, then look at Evelyn, then back at the fortune, then out the tinted window, at snow flurries swirling around lampposts, around people waiting for buses, beggars staggering directionless down city streets, and I say out loud to myself, "My luck could be worse. It really could."

"Oh honey," she says, throwing her arms around me, hugging my head. "Lunch at Le Cirque? You're the best. You're not the Grinch. I take it back. Thursday? Is Thursday good for you? Oh no. I can't do it Thursday. Herbal wrap. But how's Friday? And do we really want to go to Le Cirque? How about—"

I push her off me and knock on the divider, rapping my knuckles against it loudly until the driver lowers it. "Sid, I mean Earle, whoever, this isn't the way to Chernoble."

"Yes it is, Mr. Bateman—"

"Hey!"

"I mean Mr. *Halberstam*. Avenue C, right?" He coughs politely.

"I suppose," I say, staring out the window. "I don't recognize anything."

"Avenue C?" Evelyn looks up from marveling at the necklace Paul Owen bought Meredith. "What's Avenue C? C as in ... Cartier, I take it?"

"It's hip," I assure her. "It's totally hip."

"Have you been there?" she asks.

"Millions of times," I mutter.

"Chernoble? No, *not* Chernoble," she whines. "Honey, it's *Christmas*."

"What in the hell does *that* mean?" I ask.

"Limo driver, oh limo driver ..." Evelyn leans forward, balancing herself on my knees. "Limo driver, we're going to the Rainbow Room. Driver, to the Rainbow Room, please."

I push her back and lean forward. "Ignore her. Chernoble. ASAP." I press the button and the divider goes back up.

"Oh Patrick. It's *Christmas*," she whines.

"You keep saying that as if it *means* something," I say, staring right at her.

"But it's *Christmas*," she whines again.

"I can't *stand* the Rainbow Room," I say, adamant.

"Oh why *not*, Patrick?" she whines. "They have the *best* Waldorf salad in town at the Rainbow Room. Did you like mine? Did you like my Waldorf salad, honey?"

"Oh my god," I whisper, covering my face with both hands.

"Honestly. Did you?" she asks. "The only thing I really worried about was *that* and the chestnut stuffing . . ." She pauses. "Well, because the chestnut stuffing was . . . well, gross, you know—"

"I don't want to go the the Rainbow Room," I interrupt, my hands still covering my face, "because I can't score drugs there."

"Oh . . ." She looks me over, disapprovingly. "Tsk, tsk, tsk. Drugs, Patrick? What kind of, ahem, drugs, are we talking about?"

"Drugs, Evelyn. Cocaine. *Drugs*. I want to do some cocaine tonight. Do you understand?" I sit up and glare at her.

"Patrick," she says, shaking her head, as if she's lost faith in me.

"I can see you're confused," I point out.

"I just don't want any part of it," she says.

"You don't have to do any of it," I tell her. "Maybe you're not even invited to do any of it."

"I just don't understand why you have to ruin this time of year for me," she says.

"Think of it as . . . *frost*. As Christmas frost. As expensive Christmas *frost*," I say.

"Well . . ." she says, lighting up. "It's kind of exciting to slum, isn't it?"

"Thirty bucks at the door *apiece* is not exactly slumming, Evelyn." Then I ask, suspiciously, "Why wasn't Donald Trump invited to your party?"

"Not Donald Trump *again*," Evelyn moans. "Oh god. Is that why you were acting like such a buffoon? This obsession has *got* to end!" she practically shouts. "That's why you were acting like such an ass!"

"It was the Waldorf salad, Evelyn," I say, teeth clenched. "It was the Waldorf salad that was making me act like an ass!"

"Oh my god. You mean it, too!" She throws her head back in despair. "I knew it, I knew it."

"But you didn't even make it!" I scream. "It was *catered*!"

"Oh god," she wails. "I can't believe it."

The limousine pulls up in front of Club Chernoble, where a

crowd ten deep waits standing outside the ropes in the snow. Evelyn and I get out, and using Evelyn, much to her chagrin, as a blocker, I push my way through the crowd and luckily spot someone who looks exactly like Jonathan Leatherdale, about to be let in, and really shoving Evelyn, who's still holding on to her Christmas present, I call out to him, "Jonathan, hey Leatherdale," and suddenly, predictably, the whole crowd starts shouting, "Jonathan, hey Jonathan." He spots me as he turns around and calls out, "Hey Baxter!" and winks, giving me the thumbs-up sign, but it's not to me, it's to someone else. Evelyn and I pretend we're with his party anyway. The doorman closes the ropes on us, asks, "You two come in that limo?" He looks over at the curb and motions with his head.

"Yes." Evelyn and I both nod eagerly.

"You're in," he says, lifting the ropes.

We walk in and I lay out sixty dollars; not a single drink ticket. The club is predictably dark except for the flashing strobe lights, and even with them, all I can really see is dry ice pumping out of a fog machine and one hardbody dancing to INXS's "New Sensation," which blasts out of speakers at a pitch that vibrates the body. I tell Evelyn to go to the bar and get us two glasses of champagne. "Oh of course," she shouts back, heading tentatively toward one thin white strip of neon, the only light illuminating what might be a place where alcohol is served. In the meantime I score a gram from someone who looks like Mike Donaldson, and after debating for ten minutes while checking out this hardbody whether I should ditch Evelyn or not, she comes up with two flutes full of champagne, indignant, sad-faced. "It's Korbel," she shouts. "Let's *leave*." I shake my head negative and shout back, "Let's go to the rest rooms." She follows.

The one bathroom at Chernoble is unisex. Two other couples are already there, one of them in the only stall. The other couple is, like us, impatiently waiting for the stall to empty. The girl is wearing a silk jersey halter top, a silk chiffon skirt and silk sling-backs, all by Ralph Lauren. Her boyfriend is wearing a suit tailored by, I think, William Fioravanti or Vincent Nicolosi or Scali—some wop. Both are holding champagne glasses: his, full; hers, empty. It's quiet except for the sniffling and muted laughter coming from the stall, and the bathroom's door is thick enough to block out the music except for the deep thumping drumbeat. The guy taps his foot expectantly. The girl keeps sighing and tossing her hair over her shoulder in these strangely enticing jerky head movements; then she looks over at Evelyn and me and whispers something to her boyfriend. Finally, after she whispers something to him again, he nods and they leave.

"Thank *god*," I whisper, fingering the gram in my pocket; then, to Evelyn, "Why are you so quiet?"

"The Waldorf salad," she murmurs, not looking at me. "Damnit."

There's a click, the door to the stall opens and a young couple—the guy wearing a double-breasted wool cavalry twill suit, cotton shirt and silk tie, all by Givenchy, the girl wearing a silk taffeta dress with ostrich hem by Geoffrey Beene, vermeil earrings by Stephen Dweck Moderne and Chanel grosgrain dance shoes—walks out, discreetly wiping each other's noses, staring at themselves in the mirror before leaving the rest room, and just as Evelyn and I are about to walk into the stall they've vacated, the first couple rushes back in and attempts to overtake it.

"*Excuse* me," I say, my arm outstretched, blocking the entrance. "*You* left. It's uh, our turn, you know?"

"Uh, no, I don't think so," the guy says mildly.

"Pat*rick*," Evelyn whispers behind me. "Let them . . . you know."

"Wait. No. It's *our* turn," I say.

"Yeah, but *we* were waiting first."

"Listen, I don't *want* to start a fight—"

"But you *are*," the girlfriend says, bored yet still managing a sneer.

"Oh my," Evelyn murmurs behind me, looking over my shoulder.

"Listen, we should just do it here," the girl, who I wouldn't mind fucking, spits out.

"What a *bitch*," I murmur, shaking my head.

"Listen," the guy says, relenting. "While we're arguing about this, one of us could be *in* there."

"Yeah," I say. "*Us.*"

"Oh Christ," the girl says, hands on hips, then to Evelyn and me, "I can't believe who they're letting in now."

"*You* are a bitch," I murmur, disbelieving. "Your attitude *sucks*, you know that?"

Evelyn gasps and squeezes my shoulder. "*Patrick.*"

The guy has already started snorting his coke, spooning the powder out of a brown vial, inhaling then laughing after each hit, leaning against the door.

"Your girlfriend's a *total* bitch," I tell the guy.

"*Patrick*," Evelyn says. "Stop it."

"She's a bitch," I say, pointing at her.

"*Patrick*, apologize," Evelyn says.

The guy goes into hysterics, his head thrown back, sniffing in loudly, then he doubles up and tries to catch his breath.

"Oh my *god*," Evelyn says, appalled. "Why are you laughing? *Defend* her."

"Why?" the guy asks, then shrugs, both nostrils ringed with white powder. "He's *right*."

"I'm leaving, Daniel," the girl says, near tears. "I can't handle *this*. I can't handle *you*. I can't handle *them*. I warned you at Bice."

"Go ahead," the guy says. "Go. Just do it. Take a hike. I don't care."

"Patrick, what have you started?" Evelyn asks, backing away from me. "This is unacceptable," and then, looking up at the fluorescent bulbs, "And so is this lighting. I'm leaving." But she stands there, waiting.

"I'm leaving, Daniel," the girl says. "Did you *hear* me?"

"Go *ahead*. Forget it," Daniel says, staring at his nose in the mirror, waving her away. "I said take a hike."

"I'm using the stall," I tell the room. "Is this okay? Does anybody mind?"

"Aren't you going to defend your girlfriend?" Evelyn asks Daniel.

"Jesus, what do you want me to do?" He looks at her in the mirror, wiping his nose, sniffing again. "I bought her dinner. I introduced her to Richard Marx. Jesus Christ, what else does she want?"

"Beat the shit out of him?" the girl suggests, pointing at me.

"Oh honey," I say, shaking my head, "the things I could do to you with a coat hanger."

"Goodbye, Daniel," she says, pausing dramatically. "I'm out of here."

"Good," Daniel says, holding up the vial. "More for moi."

"And don't try calling me," she screams, opening the door. "My answering machine is on tonight and I'm screening all calls!"

"Patrick," Evelyn says, still composed, prim. "I'll be outside."

I wait a moment, staring at her from inside the stall, then at the girl standing in the doorway. "Yeah, so?"

"Patrick," Evelyn says, "don't say something you'll regret."

"Just go," I say. "Just leave. Take the limo."

"Patrick—"

"Leave," I roar. "The Grinch says leave!"

I slam the door of the stall and start shoveling the coke from the envelope into my nose with my platinum AmEx. In between my gasps I hear Evelyn leave, sobbing to the girl, "He made me walk out of my own Christmas party, can you believe it? My Christmas party?" And I hear the girl sneer "Get a life" and I start laughing raucously, banging my head against the side of the stall, and then I hear the guy do a couple more hits, then he splits, and after finishing most of the gram I peek out from over the stall to see if Evelyn's still hanging around, pouting, chewing her lower lip sorrowfully—oh boo hoo hoo, baby—but she hasn't come back, and then I get an image of Evelyn and Daniel's girlfriend on a bed somewhere with the girl spreading Evelyn's legs, Evelyn on all fours, licking her asshole, fingering her cunt, and this makes me dizzy and I head out of the rest room into the club, horny and desperate, lusting for contact.

But it's later now and the crowd has changed—it's now filled with more punk rockers, blacks, fewer Wall Street guys, more bored rich girls from Avenue A lounging around, and the music has changed; instead of Belinda Carlisle singing "I Feel Free" it's some black guy rapping, if I'm hearing this correctly, something called "Her Shit on His Dick" and I sidle up to a couple of hardbody rich girls, both of them wearing skanky Betsey Johnson-type dresses, and I'm wired beyond belief and I start off with a line like "Cool music—haven't I seen you at Salomon Brothers?" and one of them, one of these girls, sneers and says, "Go back to Wall Street," and the one with the nose ring says, "Fucking yuppie."

And they say this even though my suit looks black in the darkness of the club and my tie—paisley, Armani, silk—is loosened.

"Hey," I say, grinding my teeth. "You may think I'm a really disgusting yuppie but I'm not, *really*," I tell them, swallowing rapidly, wired out of my head.

Two black guys are sitting with them at the table. Both sport faded jeans, T-shirts, and leather jackets. One has reflector sunglasses on, the other has a shaved head. Both are glaring at me. I stick out my hand at a crooked angle, trying to mimic a rapper. "Hey," I say. "I'm fresh. The freshest, y'know . . . like uh, def . . . the deffest." I take a sip of champagne. "You know . . . *def*."

To prove this I spot a black guy with dreadlocks and I walk up to him and exclaim "Rasta Man!" and hold out my hand, anticipating a high-five. But the nigger just stands there.

"I mean"—I cough—"*Mon*," and then, with less enthusiasm, "We be, uh, jamming . . ."

He brushes past me, shaking his head. I look back at the girls. They shake their heads—a warning to me not to come back over. I turn my gaze to a hardbody who's dancing by herself next to a column, then I finish my champagne and walk up to her, asking for a phone number. She smiles. Exit.

NELL'S

Midnight. I'm sitting in a booth at Nell's with Craig McDermott and Alex Taylor—who has just passed out—and three models from Elite: Libby, Daisy and Caron. It's nearing summer, mid-May, but the club is air-conditioned and cool, the music from the light jazz band drifts through the half-empty room, ceiling fans are whirring, a crowd twenty deep waits outside in the rain, a surging mass. Libby is blond and wearing black grosgrain high-heeled evening shoes with exaggeratedly pointed toes and red satin bows by Yves Saint Laurent. Daisy is blonder and wearing black satin tapered-toe pumps set off by splattered-silver sheer black stockings by Betsey Johnson. Caron is platinum blond and wearing stack-heeled leather boots with a pointed patent-leather toe and wool tweed turned-over calf by Karl Lagerfeld for Chanel. All three of them have on skimpy

black wool-knit dresses by Giorgio di Sant'Angelo and are drinking
champagne with cranberry juice and peach schnapps and smoking
German cigarettes—but I don't complain, even though I think it
would be in Nell's best interest if a nonsmoking section was
initiated. Two of them are wearing Giorgio Armani sunglasses.
Libby has jet lag. Of the three, Daisy is the only one I even remotely
want to fuck. Earlier in the day, after a meeting with my lawyer
about some bogus rape charges, I had an anxiety attack in Dean &
Deluca which I worked off at Xclusive. Then I met the models for
drinks at the Trump Plaza. This was followed by a French movie
that I completely did not understand, but it was fairly chic anyway,
then dinner at a sushi resturant called Vivids near Lincoln Center
and a party at one of the models' ex-boyfriend's loft in Chelsea,
where bad, fruity sangria was served. Last night I had dreams that
were lit like pornography and in them I fucked girls made of
cardboard. *The Patty Winters Show* this morning was about Aerobic
Exercise.

   I'm wearing a two-button wool suit with pleated trousers by
Luciano Soprani, a cotton shirt by Brooks Brothers and a silk tie
by Armani. McDermott's got on this wool suit by Lubiam with a
linen pocket square by Ashear Bros., a Ralph Lauren cotton shirt
and a silk tie by Christian Dior and he's about to toss a coin to see
which one of us is going downstairs to fetch the Bolivian Marching
Powder since *neither* one of us wants to sit here in the booth with
the girls because though we probably want to fuck them, we don't
want to, in fact *can't*, we've found out, talk to them, not even
condescendingly—they simply have *nothing* to say and, I mean, I
know we shouldn't be surprised by this but still it's somewhat
disorienting. Taylor is sitting up but his eyes are closed, his mouth
slightly open, and though McDermott and I originally thought he
was protesting the girls' lack of verbal skills by pretending to be
asleep, it dawns on us that perhaps he's authentically shitfaced (he's
been near incoherent since the three sakes he downed at Vivids),
but none of the girls pay any attention, except maybe Libby since
she's sitting next to him, but it's doubtful, very doubtful.

   "Head, heads, heads," I mutter under my breath.

   McDermott flips the quarter.

   "Tails, tails, tails," he chants, then he slaps his hand over the
coin after it lands on his napkin.

"Heads, heads, heads," I hiss, praying.

He lifts his palm. "It's tails," he says, looking at me.

I stare at the quarter for a long time before asking, "Do it again."

"So long," he says, looking over at the girls before getting up, then he glances at me, rolls his eyes, gives his head a curt shake. "Listen," he reminds me. "I want another martini. Absolut. Double. No olive."

"Hurry," I call after him, then under my breath, watching as he waves gaily from the top of the stairs, "Fucking moron."

I turn back to the booth. Behind us, a table of Eurotrash hardbodies that suspiciously resemble Brazilian transvestites shriek in unison. Let's see . . . Saturday night I'm going to a Mets game with Jeff Harding and Leonard Davis. I'm renting Rambo movies on Sunday. The new Lifecycle will be delivered on Monday . . . I stare at the three models for an agonizing amount of time, minutes, before saying anything, noticing that someone has ordered a plate of papaya slices and someone else a plate of asparagus, though both remain untouched. Daisy carefully looks me over, then aims her mouth in my direction and blows smoke toward my head, exhaling, and it floats over my hair, missing my eyes, which are protected anyway by the Oliver Peoples nonprescription redwood-framed glasses I've been wearing most of the night. Another one, Libby, the bimbo with jet lag, is trying to figure out how to unfold her napkin. My frustration level is surprisingly low, because things could be worse. After all, these could be *English* girls. We could be drinking . . . *tea*.

"So!" I say, clapping my hands together, trying to seem alert. "It was hot out today. No?"

"Where did Greg go?" Libby asks, noticing McDermott's absence.

"Well, Gorbachev is downstairs," I tell her. "McDermott, *Greg*, is going to sign a peace treaty with him, between the United States and Russia." I pause, trying to gauge her reaction, before adding, "McDermott's the one behind glasnost, you know."

"Well . . . yeah," she says, her voice impossibly toneless, nodding. "But he told me he was in mergers and . . . aqua-sessions."

I'm looking over at Taylor, who's still sleeping. I snap one of his suspenders but there's no reaction, no movement, then I turn back to Libby. "You're not confused, are you?"

"No," she says, shrugging. "Not really."

"Gorbachev's not downstairs," Caron says suddenly.

"Are you lying?" Daisy asks, smiling.

I'm thinking: Oh boy. "Yes. Caron's right. Gorbachev's not downstairs. He's at Tunnel. Excuse me. Waitress?" I grab at a passing hardbody who's wearing a Bill Blass navy lace gown with a silk organza ruffle. "I'll have a J&B on the rocks and a butcher knife or something sharp from the kichen. Girls?"

None of them say anything. The waitress is staring at Taylor. I look over at him, then back at the hardbody waitress, then back at Taylor. "Bring him the, um, grapefruit sorbet and, oh, let's say, a Scotch, okay?"

The waitress just stares at him.

"Ahem, honey?" I wave my hand in front of her face. "J&B? On the rocks?" I tell her, enunciating over the jazz band, who are in the middle of a fine rendition of "Take Five."

She finally nods.

"And bring them"—I gesture toward the girls—"whatever it was they're drinking. Ginger ale? Wine cooler?"

"No," Libby says. "It's champagne." She points, then says to Caron, "Right?"

"I guess." Caron shrugs.

"With peach schnapps," Daisy reminds her.

"Champagne," I repeat, to the waitress. "With, uh-huh, peach schnapps. Catch that?"

Waitress nods, writes something down, leaves, and I'm checking out her ass as she walks away, then I look back at the three of them, studying each one very carefully for any signs, a flicker of betrayal that would cross their faces, the one gesture that would give away this robot act, but it's pretty dark in Nell's and my hope—that this is the case—is just wishful thinking and so I clap my hands together again and breathe in. "So! It was really hot out today. Right?"

"I need a new fur," Libby sighs, staring into her champagne glass.

"Full length or ankle length?" Daisy asks in the same toneless voice.

"A stole?" Caron suggests.

"Either a full length or . . ." Libby stops and thinks hard for a minute. "I saw this short, cuddly wrap . . ."

"But mink, right?" Daisy asks. "Definitely *mink*?"

"Oh yeah. Mink," Libby says.

"Hey Taylor," I whisper, nudging him. "Wake up. They're talking. You've gotta see this."

"But *which* kind?" Caron's on a roll.

"Don't you find some minks are too . . . *fluffy*?" Daisy asks.

"Some minks *are* too fluffy." Libby this time.

"Silver fox is *very* popular," Daisy murmurs.

"Beige tones are also increasingly popular," Libby says.

"Which ones are those?" someone asks.

"Lynx. Chinchilla. Ermine. Beaver—"

"Hello?" Taylor wakes up, blinking. "I'm here."

"Go back to sleep, Taylor," I sigh.

"Where's Mr. McDermott?" he asks, stretching.

"Wandering around downstairs. Looking for coke." I shrug.

"Silver fox is very popular," one of them says.

"Raccoon. Fitch. Squirrel. Muskrat. Mongolian lamb."

"Am I dreaming," Taylor asks me, "or . . . am I really hearing an actual conversation?"

"Well, I suppose what passes for one." I wince. "Shhh. Listen. It's happening."

At the sushi restaurant tonight McDermott, in a state of total frustration, asked the girls if they knew the names of any of the nine planets. Libby and Caron guessed the moon. Daisy wasn't sure but she actually guessed . . . Comet. Daisy thought that Comet was a planet. Dumbfounded, McDermott, Taylor and I all assured her that it was.

"Well, it's easy to find a good fur now," Daisy says slowly. "Since more ready-to-wear designers have now entered the fur field, the range increases because each designer selects different pelts to give his collection an individual character."

"It's all so scary," Caron says, shivering.

"Don't be intimidated," Daisy says. "Fur is only an accessory. *Don't* be intimidated by it."

"But a luxurious accessory," Libby points out.

I ask the table, "Has anyone ever played around with a TEC

nine-millimeter Uzi? It's a gun. No? They're particularly useful because this model has a threaded barrel for attaching silencers and barrel extensions." I say this nodding.

"Furs shouldn't be intimidating." Taylor looks over at me and blankly says, "I'm gradually uncovering some startling information here."

"But a luxurious accessory," Libby points out.

The waitress reappears, setting the drinks down along with a bowl of grapefruit sorbet. Taylor looks at it and says, blinking, "I didn't order this."

"Yes you did," I tell him. "In your sleep you ordered this. You ordered this in your sleep."

"No I didn't," he says, unsure.

"I'll eat it," I say. "Just listen." I'm tapping my fingers against the table loudly.

"Karl Lagerfeld hands down," Libby's saying.

"Why?" Caron.

"He created the Fendi collection, of course," Daisy says, lighting a cigarette.

"I like the Mongolian lamb mixed with mole or"—Caron stops to giggle—"this black leather jacket lined with Persian lamb."

"What do you think of Geoffrey Beene?" Daisy asks her.

Caron ponders this. "The white satin collars . . . i*ffy*."

"But he does *marv*elous things with Tibetan lambs," Libby says.

"Carolina Herrera?" Caron asks.

"No, no, too fluffy," Daisy says, shaking her head.

"Too schoolgirl," Libby agrees.

"James Galanos has the most wonderful Russian lynx bellies, though," Daisy says.

"And don't forget Arnold Scaasi. The white ermine," Libby says. "To *die* for."

"Really?" I smile and lift my lips into a depraved grin. "To die for?"

"To die for," Libby says again, affirmative about something for the first time all night.

"I think you'd look adorable in, oh, a Geoffrey Beene, Taylor," I whine in a high, faggy voice, flopping a limp wrist on his shoulder, but he's sleeping again so it doesn't matter. I remove the hand with a sigh.

"That's Miles . . ." Caron peers over at some aging gorilla in the next booth with a graying crew cut and an eleven-year-old bimbo balanced on his lap.

Libby turns around to make sure. "But I thought he was filming that Vietnam movie in Philadelphia."

"No. The *Philippines*," Caron says. "It wasn't in Philadelphia."

"Oh yeah," Libby says, then, "Are you sure?"

"Yeah. In fact it's over," Caron says in a tone that's completely undecided. She blinks. "In fact it's . . . out." She blinks again. "In fact I think it came out . . . last year."

The two of them are looking over at the next booth disinterestedly, but when they turn back to our table, their eyes falling on the sleeping Taylor, Caron turns to Libby and sighs. "Should we go over and say hello?"

Libby nods slowly, her features quizzical in the candlelight, and stands up. "Excuse us." They leave. Daisy stays, sips Caron's champagne. I imagine her naked, murdered, maggots burrowing, feasting on her stomach, tits blackened by cigarette burns, Libby eating this corpse out, then I clear my throat. "So it was really hot out today, wasn't it?"

"It was," she agrees.

"Ask me a question," I tell her, feeling suddenly, well, spontaneous.

She inhales on the cigarette, then blows out. "So what do you do?"

"What do you think I do?" And frisky too.

"A model?" She shrugs. "An actor?"

"No," I say. "Flattering, but no."

"Well?"

"I'm into, oh, murders and executions mostly. It depends." I shrug.

"Do you like it?" she asks, unfazed.

"Um . . . It depends. Why?" I take a bite of sorbet.

"Well, most guys I know who work in mergers and acquisitions don't really like it," she says.

"That's *not* what I said," I say, adding a forced smile, finishing my J&B. "Oh, forget it."

"Ask *me* a question," she says.

"Okay. Where do you . . ." I stop for a moment, stuck, then, "summer?"

"Maine," she says. "Ask me something else."

"Where do you work out?"

"Private trainer," she says. "How about you?"

"Xclusive," I say. "On the Upper West Side."

"Really?" She smiles, then notices someone behind me, but her expression doesn't change, and her voice remains flat. "Francesca. Oh my god. It's Francesca. Look."

"Daisy! And Patrick, you *devil*!" Francesca screeches. "Daisy, what in god's name are you doing with a *stud* like Batman?" She overtakes the booth, sliding in with this bored blond girl I don't recognize. Francesca is wearing a velvet dress by Saint Laurent Rive Gauche and the girl I don't recognize is wearing a wool dress by Geoffrey Beene. Both are wearing pearls.

"Hello, Francesca," I say.

"Daisy, oh my god. Ben and Jerry's *here*. I *love* Ben and Jerry," I think is what she says, all in a breathless rush, shouting over the light din—actually, drowning out the light din—of the jazz band. "Don't you *love* Ben and Jerry?" she asks, her eyes wide, and then she rasps out to a passing waitress, "*Orange* juice! I need *orange* juice! Jesus fucking Christ the help here has *got* to go. Where's Nell? I'll tell her," she mutters, looking around the room, then turns to Daisy. "How's my face? Bateman, *Ben and Jerry* are *here*. Don't sit there like an idiot. Oh god I'm kidding. I adore Patrick but come on, Batman, look lively, you stud, Ben and Jerry are here." She winks lasciviously then wets both lips with her tongue. Francesca writes for *Vanity Fair*.

"But I already . . ." I stop and look down at my sorbet, troubled. "I already ordered this grapefruit sorbet." Gloomily I point at the dish, confused. "I don't want any ice cream."

"For Christ sakes, Bateman, *Jagger* is here. Mick. Jerry. *You* know," Francesca says, talking to the booth but constantly scanning the room. Daisy's expression hasn't changed once all evening. "What a y-u-p-p-i-e," she spells to the blond girl, then Francesca's eyes land on my sorbet. I pull it toward me protectively.

"Oh yeah," I say. "'*Just another night, just another night with you . . .*'" I sing, sort of. "I know who he is."

"You look thin, Daisy, you're making me sick. Anyway, this is Alison Poole, who is also too thin and makes me sick," Francesca says, lightly slapping my hands covering the sorbet, pulling the dish back toward her. "And this is Daisy Milton and Patrick—"

"We've met," Alison says, glaring at me.

"Hi, Alison. Pat Bateman," I say, holding out my hand.

"We've *met*," she says again, glaring harder.

"Uh . . . we have?" I ask.

Francesca screams, "God, look at that profile of Bateman's. Totally *Roman*. And those *lashes!*" she shrieks.

Daisy smiles approvingly, I play it cool, ignoring them.

I recognize Alison as a girl I did last spring while at the Kentucky Derby with Evelyn and her parents. I remember she screamed when I tried to push my entire arm, gloved and slathered with Vaseline, toothpaste, anything I could find, up into her vagina. She was drunk, wasted on coke, and I had tied her up with wire, slapped duct tape all over her mouth, her face, her breasts. Francesca has given me head before. I don't remember the place, or when, but she's given me head and liked it. I suddenly remember, painfully, that I would have liked to see Alison bleed to death that afternoon last spring but something stopped me. She was so high— "oh my god," she kept moaning during those hours, blood bubbling out of her nose—she never wept. Maybe that was the problem; maybe that was what saved her. I won a lot of money that weekend on a horse called Indecent Exposure.

"Well . . . Hi." I smile weakly but soon regain my confidence. Alison would never have told anyone that story. Not a soul could've possibly heard about that lovely, horrible afternoon. I grin at her in the darkness of Nell's. "Yeah, I remember you. You were a real . . ." I pause, then growl, "manhandler."

She says nothing, just looks at me like I'm the opposite of civilization or something.

"Jesus. Is Taylor sleeping or just dead?" Francesca asks while gobbling up what's left of my sorbet. "Oh my God, did anyone read Page Six today? I was in it, so was Daisy. And Taffy too."

Alison gets up without looking over at me. "I'm going to find Skip downstairs and dance." She walks away.

McDermott comes back and gives Alison, who's squeezing past him, the once-over before taking the seat next to mine.

"Any luck?" I ask.

"No dice," he says, wiping his nose. He lifts my drink to his face and sniffs it, then takes a sip and lights one of Daisy's cigarettes. He looks back at me while lighting it and introduces himself to Francesca before looking back at me. "Don't look so, you know, *astounded*, Bateman. It *hap*pens."

I pause, staring at him, before asking, "Are you, uh, like, shitting me, McDermott?"

"No," he says. "No luck."

I pause again, then look down at my lap and sigh. "Look, McDermott, I've pulled this act before. I know what you're doing."

"I fucked her." He sniffs again, pointing at some girl in one of the booths up front. McDermott's sweating profusely and reeks of Xeryus.

"You did? Wow. Now listen to me," I say, then notice something out of the corner of my eye. "*Francesca . . .*"

"What?" She looks up, a dribble of sorbet running down her chin.

"You're eating my sorbet?" I point at the dish.

She swallows, glaring at me. "Lighten up, Bateman. What do you want from me, you goregous stud? An AIDS test? Oh my god, speaking of which, that guy over there, Krafft? Yep. No loss."

The guy Francesca pointed out is sitting in a booth near the stage where the jazz band plays. His hair is slicked back over a very boyish face and he's wearing a suit with pleated trousers and a silk shirt with light gray polka dots by Comme des Garçons Homme and sipping a martini and it's not difficult to imagine him in someone's bedroom tonight, lying, probably to the girl he's sitting with: blond, big tits, wearing a metal-studded dress by Giorgio di Sant'Angelo.

"Should we tell her?" someone asks.

"Oh no," Daisy says. "Don't. She looks like a real bitch."

"Listen to me, McDermott." I lean in toward him. "You *have* drugs. I can see it in your eyes. Not to mention that fucking sniffing."

"Nope. *Negatif.* Not tonight, honey." He wags his head.

Applause for the jazz band—the whole table claps, even Taylor, whom Francesca has inadvertently woken up, and I turn away from McDermott, heavily pissed, and bring my hands together like everyone else. Caron and Libby walk up to the table and Libby says, "Caron's got to go to Atlanta tomorrow. *Vogue* shoot. We have to leave." Someone gets the check and McDermott puts it on his gold AmEx card, which conclusively proves that he's high on coke since he's a famous tightwad.

Outside it's muggy and there's a faint drizzle, almost like a mist, lightning but no thunder. I trail McDermott, hoping to confront him, almost bumping into someone in a wheelchair who I remember rolling up to the ropes when we first arrived and the guy's still sitting there, wheels moving up then backing away, up then back on the pavement, totally ignored by the doormen.

"McDer*mott*," I call. "What are you doing? Give me your *drugs*."

He turns, facing me, and breaks into this weird jig, twirling around, then just as abruptly he stops and walks over to a black woman and child who are sitting in the doorway of the closed deli next to Nell's and predictably she's begging for food, a predictable cardboard sign at her feet. It's hard to tell if the kid, six or seven, is black or not, even if it's really hers, since the light outside Nell's is too bright, really unflattering, and tends to make everyone's skin look the same yellowish, washed-out color.

"What are they *doing*?" Libby says, staring, transfixed. "Don't they know they need to stand closer to the ropes?"

"*Libby*, come *on*," Caron says, pulling her toward two taxis at the curb.

"McDermott?" I ask. "What in the *hell* are you doing?"

McDermott's eyes are glazed over and he's waving a dollar bill in front of the woman's face and she starts sobbing, pathetically trying to grab at it, but of course, typically, he doesn't give it to her. Instead he ignites the bill with matches from Canal Bar and relights the half-smoked cigar clenched between his straight white teeth— probably caps, the jerk.

"How . . . gentrifying of you, McDermott," I tell him.

Daisy is leaning against a white Mercedes parked next to the curb. Another Mercedes, this one a limo, black, is double-parked next to the white one. There's more lightning. An ambulance screams down Fourteenth Street. McDermott walks by Daisy and kisses her hand before hopping in the second cab.

I'm left standing in front of the black woman, Daisy staring.

"Jesus," I mutter, then, "Here . . ." I hand the black woman a book of matches from Lutèce before realizing the mistake, then find a book of matches from Tavern on the Green and toss them at the kid and pluck the other matchbook from her dirty, scabbed fingers.

"Jesus," I mutter again, walking over to Daisy.

"There are *no more cabs*," she says, hands on hips. Another flash of lightning causes her to jerk her head around, whining, "Where's the pho*tog*raphers? Who's taking the *pic*tures?"

"Taxi!" I whistle, trying to wave down a passing cab.

Another bolt of lightning rips across the sky above Zeckendorf Towers and Daisy squeals, "Where *is* the photographer? *Patrick*. Tell them to *stop*." She's confused, her head moving left, right, behind, left, right. She lowers her sunglasses.

"Oh my god," I mutter, my voice building to a shout. "It's *light*ning. Not a photographer. *Lightning!*"

"Oh right, *I'm* supposed to believe *you*. You said Gorbachev was downstairs," she says accusingly. "I don't believe you. I think the press is here."

"Jesus, here's a cab. *Hey, taxi.*" I whistle at an oncoming cab that has just turned off Eighth Avenue, but someone taps my shoulder and when I turn around, Bethany, a girl I dated at Harvard and who I was subsequently dumped by, is standing in front of me wearing a lace-embroidered sweater and viscose-crepe trousers by Christian Lacroix, an open white umbrella in one hand. The cab I was trying to hail whizzes by.

"Bethany," I say, stunned.

"Patrick." She smiles.

"Bethany," I say again.

"How are you, Patrick?" she asks.

"Um, well, um, I'm fine," I stutter, after an awkward byte of silence. "And you?"

"Really well, thanks," she says.

"You know . . . well, were you in there?" I ask.

"Yeah, I was." She nods, then, "It's good to see you."

"Are you . . . living here?" I ask, gulping. "In Manhattan?"

"Yes." She smiles. "I'm working at Milbank Tweed."

"Oh, well . . . great." I look back over at Daisy and I'm suddenly angry, remembering the lunch in Cambridge, at Quarters, where Bethany, her arm in a sling, a faint bruise above her cheek, ended it all, then, just as suddenly, I'm thinking: My hair, oh god, my *hair*, and I can feel the drizzling ruining it. "Well, I gotta go."

"You're at P & P, right?" she asks, then, "You look great."

Spotting another cab approaching, I back away. "Yeah, well, you know."

"Let's have lunch," she calls out.

"What could be more fun?" I say, unsure. The cab has noticed Daisy and stopped.

"I'll call you," she says.

"Whatever," I say.

Some black guy has opened the cab door for Daisy and she steps in daintily and the black guy holds it open for me too while I get in, waving, nodding to Bethany. "A tip, mister," the black guy asks, "from you and the pretty lady?"

"Yeah," I growl, trying to check my hair in the cabdriver's rearview mirror. "Here's a tip: get a *real* job, you dumb fucking nigger." Then I slam the door myself and tell the cabdriver to take us to the Upper West Side.

"Didn't you think it was interesting in that movie tonight how they were spies but they weren't spies?" Daisy asks.

"And you can drop her off in Harlem," I tell the driver.

I'm in my bathroom, shirtless in front of the Orobwener mirror, debating whether to take a shower and wash my hair since it looks shitty due to the rain. Tentatively I smooth some mousse into it then run a comb over the mousse. Daisy sits in the Louis Montoni brass and chrome chair by the futon, spooning Macadamia Brittle Häagen-Dazs ice cream into her mouth. She is wearing only a lace bra and a garter belt from Bloomingdale's.

"You know," she calls out, "my ex-boyfriend Fiddler, at the party earlier tonight, he couldn't understand what I was doing there with a yuppie."

I'm not really listening, but while staring at my hair, I manage, "Oh. Really?"

"He said . . ." She laughs. "He said you gave him bad vibes."

I sigh, then make a muscle. "That's . . . too bad."

She shrugs and offhandedly admits, "He used to do a lot of cocaine. He used to beat me up."

I suddenly start paying attention, until she says, "But he never touched my face."

I walk into the bedroom and start undressing.

"You think I'm dumb, don't you?" she asks, staring at me, her legs, tan and aerobicized, slung over one of the chair's arms.

"What?" I slip my shoes off, then bend down to pick them up.

"You think I'm dumb," she says. "You think all models are dumb."

"No," I say, trying to contain my laughter. "I really don't."

"You do," she insists. "I can tell."

"I think you are . . ." I stand there, my voice trailing off.

"Yes?" She's grinning, waiting.

"I think you are totally brilliant and incredibly . . . brilliant," I say in monotone.

"That's nice." She smiles serenely, licking the spoon. "You have, well, a tender quality about you."

"Thanks." I take my pants off and fold them neatly, hanging them along with the shirt and tie over a black steel Philippe Stark clothes hanger. "You know, the other day I caught my maid stealing a piece of bran toast from my wastebasket in the kitchen."

Daisy takes this in, then asks, "Why?"

I pause, staring at her flat, well-defined stomach. Her torso is completely tan and muscular. So is mine. "Because she said she was hungry."

Daisy sighs and licks the spoon thoughtfully.

"You think my hair looks okay?" I'm still standing there, in just my Calvin Klein jockey shorts, hard-on bulging, and a fifty-dollar pair of Armani socks.

"Yeah." She shrugs. "Sure."

I sit on the edge of the futon and peel off the socks.

"I beat up a girl today who was asking people on the street for money." I pause, then measure each of the following words carefully. "She was young and seemed frightened and had a sign that explained she was lost in New York and had a child, though I didn't see it. And she needed money, for food or something. For a bus ticket to Iowa. Iowa. I think it was Iowa and . . ." I stop for a moment, balling the socks up, then unballing them.

Daisy stares at me blankly for a minute, before asking, "And then?"

I pause, distracted, and then stand up. Before walking into the bathroom I mutter, "And then? I beat the living shit out of her."

I open the medicine cabinet for a condom and as I reenter the bedroom, say, "She had misspelled *disabled*. I mean, that's not the reason I did what I did but . . . you know." I shrug. "She was too ugly to rape."

Daisy stands up, placing the spoon next to the Häagen-Dazs carton on the Gilbert Rhode-designed nightstand.

I point. "No. Put it in the carton."

"Oh, sorry," she says.

She admires a Palazzetti vase while I slip on the condom. I get on top of her and we have sex and lying beneath me she is only a shape, even with all the halogen lamps burning. Later, we are lying on opposite sides of the bed. I touch her shoulder.

"I think you should go home," I say.

She opens her eyes, scratches her neck.

"I think I might . . . hurt you," I tell her. "I don't think I can control myself."

She looks over at me and shrugs. "Okay. Sure." Then she starts to get dressed. "I don't want to get too involved anyway," she says.

"I think something bad is going to happen," I tell her.

She pulls her panties on, then checks her hair in the Nabolwev mirror and nods. "I understand."

After she's dressed and minutes of pure, hard silence have passed, I say, not unhopefully, "You don't want to get hurt, do you?"

She buttons up the top of her dress and sighs, without looking over at me. "That's why I'm leaving."

I say, "I think I'm losing it."

PAUL OWEN

I screened calls all morning long in my apartment, taking none of them, glaring tiredly at a cordless phone while sipping cup after cup of decaf herbal tea. Afterwards I went to the gym, where I worked out for two hours; then I had lunch at the Health Bar and could barely eat half of an endive-with-carrot-dressing salad I ordered. I stopped at Barney's on my way back from an abandoned

loft building I had rented a unit in somewhere around Hell's
Kitchen. I had a facial. I played squash with Brewster Whipple at
the Yale Club and from there made reservations for eight o'clock
under the name of Marcus Halberstam at Texarkana, where I'm
going to meet Paul Owen for dinner. I choose Texarkana because I
know that a lot of people I have dealings with are not going to be
eating there tonight. Plus I'm in the mood for their chili-wrapped
pork and one or two Dixie beers. It's June and I'm wearing a two-
button linen suit, a cotton shirt, a silk tie and leather wing-tips, all
by Armani. Outside Texarkana a cheerful black bum motions for
me, explaining that he's Bob Hope's younger brother, No Hope. He
holds out a Styrofoam coffee cup. I think this is funny so I give him
a quarter. I'm twenty minutes late. From an open window on Tenth
Street I can hear the last strains of "A Day in the Life" by the
Beatles.

The bar in Texarkana is empty and in the dining area only four
or five tables have people at them. Owen is at a booth in the back,
complaining bitterly to the waiter, grilling him, demanding to know
the exact reasons why they are out of the crawfish gumbo tonight.
The waiter, a not-bad-looking faggot, is at a loss and helplessly lisps
an excuse. Owen is in no mood for pleasantries, but then neither
am I. As I sit down, the waiter apologizes once more and then
takes my drink order. "J&B, *straight*," I stress. "*And* a Dixie beer."
He smiles while writing this down—the bastard even bats his eyelashes—and when I'm about to warn him not to attempt small talk
with me, Owen barks out his drink order, "Double Absolut martini,"
and the fairy splits.

"This is really a beehive of, uh, activity, Halberstam," Owen
says, gesturing toward the near-empty room. "This place is hot, *very*
hot."

"Listen, the mud soup and the charcoal arugula are *outrageous*
here," I tell him.

"Yeah, well," he grumbles, staring into his martini glass. "You're
late."

"Hey, I'm a child of divorce. Give me a break," I say, shrugging,
thinking: Oh Halberstam, you *are* an asshole. And then, after I've
studied the menu, "Hmmm, I see they've omitted the pork loin
with lime Jell-O."

Owen is wearing a double-breasted silk and linen suit, a cotton shirt and a silk tie, all by Joseph Abboud, and his tan is impeccable. But he's out of it tonight, surprisingly untalkative, and his dourness drizzles over my jovial, expectant mood, dampening it considerably, and I have suddenly resorted to making comments such as "Is that Ivana Trump over there?" then, laughing, "Jeez, Patrick, I mean *Marcus*, what are you *think*ing? Why would Ivana be at Texarkana?" But this doesn't make dinner any less monotonous. It doesn't help lessen the fact that Paul Owen is exactly my age, twenty-seven, or make this whole thing any less disconcerting to me.

What I've mistaken at first for pomposity on Owen's part is actually just drunkenness. When I press for information about the Fisher account he offers useless statistical data that I already knew about: how Rothschild was originally handling the account, how Owen came to acquire it. And though I had Jean gather this information for my files *months ago*, I keep nodding, pretending that this primitive info is revelatory and saying things like "This is enlightening" while at the same time telling him "I'm utterly insane" and "I like to dissect girls." Every time I attempt to steer the conversation back to the mysterious Fisher account, he infuriatingly changes the topic back to either tanning salons or brands of cigars or certain health clubs or the best places to jog in Manhattan and he keeps guffawing, which I find totally upsetting. I'm drinking Southern beer for the first part of the meal—pre entrée, post appetizer—then switch to Diet Pepsi midway through since I need to stay slightly sober. I'm about to tell Owen that Cecelia, Marcus Halberstam's girlfriend, has two vaginas and that we plan to wed next spring in East Hampton, but he interrupts.

"I'm feeling, er, slightly mellow," he admits, drunkenly squeezing a lime onto the table, completely missing his beer mug.

"Uh-huh." I dip a stick of jicama sparingly into a rhubarb mustard sauce, pretending to ignore him.

He's so drunk by the time dinner is over that I (1) make him pay the check, which comes to two hundred and fifty dollars, (2) make him admit what a dumb son-of-a-bitch he really is, and (3) get him back to my place, where he makes himself *another* drink—he actually opens a bottle of Acacia I thought I had hidden, with a Mulazoni sterling silver wine opener that Peter Radloff bought me after we completed the Heatherberg deal. In my bathroom I take out the ax I'd stashed in the shower, pop two five-milligram Valium, washing them down with a tumblerful of Plax, and then I move into the foyer, where I put on a cheap raincoat I picked up at Brooks Brothers on Wednesday and move toward Owen, who is bent over near the stereo system in the living room looking through my CD collection—all the lights in the apartment on, the venetian blinds closed. He straightens up and walks slowly backward, sipping from his wineglass, taking in the apartment, until he seats himself in a white aluminum folding chair I bought at the Conran's Memorial Day sale weeks ago, and finally he notices the newspapers—copies of *USA Today* and *W* and *The New York Times*—spread out beneath him, covering the floor, to protect the polished white-stained oak from his blood. I move toward him with the ax in one hand, and with the other I button up the raincoat.

"Hey, Halberstam," he asks, managing to slur both words.

"Yes, Owen," I say, drawing near.

"Why are there, um, copies of the Style section all over the place?" he asks tiredly. "Do you have a dog? A chow or something?"

"No, Owen." I move slowly around the chair until I'm facing him, standing directly in his line of vision, and he's so drunk he can't even focus in on on the ax, he doesn't even notice once I've raised it high above my head. Or when I change my mind and lower it to my waist, almost holding it as if it's a baseball bat and I'm about to swing at an oncoming ball, which happens to be Owen's head.

Owen pauses, then says, "Anyway, I used to hate Iggy Pop but now that he's so commercial I like him a lot better than—"

The ax hits him midsentence, straight in the face, its thick blade chopping sideways into his open mouth, shutting him up. Paul's eyes look up at me, then involuntarily roll back into his head, then back at me, and suddenly his hands are trying to grab at the handle, but the shock of the blow has sapped his strength. There's no blood at first, no sound either except for the newspapers under Paul's kicking feet, rustling, tearing. Blood starts to slowly pour out of the sides of his mouth shortly after the first chop, and when I pull the ax out—almost yanking Owen out of the chair by his head—and strike him again in the face, splitting it open, his arms flailing at nothing, blood sprays out in twin brownish geysers, staining my raincoat. This is accompanied by a horrible momentary hissing noise actually coming from the wounds in Paul's skull, places where bone and flesh no longer connect, and this is followed by a rude farting noise caused by a section of his brain, which due to pressure forces itself out, pink and glistening, through the wounds in his face. He falls to the floor in agony, his face just gray and bloody, except for one of his eyes, which is blinking uncontrollably; his mouth is a twisted red-pink jumble of teeth and meat and jawbone, his tongue hangs out of an open gash on the side of his cheek, connected only by what looks like a thick purple string. I scream at him only once: "Fucking stupid bastard. Fucking bastard." I stand there waiting, staring up at the crack above the Onica that the superintendent hasn't fixed yet. It takes Paul five minutes to finally die. Another thirty to stop bleeding.

I take a cab to Owen's apartment on the Upper East Side and on the ride across Central Park in the dead of this stifling June night in the back of the taxi it hits me that I'm still wearing the bloody raincoat. At his apartment I let myself in with the keys I took from the corpse's pocket and once inside I douse the coat with lighter fluid and burn it in the fireplace. The living room is very spare, minimalist. The walls are white pigmented concrete, except for one wall, which is covered with a trendy large-scale scientific drawing, and the wall facing Fifth Avenue has a long strip of faux-cowhide paneling stretched across it. A black leather couch sits beneath it.

I switch on the wide-screen thirty-one-inch Panasonic to *Late Night with David Letterman*, then move over to the answering machine to change Owen's message. While erasing the current one (Owen giving all the numbers he can be reached at—including the Seaport, *for god's sake*—while Vivaldi's *Four Seasons* plays tastefully in the background) I wonder aloud where I should send Paul, and after a few minutes of intense debating decide: London. "I'll send the bastard to England," I cackle while turning the volume down on the TV and then I leave the new message. My voice sounds similar to Owen's and to someone hearing it over the phone probably identical. Tonight Letterman has on Stupid Pet Tricks. A German shepherd with a Mets cap on peels and eats an orange. This is replayed twice, in slow motion.

Into a hand-constructed bridle leather suitcase with a khaki-colored canvas cover, extra-heavy cap corners, gold straps and locks, by Ralph Lauren, I pack a wool six-button double-breasted peak-lapel chalk-striped suit and one wool flannel navy suit, both from Brooks Brothers, along with a Mitsubishi rechargeable electric shaver, a silver-plated shoehorn from Barney's, a Tag-Heuer sports watch, a black leather Prada currency holder, a Sharp Handy-Copier, a Sharp Dialmaster, his passport in its own black leather passport case and a Panasonic portable hair dryer. I also steal for myself a Toshiba portable compact disc player with one of the discs from the original cast recording of *Les Misérables* still in it. The bathroom is done completely in white except for the Dalmatian-spot wallpaper covering one wall. I throw any toiletry articles I might've missed into a plastic Hefty bag.

Back at my apartment his body is already in rigor mortis, and after wrapping it up in four cheap terry-cloth towels I also bought at the Conran's Memorial Day sale, I place Owen head-first and fully dressed into a Canalino goose-down sleeping bag, which I zip up then drag easily into the elevator, then through the lobby, past the night doorman, down the block, where briefly I run into Arthur Crystal and Kitty Martin, who've just had dinner at Café Luxembourg. Luckily Kitty Martin is supposed to be dating Craig McDermott, who is in Houston for the night, so they don't linger, even though Crystal—the rude bastard—asks me what the general rules of wearing a white dinner jacket are. After answering him curtly I hail a taxi, effortlessly manage to swing the sleeping bag into the backseat, hop in and give the driver the address in Hell's Kitchen. Once there I carry the body up four flights of stairs until we're at the unit I own in the abandoned building and I place Owen's body into an oversize porcelain tub, strip off his Abboud suit and, after wetting the corpse down, pour two bags of lime over it.

Later, around two, in bed, I'm unable to sleep. Evelyn catches me on call waiting while I'm listening to messages on 976-TWAT and watching a tape on the VCR of this morning's *Patty Winters Show* which is about Deformed People.

"Patrick?" Evelyn asks.

I pause, then in a dull monotone calmly announce, "You have reached Patrick Bateman's number. He is unable to come to the phone right now. So please leave a message after the tone . . ." I pause, then add, "Have a nice day." I pause again, praying to god that she bought it, before emitting a pitiful "Beep."

"Oh stop it, Patrick," she says irritably. "I know it's you. What in god's name do you think you're doing?"

I hold the phone out in front of me then drop it on the floor and bang it against the nightstand. I keep pressing some of the numbers down, hoping that when I lift the receiver up to my ear I'll be greeted by a dial tone. "Hello? Hello?" I say. "Is anyone there? Yes?"

"Oh for god's sake stop it. Just *stop* it," Evelyn wails.

"Hi, Evelyn," I say cheerily, my face twisted into a grimace.

"Where have you *been* tonight?" she asks. "I thought we were supposed to have dinner. I thought we had reservations at Raw Space."

"No, Evelyn," I sigh, suddenly very tired. "We didn't. Why would you think that?"

"I thought I had it written down," she whines. "I thought my secretary had written it down for me."

"Well, one of you was wrong," I say, rewinding the tape by remote control from my bed. "Raw Space? Jesus. You . . . are . . . insane."

"Honey," she pouts. "Where *were* you tonight? I hope you didn't go to Raw Space without me."

"Oh my god," I moan. "I had to rent some videotapes. I mean I had to return some videos."

"What else did you do?" she asks, still whining.

"Well, I ran into Arthur Crystal and Kitty Martin," I say. "They just had dinner at Café Luxembourg."

"Oh really?" Chillingly, her interest perks up. "What was Kitty wearing?"

"An off-the-shoulder ball gown with velvet bodice and a floral-patterned lace skirt by Laura Marolakos, I think."

"And Arthur?"

"Same thing."

"Oh Mr. Bateman." She giggles. "I adore your sense of humor."

"Listen, it's late. I'm tired." I fake a yawn.

"Did I wake you?" she asks worriedly. "I hope I didn't wake you."

"Yes," I say. "You did. But I took your call so it's my fault, not yours."

"Dinner, honey? Tomorrow?" she asks, coyly expecting an affirmative response.

"I can't. Work."

"You practically own that damn company," she moans. "*What* work? What *work* do you do? I *don't* understand."

"Evelyn," I sigh. "*Please.*"

"Oh Patrick, let's go away this summer," she says wistfully. "Let's go to Edgartown or the Hamptons."

"I'll do that," I say. "Maybe I'll do that."

PAUL SMITH

I'm standing in Paul Smith talking to Nancy and Charles Hamilton and their two-year-old daughter, Glenn. Charles is wearing a four-button double-breasted linen suit by Redaelli, a cotton broadcloth shirt by Ascot Chang, a patterned silk tie by Eugenio Venanzi and loafers by Brooks Brothers. Nancy is wearing a silk blouse with mother-of-pearl sequins and a silk chiffon skirt by Valentino and silver earrings by Reena Pachochi. I'm wearing a six-button double-breasted chalk-striped wool suit and a patterned silk tie, both by Louis, Boston, and a cotton oxford cloth shirt by Luciano Barbera. Glenn is wearing silk Armani overalls and a tiny Mets cap. As the salesgirl rings up Charles's purchases, I'm playing with the baby while Nancy holds her, offering Glenn my platinum American Express card, and she grabs at it excitedly, and I'm shaking my head, talking in a high-pitched baby voice, squeezing her chin, waving the card in front of her face, cooing, "Yes I'm a total psychopathic murderer, oh yes I am, I like to kill people, oh yes I do, honey, little sweetie pie, yes I do . . ." After the office today I played squash with Ricky Hendricks, then had drinks with Stephen Jenkins at Fluties and I'm supposed to meet Bonnie Abbott for dinner at Pooncakes, the new Bishop Sullivan restaurant in Gramercy Park, at eight o'clock. *The Patty Winters Show* this morning was about Concentration Camp Survivors. I take out a Sony Watchman pocket TV (the FD-270) that has a 2.7 inch black-and-white miniscreen and weighs only thirteen ounces, and hold it out to Glenn. Nancy asks, "How's the shad roe at Rafaeli's?" Right now, outside this store, it's not dark yet but it is getting there.

"It's terrific," I murmur, staring happily at Glenn.

Charles signs the slip and while placing his gold American Express card back into his wallet he turns to me and recognizes someone over my shoulder.

"Hey Luis," Charles says, smiling.

I turn around.

"Hi, Charles. Hi, Nancy." Luis Carruthers kisses Nancy's cheek, then shakes the baby's hand. "Oh hiya, Glenn. My my, you look so big."

"Luis, you know Robert Chanc—" Charles starts.

"Pat Bateman," I say, putting the Watchman back in my pocket. "Forget it. We've met."

"Oh, I'm sorry. That's right. Pat Bateman," Charles says. Luis is wearing a wool-crepe suit, a cotton broadcloth shirt and a silk tie, all by Ralph Lauren. Like me, like Charles, he wears his hair slicked back and he's wearing Oliver Peoples redwood-framed glasses. Mine, at least, are nonprescription.

"Well, well," I say, shaking his hand. Luis's grip is overly firm, yet horribly sensuous at the same time. "Excuse me, I have to purchase a tie." I wave bye-bye to baby Glenn once more and move off to inspect the neckwear in the adjoining room, wiping my hand against a two-hundred-dollar bath towel that hangs on a marble rack.

Soon enough Luis wanders over and leans against the tie drawer, pretending to examine the ties like I'm doing.

"What are you doing here?" he whispers.

"Buying a tie for my brother. It's his birthday soon. Excuse me." I move down the rack, away from him.

"He must feel very lucky to have a brother like you," he says, sliding up next to me, grinning sincerely.

"Maybe, but I find him completely repellent," I say. "*You* might like him though."

"Patrick, why won't you look at me?" Luis asks, sounding anguished. "*Look* at me."

"Please, *please* leave me alone, Luis," I say, my eyes closed, both fists clenched in anger.

"Come on, let's have a drink at Sofi's and talk about this," he suggests, starting to plead.

"Talk about *what*?" I ask incredulously, opening my eyes.

"Well . . . about *us*." He shrugs.

"Did you *follow* me in here?" I ask.

"Into *where*?"

"Here. Paul Smith. Why?"

"*Me*? Follow *you*? Oh come on." He tries to laugh, scoffing at my remark. "Jesus."

"Luis," I say, forcing myself to make eye contact. "Please leave me alone. Go away."

"Patrick," he says. "I love you very much. I hope you realize this."

I moan, moving over to the shoes, smiling wanly at a salesperson.

Luis follows. "Patrick, what are we doing here?"

"Well, I'm trying to buy a tie for my brother and"—I pick up a loafer, then sigh—"and you're trying to give me head, figure it out. Jesus, I'm getting out of here."

I move back over to the tie rack, grab one without choosing and take it up to the register. Luis follows. Ignoring him, I hand the salesgirl the platinum AmEx card and tell her, "There's a bum outside the door." I point out the window at the crying homeless man with the bag of newspapers standing on a bench next to the store's entrance. "You should call the police or something." She nods thanks and runs my card through the computer. Luis just stands there, shyly staring at the ground. I sign the receipt, take the bag and inform the salesgirl, pointing at Luis, "He's not with me."

Outside I try to wave down a cab on Fifth Avenue. Luis hurries out of the store after me.

"Patrick, we've *got* to talk," he calls out over the roar of traffic. He runs up to me, grabbing my coat sleeve. I whirl around, my switchblade already open, and I jab it threateningly, warning Luis to stay back. People move out of our way, continue walking.

"Hey, whoa, Patrick," he says, holding his hands up, backing off. "Patrick . . ."

I hiss at him, still holding out the knife until a cab I flag down skids to a stop. Luis tries to get near me, his hands still up, and I keep the knife aimed at him, slicing the air with it, while I open the door to the cab and back in, still hissing, then I close the door and tell the driver head over to Gramercy Park, to Pooncakes.

BIRTHDAY, BROTHERS

I spend all day thinking about what kind of table my brother Sean and I will be seated at tonight in the Quilted Giraffe. Since it's his birthday and he happens to be in the city, my father's accountant, Charles Conroy, and the trustee of his estate, Nicholas Leigh, both called last week and mutually suggested that it would be in everyone's best interest to use this date as an excuse to find out what Sean's doing with his life and perhaps to ask a pertinent question or two. And though both of these men know I despise Sean, and that the feeling is unambiguously reciprocated, it would be a good idea to get him to come to dinner, and as a lure, as bait in case he refuses, by mentioning, not lightly, that something bad has happened. I was on a conference call to Conroy and Leigh last Wednesday afternoon.

"Something bad? Like what?" I asked, trying to concentrate on the numbers sliding across my monitor while simultaneously waving Jean away, even though she was holding a sheaf of papers I was supposed to sign. "That all Michelob breweries in the Northeast are closing? That 976-BIMBO has stopped making house calls?"

"No," Charles said, then quietly mentioned, "Tell him your mother is . . . worse."

I mulled over this tactic, then said, "He might not care."

"Tell him . . ." Nicholas paused, then cleared his throat and rather delicately proposed, "it has to do with her estate."

I looked up from the monitor, lowering my Wayfarer aviator sunglasses, and stared at Jean, then lightly fingered the Zagat guide that sat next to the monitor. Pastels would be impossible. Ditto Dorsia. Last time I called Dorsia someone had actually hung up on me even before I asked, "Well, if not next month, how about January?" and though I have vowed to get a reservation at Dorsia one day (if not during this calender year, then at least before I'm thirty), the energy I would spend attempting this feat isn't worth wasting on Sean. Besides, Dorsia's far too chic for him. I want to make him *endure* this dinner; to not be allowed the pleasure of being distracted by hardbodies on their way to Nell's; somewhere with a men's room attendant so he would have to be painfully subtle about what is now, I'm sure, his *chronic* cocaine usage. I handed the Zagat to Jean and asked her to find the most expensive restaurant in Manhattan. She made a nine o'clock reservation at the Quilted Giraffe.

"Things are worse at Sandstone," I tell Sean later this afternoon, around four o'clock. He's staying in our father's suite at the Carlyle. MTV is blasting in the background, other voices shout over its din. I can hear a shower running.

"Like what? Mom ate her pillow? What?"

"I think we should have dinner," I say.

"Dominique, cool it," he says, then places his hand over the phone and mutters something, muffled.

"Hello, Sean? What's going on?" I'm asking.

"I'll call back," he says, hanging up.

I happen to like the tie I bought Sean at Paul Smith last week and I've decided not to give it to him (though the idea of the asshole, say, hanging himself with it pleases me greatly). In fact *I* decide to wear it to the Quilted Giraffe tonight. Instead of the tie, I'm going to bring him a Casio QD-150 Quick-Dialer combination wristwatch, calculator and data bank. It dials touch-tone phones sonically when held up to a mouthpiece and it stores up to fifty names and numbers. I start laughing while putting this useless gift back into its box, thinking to myself that Sean doesn't even *have* fifty acquaintances. He couldn't even *name* fifty people. *The Patty Winters Show* this morning was about Salad Bars.

Sean calls at five from the Racquet Club and tells me to meet him at Dorsia tonight. He just talked to Brin, the owner, and reserved a table at nine. My mind is a mess. I don't know what to think or how to feel. *The Patty Winters Show* this morning was about Salad Bars.

Later, Dorsia, nine-thirty: Sean is half an hour late. The maître d' refuses to seat me until my brother arrives. My worst fear—a reality. A prime booth across from the bar sits there, empty, waiting for Sean to grace it with his presence. My rage is controlled, barely, by a Xanax and an Absolut on the rocks. While taking a piss in the men's room, I stare into a thin, weblike crack above the urinal's handle and think to myself that if I were to disappear into that crack, say somehow miniaturize and slip into it, the odds are good that no one would notice I was gone. No . . . one . . . would . . . care. In fact some, if they noticed my absence, might feel an odd, indefinable sense of relief. This is true: the world is better off with some people gone. Our lives are *not* all interconnected. That theory is a crock. Some people truly do not *need* to be here. In fact one of them, my brother, Sean, is sitting in the booth he reserved when I come out of the men's room after I've phoned the apartment and checked for messages (Evelyn's suicidal, Courtney wants to buy a chow, Luis suggests dinner on Thursday). Sean is already chain-smoking, and I'm thinking to myself: *Damn*, why didn't I request a table in the nonsmoking section? He's shaking hands with the maître d' as I walk over but doesn't even bother to introduce us. I sit down and nod. Sean nods too, having already ordered a bottle of Cristal, knowing that I'm paying; also knowing, I'm sure, that *I* know he doesn't drink champagne.

Sean, who is now twenty-three, went to Europe last fall, or at least this is what Charles Conroy said Sean told him, and though Charles *did* receive a substantial bill from the Plaza Athénée, the signature on the receipts didn't match Sean's and no one really seemed to know how long Sean was actually in France or even if he had spent real time there. Afterwards he bummed around, then reenrolled at Camden for about three weeks. Now he's in Manhattan before flying to either Palm Beach or New Orleans. Predictably, tonight he's alternately moody and insistently arrogant. He has also, I've just noticed, started to pluck his eyebrows. He no longer has only one. The overwhelming urge I have to mention this to him is quelled only by squeezing my hand into a fist so tightly that I break the skin on the palm of my hand and the biceps of my left arm bulges then rips through the cloth of the linen Armani shirt I have on.

"So you like this place?" he asks, grinning.

"My . . . favorite," I joke through clenched teeth.

"Let's order," he says, not looking at me, waving to a hardbody, who brings over two menus and a wine list while smiling appreciatively at Sean, who in turn ignores her totally. I open the menu

and—*damnit*—it's not prix fixe, which means that Sean orders
the lobster with caviar and peach ravioli as an appetizer and the
blackened lobster with strawberry sauce as an entrée—the two most
expensive items on the menu. I order the quail sashimi with grilled
brioche and the baby soft-shell crabs with grape jelly. A hardbody
opens the bottle of Cristal and pours it into crystal *tumblers*, which
I guess is supposed to be cool. After she leaves, Sean notices me
staring at him in a vaguely disapproving manner.

"What?" he asks.

"Nothing," I say.

"What ... is ... it ... Pat*rick*?" He spaces the words out,
obnoxiously.

"Lobster to start with? *And* for an entrée?"

"What do you want me to order? The Pringle Potato Chip
appetizer?"

"*Two* lobsters?"

"These matchbooks are slightly larger than the lobster they
serve here," he says. "Besides, I'm not that hungry."

"Even more of a reason."

"I'll fax you an apology."

"Still, Sean."

"Rock 'n' roll—"

"I know, I know, rock 'n' roll, deal with it, right?" I say, holding
up a hand while sipping the champagne. I wonder if it's not too late
to ask one of the waitresses to bring a piece of cake over here with
a candle in it—just to embarrass the shit out of him, to put the little
bastard in his place—but instead I put the glass down and ask,
"Listen, so, oh Jesus." I breathe in, then force out, "What did you
do today?"

"Played squash with Richard Lindquist." He shrugs contemptuously. "Bought a tuxedo."

"Nicholas Leigh and Charles Conroy want to know if you're
going to the Hamptons this summer."

"Not if I can help it," he says, shrugging.

A blond girl close enough to physical perfection, with big tits
and a *Les Misérables* playbill in one hand, wearing a long rayon
matte-jersey evening dress by Michael Kors from Bergdorf Goodman, Manolo Blahnik shoes and gold-plated chandelier earrings by
Ricardo Siberno, stops to say hello to Sean and though *I* would fuck

this girl, Sean ignores her flirtatious manner and refuses to introduce me. During this encounter Sean is completely rude, yet the girl leaves smiling, raising a gloved hand. "We'll be at Mortimer's. Later." He nods, staring at my water glass, then waves down a waiter and orders a Scotch, straight.

"Who was that?" I ask.

"Some babe who went to Stephens."

"Where did you meet her?"

"Playing pool at M.K." He shrugs.

"Is she a du Pont?" I ask.

"Why? Do you want her number?"

"No, I just wanted to know if she's a du Pont."

"She might be. I don't know." He lights another cigarette, a Parliament, with what looks like an eighteen-karat gold cigarette lighter from Tiffany's. "She might be a friend of one of the du Ponts."

I keep thinking of reasons why I'm sitting here, right now, tonight, with Sean, at Dorsia, but none come to mind. Just this infinitely recurring zero floats into view. After dinner—the food is small but very good; Sean touches nothing—I tell him that I have to meet Andrea Rothmere at Nell's and if he wants espresso or dessert, he should order it now since I have to be downtown by midnight.

"Why rush?" he asks. "Nell's isn't that hip anymore."

"Well." I falter, quickly regain composure. "We're just going to meet there. We're really going to"—my mind races, lands on something—"Chernoble." I take another sip of champagne from the tumbler.

"Big yawn. *Really* big yawn," he says, scanning the room.

"Or Contraclub East. I can't remember."

"Out. Stone Age. Prehistory." He laughs cynically.

Tense pause. "How would you know?"

"Rock 'n' roll." He shrugs. "Deal with it."

"Well, Sean, where do *you* go?"

Immediate answer. "Petty's."

"Oh yes," I murmur, having forgotten that it was already open. He whistles something, smokes a cigarette.

"We're going to a party Donald Trump's having," I lie.

"Big fun. Very big fun."

"Donald's a nice guy. You should meet him," I say. "I'll . . . introduce you to him."

"Really?" Sean asks, maybe hopefully, maybe not.

"Yeah, sure." Oh, *right*.

Now, by the time I get the check . . . let's see . . . pay it, take a cab back to my place, it will be almost midnight, which doesn't give me enough time to return yesterday's videotapes, so if I don't stop by my place I can just go in and rent another videotape, though on my membership doesn't it say that you can only take out three at a time? So this means last night I took out two (*Body Double* and *Blond, Hot, Dead*) so I *could* rent one more, but I've forgotten I'm also part of the Gold Circle Membership Plan, which means that if I've spent one thousand dollars (at least) in the last six months then I'm allowed to rent as many videos on any given night as I want, but if I still have two out now that might mean I can't take any more out, Gold Circle Member or not, if the other ones haven't been returned, but—

"Damien. You're Damien," I think I hear Sean mutter.

"What did you say?" I ask, looking up. "I didn't hear you."

"Nice tan," he sighs. "I said nice tan."

"Oh," I say, still confused about the video thing. I look down—at what, my lap? "Uh, thanks."

"Rock 'n' roll." He stamps his cigarette out. Fumes rise from the crystal ashtray, then die.

Sean knows *I* know he can probably get us into Petty's, which is the new Norman Prager club on Fifty-ninth, but I'm not going to ask him and he's not going to offer. I place my platinum American Express card over the check. Sean's eyes are glued to a hardbody by the bar in a Thierry Mugler wool jersey dress and a Claude Montana scarf, sipping from a champagne tumbler. When our waitress comes by to pick up the check and the card, I shake my head no. Sean's eyes finally fall on it, for a second, maybe more, and I wave the waitress back over and allow her to take it.

LUNCH WITH BETHANY

Today I'm meeting Bethany for lunch at Vanities, the new Evan Kiley bistro in Tribeca, and though I worked out for nearly two hours this morning and even lifted weights in my office before noon, I'm still extremely nervous. The cause is hard to locate but I've narrowed it down to one of two reasons. It's either that I'm afraid of rejection (though I can't understand why: *she* called *me*, she wants to see *me*, she wants to have lunch with *me*, she wants to fuck *me* again) or, on the other hand, it could have something to do with this new Italian mousse I'm wearing, which, though it makes my hair look fuller and smells good, feels very sticky and uncomfortable, and it's something I could easily blame my nervousness on. So we wouldn't run out of things to talk about over lunch, I tried to read a trendy new short-story collection called *Wok* that I bought at Barnes & Noble last night and whose young author was recently profiled in the Fast Track section of *New York* magazine, but every story started off with the line "When the moon hits your eye like a big pizza pie" and I had to put this slim volume back into my bookshelf and drink a J&B on the rocks, followed by two Xanax, to recover from the effort. To make up for this, before I fell asleep I wrote Bethany a poem and it took a long time, which surprised me, since I used to write her poems, long dark ones, quite often when we were both at Harvard, before we broke up. God, I'm thinking to myself as I walk into Vanities, only fifteen minutes late, I hope she hasn't ended up with Robert Hall, that dumb asshole. I pass by a mirror hung over the bar as I'm led to our table and check out my reflection—the mousse looks good. The topic on *The Patty Winters Show* this morning was Has Patrick Swayze Become Cynical or Not?

I have to stop moving as I near the table, following the maître d' (this is all happening in slow motion). She isn't facing me and I can only catch the back of her neck, her brown hair pinned up into a bun, and when she turns to gaze out the window I see only part of her profile, briefly; she looks *just like a model*. Bethany's wearing a silk gazar blouse and a silk satin skirt with crinoline. A Paloma Picasso hunter green suede and wrought-iron handbag sits in front of her on the table, next to a bottle of San Pellegrino water. She checks her watch. The couple next to our table is smoking and after I lean in behind Bethany, surprising her, kissing her cheek, I coolly ask the maître d' to reseat us in the *non*smoking section. I'm suave but loud enough for the nicotine addicts to hear me and hopefully feel a slight twinge of embarrassment about their filthy habit.

"Well?" I ask, standing there, arms crossed, tapping my foot impatiently.

"I'm afraid there is no nonsmoking section, sir," the maître d' informs me.

I stop tapping my foot and slowly scan the restaurant, the *bistro*, wondering how my hair really looks, and suddenly I wish I *had* switched mousses because since I last saw my hair, seconds ago, it feels different, as if its shape was somehow altered on the walk from bar to table. A pang of nausea that I'm unable to stifle washes warmly over me, but since I'm really dreaming all this I'm able to ask, "So you say there's *no* nonsmoking section? Is this correct?"

"Yes sir." The maître d', younger than myself, faggy, innocent, an *actor* no doubt, adds, "I'm sorry."

"Well, this is . . . very interesting. I can accept this." I reach into my back pocket for my gazelleskin wallet and press a twenty into the maître d's uncertain fist. He looks at the bill, confused, then murmurs "Thank you" and walks away as if in a daze.

"No. Thank *you*," I call out and take my seat across from Bethany, nodding courteously to the couple next to us, and though I try to ignore her for as long as etiquette allows, I can't. Bethany looks absolutely stunning, *just like a model*. Everything's murky. I'm on edge. Feverish, romantic notions—

"Didn't you smoke at Harvard?" is the first thing she says.

"Cigars," I say. "Only cigars."

"Oh," she says.

"But I quit that," I lie, breathing in hard, squeezing my hands together.

"That's good." She nods.

"Listen, did you have any trouble getting reservations?" I ask, and *I am fucking shaking*. I put my hands on the table like a fool, hoping that under her watchful gaze they will stop trembling.

"You don't need reservations here, Patrick," she says soothingly, reaching out a hand, covering one of mine with hers. "Calm down. You look like a wild man."

"I'm clam, I mean calm," I say, breathing in hard, trying to smile, and then, involuntarily, unable to stop myself, ask, "How's my hair?"

"Your hair is fine," she says. "Shhh. It's okay."

"All right. I am all right." I try to smile again but I'm sure it looks just like a grimace.

After a short pause she comments, "That's a nice suit. Henry Stuart?"

"No," I say, insulted, touching its lapel. "Garrick Anderson."

"It's very nice," she says and then genuinely concerned, "Are you okay, Patrick? You just . . . twitched."

"Listen. I'm frazzled. I just got back from Washington. I took the Trump shuttle this morning," I tell her, unable to make eye contact, all in a rush. "It was delightful. The service—really fabulous. I need a drink."

She smiles, amused, studying me in a shrewd way. "Was it?" she asks, not totally, I sense, without smugness.

"Yes." I can't really look at her and it takes immense effort to unfold the napkin, lay it across my lap, reposition it correctly, busy myself with the wineglass, praying for a waiter, the ensuing silence causing the loudest possible sound. "So did you watch *The Patty Winters Show* this morning?"

"No, I was out jogging," she says, leaning in. "It was about Michael J. Fox, right?"

"No," I correct her. "It was about Patrick Swayze."

"Oh really?" she asks, then, "It's hard to keep track. You're sure?"

"Yes. Patrick Swayze. I'm positive."

"How was it?"

"Well, it was very interesting," I tell her, breathing in air. "It was almost like a debate, about whether he's gotten cynical or not."

"Do you think he has?" she asks, still smiling.

"Well, no, I'm not sure," I start nervously. "It's an interesting question. It wasn't explored fully enough. I mean after *Dirty Dancing* I wouldn't think so, but with *Tiger Warsaw* I don't know. I might be crazy, but I thought I detected *some* bitterness. I'm not sure."

She stares at me, her expression unchanged.

"Oh, I almost forgot," I say, reaching into my pocket. "I wrote you a poem." I hand her the slip of paper. "Here." I feel sick and broken, tortured, really on the brink.

"Oh Patrick." She smiles. "How sweet."

"Well, you know," I say, looking down shyly.

Bethany takes the slip of paper and unfolds it.

"Read it," I urge enthusiastically.

She looks it over quizzically, puzzled, squinting, then she turns the page over to see if there's anything on the back. Something in her understands it's short and she looks back at the words written, scrawled in red, on the front of the page.

"It's like haiku, you know?" I say. "Read it. Go on."

She clears her throat and hesitantly begins reading, slowly, stopping often. " 'The poor nigger on the wall. Look at him.' " She pauses and squints again at the paper, then hesitantly resumes. " 'Look at the poor nigger. Look at the poor nigger . . . on . . . the . . . wall.' " She stops again, faltering, looks at me, confused, then back at the paper.

"Go on," I say, looking around for a waiter. "Finish it."

She clears her throat and staring steadily at the paper tries to read the rest of it in a voice below a whisper. " 'Fuck him . . . Fuck the nigger on the wall . . .' " She falters again, then reads the last sentence, sighing. " 'Black man . . . is . . . de . . . debil?' "

The couple at the next table have slowly turned to gaze over at us. The man looks aghast, the woman has an equally horrified expression on her face. I stare her down, glaring, until she looks back at her fucking salad.

"Well, Patrick," Bethany says, clearing her throat, trying to smile, handing the paper back to me.

"Yes?" I ask. "Well?"

"I can see that"—she stops, thinking—"that your sense of . . . social injustice is"—she clears her throat again and looks down—"still intact."

I take the paper back from her and slip it in my pocket and smile, still trying to keep a straight face, holding my body upright so she won't suspect me of cringing. Our waiter comes over to the table and I ask him what kinds of beer they serve.

"Heineken, Budweiser, Amstel Light," he recites.

"Yes?" I ask, staring at Bethany, gesturing for him to continue.

"That's, um, all, sir," he says.

"No Corona? No Kirin? No Grolsch? No Morretti?" I ask, confused, irate.

"I'm sorry, sir, but no," he says cautiously. "Only Heineken, Budweiser, Amstel Light."

"That's crazy," I sigh. "I'll have a J&B on the rocks. No, an Absolut martini. No, a J&B straight up."

"And I'll have another San Pellegrino," Bethany says.

"I'll have the same thing," I quickly add, my leg jerking up then down uncontrollably beneath the table.

"Okay. Would you like to hear the specials?" he asks.

"By all means," I spit out, then, calming down, smile reassuringly at Bethany.

"You're sure?" He laughs.

"Please," I say, unamused, studying the menu.

"For appetizers I have the sun-dried tomatoes and golden caviar with poblano chilies and I also have a fresh endive soup—"

"Wait a minute, wait a minute," I say, holding up a hand, stopping him. "Hold on a minute."

"Yes sir?" the waiter asks, confused.

"You have? You mean the *restaurant* has," I correct him. *"You* don't have any sun-dried tomatoes. The restaurant does. *You* don't have the poblano chilies. The restaurant does. Just, you know, clarify."

The waiter, stunned, looks at Bethany, who handles the situation deftly by asking him, "So how is the endive soup served?"

"Er . . . cold," the waiter says, not fully recovered from my outburst, sensing he's dealing with someone very, very on edge. He stops again, uncertain.

"Go on," I urge. "Please go on."

"It's served cold," he starts again. "And for entrées we have monkfish with mango slices and red snapper sandwich on brioche with maple syrup and"—he checks his pad again—"cotton."

"Mmmm, sounds delicious. Cotton, mmmm," I say, rubbing my hands together eagerly. "Bethany?"

"I'll have the ceviche with leeks and sorrel," Bethany says. "And the endive with . . . walnut dressing."

"Sir?" the waiter asks tentatively.

"I'll have . . ." I stop, scan the menu quickly. "I'll have the squid with pine nuts and can I have a slice of goat cheese, of *chèvre*"—I glance over at Bethany to see if she flinches at my mispronunciation—"with that and some . . . oh, some salsa on the side."

The waiter nods, leaves, we're left alone.

"Well." She smiles, then notices the table slightly shaking. "What's . . . wrong with your leg?"

"My leg? Oh." I look down at it, then back at her. "It's . . . the music. I like the music a lot. The music that's playing."

"What is it?" she asks, tilting her head, trying to catch a refrain of the New Age Muzak coming from the speakers hooked to the ceiling over the bar.

"It's . . . I think it's Belinda Carlisle," I guess. "I'm not sure."

"But . . ." she starts, then stops. "Oh, forget it."

"But what?"

"But I don't hear any singing." She smiles, looks down demurely.

I hold my leg still and pretend to listen. "But it's one of her songs," I say, then lamely add, "I think it's called 'Heaven Is a Place On Earth.' You know it."

"Listen," she says, "have you gone to any concerts lately?"

"No," I say, wishing she hadn't brought this, of all topics, up. "I don't like live music."

"*Live* music," she asks, intrigued, sipping San Pellegrino water.

"Yeah. You know. Like a band," I explain, sensing from her expression that I'm saying totally the wrong things. "Oh, I forgot. I did see U2."

"How were they?" she asks. "I liked the new CD a lot."

"They were great, just totally great. Just totally . . ." I pause, unsure of what to say. Bethany raises her eyebrows quizzically, wanting to know more. "Just totally . . . Irish."

"I've heard they're quite good live," she says, and her own voice has a light, musical lilt to it. "Who else do you like?"

"Oh you know," I say, completely stuck. "The Kingsmen. 'Louie, Louie.' That sort of stuff."

"Gosh, Patrick," she says, looking at every part of my face.

"What?" I panic, immediately touching my hair. "Too much mousse? You don't like the Kingsmen?"

"No." She laughs. "I just don't remember you being so tan back at school."

"I had a tan then, didn't I?" I ask. "I mean I wasn't Casper the Ghost or anything, was I?" I put my elbow on the table and flex my biceps, asking her to squeeze the muscle. After she touches it, reluctantly, I resume my questions. "Was I really not that tan at Harvard?" I ask mock-worriedly, but worriedly.

"No, no." She laughs. "You were definitely the George Hamilton of the class of eighty-four."

"Thanks," I say, pleased.

The waiter brings our drinks—two bottles of San Pellegrino water. Scene Two.

"So you're at Mill . . . on the water? Taffeta? What is it?" I ask. Her body, her skin tone, seem firm and rosy.

"Milbank Tweed," she says. "That's where I am."

"Well," I say, squeezing a lime into my glass. "That's just wonderful. Law school really paid off."

"And you're at . . . P & P?" she asks.

"Yes," I say.

She nods, pauses, wants to say something, debates whether she should, then asks, all in a matter of seconds: "But doesn't your family own—"

"I don't want to talk about this," I say, cutting her off. "But yes, Bethany. Yes."

"And you still work at P & P?" she asks. Each syllable is spaced so that it bursts, booming sonically, into my head.

"Yes," I say, looking furtively around the room.

"But—" She's confused. "Didn't your father—"

"Yes, of course," I say, interrupting. "Have you had the focaccia at Pooncakes?"

"*Patrick*."

"Yes?"

"What's wrong?"

"I just don't want to talk about . . ." I stop. "About work."

"Why not?"

"Because I hate it," I say. "Now listen, have you tried Pooncakes yet? I think Miller underrated it."

"Patrick," she says slowly. "If you're so uptight about work, why don't you just quit? You don't have to work."

"Because," I say, staring directly at her, "I . . . want . . . to . . . fit . . . in."

After a long pause, she smiles. "I see." There's another pause.

This one I break. "Just look at it as, well, a new approach to business," I say.

"How"—she stalls—"sensible." She stalls again. "How, um, practical."

Lunch is alternately a burden, a puzzle that needs to be solved, an obstacle, and then it floats effortlessly into the realm of relief and I'm able to give a skillful performance—my overriding intelligence tunes in and lets me know that it can sense how much she wants me, but I hold back, uncommitted. She's also holding back, but flirting nonetheless. She has made a promise by asking me to lunch and I panic, once the squid is served, certain that I will never recover unless it's fulfilled. Other men notice her as they pass by our table. Sometimes I coolly bring my voice down to a whisper. I'm hearing things—noise, mysterious sounds, inside my head; her mouth opens, closes, swallows liquid, smiles, takes me in like a magnet covered with lipstick, mentions something involving fax machines twice. I finally order a J&B on the rocks, then a cognac. She has mint-coconut sorbet. I touch, hold her hand across the table, more than a friend. Sun pours into Vanities, the restaurant empties out, it nears three. She orders a glass of chardonnay, then another, then the check. She has relaxed but something happens. My heartbeat rises and falls, momentarily stabilizes. I listen carefully. Possibilities once imagined plummet. She lowers her eyes and when she looks back at me I lower mine.

"So," she asks. "Are you seeing anyone?"

"My life is essentially uncomplicated," I say thoughtfully, caught off guard.

"What does *that* mean?" she asks.

I take a sip of cognac and smile secretly to myself, teasing her, dashing her hopes, her dreams of being reunited.

"Are you seeing anyone, Patrick?" she asks. "Come on, tell me."

Thinking of Evelyn, I murmur to myself, "Yes."

"Who?" I hear her ask.

"A very large bottle of Desyrel," I say in a faraway voice, suddenly very sad.

"*What?*" she asks, smiling, but then she realizes something and shakes her head. "I shouldn't be drinking."

"No, I'm not really," I say, snapping out of it, then, not of my own accord, "I mean, does anyone really *see* anyone? Does anyone really *see* anyone else? Did *you* ever see *me*? *See?* What does that mean? Ha! *See?* Ha! I just don't get it. Ha!" I laugh.

After taking this in, she says, nodding, "That has a certain kind of tangled logic to it, I suppose."

Another long pause and I fearfully ask the next question. "Well, are *you* seeing anyone?"

She smiles, pleased with herself, and still looking down, admits, with incomparable clarity, "Well, yes, I have a boyfriend and—"

"Who?"

"What?" She looks up.

"Who is he? What's his name?"

"Robert Hall. Why?"

"With Salomon Brothers?"

"No, he's a chef."

"With Salomon Brothers?"

"Patrick, he's a *chef*. And co-owner of a restaurant."

"Which one?"

"Does it matter?"

"No, really, which one?" I ask, then under my breath, "I want to cross it out of my Zagat guide."

"It's called Dorsia," she says, then, "Patrick, are you okay?"

Yes, my brain does explode and my stomach bursts open inwardly—a spastic, acidic, gastric reaction; stars and planets, whole galaxies made up entirely of little white chef hats, race over the film of my vision. I choke out another question.

"Why Robert Hall?" I ask. "Why him?"

"Well, I don't know," she says, sounding a little tipsy. "I guess it has to do with being twenty-seven and—"

"Yeah? So am I. So is half of Manhattan. So what? That's no excuse to marry Robert Hall."

"*Marry?*" she asks, wide-eyed, defensive. "Did I say that?"

"Didn't you say marry?"

"No, I didn't, but who knows." She shrugs. "We might."

"Ter-rific."

"As I was saying, Patrick"—she glares at me, but in a playful way that makes me sick—"I think you know that, well, time is running out. That biological clock just won't stop ticking," she says, and I'm thinking: My god, it took only *two* glasses of chardonnay to get her to admit this? Christ, what a lightweight. "I want to have children."

"With Robert Hall?" I ask, incredulous. "You might as well do it with Captain Lou Albano, for Christ sakes. I just don't get you, Bethany."

She touches her napkin, looking down and then out onto the sidewalk, where waiters are setting up tables for dinner. I watch them too. "Why do I sense hostility on your part, Patrick?" she asks softly, then sips her wine.

"Maybe because I'm hostile," I spit out. "Maybe because you sense this."

"Jesus, Patrick," she says, searching my face, genuinely upset. "I thought you and Robert were friends."

"What?" I ask. "I'm confused."

"Weren't you and Robert friends?"

I pause, doubtful. "Were we?"

"Yes, Patrick, you *were*."

"Robert Hall, Robert Hall, Robert Hall," I mutter to myself, trying to remember. "Scholarship student? President of our senior class?" I think about it a second longer, then add, "Weak chin?"

"No, Patrick," she says. "The *other* Robert Hall."

"I'm confusing him with the *other* Robert Hall?" I ask.

"Yes, Patrick," she says exasperated.

Inwardly cringing, I close my eyes and sigh. "Robert Hall. Not the one whose parents own half of, like, Washington? Not the one who was"—I gulp—"captain of the crew team? Six feet?"

"Yes," she says. "*That* Robert Hall."

"But . . ." I stop.

"Yes? But *what*?" She seems prepared to wait for an answer.

"But he was a *fag*," I blurt out.

"No, he was *not*, Patrick," she says, clearly offended.

"I'm positive he was a fag." I start nodding my head.

"Why are you so positive?" she asks, not amused.

"Because he used to let frat guys—not the ones in my house—like, you know, gang bang him at parties and tie him up and stuff. At least, you know, that's what I've heard," I say sincerely, and then, more humiliated than I have ever been in my entire life, I confess, "Listen, Bethany, he offered me a . . . you know, a blow-job once. In the, um, civics section of the library."

"Oh my god," she gasps, disgusted. "Where's the check?"

"Didn't Robert Hall get kicked out for doing his thesis on Babar? Or something like Babar?" I ask. "Babar the elephant? The, oh Jesus, *French* elephant?"

"What are you *talking* about?"

"Listen to me," I say. "Didn't he go to business school at Kellogg? At Northwestern, right?"

"He dropped out," she says without looking at me.

"Listen," I touch her hand.

She flinches and pulls back.

I try to smile. "Robert Hall's not a fag—"

"I can assure you of that," she says a tad too smugly. How can anyone get indignant over Robert Hall? Instead of saying "Oh yeah, you dumb sorry bitch" I say soothingly, "I'm sure you can," then, "Tell me about him. I want to know how things stand with the two of you," and then, smiling, furious, full of rage, I apologize. "I'm sorry."

It takes some time but she finally relents and smiles back at me and I ask her, once again, "Tell me more," and then, under my breath, smiling a rictus at her, "I'd like to slice open your beaver." The chardonnay has mellowed her, so she softens and talks freely.

I think about other things while she describes her recent past: air, water, sky, time, a moment, a point somewhere when I wanted to show her everything beautiful in the world. I have no patience for revelations, for new beginnings, for events that take place beyond the realm of my immediate vision. A young girl, a freshman, I met in a bar in Cambridge my junior year at Harvard told me early one fall that "Life is full of endless possibilities." I tried valiantly not to choke on the beer nuts I was chewing while she gushed this kidney stone of wisdom, and I calmly washed them down with the rest of a Heineken, smiled and concentrated on the

dart game that was going on in the corner. Needless to say, she did
not live to see her sophomore year. That winter, her body was
found floating in the Charles River, decapitated, her head hung
from a tree on the bank, her hair knotted around a low-hanging
branch, three miles away. My rages at Harvard were less violent
than the ones now and it's useless to hope that my disgust will
vanish—there is just *no way*.

"Oh, Patrick," she's saying. "You're still the same. I don't know
if that's good or bad."

"Say it's good."

"Why? Is it?" she asks, frowning. "Was it? Then?"

"You only knew one facet of my personality," I say. "Student."

"Lover?" she asks, her voice reminding me of someone human.

My eyes fall on her coldly, untouched. Out on the street, music
that sounds like salsa blares. The waiter finally brings the check.

"I'll pay for it," I sigh.

"No," she says, opening her handbag. "*I* invited *you*."

"But I have a platinum American Express card," I tell her.

"But so do I," she says, smiling.

I pause, then watch her place the card on the tray the check
came on. Violent convulsions seem close at hand if I do not get up.
"The women's movement. Wow." I smile, unimpressed.

Outside, she waits on the sidewalk while I'm in the men's room
throwing up my lunch, spitting out the squid, undigested and less
purple than it was on my plate. When I come out of Vanities onto
the street, putting on my Wayfarers, chewing a Cert, I murmur
something to myself, and then I kiss her on the cheek and make up
something else. "Sorry it took so long. Had to call my lawyer."

"Oh?" she acts concerned—the dumb bitch.

"Just a friend of mine." I shrug. "Bobby Chambers. He's in
prison. Some friends of his, well, mainly *me*, are trying to remount
his defense," I say with another shrug, then, changing the subject,
"Listen."

"Yes?" she asks, smiling.

"It's late. I don't want to go back to the office," I say, checking
my Rolex. The sun, setting, glints off it, momentarily blinding her.
"Why don't you come up to my place?"

"What?" She laughs.

"Why don't you come up to my place?" I suggest again.

"Patrick." She laughs suggestively. "Are you serious?"

"I have a bottle of Pouilly-Fuissé, *chilled*, huh?" I say, arching my eyebrows.

"Listen, that line might've worked at Harvard but"—she laughs, then continues—"um, we're older now and . . ." She stops.

"And . . . what?" I ask.

"I shouldn't have had that wine at lunch," she says again.

We start walking. It's a hundred degrees outside, impossible to breathe. It's not day, it's not night. The sky seems yellow. I hand a beggar on the corner of Duane and Greenwich a dollar just to impress her.

"Listen, come over," I say again, almost whining. "Come on over."

"I can't," she says. "The air-conditioning in my office is broken but I can't. I'd like to but I can't."

"Aw come on," I say, grabbing her shoulders, giving them a good-natured squeeze.

"Patrick, I have to be back at the office," she groans, protesting weakly.

"But you'll be *swelt*ering in there," I point out.

"I have no choice."

"Come on." Then, trying to entice her, "I have a 1940s Durgin Gorham four-piece sterling silver tea and coffee set I'd like to show you."

"I can't." She laughs, putting on her sunglasses.

"Beth*any*," I say, warning her.

"Listen," she says, relenting. "I'll buy you a Dove Bar. Have a Dove Bar instead."

"I'm appalled. Do you know how many grams of fat, of *sodium*, are in the chocolate covering alone?" I gasp, mock horrified.

"Come on," she says, "You don't need to worry about that."

"No, *you* come on," I say, walking in front of her for a little while so she won't sense any aggressiveness on my part. "Listen, come by for a drink and then we'll walk over to Dorsia and I'll meet Robert, okay?" I turn around, still walking, but backward now. "*Please?*"

"Patrick," she says. "You're begging."

"I really want to show you that Durgin Gorham tea set." I pause. "Please?" I pause again. "It cost me three and a half thousand dollars."

She stops walking because I stop, looks down, and when she looks back up her brow, both cheeks, are damp with a layer of perspiration, a fine sheen. She's hot. She sighs, smiling to herself. She looks at her watch.

"Well?" I ask.

"If I did . . ." she starts.

"Y-e-es?" I ask, stretching the word out.

"If I did, I have to make a phone call."

"No, negative," I say, waving down a cab. "Call from my place."

"*Patrick*," she protests. "There's a phone right over there."

"Let's go now," I say. "There's a taxi."

In the cab heading toward the Upper West Side, she says, "I shouldn't have had that wine."

"Are you drunk?"

"No," she says, fanning herself with a playbill from *Les Misérables* someone left in the backseat of the cab, which isn't air-conditioned and even with both windows open she keeps fanning herself. "Just slightly . . . tipsy."

We both laugh for no reason and she leans into me, then realizes something and pulls back. "You have a doorman, right?" she asks suspiciously.

"Yes." I smile, turned on by her unawareness of just how close to peril she really is.

Inside my apartment. She moves into the living room area, nodding her head approvingly, murmuring, "Very nice, Mr. Bateman, very nice." Meanwhile I'm locking the door, making sure it's bolted shut, then I move over to the bar and pour some J&B into a glass while she runs her hand over the Wurlitzer jukebox, inspecting it. I've started growling to myself and my hands are shaking so badly I decide to forgo any ice and then I'm in the living room, standing behind her while she looks up at the David Onica that's hung above the fireplace. She cocks her head, studying it, then she starts giggling and looks at me, puzzled, then back at the Onica, still laughing. I don't ask what's wrong—I could care less. Downing the drink in a single gulp, I move over to the Anaholian white-oak armoire where I keep a brand-new nail gun I bought last week at a hardware store near my office in Wall Street. After I've slipped on a pair of black leather gloves, I make sure the nail gun is loaded.

"Patrick?" Bethany asks, still giggling.

"Yes?" I say, then, "Darling?"

"Who hung the Onica?" she asks.

"You like it?" I ask.

"It's fine, but . . ." She stops, then says, "I'm pretty sure it's hung upside down."

"What?"

"*Who* hung the Onica?"

"I did," I say, my back still to her.

"You've hung the Onica *upside down*." She laughs.

"Hmmm?" I'm standing at the armoire, squeezing the nail gun, getting used to its weight in my gloved fist.

"I can't believe it's upside down," she says. "How long has it been this way?"

"A millennium," I whisper, turning around, nearing her.

"What?" she asks, still studying the Onica.

"I said, what in the fuck are you doing with Robert Hall?" I whisper.

"What did you say?" As if in slow motion, like in a movie, she turns around.

I wait until she's seen the nail gun and the gloved hands to scream, "*What the fuck are you doing with Robert Hall?*"

Perhaps in instinct, perhaps from memory, she makes a futile dash for the front door, crying out. Though the chardonnay has dulled her reflexes, the Scotch I've drunk has sharpened mine, and effortlessly I'm leaping in front of her, blocking her escape, knocking her unconscious with four blows to the head from the nail gun. I drag her back into the living room, laying her across the floor over a white Voilacutro cotton sheet, and then I stretch her arms out, placing her hands flat on thick wooden boards, palms up, and nail three fingers on each hand, at random, to the wood by their tips. This causes her to regain consciousness and she starts screaming. After I've sprayed Mace into her eyes, mouth, into her nostrils, I place a camel-hair coat from Ralph Lauren over her head, which drowns out the screams, sort of. I keep shooting nails into her hands until they're both covered—nails bunched together, twisted over each other in places, making it impossible for her to try and sit up.

I have to remove her shoes, which slightly disappoints me, but she's kicking at the floor violently, leaving black scuff marks on the stained white oak. During this period I keep shouting "You bitch," at her and then my voice drops to a raspy whisper and into her ear I drool the line "You fucking cunt."

Finally, in agony, after I've taken the coat off her face, she starts pleading, or at least tries to, the adrenaline momentarily overpowering the pain. "Patrick oh god stop it please oh god stop hurting me . . ." But, typically, the pain returns—it's too intense not to—and she passes out again and vomits, while unconscious, and I have to hold her head up so she doesn't choke on it and then I Mace her again. The fingers I haven't nailed I try to bite off, almost succeeding on her left thumb which I manage to chew all the flesh off of, leaving the bone exposed, and then I Mace her, needlessly, once more. I place the camel-hair coat back over her head in case she wakes up screaming, then set up the Sony palm-sized Handycam so I can film all of what follows. Once it's placed on its stand and running on automatic, with a pair of scissors I start to cut off her dress and when I get up to her chest I occasionally stab at her breasts, accidentally (not really) slicing off one of her nipples through the bra. She starts screaming again once I've ripped her dress off, leaving Bethany in only her bra, its right cup darkened with blood, and her panties, which are soaked with urine, saving them for later.

I lean in above her and shout, over her screams, "Try to scream, scream, keep screaming . . ." I've opened all the windows and the door to my terrace and when I stand over her, the mouth opens and not even screams come out anymore, just horrible, guttural, animal-like noises, sometimes interrupted by retching sounds. "Scream, honey," I urge, "keep screaming." I lean down, even closer, brushing her hair back. "No one cares. No one will help you . . ." She tries to cry out again but she's losing consciousness and she's capable of only a weak moan. I take advantage of her helpless state and, removing my gloves, force her mouth open and with the scissors cut out her tongue, which I pull easily from her mouth and hold in the palm of my hand, warm and still bleeding, seeming so much smaller than in her mouth, and throw it against the wall, where it sticks for a moment, leaving a stain, before falling to the floor with a tiny wet slap. Blood gushes out of her mouth and

I have to hold her head up so she won't choke. Then I fuck her in the mouth, and after I've ejaculated and pulled out, I Mace her some more.

Later, when she briefly regains consciousness, I put on a porkpie hat I was given by one of my girlfriends freshman year at Harvard.

"Remember *this*?" I shout, towering over her. "And look at *this*!" I scream triumphantly, holding up a cigar. "I *still* smoke cigars. Ha. See? A cigar." I light it with steady, bloodstained fingers, and her face, pale to the point of blueness, keeps contracting, twitching with pain, her eyes, dull with horror, close, then open halfway, her life reduced to nightmare.

"And another thing," I yell, pacing. "It's not Garrick Anderson either. The suit is by *Armani*! *Giorgio* Armani." I pause spitefully and, leaning into her, sneer, "And you thought it was *Henry Stuart*. Jesus." I slap her hard across the face and hiss the words "Dumb bitch," spraying her face with spit, but it's covered with so much Mace that she probably can't even feel it, so I Mace her again and then I try to fuck her in the mouth once more but I can't come so I stop.

THURSDAY

Later, the next night in fact, three of us, Craig McDermott, Courtney and myself, are in a cab heading toward Nell's and talking about Evian water. Courtney, in an Armani mink, has just admitted, giggling, that she uses Evian for ice cubes, which sparks a conversation about the differences in bottled water, and at Courtney's request we each try to list as many brands as we can.

Courtney starts, counting each name off on one of her fingers. "Well, there's Sparcal, Perrier, San Pellegrino, Poland Spring, Calistoga . . ." she stops, stuck, and looks over at McDermott for help.

He sighs, then lists, "Canadian Spring, Canadian Calm, Montclair, which is also from Canada, Vittel from France, Crodo, which is Italian . . ." He stops and rubs his chin thoughtfully, thinking of

one more, then announces it as if surprised. "Elan." And though it
seems he's on the verge of naming another one, Craig lapses into
an unilluminating silence.

"Elan?" Courtney asks.

"It's from Switzerland," he says.

"Oh," she says, then turns to me. "It's your turn, Patrick."

Staring out the window of the cab, lost in thought, the silence
I'm causing filling me with a nameless dread, numbly, by rote, I list
the following. "You forgot Alpenwasser, Down Under, Schat, which
is from Lebanon, Qubol and Cold Springs—"

"I said that one already," Courtney cuts in, accusingly.

"No," I say. "You said Poland *Spring*."

"Is that right?" Courtney murmurs, then tugging at Mc-
Dermott's overcoat, "Is he right, Craig?"

"Probably." McDermott shrugs. "I guess."

"You must also remember that one should always buy mineral
water in *glass* bottles. You shouldn't buy it in plastic ones," I say
ominously, then wait for one of them to ask me why.

"Why?" Courtney's voice is tinged with actual interest.

"Because it oxidizes," I explain. "You want it to be crisp, with
no aftertaste."

After a long, confused, Courtney-like pause, McDermott
admits, staring out the window, "He's right."

"I really don't understand the differences in water," Courtney
murmurs. She's sitting between McDermott and myself in the back
of the cab and under the mink has on a wool twill suit by Givenchy,
tights by Calvin Klein and shoes by Warren Susan Allen Edmonds.
Earlier, in this same cab, when I touched the mink suggestively,
with no intent other than to check its quality and she could sense
this, Courtney quietly asked me if I had a breath mint. I said
nothing.

"What do you mean?" McDermott inquires solemnly.

"Well," she says, "I mean what's *really* the difference between
something like spring water and natural water, for instance, or, I
mean, *is* there one?"

"*Courtney*. Natural water is any water from an underground
source," Craig sighs, still staring out the window. "Mineral content
hasn't been changed, although the water may have been disinfected

or filtered." McDermott is wearing a wool tuxedo with notched lapels by Gianni Versace, and he reeks of Xeryus.

I momentarily break out of my conscious inertia to explain further: "And in spring water, minerals may have been added or removed and it's usually filtered, not processed." I pause. "Seventy-five percent of all bottled water in America is actually spring water." I pause again, then ask the cab, "Did anyone know that?"

A long, soulless pause follows and then Courtney asks another question, this one only half finished. "The differences between distilled and purified water is . . .?"

I'm not really listening to any of this conversation, not even to myself, because I'm thinking of ways to get rid of Bethany's body, or at least debating whether or not I should keep it in my apartment another day or so. If I decide to get rid of it tonight, I can easily stuff what's left of her into a Hefy garbage bag and leave it in the stairwell; or I can exert the extra effort and drag it into the street, leaving it with the rest of the trash on the curb. I could even take it to the apartment in Hell's Kitchen and pour lime over it, smoke a cigar and watch it dissolve while listening to my Walkman, but I want to keep the men's bodies separate from the women's, and besides, I also want to watch *Bloodhungry*, the videotape I rented this afternoon—its ad line reads, "Some clowns make you laugh, but Bobo will make you die and then he'll eat your body"—and a midnight trip to Hell's Kitchen, even without a stop at Bellvue's for a small bite to eat, wouldn't give me enough time. Bethany's bones and most of her intestines and flesh will probably get dumped into the incinerator down the hall from my apartment.

Courtney, McDermott and I have just left a Morgan Stanley party that took place near the Seaport at the tip of Manhattan in a new club called Goldcard, which seemed like a vast city of its own and where I ran into Walter Rhodes, a total Canadian, whom I haven't seen since Exeter and who also, like McDermott, reeked of Xeryus, and I actually told him, "Listen, I'm trying to stay away from people. I'm avoiding even speaking to them," and then I asked to be excused. Only slightly stunned, Walter said, "Uh, sure, I, um, understand." I'm wearing a six-button double-breasted wool-crepe tuxedo with pleated trousers and a silk grosgrain bow tie, all by Valentino. Luis Carruthers is in Atlanta for the week. I did a line of coke with Herbert Gittes at Goldcard and before McDermott hailed this cab to head for Nell's I took a Halcion to get rid of the edge from the cocaine, but it hasn't sunk in yet. Courtney seems attracted to McDermott and since her Chembank card wasn't functioning tonight, at least not at the automated teller we stopped at (the reason being she uses it too often to cut lines of coke with, though she would never admit this; cocaine residue has, at various times, fucked up my card also) and McDermott's *was* working, she bypassed *mine* in favor of *his*, which means, knowing Courtney, that she wants to *fuck* McDermott. But it doesn't really matter. Even though I'm more handsome than Craig, we both look pretty much the same. Talking animals were the topic of this morning's *Patty Winters Show*. An octopus was floating in a makeshift aquarium with a microphone attached to one of its tentacles and it kept asking—or so its "trainer," who is positive that mollusks have vocal cords, assured us—for "cheese." I watched, vaguely transfixed, until I started to sob. A beggar dressed as a Hawaiian frets over a garbage can on the darkened corner of Eighth and Tenth.

"With distilled or purified water," McDermott is saying, "most of the minerals have been removed. The water has been boiled and the steam condensed into purified water."

"Whereas distilled water has a flat taste and it's usually not for drinking." I find myself yawning.

"And mineral water?" Courtney asks.

"It's not defined by the—" McDermott and I start simultaneously.

"Go ahead," I say, yawning again, causing Courtney to yawn also.

"No, you go ahead," he says apathetically.

"It's not defined by the FDA," I tell her. "It has no chemicals or salts or sugars or caffeine."

"And sparkling water gets its fizz from carbon dioxide, right?" she asks.

"Yes." Both McDermott and I nod, staring straight ahead.

"I knew that," she says hesitantly, and by the tone of her voice I can sense, without looking over, that she probably smiles when she says this.

"But only buy *naturally* sparkling water," I caution. "Because *that* means the carbon dioxide content is in the water at its source."

"Club soda and seltzer, for example, are artificially carbonated," McDermott explains.

"White Rock seltzer is an exception," I mention, nonplussed by McDermott's ridiculous, incessant one-upmanship. "Ramlösa sparkling mineral water is also very good."

The cab is about to turn onto Fourteenth Street, but maybe four or five limousines are trying to make the same right so we miss the light. I curse the driver but an old Motown song from the sixties, maybe it's the Supremes, plays muted, up front, the sound blocked by the fibreglass partition. I try to open it but it's locked and won't slide across. Courtney asks, "What kind should you drink after exercising?"

"Well," I sigh. "Whatever it is, it should be really cold."

"Because?" she asks.

"Because it's absorbed faster than if it was at room temperature." Absently I check my Rolex. "It should probably be water. Evian. But not in plastic."

"My trainer says Gatorade's okay," McDermott counters.

"But don't you think water is the best fluid replacer since it enters the bloodstream faster than *any* other liquid?" I can't help but add, "*Buddy?*"

I check my watch again. If I have one J&B on the rocks at Nell's I can make it home in time to watch all of *Bloodhungry* by two. Again it's silent in the cab, which moves steadily toward the crowd outside the club, the limousines dropping off passengers then moving on, each of us concentrating on that, and also on the sky above the city, which is heavy, looming with dark clouds. The limousines keep blaring their horns at each other, solving nothing. My throat, because of the coke I did with Gittes, feels parched and I swallow, trying to wet it. Posters for a sale at Crabtree & Evelyn line the boarded windows of abandoned tenement buildings on the other side of this street. Spell "mogul," Bateman. How do you spell mogul? M-o-g-u-l. Mo-gul. Mog-ul. Ice, ghosts, aliens—

"I don't like Evian," McDermott says somewhat sadly. "It's too sweet." He looks so miserable when he admits this that it moves me to agree.

Glancing over at him in the darkness of the cab, realizing he's probably going to end up in bed with Courtney tonight, I feel an instantaneous moment of pity for him.

"Yes, McDermott," I say slowly. "Evian *is* too sweet."

Earlier, there was so much of Bethany's blood pooled on the floor that I could make out my reflection in it while I reached for one of my cordless phones, and I watched myself make a haircut appointment at Gio's. Courtney breaks my trance by admitting, "I was afraid to try Pellegrino for the first time." She looks over at me nervously—expecting me to . . . what, agree?—then at McDermott, who offers her a wan, tight smile. "But once I did, it was . . . fine."

"How courageous," I murmur, yawning again, the cab inching its way toward Nell's, then, raising my voice, "Listen, does anyone know of a device you can hook up to your phone to simulate that call-waiting sound?"

Back at my place I stand over Bethany's body, sipping a drink contemplatively, studying its condition. Both eyelids are open half-way and her lower teeth look as if they're jutting out since her lips have been torn—actually bitten—off. Earlier in the day I had sawed off her left arm, which is what finally killed her, and right now I pick it up, holding it by the bone that protrudes from where her hand used to be (I have no idea where it is now: the freezer? the closet?), clenching it in my fist like a pipe, flesh and muscle still clinging to it though a lot of it has been hacked or gnawed off, and I bring it down on her head. It takes very few blows, five or six at most, to smash her jaw open completely, and only two more for her face to cave in on itself.

WHITNEY HOUSTON

Whitney Houston burst onto the music scene in 1985 with her self-titled LP which had four number one hit singles on it, including "The Greatest Love of All," "You Give Good Love" and "Saving All My Love for You," plus it won a Grammy Award for best pop vocal performance by a female and two American Music Awards, one for best rhythm and blues single and another for best rhythm and blues video. She was also cited as best new artist of the year by *Billboard* and by *Rolling Stone* magazine. With all this hype one might expect the album to be an anticlimatic, lackluster affair, but the surprise is that *Whitney Houston* (Arista) is one of the warmest, most complex and altogether satisfying rhythm and blues records of the decade and Whitney herself has a voice that defies belief. From the elegant, beautiful photo of her on the cover of the album (in a gown by Giovanne De Maura) and its fairly sexy counterpart on the back (in a bathing suit by Norma Kamali) one knows that this isn't going to be a blandly professional affair; the record *is* smooth but intense and Whitney's voice leaps across so many boundaries and is so versatile (though she's mainly a *jazz* singer) that it's hard to take in the album on a first listening. But you won't want to. You'll want to savor it over many.

It opens with "You Give Good Love" and "Thinking About You," both produced and arranged by Kashif, and they emanate warm, lush jazz arrangements but with a contemporary synthesized beat and though they're both really good songs, the album doesn't get kicking until "Someone for Me" which was produced by Jermaine Jackson, where Whitney sings longingly against a jazz-disco background and the difference between her longing and the sprightliness of the song is very moving. The ballad "Saving All My Love for You" is the sexiest, most romantic song on the record. It also has a killer saxophone solo by Tom Scott and one can hear the influences of sixties girl-group pop in it (it was cowritten by Gerry Goffin) but the sixties girl groups were never this emotional or sexy (or as well produced) as this song is. "Nobody Loves Me Like You Do" is a glorious duet with Jermaine Jackson (who also produced it) and just one example of how sophisticated lyrically this album is. The last thing it suffers from is a paucity of decent lyrics which is what usually happens when a singer doesn't write her own material and has to have her producer choose it. But Whitney and company have picked well here.

The dance single "How Will I Know" (my vote for best dance song of the 1980s) is a joyous ode to a girl's nervousness about whether another guy is interested in her. It's got a great keyboard riff and it's the only track on the album produced by wunderkind producer Narada Michael Walden. My own personal favourite ballad (aside from "The Greatest Love of All"—her crowning achievement) is "All at Once" which is about how a young woman realizes all at once her lover is fading away from her and it's accompanied by a gorgeous string arrangement. Even though nothing on the album sounds like filler, the only track that might come close is "Take Good Care of My Heart," another duet with Jermaine Jackson. The problem is that it strays from the album's jazz roots and seems too influenced by 1980s dance music.

But Whitney's talent is restored with the overwhelming "The Greatest Love of All," one of the best, most powerful songs ever written about self-preservation and dignity. From the first line (Michael Masser and Linda Creed are credited as the writers) to the last, it's a state-of-the-art ballad about believing in yourself. It's a powerful statement and one that Whitney sings with a grandeur that approaches the sublime. Its universal message crosses all boundaries and instills one with the hope that it's not too late for us to better ourselves, to act kinder. Since it's impossible in the world we live in to empathize with others, we can always empathize with ourselves. It's an important message, crucial really, and it's beautifully stated on this album.

Her second effort, *Whitney* (Arista: 1987), had four number one singles, "I Wanna Dance with Somebody," "So Emotional," "Didn't We Almost Have It All?" and "Where Do Broken Hearts Go?" and was mostly produced by Narada Michael Walden and though it's not as serious an effort as *Whitney Houston* it's hardly a victim of Sophomore Slump. It starts off with the bouncy, danceable "I Wanna Dance with Somebody (Who Loves Me)" which is in the same vein as the last album's irrepressible "How Will I Know." This is followed by the sensuous "Just the Lonely Talking Again" and it reflects the serious jazz influence that permeated the first album and one can also sense a newfound artistic maturity in Whitney's voice—she did all the vocal arrangements on this album—and this is all very evident on "Love Will Save the Day" which is the most ambitious song Whitney's yet performed. It was produced by Jellybean Benitez and it pulsates with an uptempo intensity and like most of the songs on this album it reflects a grownup's awareness of the world we all live in. She sings and we believe it. This is quite a change from the softer, little-girl image that was so appealing on the first album.

She projects an even more adult image on the Michael Masser-produced "Didn't We Almost Have It All," a song about meeting up with a long-lost lover and letting him know your feelings about the past affair, and it's Whitney at her most poetic. And as on most of the ballads there's a gorgeous string arrangement. "So Emotional" is in the same vein as "How Will I Know" and "I Wanna Dance with Somebody" but it's even more rock-influenced and, like all the songs on *Whitney*, played by a terrific backup studio band with Narada on drum machine, Wolter Afanasieff on the synthesizer and synth bass, Corrado Rustici on synth guitar, and someone listed as Bongo Bob on percussion programming and drum sampling. "Where You Are" is the only song on the album produced by Kashif and it bears his indelible imprint of professionalism—it has a smooth, gleaming sound and sheen to it with a funky sax solo by Vincent Henry. It sounded like a hit single to me (but then all the songs on the album do) and I wondered why it wasn't released as one.

"Love Is a Contact Sport" is the album's real surprise—a big-sounding, bold, sexy number that, in terms of production, is the album's centerpiece, and it has great lyrics along with a good beat. It's one of my favorites. On "You're Still My Man" you can hear how clearly Whitney's voice is like an instrument—a flawless, warm machine that almost overpowers the sentiment of her music, but the lyrics and the melodies are too distinctive, too strong to let any singer, even one of Whitney's caliber, overshadow them. "For the Love of You" shows off Narada's brilliant drum programming capabilities and its jazzy modern feel harks back not only to purveyors of modern jazz like Michael Jackson and Sade but also to other artists, like Miles Davis, Paul Butterfield and Bobby McFerrin.

"Where Do Broken Hearts Go" is the album's most powerful emotional statement of innocence lost and trying to regain the safety of childhood. Her voice is as lovely and controlled as it ever has been and it leads up to "I Know Him So Well," the most moving moment on the record because it's first and foremost a duet with her mother, Cissy. It's a ballad about . . . who?—a lover shared? a long-lost father?—with a combination of longing, regret, determination and beauty that ends the album on a graceful, perfect note. We can expect new things from Whitney (she made a stunning gift to the 1988 Olympics with the ballad "One Moment in Time") but even if we didn't, she would remain the most exciting and original black jazz voice of her generation.

DINNER WITH SECRETARY

Monday night at eight o'clock. I'm in my office attempting yesterday's *New York Times* Sunday crossword puzzle, listening to rap music on the stereo, trying to fathom its popularity, since a little blond hardbody I met at Au Bar two nights ago told me that rap is all she listens to, and though later I beat the living shit out of her at someone's apartment in the Dakota (she was almost decapitated; hardly a strange experience for me), earlier this morning her taste in music haunted my memory and I had to stop at Tower Records on the Upper West Side and buy ninety dollars' worth of rap CDs but, as expected, I'm at a loss: niggerish voices uttering ugly words like *digit, pudding, chunk*. Jean sits at her desk, which is piled high with reams of documents that I want her to go over. Today has not been bad: I worked out for two hours before the office; the new Tobison Hirsch restaurant called Finna opened in Chelsea; Evelyn left two messages on my answering machine and another with Jean letting me know that she'll be in Boston for most of the week; and best of all, *The Patty Winters Show* this morning was in two parts. The first was an exclusive interview with Donald Trump, the second was a report on women who've been tortured. I'm supposed to have dinner with Madison Grey and David Campion at Café Luxembourg, but at eight-fifteen I find out that Luis Carruthers is going to be dining with us so I call up Campion, the dumb bastard, and cancel, then spend minutes debating about what I should do with the rest of the evening. Looking out my window, I realize that within moments the sky above this city will be completely dark.

Jean peers into my office, knocking gently on the half-open door. I pretend not to acknowledge her presence, though I'm not sure why, since I'm kind of lonely. She moves up to the desk. I'm still staring at the crossword puzzle with my Wayfarers on, stunned but for no real reason.

She places a file on top of the desk before asking "Doin' the crossword?" dropping the g in "doing"—pathetic gesture of intimacy, an irritating stab at forced friendliness. I gag inwardly, then nod without looking up at her.

"Need help?" she asks, moving cautiously around the desk to where I sit, and she leans over my shoulder to offer assistance. I've already filled in every space with either the word *meat* or *bone* and she emits only a slight gasp when noticing this, and when she sees the pile of No. 2 pencils I've snapped in half lying on my desk she dutifully picks them up and walks out of the room.

"Jean?" I call.

"Yes, Patrick?" She reenters the office trying to downplay her eagerness.

"Would you like to accompany me to dinner?" I ask, still staring at the crossword, gingerly erasing the *m* in one of the many *meats* I've filled the puzzle with. "That is, if you're not . . . doing anything."

"Oh no," she answers too quickly and then, I think, realizing this quickness, says, "I have no plans."

"Well, isn't this a coincidence," I ask, looking up, lowering my Wayfarers.

She laughs lightly but there's a real urgency in it, something uncomfortable, and this does little in the way of making me feel less sick.

"I guess," she shrugs.

"I also have tickets to a . . . a Milla Vanilla concert, if you'd like to go," I tell her casually.

Confused, she asks, "Really? Who?"

"Milla . . . Vanilla," I repeat slowly.

"Milla . . . Vanilla?" she asks uncomfortably.

"Milla . . . Vanilla," I say. "I think that's what their name is."

She says, "I'm not sure."

"About going?"

"No . . . of the name." She concentrates, then says, "I think they're called . . . Milli Vanilli."

I pause for a long time before saying, "Oh."

She stands there, nods once.

"It doesn't matter," I say—I don't have any tickets to it anyway. "It's months from now."

"Oh," she says, nodding again. "Okay."

"Listen, where should we go?" I lean back and pull my Zagat from the desk's top drawer.

She pauses, afraid of what to say, taking my question as a test she needs to pass, and then, unsure she's chosen the right answer, offers, "Anywhere you want?"

"No, no, no." I smile, leafing through the booklet. "How about anywhere *you* want?"

"Oh Patrick," she sighs. "I can't make this decision."

"No, come on," I urge. "Anywhere you want."

"Oh I can't." Helplessly, she sighs again. "I don't know."

"Come on," I urge her, "where do you want to go? Anywhere you want. Just say it. I can get us in anywhere."

She thinks about it for a long time and then, sensing her time is running out, timidly asks, trying to impress me, "What about . . . Dorsia?"

I stop looking through the Zagat guide and without glancing up, smiling tightly, stomach dropping, I silently ask myself, Do I really want to say no? Do I really want to say I can't possibly get us in? Is that what I'm really prepared to do? Is that what I really want to do?

"So-o-o-o," I say, placing the book down, then nervously opening it up again to find the number. "Dorsia is where Jean wants to go . . ."

"Oh I don't know," she says, confused. "No, we'll go anywhere you want."

"Dorsia is . . . fine," I say casually, picking up the phone, and with a trembling finger very quickly dial the seven dreaded numbers, trying to remain cool. Instead of the busy signal I'm expecting, the phone actually rings at Dorsia and after two rings the same harassed voice I've grown accustomed to for the past three months answers, shouting out, "Dorsia, yes?" the room behind the voice a deafening hum.

"Yes, can you take two tonight, oh, let's say, in around twenty minutes?" I ask, checking my Rolex, offering Jean a wink. She seems impressed.

"We are totally booked," the maître d' shouts out smugly.

"Oh, really?" I say, trying to look pleased, on the verge of vomiting. "That's great."

"I said we are totally booked," he shouts.

"Two at nine?" I say. "Perfect."

"There are no tables available tonight," the maître d', unflappable, drones. "The waiting list is also totally booked." He hangs up.

"See you then." I hang up too, and with a smile that tries its best to express pleasure at her choice, I find myself fighting for breath, every muscle tensed sharply. Jean is wearing a wool jersey and flannel dress by Calvin Klein, an alligator belt with a silver buckle by Barry Kieselstein Cord, silver earrings and clear stockings also by Calvin Klein. She stands there in front of the desk, confused.

"Yes?" I ask, walking over to the coatrack. "You're dressed . . . okay."

She pauses. "You didn't give them a name," she says softly.

I think about this while putting on my Armani jacket and while reknotting my Armani silk tie, and without stammering I tell her, "They . . . know me."

While the maître d' seats a couple who I'm pretty sure are Kate Spencer and Jason Lauder, Jean and I move up to his podium, where the reservation book lies open, names absurdly legible, and leaning over it casually I spot the only name for two at nine without a line drawn through it, which happens to be—oh Jesus—*Schrawtz*. I sigh, and tapping my foot, my mind racing, I try to concoct some kind of feasible plan. Suddenly I turn to Jean and say, "Why don't you go to the women's room."

She's looking around the restaurant, taking it in. Chaos. People are waiting ten deep at the bar. The maître d' seats the couple at a table in the middle of the room. Sylvester Stallone and a bimbo sit in the front booth that Sean and I sat in just weeks before, much to my sickened amazement, and his bodyguards are piled into the booth next to that, and the owner of Petty's, Norman Prager, lounges in the third. Jean turns her head to me and shouts "What?" over the din.

"Don't you want to use the ladies' room?" I ask. The maître d' nears us, picking his way through the packed restaurant, unsmiling.

"Why? I mean . . . do I?" she asks, totally confused.

"Just . . . go," I hiss, desperately squeezing her arm.

"But I don't need to go, Patrick," she protests.

"Oh Christ," I mutter. Now it's too late anyway.

The maître d' walks up to the podium and inspects the book, takes a phone call, hangs up in a matter of seconds, then looks us over, not exactly displeased. The maître d' is at least fifty and has a ponytail. I clear my throat twice to get his full attention, make some kind of lame eye contact.

"Yes?" he asks, as if harassed.

I give him a dignified expression before sighing inside. "Reservations at nine . . ." I gulp. "For two."

"Ye-e-es?" he asks suspiciously, drawing the word out. "Name?" he says, then turns to a passing waiter, eighteen and model handsome, who'd asked, "Where's da ice?" He's glaring and shouting, "Not . . . now. Okay? How many times do you need to be told?" The waiter shrugs, humbly, and then the maître d' points off toward the bar, "Da *ice* is over dere!" He turns back to us and I am genuinely frightened.

"Name," he commands.

And I'm thinking: Of all the fucking names, why *this* one? "Um, Schrawtz"—oh god—"Mr. and Mrs. Schrawtz." My face, I'm sure, is ashen and I say the name mechanically, but the maître d' is too busy to not buy it and I don't even bother to face Jean, who I'm sure is totally bewildered by my behavior as we're led to the Schrawtzes' table, which I'm sure probably sucks though I'm relieved anyway.

Menus already lie on the table but I'm so nervous the words and even the prices look like hieroglyphics and I'm completely at a loss. A waiter takes our drink order—the same one who couldn't locate the ice—and I find myself saying things, without listening to Jean, like "Protecting the ozone layer is a really cool idea" and telling knock-knock jokes. I smile, fixing it on my face, in another country, and it takes no time at all—minutes, really, the waiter doesn't even get a chance to tell us about the specials—for me to notice the tall, handsome couple by the podium conferring with the maître d', and after sighing very deeply, light-headed, stammering, I mention to Jean, "Something bad is happening."

She looks up from the menu and puts down the iceless drink she's been sipping. "Why? What's wrong?"

The maître d' is glaring over at us, at *me*, from across the room as he leads the couple toward our table. If the couple had been short, dumpy, excessively Jewish, I could've kept this table, even without the aid of a fifty, but this couple looks like they've just strolled out of a Ralph Lauren ad, and though Jean and I do too (and so does the rest of the whole goddamn restaurant), the man is wearing a tuxedo and the girl—a totally fuckable babe—is covered with jewels. This is reality, and as my loathsome brother Sean would say, I have to deal with it. The maître d' now stands at the table, hands clasped behind his back, unamused, and after a long pause asks, "Mr. and Mrs. . . . *Schrawtz?*"

"Yes?" I play it cool.

He just stares. This is accompanied by an abnormal silence. His ponytail, gray and oily, hangs like some kind of malignancy below his collar.

"You know," I finally say, somewhat suavely, "I happen to know the chef."

He continues staring. So, no doubt, does the couple behind him.

After another long pause, for no real reason, I ask, "Is he . . . in Aspen?"

This is getting nowhere. I sigh and return to Jean, who looks completely mystified. "Let's go, okay?" She nods dumbly. Humiliated, I take Jean's hand and we get up—she slower than I—brushing past the maître d' and the couple, and make our way back through the crowded restaurant and then we're outside and I'm utterly devastated and murmuring robotically to myself "I should have known better I should have known better I should," but Jean skips down the street laughing, pulling me along, and when I finally notice her unexpected mirth, between giggles she lets out "That was *so* funny" and then, squeezing my clenched fist, she lets me know "Your sense of humor is so *spontaneous*." Shaken, walking stiffly by her side, ignoring her, I ask myself "Where . . . to . . . now?" and in seconds come up with an answer—Arcadia, toward which I find myself guiding us.

After someone who I think is Hamilton Conway mistakes me for someone named Ted Owen and asks if I can get him into Petty's tonight—I tell him, "I'll see what I can do," then turn what's left of my attention to Jean, who sits across from me in the near-empty dining room of Arcadia—after he leaves, only five of the restaurant's tables have people at them. I've ordered a J&B on the rocks. Jean's sipping a glass of white wine and talking about how what she really wants to do is "get into merchant banking" and I'm thinking: Dare to dream. Someone else, Frederick Dibble, stops by and congratulates me on the Larson account and then has the nerve to say, "Talk to you later, Saul." But I'm in a daze, millions of miles away, and Jean doesn't notice; she's talking about a new novel she's been reading by some young author—its cover, I've seen, slathered with neon; its subject, lofty suffering. Accidentally I think she's talking about something else and I find myself saying, without really looking over at her, "You need a tough skin to survive in this city." She flushes, seems embarrassed and takes another sip of the wine, which is a nice sauvignon blanc.

"You seem distant," she says.

"What?" I ask, blinking.

"I said you seem distant," she says.

"No," I sigh. "I'm still my same kooky self."

"That's good." She smiles—am I dreaming this?—relieved.

"So listen," I say, trying to focus in on her, "what do you really want to do with your life?" Then, remembering how she was droning on about a career in merchant banking, I add, "Just briefly, you know, summarize." Then I add, "And don't tell me you enjoy working with children, okay?"

"Well, I'd like to travel," she says. "And maybe go back to school, but I really don't know . . ." She pauses thoughtfully and announces, sincerely, "I'm at a point in my life where there seems to be a lot of possibilities, but I'm so . . . I don't know . . . unsure."

"I think it's also important for people to realize their limitations." Then, out of the blue I ask, "Do you have a boyfriend?"

She smiles shyly, blushes, and then says, "No. Not really."

"Interesting," I murmur. I've opened my menu and I'm studying tonight's prix fixe dinner.

"Are *you* seeing anyone?" she ventures timidly. "I mean, seriously?"

I decide on the pilot fish with tulips and cinnamon, evading the question by sighing. "I just want to have a meaningful relationship with someone special," and before she's allowed to respond I ask her what she's going to order.

"I think the mahi-mahi," she says and then, squinting at the menu, "with ginger."

"I'm having the pilot fish," I say. "I'm developing a taste for them. For . . . pilot fish," I say, nodding.

Later, after a mediocre dinner, a bottle of expensive California cabernet sauvignon and a crème brûlée that we share, I order a glass of fifty-dollar port and Jean sips a decaffeinated espresso and when she asks where the restaurant got its name, I tell her, and I don't make anything ridiculous up—though I'm tempted, just to see if she'd believe it anyway. Sitting across from Jean right now in the darkness of Arcadia, it's very easy to believe that she would swallow any kind of misinformation I push her way—the crush she has on me rendering her powerless—and I find this lack of defense oddly unerotic. I could even explain my pro-apartheid stance and have her find reasons why she too should share it and invest large sums of money in racist corporations tha—

"Arcadia was an ancient region in Peloponnesus, Greece, which was founded in 370 B.C., and it was completely surrounded by mountains. Its chief city was . . . Megalopolis, which was also the center of political activity and the capital of the Arcadian confeder-acy . . ." I take a sip of the port, which is thick, strong, expensive. "It was destroyed during the Greek war of independence . . ." I pause again. "Pan was worshiped originally in Arcadia. Do you know who Pan was?"

Never taking her eyes of me, she nods.

"His revels were very similar to those of Bacchus," I tell her. "He frolicked with nymphs at night but he also liked to . . . frighten travelers during the day . . . Hence the word *pan-ic*." Blah blah blah. I'm amused that I've retained this knowledge and I look up from the port I've been staring thoughtfully into and smile at her. She's silent for a long time, confused, unsure of how to respond, but eventually she looks deeply into my eyes and says, haltingly, leaning across the table, "That's . . . so . . . interesting," which is all that comes out of her mouth, is all she has to say.

Eleven thirty-four. We stand on the sidewalk in front of Jean's apartment on the Upper East Side. Her doorman eyes us warily and fills me with a nameless dread, his gaze piercing me from the lobby. A curtain of stars, miles of them, are scattered, glowing, across the sky and their multitude humbles me, which I have a hard time tolerating. She shrugs and nods after I say something about forms of anxiety. It's as if her mind is having a hard time communi-cating with her mouth, as if she is searching for a rational analysis of who I am, which is, of course, an impossibility: there . . . is . . . no . . . key.

"Dinner was wonderful," she says. "Thank you very much."

"Actually, the food was mediocre, but you're welcome." I shrug.

"Do you want to come up for a drink?" she asks too casually, and even though I'm critical of her approach it doesn't necessarily mean that I don't want to go up—but something stops me, something quells the bloodlust: the doorman? the way the lobby is lit? her lipstick? Plus I'm beginning to think that pornography is so much less complicated than actual sex, and because of this lack of complication, so much more pleasurable.

"Do you have any peyote?" I ask.

She pauses, confused. "What?"

"Just a joke," I say, then, "Listen, I want to watch *David Letterman* so . . ." I pause, unsure as to why I'm lingering. "I should go."

"You can watch it . . ." She stops, then suggests, "at my place."

I pause before asking, "Do you have cable?"

"Yes." She nods. "I have cable."

Stuck, I pause again, then pretend to mull it over. "No, it's okay. I like to watch it . . . without cable."

She offers a sad, perplexed glance. "What?"

"I have to return some videotapes," I explain in a rush.

She pauses. "Now? It's"—she checks her watch—"almost midnight."

"Well, yeah," I say, considerably detached.

"Well, I guess . . . it's good night then," she says.

What kind of books does Jean read? Titles race through my mind: *How to Make a Man Fall in Love with You. How to Keep a Man in Love with You Forever. How to Close a Deal: Get Married. How to Be Married One Year from Today. Supplicant.* In my overcoat pocket I finger the ostrich condom case from Luc Benoit I bought last week but, er, no.

After awkwardly shaking hands she asks, still holding mine, "Really? You don't have cable?"

And though it has been in no way a romantic evening, she embraces me and this time emanates a warmth I'm not familiar with. I am so used to imagining everything happening the way it occurs in movies, visualizing things falling somehow into the shape of events on a screen, that I almost hear the swelling of an orchestra, can almost hallucinate the camera panning low around us, fireworks bursting in slow motion overhead, the seventy-millimeter image of her lips parting and the subsequent murmur of "I *want* you" in Dolby sound. But my embrace is frozen and I realize, at first distantly and then with greater clarity, that the havoc raging inside me is gradually subsiding and she is kissing me on the mouth and this jars me back into some kind of reality and I lightly push her away. She glances up at me fearfully.

"Listen, I've got to go," I say, checking my Rolex. "I don't want to miss . . . Stupid Pet Tricks."

"Okay," she says, composing herself. "Bye."

"Night," I say.

We both head off in our separate directions, but suddenly she calls out something.

I turn around.

"Don't forget you have a breakfast meeting with Frederick Bennet and Charles Rust at '21,'" she says from the door, which the doorman is holding open for her.

"Thanks," I call out, waving. "It slipped my mind completely."

She waves back, disappearing into the lobby.

On my way over to Park Avenue to find a cab I pass an ugly, homeless bum—a member of the genetic underclass—and when he softly pleads for change, for "anything," I notice the Barnes & Noble book bag that sits next to him on the steps of the church he's begging on and I can't help but smirk, out loud, "Oh right, like *you* read . . ." and then, in the back of the cab on the way across town to my apartment, I imagine running around Central Park on a cool spring afternoon with Jean, laughing, holding hands. We buy balloons, we let them go.

DETECTIVE

May slides into June which slides into July which creeps toward August. Because of the heat I've had intense dreams the last four nights about vivisection and I'm doing nothing now, vegetating in my office with a sickening headache and a Walkman with a soothing

Kenny G CD playing in it, but the bright midmorning sunlight floods the room, piercing my skull, causing my hangover to throb, and because of this, there's no workout this morning. Listening to the music I notice the second light on my phone blinking off and on, which means that Jean is buzzing me. I sigh and carefully remove the Walkman.

"What is it?" I ask in monotone.

"Um, Patrick?" she begins.

"Ye-es, Je-an?" I ask condescendingly, spacing the two words out.

"Patrick, a Mr. Donald Kimball is here to see you," she says nervously.

"Who?" I snap, distracted.

She emits a small sigh of worry, then, as if asking, lowers her voice. "*Detective* Donald Kimball?"

I pause, staring out the window into sky, then at my monitor, then at the headless woman I've been doodling on the back cover of this week's *Sports Illustrated*, and I run my hand over the glossy finish of the magazine once, twice, before tearing the cover off and crumpling it up. Finally I start, "Tell him . . ." Then, mulling it over, rethinking my options, I stop and begin again. "Tell him I'm at lunch."

Jean pauses, then whispers. "Patrick . . . I think he knows you're here." During my protracted silence, she adds, still hushed, "It's ten-thirty."

I sigh, stalling again, and in a contained panic tell Jean, "Send him in, I guess."

I stand up, walk over to the Jodi mirror that hangs next to the George Stubbs painting and check my hair, running an oxhorn comb through it, then, calmly, I pick up one of my cordless phones and, preparing myself for a tense scene, pretend to be talking with John Akers, and I start enunciating clearly into the phone before the detective enters the office.

"Now, John . . ." I clear my throat. "You've got to wear clothes in proportion to your physique," I begin, talking to nobody. "There are definitely *dos* and *don'ts*, good buddy, of wearing a bold-striped shirt. A bold-striped shirt calls for solid-colored or discreetly patterned suits and ties . . ."

The door to the office opens and I wave in the detective, who is surprisingly young, maybe my age, wearing a linen Armani suit not unlike mine, though his is slightly disheveled in a hip way, which worries me. I offer a reassuring smile.

"And a shirt with a high yarn count means it's more durable than one that doesn't . . . Yes, I know . . . But to determinate this you've got to examine the material's *weave* . . ." I point to the Mark Schrager chrome and teak chair on the opposite side of my desk, silently urging him to sit.

"Tightly woven fabric is created not only by using a lot of yarn but by using yarn of high-quality fibers, both long and thin, which . . . yes . . . which are . . . which fabricate a close weave as opposed to short and stubbly fibers, like those found in tweed. And loosely *woven* fabrics such as knits are extremely delicate and should be treated with great care . . ." Because of the detective's arrival, it seems unlikely that this will be a good day and I eye him warily as he takes the seat and crosses his legs in a way that fills me with a nameless dread. I realize I've been quiet too long when he turns around to see if I'm off the phone.

"Right, and . . . yes, John, right. And . . . yes, always tip the stylist fifteen percent . . ." I pause. "No, the owner of the salon shouldn't be tipped . . ." I shrug at the detective hopelessly, rolling my eyes. He nods, smiles understandingly and recrosses his legs. Nice socks. Jesus. "The girl who washes the hair? It depends. I'd say a dollar or two . . ." I laugh. "Depends on what she looks like . . ." I laugh harder. "And yeah, what else she washes . . ." I pause again, then say, "Listen, John, I've got to go. T. Boone Pickens just walked in . . ." I pause, grinning like an idiot, then laugh. "Just joking . . ." Another pause. "No, don't tip the owner of the salon." I laugh once more, then, finally, "Okay, John . . . right, got it." I hang up the phone, push its antenna down and then, uselessly stressing my normality, say, "Sorry about that."

"No, *I'm sorry*," he says, genuinely apologetic. "I should've made an appointment." Gesturing toward the cordless phone I'm placing back in its recharging cradle, he asks, "Was that, uh, anything important?"

"Oh that?" I ask, moving towards my desk, sinking into my chair. "Just mulling over business problems. Examining opportunities . . . Exchanging rumors . . . Spreading gossip." We both laugh. The ice breaks.

"Hi," he says, sitting up, holding out his hand. "I'm Donald Kimball."

"Hi. Pat Bateman." I take it, squeezing it firmly. "Nice to meet you."

"I'm sorry," he says, "to barge in on you like this, but I was supposed to talk to Luis Carruthers and he wasn't in and . . . well, you're here, so . . ." He smiles, shrugs. "I know how busy you guys can get." He averts his eyes from the three copies of *Sports Illustrated* that lie open atop my desk, covering it, along with the Walkman. I notice them too, then close all three issues and slip them into the desk's top drawer along with the still-running Walkman.

"So," I start, trying to come off as friendly and conversational as possible. "What's the topic of discussion?"

"Well," he starts. "I've been hired by Meredith Powell to investigate the disappearance of Paul Owen."

I nod thoughtfully before asking, "You're not with the FBI or anything, are you?"

"No, no," he says. "Nothing like that. I'm just a private investigator."

"Ah, I see . . . Yes." I nod again, still not relieved. "Paul's disappearance . . . yes."

"So it's nothing *that* official," he confides. "I just have some basic questions. About Paul Owen. About yourself—"

"Coffee?" I ask suddenly.

As if unsure, he says, "No, I'm okay."

"Perrier? San Pellegrino?" I offer.

"No, I'm okay," he says again, opening a small black notebook he's taken out of his pocket along with a gold Cross pen. I buzz Jean.

"Yes, Patrick?"

"Jean can you bring Mr. . . ." I stop, look up.

He looks up too. "Kimball."

". . . Mr. Kimball a bottle of San Pelle—"

"Oh no, I'm okay," he protests.

"It's no problem," I tell him.

I get the feeling he's trying not to stare at me strangely. He turns back to his notebook and writes something down, then crosses something out. Jean walks in almost immediately and she places the bottle of San Pellegrino and a Steuben etched-glass tumbler on my desk in front of Kimball. She gives me a fretful, worried glance, which I scowl at. Kimball looks up, smiles and nods at Jean, who I notice is not wearing a bra today. Innocently, I watch her leave, then return my gaze to Kimball, clasping my hands together, sitting up. "Well, what's the topic of discussion?" I say again.

"The disappearance of Paul Owen," he says, reminding me.

"Oh right. Well, I haven't heard anything about the disappearance or anything . . ." I pause, then try to laugh. "Not on Page Six at least."

Kimball smiles politely. "I think his family wants this kept quiet."

"Understandable." I nod at the untouched glass and bottle, and then look up at him. "Lime?"

"No, really," he says. "I'm okay."

"You sure?" I ask. "I can always get you a lime."

He pauses briefly, then says, "Just some preliminary questions that I need for my own files, okay?"

"Shoot," I say.

"How old are you?" he asks.

"Twenty-seven," I say. "I'll be twenty-eight in October."

"Where did you go to school?" He scribbles something in his book.

"Harvard," I tell him. "Then Harvard Business School."

"Your address?" he asks, looking only at his book.

"Fifty-five West Eighty-first Street," I say. "The American Gardens Building."

"Nice." He looks up, impressed. "Very nice."

"Thanks." I smile, flattered.

"Doesn't Tom Cruise live there?" he asks.

"Yup." I squeeze the bridge of my nose. Suddenly I have to close my eyes tightly.

I hear him speak. "Pardon me, but are you okay?"

Opening my eyes, both of them tearing, I say, "Why do you ask?"

"You seem . . . *nervous*."

I reach into a drawer in my desk and bring out a bottle of aspirin.

"Nuprin?" I offer.

Kimball looks at the bottle strangely and then back at me before shaking his head. "Uh . . . no thanks." He's taken out a pack of Marlboros and absently lays it next to the San Pellegrino bottle while studying something in the book.

"Bad habit," I point out.

He looks up and, noticing my disapproval, smiles sheepishly. "I know. I'm sorry."

I stare at the box.

"Do you . . . would you rather I not smoke?" he asks, tentative.

I continue to stare at the cigarette packet, debating. "No . . . I guess it's okay."

"You sure?" he asks.

"No problem." I buzz Jean.

"Yes, Patrick?"

"Bring us an ashtray for Mr. Kimball, please," I say.

In a matter of seconds, she does.

"What can you tell me about Paul Owen?" he finally asks, after Jean leaves, having placed a Fortunoff crystal ashtray on the desk next to the untouched San Pellegrino.

"Well," I cough, swallowing two Nuprin, dry. "I didn't know him that well."

"How well *did* you know him?" he asks.

"I'm . . . at a loss," I tell him, somewhat truthfully. "He was part of that whole . . . Yale thing, you know."

"*Yale* thing?" he asks, confused.

I pause, having no idea what I'm talking about. "Yeah . . . Yale thing."

"What do you mean . . . Yale thing?" Now he's intrigued.

I pause again—what *do* I mean? "Well, I think, for one, that he was probably a closet homosexual." I have no idea; doubt it considering his taste in babes. "Who did a lot of cocaine . . ." I pause, then add, a bit shakily. "*That* Yale thing." I'm sure I say this bizarrely, but there's no other way to put it.

It's very quiet in the office right now. The room suddenly seems cramped and sweltering and even though the air-conditioning is on full blast, the air seems fake, recycled.

"So . . ." Kimball looks at his book helplessly. "There's nothing you can tell me about Paul Owen?"

"Well," I sigh. "He led what I suppose was an orderly life, I guess." Really stumped, I offer, "He . . . ate a balanced diet."

I'm sensing frustration on Kimball's part and he asks, "What kind of man was he? Besides"—he falters, tries to smile—"the information you've just given."

How could I describe Paul Owen to this guy? Boasting, arrogant, cheerful dickhead who constantly weaseled his way out of checks at Nell's? That I'm heir to the unfortunate information that his penis had a name and that name was *Michael*? No. Calmer, Bateman. I think that I'm smiling.

"I hope I'm not being cross-examined here," I manage to say.

"Do you feel that way?" he asks. The question sounds sinister but isn't.

"No," I say carefully. "Not really."

Maddeningly he writes something else down, then asks, without looking up, chewing on the tip of the pen, "Where did Paul hang out?"

"Hang . . . out?" I ask.

"Yeah," he says. "You know . . . hang out."

"Let me think," I say, tapping my fingers across my desk. "The Newport. Harry's. Fluties. Indochine. Nell's. Cornell Club. The New York Yacht Club. The regular places."

Kimball looks confused. "He had a yacht?"

Stuck, I casually say, "No. He just hung out there."

"And where did he go to school?" he asks.

I pause. "Don't you know this?"

"I just wanted to know if you know," he says without looking up.

"Er, Yale," I say slowly. "Right?"

"Right."

"And then to business school at Columbia," I add, "I *think*."

"Before all that?" he asks.

"If I remember correctly, Saint Paul's . . . I mean—"

"No, it's okay. That's not really pertinent," he apologizes. "I just have no other questions, I guess. I don't have a lot to go on."

"Listen, I just . . .," I start softly, tactfully. "I just want to help."

"I understand," he says.

Another long pause. He marks something down but it doesn't seem important.

"Anything else you can tell me about Owen?" he asks, sounding almost timid.

I think about it, then feebly announce, "We were both seven in 1969."

Kimball smiles. "So was I."

Pretending to be interested in the case, I ask, "Do you have any witnesses or fingerprints—"

He cuts me off, tiredly. "Well, there's a message on his answering machine saying he went to London."

"Well," I ask then, hopefully, "maybe he did, huh?"

"His girlfriend doesn't think so," Kimball says tonelessly.

Without even beginning to understand, I imagine, what a speck Paul Owen was in the overall enormity of things.

"But . . ." I stop. "Has anyone seen him in London?"

Kimball looks at his book, flips a page and then, looking back at me, says, "Actually, yes."

"Hmmm," I say.

"Well, I've had a hard time getting an accurate verification," he admits. "A . . . Stephen Hughes says he saw him at a restaurant there, but I checked it out and what happened is, he mistook a Hubert Ainsworth for Paul, so . . ."

"Oh," I say.

"Do you remember where you were on the night of Paul's disappearance?" He checks his book. "Which was on the twenty-fourth of June?"

"Gosh . . . I guess . . ." I think about it. "I was probably return-ing videotapes." I open my desk drawer, take out my datebook and looking through December announce, "I had a date with a girl named Veronica . . ." I'm completely lying, totally making this up.

"Wait," he says, confused, looking at his book. "That's . . . not what I've got."

My thigh muscles tense. "What?"

"That's not the information I've received," he says.

"Well . . ." I'm suddenly confused and scared, the Nuprin bitter in my stomach. "I . . . Wait . . . What information *have* you received?"

"Let's see . . ." He flips through his pad, finds something. "That you were with—"

"Wait." I laugh. "I *could* be wrong . . ." My spine feels damp.

"Well . . ." He stops. "When was the last time you were with Paul Owen?" he asks.

"We had"—oh my god, Bateman, think up something—"gone to a new musical that just opened, called . . . *Oh Africa, Brave Africa*." I gulp. "It was . . . a laugh riot . . . and that's about it. I think we had dinner at Orso's . . . no, Petaluma. No, Orso's." I stop. "The . . . last time I *physically* saw him was . . . at an automated teller. I can't remember which . . . just one that was near, um, Nell's."

"But the night he disappeared?" Kimball asks.

"I'm not really sure," I say.

"I think maybe you've got your dates mixed up," he says, glancing at his book.

"But how?" I ask. "Where do *you* place Paul that night?"

"According to his datebook, and this was verified by his secretary, he had dinner with . . . Marcus Halberstam," he says.

"And?" I ask.

"I've questioned him."

"Marcus?"

"Yes. And he denies it," Kimball says. "Though at first he couldn't be sure."

"But Marcus denied it?"

"Yes."

"Well, does Marcus have an alibi?" I have a heightened receptivity to his answers now.

"Yes."

Pause.

"He *does*?" I ask. "You're sure?"

"I checked it out," he says with an odd smile. "It's clean."

Pause.

"Oh."

"Now where were *you*?" He laughs.

I laugh too, though I'm not sure why. "Where was Marcus?" I'm almost giggling.

Kimball keeps smiling as he looks me over. "He wasn't with Paul Owen," he says enigmatically.

"So who was he with?" I'm laughing still, but I'm also very dizzy.

Kimball opens his book and for the first time gives me a slightly hostile look. "He was at Atlantis with Craig McDermott, Frederick Dibble, Harry Newman, George Butner and"—Kimball pauses, then looks up—"you."

In this office right now I am thinking about how long it would take a corpse to disintegrate right in this office. In this office these are the things I fantasize about while dreaming: Eating ribs at Red, Hot and Blue in Washington, D.C. If I should switch shampoos. What really is the best dry beer? Is Bill Robinson an overrated designer? What's wrong with IBM? Ultimate luxury. Is the term "playing hardball" an adverb? The fragile peace of Assisi. Electric light. The epitome of luxury. Of ultimate luxury. The bastard's wearing the same damn Armani linen suit I've got on. How easy it would be to scare the living wits out of this fucking guy. Kimball is utterly unaware of how truly vacant I am. There is no evidence of animate life in this office, yet still he takes notes. By the time you finish reading this sentence, a Boeing jetliner will take off or land somewhere in the world. I would like a Pilsner Urquell.

"Oh right," I say. "Of course . . . We had wanted Paul Owen to come," I say, nodding my head as if just realizing something. "But he said he had plans . . ." Then, lamely, "I guess I had dinner with Victoria the . . . following night."

"Listen, like I said, I was just hired by Meredith." He sighs closing his book.

Tentatively, I ask, "Did you know that Meredith Powell is dating Brock Thompson?"

He shrugs, sighs. "I don't know about that. All I know is that Paul Owen owes her supposedly a lot of money."

"Oh?" I say, nodding. "Really?"

"Personally," he says, confiding, "I think the guy went a little nutso. Split town for a while. May he *did* go to London. Sightseeing. Drinking. Whatever. Anyway, I'm pretty sure he'll turn up sooner or later."

I nod slowly, hoping to look suitably bewildered.

"Was he involved at all, do you think, in, say, occultism or Satan worship?" Kimball asks seriously.

"Er, what?"

"I know it sounds like a lame question but in New Jersey last month—I don't know if you've heard about this, but a young stockbroker was recently arrested and charged with murdering a young Chicano girl and performing voodoo rituals with, well, various body parts—"

"Yikes!" I exclaim.

"And I mean . . ." He smiles sheepishly again. "Have you heard anything about this?"

"Did the guy deny doing it?" I ask, tingling.

"Right." Kimball nods.

"That was an interesting case," I manage to say.

"Even though the guy says he's innocent he still thinks he's Inca, the bird god, or something," Kimball says, scrunching his features up.

We both laugh out loud about this.

"No," I finally say. "Paul wasn't into that. He followed a balanced diet and—"

"Yeah, I know, and was into that whole Yale thing," Kimball finishes tiredly.

There is a long pause that, I think, might be the longest one so far.

"Have you consulted a psychic?" I ask.

"No." He shakes his head in a way that suggests he's considered it. Oh *who cares*?

"Had his apartment been burglarized?" I ask.

"No, it actually hadn't," he says. "Toiletries were missing. A suit was gone. So was some luggage. That's it."

"Do you suspect foul play?"

"Can't say," he says. "But like I told you, I wouldn't be surprised if he's just hiding out someplace."

"I mean no one's dealing with the homicide squad yet or anything, right?" I ask.

"No, not yet. As I said, we're not sure. But . . ." He stops, looks dejected. "Basically no one has seen or heard anything."

"That's so typical, isn't it?" I ask.

"It's just strange," he agrees, staring out the window, lost. "One day someone's walking around, going to work, *alive*, and then . . ." Kimball stops, fails to complete the sentence.

"Nothing," I sigh, nodding.

"People just . . . disappear," he says.

"The earth just opens up and swallows people," I say, somewhat sadly, checking my Rolex.

"Eerie." Kimball yawns, stretching. "Really eerie."

"Ominous." I nod my agreement.

"It's just"—he sighs, exasperated—"futile."

I pause, unsure of what to say, and come up with "Futility is . . . hard to deal with."

I am thinking about nothing. It's silent in the office. To break it, I point out a book on top of the desk, next to the San Pellegrino bottle. *The Art of the Deal*, by Donald Trump.

"Have you read it?" I ask Kimball.

"No," he sighs, but politely asks, "Is it any good?"

"It's very good," I say, nodding.

"Listen." He sighs again. "I've taken up enough of your time." He pockets the Marlboros.

"I have a lunch meeting with Cliff Huxtable at The Four Seasons in twenty minutes anyway," I lie, standing up. "I have to go too."

"Isn't The Four Seasons a little far uptown?" He looks concerned, also getting up. "I mean aren't you going to be late?"

"Um, no," I stall. "There's one . . . down here."

"Oh really?" he asks. "I didn't know that."

"Yes," I say, leading him to the door. "It's very good."

"Listen," he says, turning to face me. "If anything occurs to you, any information at all . . ."

I hold up a hand. "Absolutely. I'm one hundred percent with you," I say solemnly.

"Great," the ineffectual one says, relieved. "And thanks for your, uh, time, Mr. Bateman."

Moving him toward the door, my legs wobbly, astronaut-like, leading him out of the office, though I'm empty, devoid of feeling, I still sense—without deluding myself—that I've accomplished something and then, anticlimactically, we talk for a few minutes more about razor-burn balms and tattersall shirts. There was an odd general lack of urgency to the conversation that I found soothing— nothing happened at all—but when he smiles, hands me his card, leaves, the door closing sounds to me like a billion insects screaming, pounds of bacon sizzling, a vast emptiness. And after he leaves the building (I have Jean buzz Tom at Security to make sure) I call someone recommended by my lawyer, to make sure none of my phones are wiretapped, and after a Xanax I'm able to meet with my nutritionist at an expensive, upscale health-food restaurant called Cuisine de Soy in Tribeca, and while sitting beneath the dolphin, stuffed and shellacked, that hangs over the tofu bar, its body bent into an arc, I'm able to ask the nutritionist questions like "Okay, so give me the muffin lowdown" without cringing. Back at the office two hours later, I find out that none of my phones are tapped.

I also run into Meredith Powell later this week, on Friday night, at Ereze with Brock Thompson, and though we talk for ten minutes, mostly about why neither one of us is in the Hamptons, with Brock glaring at me the entire time, she doesn't mention Paul Owen once. I'm having an excruciatingly slow dinner with my date, Jeannette. The restaurant is flashy and new and the meal inches along, drags by. The portions are meager. I grow increasingly agitated. Afterwards I want to bypass M.K., even though Jeanette complains because she wants to dance. I'm tired and I need to rest. At my apartment I lie in bed, too distracted to have sex with her, so she leaves, and after watching a tape of this morning's *Patty Winters Show*, which is about the best restaurants in the Middle East, I pick up my cordless phone and tentatively, reluctantly, call Evelyn.

SUMMER

Most of the summer I spent in a stupor, sitting either in my office or in new restaurants, in my apartment watching videotapes or in the backs of cabs, in nightclubs that just opened or in movie theaters, at the building in Hell's Kitchen or in new restaurants. There were four major air disasters this summer, the majority of them captured on videotape, almost as if these events had been planned, and repeated on television endlessly. The planes kept crashing in slow motion, followed by countless roaming shots of the wreckage and the same random views of the burned, bloody carnage, weeping rescue workers retrieving body parts. I started using Oscar de la Renta men's deodorant, which gave me a slight rash. A movie about a small talking bug was released to great fanfare and grossed over two hundred million dollars. The Mets were doing

badly. Beggars and homeless seemed to have multiplied in August
and the ranks of the unfortunate, weak and aged lined the streets
everywhere. I found myself asking too many summer associates at
too many dinners in flashy new restaurants before taking them to
Les Misérables if anyone had seen *The Toolbox Murders* on HBO
and silent tables would stare back at me, before I would cough
politely and summon the waiter over for the check, or I'd ask for
sorbet or, if this was earlier in the dinner, for another bottle of San
Pellegrino, and then I'd ask the summer associates, "No?" and
assure them, "It was quite good." My platinum American Express
card had gone through so much use that it snapped in half, self-
destructed, at one of those dinners, when I took two summer
associates to Restless and Young, the new Pablo Lester restaurant
in midtown, but I had enough cash in my gazelleskin wallet to pay
for the meal. *The Patty Winters Shows* were all repeats. Life
remained a blank canvas, a cliché, a soap opera. I felt lethal, on the
verge of frenzy. My nightly bloodlust overflowed into my days and I
had to leave the city. My mask of sanity was a victim of impending
slippage. This was the bone season for me and I needed a vacation.
I needed to go to the Hamptons.

I suggested this to Evelyn and, like a spider, she accepted.

The house we stayed at was actually Tim Price's, which Evelyn
had the keys to for some reason, but in my stupefied state I refused
to ask for specifics.

Tim's house was on the water in East Hampton and was
adorned with many gable roofs and was four stories high, all
connected by a galvanized-steel staircase, and had what at first I
thought was a Southwestern motif but wasn't. The kitchen was one
thousand square feet of pure minimalist design; one wall held
everything; two huge ovens, massive cupboards, a walk-in freezer, a
three-door refrigerator. An island of custom-crafted stainless steel
divided the kitchen into three separate spaces. Four of the nine
bathrooms contained trompe l'oeil paintings and five of them had
antique lead ram's heads that hung over the sink, water spouting
from their mouths. All the sinks and bathtubs and showers were
antique marble and the floors were composed of tiny marble
mosaics. A television was built into a wall alcove above the master
bathtub. Every room had a stereo. The house also contained twelve
Frank Lloyd Wright standing lamps, fourteen Josef Heffermann

club chairs, two walls of floor-to-ceiling videocassette cases and another wall stacked solely with thousands of compact discs encased in glass cabinets. A chandelier by Eric Schmidt hung in the front entranceway, below it stood an Atomic Ironworks steel moose hatrack by a young sculptor I'd never heard of. A round nineteenth-century Russian dining table sat in a room adjacent to the kitchen, but had no chairs. Spooky photographs by Cindy Sherman lined the walls everywhere. There was an exercise room. There were eight walk-in closets, five VCRs, a Noguchi glass and walnut dining table, a hall table by Marc Schaffer and a fax machine. There was a topiary tree in the master bedroom next to a Louis XVI window bench. An Eric Fischl painting hung over one of the marble fireplaces. There was a tennis court. There were two saunas and an indoor jacuzzi in a small guesthouse that sat by the pool, which was black-bottomed. There were stone columns in odd places.

I really tried to make things work the weeks we were out there. Evelyn and I rode bicycles and jogged and played tennis. We talked about going to the south of France or to Scotland; we talked about driving through Germany and visiting unspoiled opera houses. We went windsurfing. We talked about only romantic things: the light on eastern Long Island, the moonrise in October over the hills of the Virginia hunt country. We took baths together in the big marble tubs. We had breakfast in bed snuggling beneath cashmere blankets after I'd poured imported coffee from a Melior pot into Hermès cups. I woke her up with fresh flowers. I put notes in her Louis Vuitton carry bag before she left for her weekly facials in Manhattan. I bought her a puppy, a small black chow, which she named NutraSweet and fed dietetic chocolate truffles to. I read long passages aloud from *Doctor Zhivago* and *A Farewell to Arms* (my favorite Hemingway). I rented movies in town that Price didn't own, mostly comedies from the 1930s, and played them on one of the many VCRs, our favorite being *Roman Holiday*, which we watched twice. We listened to Frank Sinatra (only his 1950s period) and Nat King Cole's *After Midnight*, which Tim had on CD. I bought her expensive lingerie, which sometimes she wore.

After skinny-dipping in the ocean late at night, we would come into the house, shivering, draped in huge Ralph Lauren towels, and we'd make omelets and noodles tossed with olive oil and truffles and porcini mushrooms; we'd make soufflés with poached pears and cinnamon fruit salads, grilled polenta with peppered salmon, apple and berry sorbet, mascarpone, red beans with arrozo wrapped in romaine lettuce, bowls of salsa and skate poached in balsamic vinegar, chilled tomato soup and risottos flavored with beets and lime and asparagus and mint, and we drank lemonade or champagne or well-aged bottles of Château Margaux. But soon we stopped lifting weights together and swimming laps and Evelyn would eat only the dietetic chocolate truffles that NutraSweet hadn't eaten, complaining about weight she hadn't gained. Some nights I would find myself roaming the beaches, digging up baby crabs and eating handfuls of sand—this was in the middle of the night when the sky was so clear I could see the entire solar system and the sand, lit by it, seemed almost lunar in scale. I even dragged a beached jellyfish back to the house and microwaved it early one morning, predawn, while Evelyn slept, and what I didn't eat of it I fed to the chow.

Sipping bourbon, then champagne, from cactus-etched highball glasses, which Evelyn would set on adobe coasters and into which she would stir raspberry cassis with papier-mâché jalapeño-shaped stirrers, I would lie around, fantasizing about killing someone with an Allsop Racer ski pole, or I would stare at the antique weather vane that hung above one of the fireplaces, wondering wild-eyed if I could stab anyone with it, then I'd complain aloud, whether Evelyn was in the room or not, that we should have made reservations at Dick Loudon's Stratford Inn instead. Evelyn soon started talking only about spas and cosmetic surgery and then she hired a masseur, some scary faggot who lived down the road with a famous book publisher and who flirted openly with me. Evelyn went back to the city three times that last week we were in the Hamptons, once for a manicure and a pedicure and a facial, the second time for a one-on-one training session at Stephanie Herman, and finally to meet with her astrologer.

"Why helicopter in?" I asked in a whisper.

"What do you want me to do?" she shrieked, popping another dietetic truffle into her mouth. "Rent a *Volvo*?"

While she was gone I would vomit—just to do it—into the rustic terracotta jars that lined the patio in front or I would drive into town with the scary masseur and collect razor blades. At night I'd place a faux-concrete and aluminum-wire sconce by Jerry Kott over Evelyn's head and since she'd be so knocked out on Halcion she wouldn't brush it off, and though I laughed at this, while the sconce rose evenly with her deep breathing, soon it made me sad and I stopped placing the sconce over Evelyn's head.

Everything failed to subdue me. Soon everything seemed dull: another sunrise, the lives of heroes, falling in love, war, the discoveries people made about each other. The only thing that didn't bore me, obviously enough, was how much money Tim Price made, and yet in its obviousness it did. There wasn't a clear, identifiable emotion within me, except for greed and, possibly, total disgust. I had all the characteristics of a human being—flesh, blood, skin, hair—but my depersonalization was so intense, had gone so deep, that the normal ability to feel compassion had been eradicated, the victim of a slow, purposeful erasure. I was simply imitating reality, a rough resemblance of a human being, with only a dim corner of my mind functioning. Something horrible was happening and yet I couldn't figure out why—I couldn't put my finger on it. The only thing that calmed me was the satisfying sound of ice being dropped into a glass of J&B. Eventually I drowned the chow, which Evelyn didn't miss; she didn't even notice its absence, not even when I threw it in the walk-in freezer, wrapped in one of her sweaters from Bergdorf Goodman. We had to leave the Hamptons because I would find myself standing over our bed in the hours before dawn, with an ice pick gripped in my fist, waiting for Evelyn to open her eyes. At my suggestion, one morning over breakfast, she agreed, and on the last Sunday before Labor Day we returned to Manhattan by helicopter.

GIRLS

"I thought the pinto beans with salmon and mint were really, really . . . you know," Elizabeth says, walking into the living room of my apartment and in one graceful movement kicking off both satin and suede Maud Frizon pumps and flopping onto the couch, "good, but Pat*rick*, my god it was expen*sive* and," then, bristling, she bitches, "it was *only* pseudo nouvelle."

"Was it my imagination or were there goldfish on the tables?" I ask, undoing my Brooks Brothers suspenders while searching the refrigerator for a bottle of sauvignon blanc. "Anyway, *I* thought it was hip."

Christie has taken a seat on the long, wide sofa, away from Elizabeth, who stretches out lazily.

"*Hip*, Patrick?" she calls out. "Donald *Trump* eats there."

I locate the bottle and stand it on the counter and, before finding a wine opener, stare at her blankly from across the room. "Yes? Is this a sarcastic comment?"

"Guess," she moans and follows it with a "Duh" so loud that Christie flinches.

"Where are you working now, Elizabeth?" I ask, closing drawers. "Polo outlet or something?"

Elizabeth cracks up at this and says blithely, while I uncork the Acacia, "I don't have to work, Bateman," and after a beat she adds, bored, "You of all people should know how *that* feels, Mr. Wall Street." She's checking her lipstick in a Gucci compact; predictably it looks perfect.

Changing the subject, I ask, "Who chose that place anyway?" I pour the two girls wine and then make myself a J&B on the rocks with a little water. "The restaurant, I mean."

"Carson did. Or maybe Robert." Elizabeth shrugs and then after snapping the compact shut, staring intently at Christie, asks, "You look really familiar. Did you go to Dalton?"

Christie shakes her head no. It's almost three in the morning. I'm grinding up a tab of Ecstasy and watching it dissolve in the wineglass I plan to hand Elizabeth. This morning's topic on *The Patty Winters Show* was People Who Weigh Over Seven Hundred Pounds—What Can We Do About Them? I switch on the kitchen lights, find two more tabs of the drug in the freezer, then shut the lights off.

Elizabeth is a twenty-year-old hardbody who sometimes models in Georges Marciano ads and who comes from an old Virginia banking family. We had dinner earlier tonight with two friends of hers, Robert Farrell, twenty-seven, a guy who's had a rather sketchy career as a financier, and Carson Whitall, who was Robert's date. Robert wore a wool suit by Belvest, a cotton shirt with French cuffs by Charvet, an abstract-patterned silk-crepe tie by Hugo Boss and sunglasses by Ray-Ban that he insisted on wearing during the meal. Carson wore a suit by Yves Saint Laurent Rive Gauche and a pearl necklace with matching pearl and diamond earrings by Harry Winston. We had dinner at Free Spin, the new Albert Lioman restaurant in the Flatiron district, then took the limousine to Nell's, where I excused myself, assuring an irate Elizabeth I'd be right back, and directed the chauffeur to the meat-packing district, where I picked up Christie. I made her wait in the back of the locked limousine while I reentered Nell's and had drinks with Elizabeth and Carson and Robert in one of the booths up front, empty since the place had no celebrities in it tonight—a bad sign. Finally, at two-thirty, while Carson bragged drunkenly about her monthly flower bill, Elizabeth and I split. She was so pissed off about something Carson told her was in the latest issue of *W* that she didn't even question Christie's presence.

In the ride back toward Nell's Christie had admitted that she was still upset about the last time we shared together, and that she had major reservations about tonight, but the money I've offered is simply too good to pass up and I promised her that nothing like last time will be repeated. Though she was still scared, a few shots of vodka in the back of the limo along with the money I'd given her so far, over sixteen hundred dollars, relaxed her like a tranquilizer. Her moodiness turned me on and she acted like a total sex kitten when I first handed her the cash amount—six bills attached to a Hughlans silver money clip—but after I urged her into the limo she told me that she might need surgery after what happened last time, or a lawyer, so I wrote out a check to cash in the amount of one thousand dollars, but since I knew it would never be cashed I didn't have a panic attack about it or anything. Looking over at Elizabeth right now, in my apartmnt, I'm noticing how well endowed she is in the chest area and I'm hoping that after the Ecstasy hits her system I can convince the two girls to have sex in front of me.

Elizabeth is asking Christie if she's ever met some asshole named Spicey or been to Au Bar. Christie is shaking her head. I hand Elizabeth the Ecstasy-laden sauvignon blanc while she stares at Christie like she was from Neptune, and after recovering from Christie's admission she yawns. "Anyway, Au Bar *sucks* now. It's terrible. I went to a birthday party there for Malcolm Forbes. Oh my god, *please*." She downs the wine, grimacing. I take a seat in one of the chrome and oak Sottsass chairs and reach over to the ice bucket that sits on the glass-top coffee table, adjusting the bottle of wine in order to chill it better. Immediately Elizabeth makes a move for it, pouring herself another glass. I dissolve two more tabs of the Ecstasy in the bottle before bringing it into the living room. A sullen Christie sips her untainted wine cautiously and tries not to stare at the floor; she still seems scared, and finding the silence unbearable or incriminating she asks Elizabeth where she met me.

"Oh god," Elizabeth starts, moaning as if she falsely remembered something embarrassing. "I met Patrick at, oh god, the Kentucky Derby in '86—no, '87, and . . ." She turns to me. "You were hanging out with that bimbo Alison something . . . Stoole?"

"Poole, honey," I reply calmly. "Alison Poole."

"Yeah, that was her name," she says, then with unmasked sarcasm, "Hot number."

"What do you mean by that?" I ask, offended. "She *was* a hot number."

Elizabeth turns to Christie and unfortunately says, "If you had an American Express card she'd give you a blow-job," and I'm hoping to god that Christie doesn't look over at Elizabeth, confused, and say "But we don't take credit cards." To make sure this doesn't happen, I bellow "Oh, bullshit," but good-naturedly.

"Listen," Elizabeth tells Christie, holding her hand out like a fag offering gossipy information. "This girl worked at a tanning salon, and"—and in the same sentence, without changing tone—"what do you do?"

After a long silence, Christie turning redder and even more scared, I say, "She's . . . my cousin."

Slowly, Elizabeth takes this in and says, "Uh-huh?"

After another long silence, I say, "She's . . . from France."

Elizabeth looks at me skeptically—like I'm completely crazy—but chooses not to pursue this line of questioning and asks instead, "Where's your phone? I've *got* to call Harley."

I move over to the kitchen and bring the cordless phone to her, pulling up its antenna. She dials a number and, while waiting for someone to answer, stares at Christie. "Where do you summer?" she asks. "Southampton?"

Christie looks at me and then back at Elizabeth and quietly says, "No."

"Oh *god*," Elizabeth wails, "it's his *machine*."

"Elizabeth." I point at my Rolex. "It's *three* in the morning."

"He's a goddamn *drug* dealer," she says, exasperated. "These are his peak hours."

"Don't tell him you're here," I warn.

"Why would I?" she asks. Distracted, she reaches for her wine and downs another full glass and makes a face. "This tastes weird." She checks the label, then shrugs. "Harley? It's me. I need your services. Translate that any way you'd like. I'm at—" She looks over at me.

"You're at Marcus Halberstam's," I whisper.

"Who?" Leaning in, she grins mischievously.

"Mar-cus Hal-ber-stam," I whisper again.

"I want the *number*, idiot." She waves me away and continues, "Anyway, I'm at Mark Hammerstein's and I'll try you later and if I don't see you at Canal Bar tomorrow night I'm going to sic my hairdresser on you. Bon voyage. How do I hang this thing up?" she asks, even though she expertly pushes the antenna down and presses the Off button, tossing the phone onto the Schrager chair that I've moved next to the jukebox.

"See." I smile. "You did it."

Twenty minutes later Elizabeth is squirming on the couch and I'm trying to coerce her into having sex with Christie in front of me. What started out as a casual suggestion is now at the forefront of my brain and I'm insistent. Christie stares impassively at a stain I hadn't noticed on the white-oak floor, her wine mostly untouched.

"But I'm *not* a lesbian," Elizabeth protests again, giggling. "I'm *not* into girls."

"Is this a *firm* no?" I ask, staring at her glass, then at the near-empty bottle of wine.

"Why'd you think I'd be into *that*?" she asks. Because of the Ecstasy, the question is flirtatious and she seems genuinely interested. Her foot is rubbing against my thigh. I've moved over to the couch, sitting between the two girls, and I'm massaging one of her calves.

"Well, you went to Sarah Lawrence for one thing," I tell her. "You never know."

"Those are Sarah Lawrence *guys*, Patrick," she points out, giggling, rubbing harder, causing friction, heat, everything.

"Well, I'm sorry," I admit. "I don't usually deal with a lot of guys who wear panty hose on the Street."

"Patrick, *you* went to Patrick, I mean, Harvard, oh god, I'm *so* drunk. Anyway, listen, I mean, wait—" She pauses, takes a deep breath, mumbles an unintelligible remark about feeling bizarre, then, after closing her eyes, opens them and asks, "Do you have any coke?"

I'm staring at her glass, noticing that the dissolved Ecstasy has slightly changed the color of the wine. She follows my gaze and takes a gulp of it as if it were some kind of elixir that could soothe her increasing agitation. She leans her head back, woozily, on one of the pillows on the couch. "Or Halcion. I'd take a Halcion."

"Listen, I would just like to see . . . the two of you . . . get it on," I say innocently. "What's wrong with that? It's totally disease-free."

"Patrick." She laughs. "You're a lunatic."

"Come on," I urge. "Don't you find Christie attractive?"

"Let's not get lewd," she says, but the drug is kicking in and I can sense that she's excited but doesn't want to be. "I'm in no mood to have lewd conversation."

"Come on," I say. "I think it would be a turn-on."

"Does he do this all the time?" Elizabeth asks Christie.

I look over at Christie.

Christie shrugs, noncommittal, and studies the back of a compact disc before setting it on the table next to the stereo.

"Are you telling me you've never gotten it on with a girl?" I ask, touching a black stocking, then, beneath it, a leg.

"But I'm *not* a lesbian," she stresses. "And no, I never have."

"*Never?*" I ask, arching my eyebrows. "Well, there's always a first time . . ."

"You're making me feel weird," Elizabeth moans, losing control of her facial features.

"*I'm* not," I say, shocked.

Elizabeth is making out with Christie, both of them naked on my bed, all the lights in the room burning, while I sit in the Louis Montoni chair by the side of the futon, watching them very closely, occasionally repositioning their bodies. Now I make Elizabeth lie on her back and hold both legs up, open, spreading them as wide as possible, and then I push Christie's head down and make her lap at her cunt—not suck on it but lap at it, like a thirsty dog—while fingering the clit, then, with her other hand, she sticks two fingers into the open, wet cunt, while her tongue replaces the fingers and then she takes the dripping fingers she's fucked Elizabeth's cunt with and forces them into Elizabeth's mouth, making her suck on them. Then I have Christie lie on top of Elizabeth and make her suck and bite at Elizabeth's full, swollen tits, which Elizabeth is also squeezing, and then I tell the two of them to kiss each other, hard, and Elizabeth takes the tongue that's been licking at her own small, pink cunt into her mouth hungrily, like an animal, and uncontrollably they start humping each other, pressing their cunts together, Elizabeth moaning loudly, wrapping her legs around Christie's hips, bucking up against her, Christie's legs spread in such a way that, from behind, I can see her cunt, wet and spread, and above it, her hairless pink asshole.

Christie sits up and turns herself around and while still on top of Elizabeth presses her cunt into Elizabeth's gasping face and soon, like in a movie, like animals, the two of them start feverishly licking and fingering each other's cunts. Elizabeth, totally red-faced, her neck muscles straining like a mad-woman's, tries to bury her head in Christie's pussy and then spreads Christie's ass cheeks open and starts tonguing the hole there, making guttural sounds. "Yeah," I say in monotone. "Stick your tongue up that bitch's asshole."

While this is going on I'm greasing with Vaseline a large white dildo that's connected to a belt. I stand up and hoist Christie off Elizabeth, who is writhing mindlessly on the futon, and I attach the belt around Christie's waist, and then I turn Elizabeth around and position her on all fours and I make Christie fuck her with it doggy style, while I finger Christie's cunt, then her clit, then her asshole, which is so wet and loose from Elizabeth's saliva I'm able to force my index finger into it effortlessly and her sphincter tightens, relaxes, then contracts around it. I make Christie pull the dildo out of Elizabeth's cunt and have Elizabeth lie on her back while Christie fucks her in the missionary position. Elizabeth is fingering her clit while madly French-kissing Christie until, involuntarily, she brings her head back, legs wrapped around Christie's pumping hips, her face tense, her mouth open, her lipstick smeared by Christie's cunt juice, and she yells "oh god I'm coming I'm coming fuck me I'm coming" because I told both of them to let me know when they had orgasms and to be very vocal about it.

Soon it's Christie's turn and Elizabeth eagerly straps on the dildo and fucks Christie's cunt with it while I spread Elizabeth's asshole and tongue it and soon she pushes me away and starts fingering herself desperately. Then Christie puts the dildo on again and she fucks Elizabeth in the ass with it while Elizabeth fingers her clit, bucking her ass up against the dildo, grunting, until she has another orgasm. After pulling the dildo from her ass I make Elizabeth suck on it before she straps it on again and while Christie lies on her back Elizabeth pushes it easily into her cunt. During this I lick Christie's tits and suck hard on each nipple until both of them are red and stiff. I keep fingering them to make sure they stay that way. During this Christie has kept on a pair of thigh-high suede boots from Henri Benedel that I've made her wear.

Elizabeth, naked, running from the bedroom, blood already on her, is moving with difficulty and she screams out something garbled. My orgasm has been prolonged and its release was intense and my knees are weak. I'm naked too, shouting "You bitch, you piece of bitch trash" at her and since most of the blood is coming from her feet, she slips, manages to get up, and I strike out at her with the already wet butcher knife that I'm gripping in my right hand, clumsily, slashing her neck from behind, severing something, some veins. When I strike out a second time while she's trying to escape, heading for the door, blood shoots even into the living room, across the apartment, splattering against the tempered glass and the laminated oak panels in the kitchen. She tries to run forward but I've cut her jugular and it's spraying everywhere, blinding both of us momentarily, and I'm leaping at her in a final attempt to finish her off. She turns to face me, her features twisted in anguish, and her legs give out after I punch her in the stomach and she hits the floor and I slide in next to her. After I've stabbed her five or six times—the blood's spurting out in jets; I'm leaning over to inhale its perfume—her muscles stiffen, become rigid, and she goes into her death throes; her throat becomes flooded with dark-red blood and she thrashes around as if tied up, but she isn't and I have to hold her down. Her mouths fills with blood that cascades over the sides of her cheeks, over her chin. Her body, shaking spasmodically, resembles what I imagine an epileptic goes through in a fit and I hold down her head, rubbing my dick, stiff, covered with blood, across her choking face, until she's motionless.

Back in my bedroom, Christie lies on the futon, tied to the legs of the bed, bound up with rope, her arms above her head, ripped pages from last month's *Vanity Fair* stuffed into her mouth. Jumper cables hooked up to a battery are clipped to both breasts, turning them brown. I had been dropping lit matches from Le Relais onto her belly and Elizabeth, delirious and probably overdosing on the Ecstasy, had been helping before I turned on her and chewed at one of her nipples until I couldn't control myself and bit it off, swallowing. For the first time I notice just how small and delicately structured Christie is, was. I start kneading her breasts with a pair of pliers, then I'm mashing them up, things are moving fast, I'm making hissing noises, she spits out the pages from the magazine, tries to bite my hand. I laugh when she dies, before she does she starts crying, then her eyes roll back in some kind of horrible dream state.

In the morning, for some reason, Christie's battered hands are swollen to the size of footballs, the fingers are indistinguishable from the rest of her hand and the smell coming from her burnt corpse is jolting and I have to open the venetian blinds which are splattered with burnt fat from when Christie's breasts burst apart, electrocuting her, and then the windows, to air out the room. Her eyes are wide open and glazed over and her mouth is lipless and black and there's also a black pit where her vagina should be (though I don't remember doing anything to it) and her lungs are visible beneath the charred ribs. What is left of Elizabeth's body lies crumpled in the corner of the living room. She's missing her right arm and chunks of her right leg. Her left hand, chopped off at the wrist, lies clenched on top of the island in the kitchen, in its own small pool of blood. Her head sits on the kitchen table and its blood-soaked face—even with both eyes scooped out and a pair of Alain Mikli sunglasses over the holes—looks like it's frowning. I get very tired looking at it and though I didn't get any sleep last night and I'm utterly spent, I still have a lunch appointment at Odeon with Jem Davies and Alana Burton at one. That's very important to me and I have to debate whether I should cancel it or not.

CONFRONTED BY FAGGOT

Autumn: a Sunday around four o'clock in the afternoon. I'm at Barney's, buying cuff links. I had walked into the store at two-thirty, after a cold, tense brunch with Christie's corpse, rushed up to the front counter, told a salesclerk, "I need a whip. Really." In addition to the cuff links, I've bought an ostrich travel case with double-zippered openings and vinyl lining, an antique silver, crocodile and glass pill jar, an antique toothbrush container, a badger-bristle toothbrush and a faux-tortoiseshell nailbrush. Dinner last night? At Splash. Not much to remember: a watery Bellini, soggy arugula salad, a sullen waitress. Afterwards I watched a repeat of an old *Patty Winters Show* that I found on what I originally thought was a videotape of the torture and subsequent murder of two escort girls from last spring (the topic was Tips on How Your Pet Can Become a Movie Star). Right now I'm in the middle of purchasing a belt—not for myself—as well as three ninety-dollar ties, ten hand-kerchiefs, a four-hundred-dollar robe and two pairs of Ralph Lauren pajamas, and I'm having it all mailed to my apartment except for the handkerchiefs, which I'm having monogrammed then sent to P & P. I've already made somewhat of a scene in the ladies' shoe department and, embarrassingly, was chased out by a distressed salesperson. At first it's only a sense of vague uneasiness and I'm unsure of its cause, but then it feels, though I can't be positive, as if I'm being followed, as if someone has been tracking me throughout Barney's.

Luis Carruthers is, I suppose, incognito. He's wearing some kind of jaguar-print silk evening jacket, deerskin gloves, a felt hat, aviator sunglasses, and he's hiding behind a column, pretending to inspect a row of ties, and, gracelessly, he gives me a sidelong glance. Leaning down, I sign something, a bill I think, and fleetingly Luis's presence forces me to consider that maybe a life connected to this city, to Manhattan, to my job, is *not* a good idea, and suddenly I imagine Luis at some horrible party, drinking a nice dry rosé, fags clustered around a baby grand, show tunes, now he's holding a flower, now he has a feather boa draped around his neck, now the pianist bangs out something from *Les Miz*, darling.

"Patrick? Is that you?" I hear a tentative voice inquire.

Like a smash cut from a horror movie—a jump zoom—Luis Carruthers appears, suddenly, without warning, from behind his column, slinking and jumping at the same time, if that's possible. I smile at the salesgirl, then awkwardly move away from him and over to a display case of suspenders, in dire need of a Xanax, a Valium, a Halcion, a Frozfruit, *anything*.

I don't, *can't*, look at him, but I sense he's moved closer to me. His voice confirms it.

"Patrick? . . . Hello?"

Closing my eyes, I move a hand up to my face and mutter, under my breath, "Don't make me say it, Luis."

"Patrick?" he says, feigning innocence. "What do you mean?" A hideous pause, then, "Patrick . . . Why aren't you looking at me?"

"I'm ignoring you, Luis." I breathe in, calming myself by checking the price tag on an Armani button-up sweater. "Can't you tell? I'm ignoring you."

"Patrick, can't we just talk?" he asks, almost whining. "*Patrick*— look at me."

After another sharp intake of breath, sighing, I admit, "There is *nothing, noth-ing* to talk—"

"We can't go on like this," he impatiently cuts me off. "*I* can't go on like this."

I mutter. I start walking away from him. He follows, insistent.

"Anyway," he says, once we've reached the other side of the store, where I pretend to look through a row of silk ties but everything's blurry, "you'll be glad to know that I'm transferring . . . out of state."

Something rises off me and I'm able to ask, but still without looking at him, "Where?"

"Oh, a different branch," he says, sounding remarkably relaxed, probably due to the fact that I actually inquired about the move. "In Arizona."

"Ter-rific," I murmur.

"Don't you want to know why?" he asks.

"No, not really."

"Because of *you*," he says.

"Don't say that," I plead.

"Because of *you*," he says again.

"*You* are *sick*," I tell him.

"If I'm sick it's because of *you*," he says too casually, checking his nails. "Because of you I am sick and I will not get better."

"You have distorted this obsession of yours way out of proportion. Way, *way* out of proportion," I say, then move over to another aisle.

"But I know you have the same feelings I do," Luis says, trailing me. "And I know that just because . . ." He lowers his voice and shrugs. "Just because you won't admit . . . certain feelings you have doesn't mean you don't have them."

"What are you trying to say?" I hiss.

"That I know you feel the same way I do." Dramatically, he whips off his sunglasses, as if to prove a point.

"You have reached . . . an inaccurate conclusion," I choke. "You are . . . obviously unsound."

"Why?" he asks. "Is it so wrong to love you, Patrick?"

"Oh . . . my . . . god."

"To *want* you? To want to be with you?" he asks. "Is that so wrong?"

I can feel him staring helplessly into me, that he's near total emotional collapse. After he finishes, except for a long silence I have no answer. Finally I counter this by hissing, "What is this continuing inability you have to evaluate this situation rationally?" I pause. "Huh?"

I lift my head up from the sweaters, the ties, whatever, and glance at Luis. In that instant he smiles, relieved that I'm acknowledging his presence, but the smile soon becomes fractured and in the dark inner recesses of his fag mind he realizes something and starts crying. When I calmly walk over to a column so I can hide behind it, he follows and roughly grabs my shoulder, spinning me around so I'm facing him: Luis blotting out reality.

At the same time I ask Luis to "Go away" he sobs, "Oh god, Patrick, why don't you *like* me?" and then, unfortunately, he falls to the floor at my feet.

"Get up," I mutter, standing there. "Get *up*."

"Why can't we be together?" he sobs, pounding his fist on the floor.

"Because I . . . don't"—I look around the store quickly to make sure no one is listening; he reaches for my knee, I brush his hand away—"find you . . . sexually attractive," I whisper loudly, staring down at him. "I can't believe I actually said that," I mumble to myself, to no one, and then shake my head, trying to clear it, things reaching a level of confusion that I'm incapable of registering. I tell Luis, "Leave me alone, please," and I start to walk away.

Unable to grasp this request, Luis grabs at the hem of my Armani silk-cloth trench coat and, still lying on the floor, cries out, "Please, Patrick, *please* don't leave me."

"Listen to me," I tell him, kneeling down, trying to haul Luis up off the floor. But this causes him to shout out something garbled, which turns into a wail that rises and reaches a crescendo that catches the attention of a Barney's security guard standing by the store's front entrance, who starts making his way over.

"Look what you've done," I whisper desperately. "Get up. *Get up.*"

"Is everything okay?" The security guard, a big black guy, is looking down at us.

"Yes, thank you," I say, glaring at Luis. "Everything's *fine.*"

"No-o-o-o," Luis wails, racked with sobs.

"Yes," I reiterate, looking up at the guard.

"You sure?" the guard asks.

Smiling professionally, I tell him, "Please just give us a minute. We need some privacy." I turn back to Luis. "Now come on, Luis. Get up. You're slobbering." I look back up at the security guard and mouth, holding up a hand, while nodding, "Just a minute, please."

The security guard nods unsurely and moves hesitantly back to his post.

Still kneeling, I grab Luis by his heaving shoulders and calmly tell him, my voice lowered, as threatening as possible, as if speaking to a child about to be punished, "Listen to me, Luis. If you do not stop crying, you fucking pathetic *faggot*, I am going to slit your fucking throat. Are you listening to me?" I slap him lightly on the face a couple of times. "I can't be more emphatic."

"Oh just kill me," he wails, his eyes closed, nodding his head back and forth, retreating further into incoherence; then he blubbers, "If I can't have you, I don't want to live. I want to *die*."

My sanity is in danger of fading, right here in Barney's, and I grab Luis by the collar, scrunching it up in my fist, and pulling his face very close to mine, I whisper, under my breath, "Listen to me, Luis. Are you listening to me? I usually don't warn people, Luis. So-be-thankful-I-am-warning-you."

His rationality shot to hell, making guttural noises, his head bent down shamefully, he offers a response that's barely audible. I grab his hair—it's stiff with mousse; I recognize the scent as Cactus, a new brand—and yanking his head up, snarling, I spit out, "Listen, you *want* to *die*? I'll do it, Luis. I've done it before and I will fucking *gut* you, *rip* your fucking stomach open and cram your intestines down your fucking faggot throat until you *choke* on them."

He's not listening. Still on my haunches, I just stare him in disbelief.

"Please, Patrick, please. Listen to me, I've figured it all out. I'm quitting P & P, you can too, and, and we'll relocate to Arizona, and then—"

"Shut up, Luis." I shake him. "Oh my god, just shut up."

I quickly stand, brushing myself off, and when I think his outburst has subsided and I'm able to walk away, Luis grabs at my right ankle and tries to hang on as I'm leaving Barney's and I end up dragging him along for six feet before I have to kick him in the face, while smiling helplessly at a couple who are browsing near the sock department. Luis looks up at me, imploring, the beginnings of a small gash forming on his left cheek. The couple move away.

"*I love you*," he miserably wails. "I love you."

"I'm *convinced*, Luis," I shout at him. "You've *convinced* me. Now get up."

Luckily, a salesperson, alarmed by the scene Luis has made, intervenes and helps him up.

A few minutes later, after he's sufficiently calmed down, the two of us are standing just inside Barney's main entrance. He has a handkerchief in one hand, his eyes are shut tightly, a bruise slowly forms, swelling beneath his left eye. He seems composed.

"Just, you know, have the guts to face, uh, reality," I tell him.

Anguished, he stares out the revolving doors at the warm falling rain and then, with a mournful sigh, turns to me. I'm looking at the rows, the endless rows of ties, then at the ceiling.

KILLING CHILD AT ZOO

A string of days pass. During the nights I've been sleeping in twenty-minute intervals. I feel aimless, things look cloudy, my homicidal compulsion, which surfaces, disappears, surfaces, leaves again, lies barely dormant during a quiet lunch at Alex Goes to Camp, where I have the lamb sausage salad with lobster and white beans sprayed with lime and foie gras vinegar. I'm wearing faded jeans, an Armani jacket, and a white, hundred-and-forty-dollar Commes des Garçons T-shirt. I make a phone call to check my messages. I return some videotapes. I stop at an automated teller. Last night, Jeanette asked me, "Patrick, why do you keep razor blades in your wallet?" *The Patty Winters Show* this morning was about a boy who fell in love with a box of soap.

Unable to maintain a credible public persona, I find myself roaming the zoo in Central Park, restlessly. Drug dealers hang out along the perimeter by the gates and the smell of horse shit from passing carriages drifts over them into the zoo, and the tips of skyscrapers, apartment buildings on Fifth Avenue, the Trump Plaza, the AT&T building, surround the park which surrounds the zoo and heightens its unnaturalness. A black custodian mopping the floor in the men's room asks me to flush the urinal after I use it. "Do it yourself, nigger," I tell him and when he makes a move toward me, the flash of a knifeblade causes him to back off. All the information booths seem closed. A blind man chews, feeds, on a pretzel. Two drunks, faggots, console each other on a bench. Nearby a mother breast-feeds her baby which awakens something awful in me.

The zoo seems empty, devoid of life. The polar bears look stained and drugged. A crocodile floats morosely in an oily makeshift pond. The puffins stare sadly from their glass cage. Toucans have beaks as sharp as knives. The seals stupidly dive off rocks into swirling black water, barking mindlessly. The zookeepers feed them dead fish. A crowd gathers around the tank, mostly adults, a few accompanied by children. On the seals' tank a plaque warns: COINS CAN KILL—IF SWALLOWED, COINS CAN LODGE IN AN ANIMAL'S STOMACH AND CAUSE ULCERS, INFECTIONS AND DEATH. DO NOT THROW COINS IN THE POOL. So what do I do? Toss a handful of change into the tank when none of the zookeepers are watching. It's not the seals I hate—it's the audience's enjoyment of them that bothers me. The snowy owl has eyes that look just like mine, especially when it widens them. And while I stand there, staring at it, lowering my sunglasses, something unspoken passes between me and the bird—there's this weird kind of tension, a bizarre pressure, that fuels the following, which starts, happens, ends, very quickly.

In the darkness of the penguin habitat—Edge of the Icepack is what the zoo pretentiously calls it—it's cool, in sharp contrast to the humidity outside. The penguins in the tank glide lazily underwater past the glass walls where spectators crowd in to stare. The penguins on the rocks, not swimming, look dazed, stressed out, tired and bored; they mostly yawn, sometimes stretching. Fake penguin noises, cassettes probably, play over a sound system and someone has turned up the volume because it's so crowded in the room. The penguins are cute, I guess. I spot one that looks like Craig McDermott.

A child, barely five, finishes eating a candy bar. His mother tells him to throw the wrapper away, then resumes talking to another woman, who is with a child around the same age, the three of them staring into the dirty blueness of the penguin habitat. The first child moves toward the trash can, located in a dim corner in the back of the room, that I am now crouching behind. He stands on tiptoes, carefully throwing the wrapper into the trash. I whisper something. The child spots me and just stands there, away from the crowd, slightly scared but also dumbly fascinated. I stare back.

"Would you like . . . a cookie?" I ask, reaching into my pocket.

He nods his small head, up, then down, slowly, but before he can answer, my sudden lack of care crests in a massive wave of fury and I pull the knife out of my pocket and I stab him, quickly, in the neck.

Bewildered, he backs into the trash can, gurgling like an infant, unable to scream or cry out because of the blood that starts spurting out of the wound in his throat. Though I'd like to watch this child die, I push him down behind the garbage can, then casually mingle in with the rest of the crowd and touch the shoulder of a pretty girl, and smiling I point to a penguin preparing to make a dive. Behind me, if one were to look closely, one could see the child's feet kicking in back of the trash can. I keep an eye on the child's mother, who after a while notices her son's absence and starts scanning the crowd. I touch the girl's shoulder again, and she smiles at me and shrugs apologetically, but I can't figure out why.

When the mother finally notices him she doesn't scream because she can see only his feet and assumes that he's playfully hiding from her. At first she seems relieved that she's spotted him, and moving toward the trash can she coos, "Are you playing hide-and-seek, honey?" But from where I stand, behind the pretty girl, who I've already found out is foreign, a tourist, I can see the exact moment when the expression on the mother's face changes into fear, and slinging her purse over her shoulder she pulls the trash can away, revealing a face completely covered in red blood and the child's having trouble blinking its eyes because of this, grabbing at his throat, now kicking weakly. The mother makes a sound that I cannot describe—something high-pitched that turns into screaming.

After she falls to the floor beside the body, a few people turning around, I find myself shouting out, my voice heavy with emotion, "I'm a doctor, move back, I'm a doctor," and I kneel beside the mother before an interested crowd gathers around us and I pry her arms off the child, who is now on his back struggling vainly for breath, the blood coming evenly but in dying arcs out of his neck and onto his Polo shirt, which is drenched with it. And I have a vague awareness during the minutes I hold the child's head, reverently, careful not to bloody myself, that if someone makes a phone call or if a real doctor is at hand, there's a good chance the child can be saved. But this doesn't happen. Instead I hold it, mindlessly, while the mother—homely, Jewish-looking, overweight, pitifully trying to appear stylish in designer jeans and an unsightly leaf-patterned black wool sweater—shrieks *do something, do something, do something*, the two of us ignoring the chaos, the people who start screaming around us, concentrating only on the dying child.

Though I am satisfied at first by my actions, I'm suddenly jolted with a mournful despair at how useless, how extraordinarily painless, it is to take a child's life. This thing before me, small and twisted and bloody, has no real history, no worthwhile past, nothing is really lost. It's so much worse (and more pleasurable) taking the life of someone who has hit his or her prime, who has the beginnings of a full history, a spouse, a network of friends, a career, whose death will upset far more people whose capacity for grief is limitless than a child's would, perhaps ruin many more lives than just the meaningless, puny death of this boy. I'm automatically seized with an almost overwhelming desire to knife the boy's mother too, who is in hysterics, but all I can do is slap her face harshly and shout for her to calm down. For this I'm given no disapproving looks. I'm dimly aware of light coming into the room, of a door being opened somewhere, of the presence of zoo officials, a security guard, someone—one of the tourists?—taking flash pictures, the penguins freaking out in the tank behind us, slamming themselves against the glass in a panic. A cop pushes me away, even though I tell him I'm a physician. Someone drags the boy outside, lays him on the ground and removes his shirt. The boy gasps, dies. The mother has to be restrained.

I feel empty, hardly here at all, but even the arrival of the police seems an insufficient reason to move and I stand with the crowd outside the penguin habitat, with dozens of others, taking a long time to slowly blend in and then back away; until finally I'm walking down Fifth Avenue, surprised by how little blood has stained my jacket, and I stop in a bookstore and buy a book and then at a Dove Bar stand on the corner of Fifty-sixth Street, where I buy a Dove Bar—a coconut one—and I imagine a hole, widening in the sun, and for some reason this breaks the tension I started feeling when I first noticed the snowy owl's eyes and then when it recurred after the boy was dragged out of the penguin habitat and I walked away, my hands soaked with blood, uncaught.

GIRLS

My appearances in the office the last month or so have been sporadic to say the least. All I seem to want to do now is work out, lifting weights, mostly, and secure reservations at new restaurants I've already been to, then cancel them. My apartment reeks of rotten fruit, though actually the smell is caused by what I scooped out of Christie's head and poured into a Marco glass bowl that sits on a counter near the entranceway. The head itself lies covered with brain pulp, hollow and eyeless, in the corner of the living room beneath the piano and I plan to use it as a jack-o'-lantern on Halloween. Because of the stench I decide to use Paul Owen's apartment for a little tryst I have planned for tonight. I've had the premises scanned for surveillance devices; disappointingly, there were none. Someone I talk to through my lawyer tells me that Donald Kimball, the private investigator, has heard that Owen really *is* in London, that someone spotted him twice in the lobby of Claridge's, once each at a tailor on Savile Row and at a trendy new restaurant in Chelsea. Kimball flew over two nights ago, which means no one is keeping watch over the apartment anymore, and the keys I stole from Owen still function so I was able to bring the tools (a power drill, a bottle of acid, the nail gun, knives, a Bic lighter) over there after lunch. I hire two escort girls from a reputable if somewhat sleazy private establishment I've never used before, charging them on Owen's gold American Express card which, I suppose because everyone thinks Owen is now in London, no one has put a trace on, though there is one on his platinum AmEx. *The Patty Winters Show* today was—ironically, I thought—about Princess Di's beauty tips.

Midnight. The conversation I have with the two girls, both very young, blond hardbodies with big tits, is brief, since I'm having a difficult time containing my disordered self.

"You live in a palace, mister," one of the girls, Torri, says in a baby's voice, awed by Owen's ridiculous-looking condo. "It's a real palace."

Annoyed, I shoot her a glance. "It's not *that* nice."

While making drinks from Owen's well-stocked bar, I mention to both of them that I work on Wall Street, at Pierce & Pierce. Neither seems particularly interested. Again, I find myself hearing a voice—one of theirs—asking if that's a shoe store. Tiffany flips through an issue of *GQ* that's three months old, sitting on the black leather couch beneath the strip of faux-cowhide paneling, and she's looking confused, like she doesn't understand something, anything. I'm thinking, Pray, you bitch, just pray, and then I have to admit to myself what a turn-on it is encouraging these girls to debase themselves in front of me for what amounts to pocket change. I also mention, after pouring them another drink, that I went to Harvard, and then I ask, after a pause, "Ever hear of it?"

I'm shocked when Torri answers, "I had a business acquaintance who said he went there." She shrugs dumbly.

"A client?" I ask, interested.

"Well," she starts nervously. "Let's just say a business acquaintance."

"Was this a pimp?" I ask—then the weird part happens.

"Well"—she stalls again before continuing—"let's just call him a business acquaintance." She sips from her glass. "He *said* he went to Harvard, but . . . I didn't believe him." She looks over at Tiffany, then back at me. Our mutual silence encourages her to keep talking and she continues haltingly. "He had, like, this monkey. And I would have to watch this monkey in . . . his apartment." She stops, starts, continues in monotone, occasionally gulping. "I'd want to watch TV all day, 'cause there was nothing else to do while the guy was out . . . and while I tried to keep an eye on the monkey. But there was . . . something wrong with this monkey." She stops and takes a deep breath. "The monkey would only watch . . ." Again she stops, takes in the room, a quizzical expression creasing her face as if she's not sure she should be telling us this story; if we, me and the other bitch, should be privy to this information. And I brace myself for something shocking, something revelatory, a connection. "It would only watch . . ." She sighs, then in a sudden rush admits, "*The Oprah Winfrey Show* and that's all it would watch. The guy had tapes and tapes of it and he had made all of them for this monkey"—now she looks over at me, imploringly, as if she's losing her mind here, right now in Owen's apartment and wants me to, what, verify it?—"with the commercials edited out. One time I tried to . . . turn the channel, turn one of the tapes off . . . if I wanted to watch a soap instead or something . . . but"—she finishes her drink and rolling her eyes, obviously upset by this story, continues bravely—"the monkey would s-s-screech at me and it would only calm down when Oprah was on." She swallows, clears her throat, looks like she's going to cry but doesn't. "And you know, you try to turn the channel and that d-damn monkey would try to scratch you," she concludes bitterly and hugs herself, shivering, uselessly trying to warm herself.

Silence. Arctic, frigid, utter silence. The light burning over us in the apartment is cold and electric. Standing there, I look at Torri then at the other girl, Tiffany, who looks queasy.

I finally say something, stumbling over my own words. "I don't care . . . whether you've led a . . . decent life . . . or not."

Sex happens—a hardcore montage. After I shave Torri's pussy she lies on her back on Paul's futon and spreads her legs while I finger her and suck it off, sometimes licking her asshole. Then Tiffany sucks my cock—her tongue is hot and wet and she keeps flicking it over the head, irritating me—while I call her a nasty whore, a bitch. Fucking one of them with a condom while the other sucks my balls, lapping at them, I stare at the Angelis silk-screen print hanging over the bed and I'm thinking about pools of blood, geysers of the stuff. Sometimes it's very quiet in the room except for the wet sounds my cock makes slipping in and out of one of the girls' vaginas. Tiffany and I take turns eating Torri's hairless cunt and asshole. The two of them come, yelling simultaneously, in a sixty-nine position. Once their cunts are wet enough I bring out a dildo and let the two of them play with it. Torri spreads her legs and fingers her own clit while Tiffany fucks her with the huge, greased dildo, Torri urging Tiffany to fuck her cunt harder with it, until finally, gasping, she comes.

Again I make the two of them eat each other out but it starts failing to turn me on—all I can think about is blood and what their blood will look like and though Torri knows what to do, how to eat pussy, it doesn't subdue me and I push her away from Tiffany's cunt and start licking and biting at the pink, soft, wet cuntness while Torri spreads her ass and sits on Tiffany's face while fingering her own clit. Tiffany hungrily tongues her pussy, wet and glistening, and

Torri reaches down and squeezes Tiffany's big, firm tits. I'm biting hard, gnawing at Tiffany's cunt, and she starts tensing up. "Relax," I say soothingly. She starts squealing, trying to pull away, and finally she screams as my teeth rip into her flesh. Torri thinks Tiffany is coming and grinds her own cunt harder onto Tiffany's mouth, smothering her screams, but when I look up at Torri, blood covering my face, meat and pubic hair hanging from my mouth, blood pumping from Tiffany's torn cunt onto the comforter, I can feel her sudden rush of horror. I use Mace to blind both of them momentarily and then I knock them unconscious with the butt of the nail gun.

Torri awakens to find herself tied up, bent over the side of the bed, on her back, her face covered with blood because I've cut her lips off with a pair of nail scissors. Tiffany is tied up with six pairs of Paul's suspenders on the other side of the bed, moaning with fear, totally immobilized by the monster of reality. I want her to watch what I'm going to do to Torri and she's propped up in a way that makes this unavoidable. As usual, in an attempt to understand these girls I'm filming their deaths. With Torri and Tiffany I use a Minox LX ultra-miniature camera that takes 9.5mm film, has a 15mm f/3.5lens, an exposure meter and a built-in neutral density filter and sits on a tripod. I've put a CD of the Traveling Wilburys into a portable CD player that sits on the headboard above the bed, to mute any screams.

I start by skinning Torri a little, making incisions with a steak knife and ripping bits of flesh from her legs and stomach while she screams in vain, begging for mercy in a high thin voice, and I'm hoping that she realizes her punishment will end up being relatively light compared to what I've planned for the other one. I keep spraying Torri with Mace and then I try to cut off her fingers with nail scissors and finally I pour acid onto her belly and genitals, but none of this comes close to killing her, so I resort to stabbing her in the throat and eventually the blade of the knife breaks off in what's left of her neck, stuck on bone, and I stop. While Tiffany watches, finally I saw the entire head off—torrents of blood splash against the walls, even the ceiling—and holding the head up like a prize, I take my cock, purple with stiffness, and lowering Torri's head to my lap I push it onto her bloodied mouth and start fucking it, until I come, exploding into it. Afterwards I'm so hard I can even walk around the blood-soaked room carrying the head, which feels warm and weightless, on my dick. This is amusing for a while but I need to rest so I remove the head, placing it in Paul's oak and teak armoire, and then I'm sitting in a chair, naked, covered with blood, watching HBO on Owen's TV, drinking a Corona, complaining out loud, wondering why Owen doesn't have Cinemax.

Later—now—I'm telling Tiffany, "I'll let you go, shhh . . ." and I'm stroking her face, which is slick, owing to tears and Mace, gently, and it burns me that she actually looks up hopefully for a moment before she sees the lit match I'm holding in my hand that I've torn from a matchbook I picked up in the bar at Palio's where I was having drinks with Robert Farrell and Robert Prechter last Friday, and I lower it to her eyes, which she instinctively closes, singeing both eyelashes and brows, then I finally use a Bic lighter and hold it up to both sockets, making sure they stay open with my fingers, burning my thumb and pinkie in the process, until the eyeballs burst. While she's still conscious I roll her over, and spreading her ass cheeks, I nail a dildo that I've tied to a board deep into her rectum, using the nail gun. Then, turning her over again, her body weak with fear, I cut all the flesh off around her mouth and using the power drill with a detachable, massive head I widen that hole while she shakes, protesting, and once I'm satisfied with the size of the hole I've created, her mouth open as wide as possible, a reddish-black tunnel of twisted tongue and loosened teeth, I force my hand down, deep into her throat, until it disappears up to my wrist—all the while her head shakes uncontrollably, but she can't bite down since the power drill ripped her teeth out of her gums—and grabs at the veins lodged there like tubes and I loosen them with my fingers and when I've gotten a good grip on them violently yank them out through her open mouth, pulling until the neck caves in, disappears, the skin tightens and splits though there's little blood. Most of the neck's innards, including the jugular, hang out of her mouth and her whole body starts twitching, like a roach on its back, shaking spasmodically, her melted eyes running down her face mixing with the tears and Mace, and then quickly, not wanting to waste time, I turn off the lights and in the dark before she dies I rip open her stomach with my bare hands. I can't tell what I'm doing with them but it's making wet snapping sounds and my hands are hot and covered with something.

The aftermath. No fear, no confusion. Unable to linger since there are things to be done today: return videotapes, work out at the gym, a new British musical on Broadway I promised Jeanette I'd take her to, a dinner reservation to be made somewhere. What's left of both bodies is in early rigor mortis. Part of Tiffany's body—I think it's her even though I'm having a hard time telling the two apart—has sunken in and her ribs jut out, most broken in half, from what's left of her stomach, both breasts having been pierced by them. A head has been nailed to the wall, fingers lie scattered or arranged in some kind of circle around the CD player. One of the bodies, the one on the floor, has been defecated on and seems to be covered with teeth marks where I had bitten into it, savagely. With the blood from one of the corpses' stomachs that I dip my hand into, I scrawl, in dripping red letters above the faux-cowhide paneling in the living room, the words I AM BACK and below it a scary drawing which looks like this

RAT

The following are delivered mid-October.

An audio receiver, the Pioneer VSX-9300S, which features an integrated Dolby Prologic Surround Sound processor with digital delay, plus a full-function infrared remote control that masters up to 154 programmed functions from any other brand's remote and generates 125 watts of front speaker power as well as 30 watts in back.

An analog cassette deck by Akai, the GX-950B, which comes complete with manual bias, Dolby recording level controls, a built-in calibrated tone generator and a spot-erase editing system enabling one to mark the beginning and end points of a certain musical passage, which can then be erased with a single push of a button. The three-head design features a self-enclosed tape unit, resulting in minimized interference, and its noise-reduction setup is fortified with Dolby HX-Pro while its front-panel controls are activated by a full-function wireless remote.

A multidisc CD player by Sony, the MDP-700, which spins both audios and videos—anything from three-inch digital audio singles to twelve-inch video discs. It contains a still-frame slow motion multispeed visual/audio laser that incorporates four-times-over sampling and a dual-motor system that helps ensure consistent disc rotation while the disc-protect system helps prevent the discs from warping. An automatic music sensor system lets you make up to ninety-nine track selections while an auto chapter search allows you to scan up to seventy-nine segments of a video disc. Included is a ten-key remote control joy-shuttle dial (for frame-by-frame search) and a memory stop. This also has two sets of gold-plated A-V jacks for topnotch connections.

A high-performance cassette deck, the DX-5000 from NEC, which combines digital special effects with excellent hi-fi, and a connected four-head VHS-HQ unit, which comes equipped with a twenty-one-day eight-event programmer, MTS decoding and a 140 cable-ready channels. An added bonus: a fifty-function unified remote control lets me zap out TV commercials.

Included in the Sony CCD-V200 8mm camcorder is a seven-color wipe, a character generator, an edit switch that's also capable of time-lapse recording, which allows me to, say, record a decomposing body at fifteen-second intervals or tape a small dog as it lies in convulsions, poisoned. The audio has built-in digital stereo record/playback, while the zoom lens has four-lux minimum illumination and six variable shutter speeds.

A new TV monitor with a twenty-seven-inch screen, the CX-2788 from Toshiba, has a built-in MTS decoder, a CCD comb filter, programmable channel scan, a super-VHS connection, seven watts per channel of power, with an additional ten watts dedicated to drive a subwoofer for extra low-frequency oomph, and a Carver Sonic Holographing sound system that produces a unique stereo 3-D sound effect.

Pioneer's LD-ST disc player with wireless remote and the Sony MDP-700 multidisc player with digital effects and universal-wireless-remote programming (one for the bedroom, one for the living room), which play all sizes and formats of audio and video discs—eight-inch and twelve-inch laser discs, five-inch CD video discs and three- and five-inch compact discs—in two autoload drawers. The LD-W1 from Pioneer holds two full-sized discs and plays both sides sequentially with only a several-second lag per side during the changeover so you don't have to change or flip the discs. It also has digital sound, wireless remote and a programmable memory. Yamaha's CDV-1600 multidisc player handles all disc formats and has a fifteen-selection random-access memory and a wireless remote.

A pair of Threshold monoblock amplifiers that cost close to $15,000 are also delivered. And for the bedroom, a bleached oak cupboard to store one of the new televisions arrives on Monday. A tailored cotton-upholstered sofa framed by eighteenth-century Italian bronze and marble busts on contemporary painted wood pedestals arrives on Tuesday. A new bed headboard (white cotton covered with beige brass nail trim) also arrives on Tuesday. A new Frank Stella print for the bathroom arrives on Wednesday along with a new Superdeluxe black suede armchair. The Onica, which I'm selling, is being replaced by a new one: a huge portrait of a graphic equalizer done in chrome and pastels.

I'm talking to the delivery guys from Park Avenue Sound Shop about HDTV, which isn't available yet, when one of the new black AT&T cordless phone rings. I tip them, then answer it. My lawyer, Ronald, is on the other end. I'm listening to him nodding, showing the delivery guys out of the apartment. Then I say, "The bill is three hundred dollars, Ronald. We only had coffee." A long pause, during which I hear a bizarre sloshing sound coming from the bathroom. Walking cautiously toward it, cordless phone still in hand I tell Ronald, "But yes ... Wait ... But I am ... But we only had espresso." Then I'm peering into the bathroom.

Perched on the seat of the toilet is a large wet rat that has— I'm assuming—come up out of it. It sits on the rim of the toilet bowl, shaking itself dry, before it jumps, tentatively, to the floor. It's a massive rodent and it lurches, then scrambles, across the tile, out of the bathroom's other entrance and into the kitchen, where I follow it toward the leftover pizza bag from Le Madri that for some reason sits on the floor on top of yesterday's *New York Times* near the garbage pail from Zona, and the rat, lured by the smell, takes the bag in its mouth and shakes its head furiously, like a dog would, trying to get at the leek-goat-cheese-truffle pizza, making squealing sounds of hunger. I'm on a lot of Halcion at this point so the rat doesn't bother me as much as, I suppose, it should.

To catch the rat I buy an extra-large mousetrap at a hardware store on Amsterdam. I also decide to spend the night at my family's suite at the Carlyle. The only cheese I have in the apartment is a wedge of Brie in the refrigerator and before leaving I place the entire slice—it's a really big rat—along with a sun-dried tomato and a sprinkling of dill, delicately on the trap, setting it. But when I come back the following morning, because of the rat's size, the trap hasn't killed it. The rat just lies there, stuck, squeaking, thrashing its tail, which is a horrible, oily, translucent pink, as long as a pencil and twice as thick, and it makes a slapping sound every time it hits against the white oak floor. Using a dustpan—which it takes me over a fucking *hour* to find—I corner the injured rat just as it frees itself from the trap and I pick the thing up, sending it into a panic, making it squeal even louder, hissing at me, baring its sharp, yellow rat fangs, and dump it into a Bergdorf Goodman hatbox. But then the thing claws its way out and I have to keep it in the sink, a board, heavy with unused cookbooks, covering it, and even then it almost escapes, while I sit in the kitchen thinking of ways to torture girls with this animal (unsurprisingly I come up with a lot), making a list that includes, unrelated to the rat, cutting open both breasts and deflating them, along with stringing barbed wire tightly around their heads.

ANOTHER NIGHT

McDermott and I are supposed to have dinner tonight at 1500 and he calls me around six-thirty, forty minutes before our actual reservation (he couldn't get us in any other time, except for six-ten or nine, which is when the restaurant closes—it serves Californian cuisine and its seating times are an affectation carried over from that state), and though I'm in the middle of flossing my teeth, all of my cordless phones lie by the sink in the bathroom and I'm able to pick the right one up on the second ring. So far I'm wearing black Armani trousers, a white Armani shirt, a red and black Armani tie. McDermott lets me know that Hamlin wants to come with us. I'm hungry. There's a pause.

"So?" I ask, straightening my tie. "Okay."

"So?" McDermott sighs. "Hamlin doesn't want to go to 1500."

"Why not?" I turn off the tap in the sink.

"He was *there* last night."

"So . . . what are *you*, McDermott, trying to tell *me*?"

"That we're *going* someplace else," he says.

"Where?" I ask cautiously.

"Alex Goes to Camp is where *Ham*lin suggested," he says.

"Hold on. I'm Plaxing." After swishing the antiplaque formula around my mouth and inspecting the hairline in the mirror, I spit out the Plax. "Veto. Bypass. *I* went *there* last week."

"I *know*. So did I," McDermott says. "Besides, it's cheap. So where do we go instead?"

"Didn't Hamlin have a fucking backup?" I growl, irritated.

"Er, no."

"Call him back and get one," I say, walking out of the bathroom. "I seem to have misplaced my Zagat."

"Do you want to hold or should I call you back?" he asks.

"Call me back, bozo." We hang up.

Minutes pass. The phone rings. I don't bother screening it. It's McDermott again.

"Well?" I ask.

"Hamlin doesn't have a backup and he wants to invite Luis Carruthers and what I want to know is, does this mean Courtney's coming?" McDermott asks.

"Luis can*not* come," I say.

"Why not?"

"He just *can't*." I ask, "Why does he want Luis to come?"

There's a pause. "Hold on," McDermott says. "He's on the other line. I'll ask him."

"Who?" A flash of panic. "Luis?"

"Hamlin."

While holding I move into the kitchen, over to the refrigerator, and take out a bottle of Perrier. I'm looking for a glass when I hear a click.

"Listen," I say when McDermott gets back on the line. "I don't want to see Luis *or* Courtney so, you know, dissuade them or something. Use your charm. Be charming."

"Hamlin has to have dinner with a client from Texas and—"

I cut him off. "Wait, this has nothing to do with Luis. Let Hamlin take the fag out himself."

"Hamlin wants Carruthers to come because Hamlin is supposed to be dealing with the Panasonic case, but Carruthers knows a lot more about it and that's why he wants Carruthers to come," McDermott explains.

I pause while taking this in. "If Luis comes I'll kill him. I swear to god I'll kill him. I'll fucking kill him."

"Jeez, Bateman," McDermott murmurs, concerned. "You're a real humanitarian. A sage."

"No. Just . . ." I start, confused, irritated. "Just . . . sensible."

"I just want to know if Luis comes does this mean that Courtney will come too?" he wonders again.

"Tell Hamlin to invite—oh shit, I don't know." I stop. "Tell Hamlin to have dinner with the Texas guy alone." I stop again, realizing something. "Wait a minute. Does this mean Hamlin will . . . take *us* out? I mean pay for it, since it's a business dinner?"

"You know, sometimes I think you're very smart, Bateman," McDermott says. "Other times . . ."

"Oh shit, what the hell am I saying?" I ask myself out loud, annoyed. "You and I can have a goddamn *business* dinner together. Jesus. I'm not going. That's it. I'm not going."

"Not even if Luis *doesn't* come?" he asks.

"No. Nope."

"Why not?" he whines. "We *have* reservations at 1500."

"I . . . have to . . . watch *The Cosby Show*."

"Oh *tape* it for Christ sakes, you *ass*."

"Wait." I've realized something else. "Do you think Hamlin will"—I pause awkwardly—"have some drugs, perhaps . . . for the Texan?"

"What does Bateman think?" McDermott asks, the jaded asshole.

"Hmmm. I'm thinking about it. I'm thinking about this."

After a pause McDermott says, "Tick-tock, tick-tock" in singsong. "We're getting nowhere. Of *course* Hamlin is going to be carrying."

"Get Hamlin, have him . . . get him on three-way," I sputter, checking my Rolex. "Hurry. Maybe we can talk him into 1500."

"Okay," McDermott says. "Hold on."

There are four clicking noises and then I hear Hamlin saying, "Bateman, is it okay to wear argyle socks with a business suit?" He's attempting a joke but it fails to amuse me.

Sighing inwardly, my eyes closed, I answer, impatient, "Not really, Hamlin. They're too sporty. They interfere with a business image. You can wear them with casual suits. Tweeds, whatever. Now Hamlin?"

"Bateman?" And then he says, "Thank you."

"Luis *cannot* come," I tell him. "And you're welcome."

"No prob," he says. "The Texan's not coming anyway."

"Why not?" I ask.

"Hay letsyall go to See Bee Jee Bees I har that's pretty new wave. Lifestyle difference," Hamlin explains. "The Texan is not accepted until Monday. I quickly, and quite nimbly I might add, rearranged my hectic schedule. A sick father. A forest fire. An excuse."

"How does that take care of Luis?" I ask suspiciously.

"*Luis* is having dinner with the Texan tonight, which saves me a whole lotta trouble, pardner. *I'm* seeing him at Smith and Wollensky on Monday," Hamlin says, pleased with himself. "So everything is A-okay."

"Wait," McDermott asks tentatively, "does this mean that Courtney isn't coming?"

"We have missed or are going to miss our reservations at 1500," I point out. "Besides, Hamlin, you went there last night, huh?"

"Yeah," he says. "It's got passable carpaccio. Decent wren. Okay sorbets. But let's go somewhere else and, uh, then go on the search for the, uh, perfect body. Gentlemen?"

"Sounds good," I say, amused that Hamlin, for once, has the right idea. "But what is Cindy going to say about this?"

"Cindy has to go to a charity thing at the Plaza, something—"

"That's the *Trump* Plaza," I note absently, while finally opening the Perrier bottle.

"Yeah, the Trump Plaza," he says. "Something about trees near the library. Money for trees or a bush of some kind," he says, unsure. "Plants? Beats me."

"So where to?" McDermott asks.

"Who cancels 1500?" I ask.

"You do," McDermott says.

"Oh McDermott," I moan, "just do it."

"Wait," Hamlin says. "Let's decide where we're *going* first."

"Agreed." McDermott, the parliamentarian.

"I am fanatically opposed to anywhere *not* on the Upper West or Upper East side of this city," I say.

"Bellini's?" Hamlin suggests.

"Nope. Can't smoke cigars there," McDermott and I say at the same time.

"Cross that one out," Hamlin says. "Gandango?" he suggests.

"Possibility, possibility," I murmur, mulling it over. "Trump eats there."

"Zeus Bar?" one of them asks.

"Make a reservation," says the other.

"Wait," I tell them, "I'm thinking."

"Bate*man* . . ." Hamlin warns.

"I'm toying with the idea," I say.

"*Bateman* . . ."

"Wait. Let me toy for a minute."

"I'm really too irritated to be dealing with this right now," McDermott says.

"Why don't we just forget this shit and bash some Japs," Hamlin suggests. "*Then* find the perfect body."

"Not a bad idea, actually." I shrug. "Decent combo."

"What do *you* want to do, Bateman?" McDermott asks.

Thinking about it, thousands of miles away, I answer. "I want to . . ."

"Yes . . .?" they both ask expectantly.

"I want to . . . pulverize a woman's face with a large, heavy brick."

"*Besides* that," Hamlin moans impatiently.

"Okay, fine," I say, snapping out of it. "Zeus Bar."

"You sure? Right? Zeus Bar?" Hamlin concludes, he hopes.

"Guys. I am finding myself increasingly incapable of dealing with this *at all*," McDermott says. "Zeus Bar. That's final."

"Hold on," Hamlin says. "I'll call and make a reservation." He clicks off, leaving McDermott and myself on hold. It's silent for a long time before either one of us says anything.

"You know," I finally say. "It will probably be impossible to get a reservation there."

"Maybe we should go to M.K. The Texan would probably like to go to M.K.," Craig says.

"But, McDermott, the *Texan* isn't coming," I point out.

"I can't go to M.K. anyway," he says, not listening, and he doesn't mention why.

"I don't want to know about it."

We wait two more minutes for Hamlin.

"What in the hell is he doing?" I ask, then my call waiting clicks in.

McDermott hears it too. "Do you want to take that?"

"I'm thinking." It clicks again. I moan and tell McDermott to hold on. It's Jeanette. She sounds tired and sad. I don't want to get back on the other line so I ask her what she did last night.

"After you were supposed to meet me?" she asks.

I pause, unsure. "Uh, yeah."

"We ended up at Palladium which was completely empty. They were letting in people for free." She sighs. "We saw maybe four or five people."

"That you knew?" I ask hopefully.

"In . . . the . . . club," she says, spacing each word out bitterly.

"I'm sorry," I finally say. "I had to . . . return some video-tapes . . ." and then, reacting to her silence, "You know, I *would've* met you—"

"I don't want to hear about it," she sighs, cutting me off. "What are you doing tonight?"

I pause, wondering how to answer, before admitting, "Zeus Bar at nine. McDermott. Hamlin." And then, less hopefully, "Would you like to meet us?"

"I don't know," she sighs. Without a trace of softness she asks, "Do you want me to?"

"Must you insist on being so pathetic?" I ask back.

She hangs up on me. I get back on the other line.

"Bateman, Bateman, Bateman, Bateman," Hamlin is droning.

"I'm here. Shut the fuck up."

"Are we still procrastinating?" McDermott asks. "Don't procrastinate."

"I've decided I'd rather play golf," I say. "I haven't been golfing for a long time."

"Fuck golf, Bateman," Hamlin says. "We have a nine o'clock reservation at Kaktus—"

"*And* a reservation to cancel at 1500 in, um, let's see . . . twenty minutes ago, Bateman," McDermott says.

"Oh shit, Craig. *Cancel* them *now*," I say tiredly.

"God, I hate golf," Hamlin says, shuddering.

"*You* cancel them," McDermott says, laughing.

"What name are they under?" I ask, not laughing, my voice rising.

After a pause, McDermott says, "Carruthers" softly.

Hamlin and I burst out laughing.

"Really?" I ask.

"We couldn't get into Zeus Bar," Hamlin says. "So it's Kaktus."

"Hip," I say dejectedly. "I guess."

"Cheer up." Hamlin chortles.

My call waiting buzzes again and before I can even decide whether to take it or not, Hamlin makes up my mind for me. "Now if you guys don't want to go to Kaktus—"

"Wait, my call waiting," I say. "Hold on."

Jeanette is in tears. "What aren't you capable of?" she asks, sobbing. "Just tell me what you are *not* capable of."

"Baby. Jeanette," I say soothingly. "Listen, please. We'll be at Zeus Bar at ten. Okay?"

"Patrick, please," she begs. "I'm okay. I just want to talk—"

"I'll see you at nine or ten, whenever," I say. "I've gotta go. Hamlin and McDermott are on the other line."

"Okay." She sniffs, composing herself, clearing her throat. "I'll see you there. I'm really sor—"

I click back onto the other line. McDermott is the only one left.

"Where's Hamlin?"

"He got off," McDermott says. "He'll see us at nine."

"Great," I murmur. "I feel settled."

"Who was that?"

"Jeanette," I say.

I hear a faint click, then another one.

"Was that yours or mine?" McDermott asks.

"Yours," I say. "I think."

"Hold on."

I wait, impatiently pacing the length of the kitchen. McDermott clicks back on.

"It's Van Patten," he says. "I'm putting him on three-way."

Four more clicks.

"Hey Bateman," Van Patten cries out. "*Buddy*."

"Mr. Manhattan," I say. "I'm acknowledging you."

"Hey, what's the correct way to wear a cummerbund?" he asks.

"I already answered that twice today," I warn.

The two of them start talking about whether or not Van Patten can get to Kaktus by nine and I've stopped concentrating on the voices coming through the cordless phone and started watching instead, with growing interest, the rat I've bought—I still have the mutant one that emerged from the toilet—in its new glass cage, heave what's left of its acid-ridden body halfway across the elaborate Habitrail system that sits on the kitchen table, where it attempts to drink from the water holder that I filled with poisoned Evian this morning. The scene seems too pitiful to me or not pitiful enough. I can't decide. A call-waiting noise takes me out of my mindless delirium and I tell Van Patten and McDermott to please hold.

I click off, then pause before saying, "You have reached the home of Patrick Bateman. Please leave a message after—"

"Oh for god's sake, Patrick, grow *up*," Evelyn moans. "Just *stop* it. Why do you insist on doing that? Do you really think you're going to get away with it?"

"With what?" I ask innocently. "Protecting myself?"

"With torturing me," she pouts.

"Honey," I say.

"Yes?" she sniffs.

"You don't know what torture is. You don't know what you're talking about," I tell her. "You really don't know what you're talking about."

"I don't want to talk about it," she says. "It's over. Now, what are you doing for dinner tonight?" Her voice softens. "I was thinking maybe dinner at TDK at, oh, say ninish?"

"I'm eating at the Harvard Club *by myself* tonight," I say.

"Oh don't be silly," Evelyn says. "I know you're having dinner at Kaktus with Hamlin and McDermott."

"How do you know *that*?" I ask, not caring if I've been caught in a lie. "Anyway, it's Zeus Bar, not Kaktus."

"Because I just talked to Cindy," she says.

"I thought Cindy was going to this plant or tree—this bush benefit," I say.

"Oh, no, no, no," Evelyn says. "That's *next* week. Do you want to go?"

"Hold on," I say.

I get back on the line with Craig and Van Patten.

"Bateman?" Van Patten asks. "What the *fuck* are you doing?"

"How the hell does Cindy know we're having dinner at Kaktus?" I demand.

"Hamlin told her?" McDermott guesses. "I don't know. Why?"

"Because now *Evelyn* knows," I say.

"When the *fuck* is Wolfgang Puck going to open a restaurant in this goddamn city?" Van Patten asks us.

"Is Van Patten on his third six-pack of Foster's or is he still, like, working on his first?" I ask McDermott.

"The question you're asking, Patrick," McDermott begins, "is, should we exclude the women or not? Right?"

"Something is turning into nothing very quickly," I warn. "That's all I'm saying."

"Should you invite Evelyn?" McDermott asks. "Is this what you want to know?"

"No, we should *not*," I stress.

"Well, hey, I wanted to bring Elizabeth," Van Patten says timidly (mock-timidly?).

"No," I say. "No women."

"What's wrong with Elizabeth?" Van Patten asks.

"Yeah?" McDermott follows.

"She's an idiot. No, she's intelligent. I can't tell. Don't invite her," I say.

After a pause I hear Van Patten say, "I sense weirdness starting."

"Well, if not Elizabeth, what about Sylvia Josephs?" McDermott suggests.

"Nah, too old to fuck," Van Patten says.

"Oh Christ," McDermott says. "She's twenty-three."

"Twenty-*eight*," I correct.

"Really?" a concerned McDermott asks, after pausing.

"Yes," I say. "*Really.*"

McDermott's left saying "Oh."

"Shit, I just forgot," I say, slapping my hand to my forehead. "I invited Jeanette."

"Now that is one babe I would not mind, ahem, *inviting*," Van Patten says lewdly.

"Why does a nice young babe like Jeanette put up with you?" McDermott asks. "Why *does* she put up with you, Bateman?"

"I keep her in cashmere. A great deal of cashmere," I murmur, and then, "I've got to call her and tell her not to come."

"Aren't you forgetting something?" McDermott asks me.

"What?" I'm lost in thought.

"Is, like, Evelyn still on the other line?"

"Oh shit," I exclaim. "Hold on."

"Why am I even bothering with this?" I hear McDermott ask himself, sighing.

"Bring Evelyn," Van Patten cries out. "She's a babe too! Tell her to meet us at Zeus Bar at nine-thirty!"

"Okay, okay," I shout before clicking back to the other line.

"I do not appreciate this, Patrick," Evelyn is saying.

"How about meeting us at Zeus Bar at nine-thirty?" I suggest.

"Can I bring Stash and Vanden?" she asks coyly.

"Is she the one with a tattoo?" I ask back, coyly.

"No," she sighs. "No tattoo."

"Bypass. Bypass."

"Oh *Pat*rick," she whines.

"Look, you were lucky you were even invited, so just . . ." My voice trails off.

Silence, during which I don't feel bad.

"Come on, just meet us there," I say. "I'm sorry."

"Oh all right," she says, resigned. "Nine-thirty?"

I click back onto the other line, interrupting Van Patten and McDermott's conversation about whether it's proper or not to wear a blue suit as one would a navy blazer.

"Hello?" I interrupt. "Shut up. Does everyone have my un-divided attention?"

"Yes, yes, yes," Van Patten sighs, bored.

"I am calling Cindy up to get Evelyn out of coming to dinner with *us*," I announce.

"Why in the hell did you invite Evelyn in the *first* place?" one of them asks.

"We were joking, you *idiot*," the other adds.

"Er, good question," I say, stammering. "Uh, h-hold on."

I dial Cindy's number after finding it in my Rolodex. She answers after screening the call.

"Hello, Patrick," she says.

"Cindy," I say. "I need a favor."

"Hamlin's not coming to dinner with you guys," she says. "He tried calling back but your lines were all busy. Don't you guys have call waiting?"

"Of course we have call waiting," I say. "What do you think we are, barbarians?"

"Hamlin's not coming," she says again, flatly.

"What's he doing instead?" I ask. "Oiling his Top-Siders?"

"He's going out with *me*, Mr. Bateman."

"But what about your, uh, bush benefit?" I ask.

"Hamlin got it mixed up," she says.

"Pumpkin," I start.

"Yes?" she asks.

"Pumpkin, you're dating an asshole," I say sweetly.

"Thanks, Patrick. That's nice."

"Pumpkin," I warn, "you're dating the biggest dickweed in New York."

"You're telling me like I don't know this." She yawns.

"Pumpkin, you're dating a tumbling, tumbling dickweed."

"Do you know that Hamlin owns six television sets and seven VCRs?"

"Does he ever use that rowing machine I got him?" I actually wonder.

"Unused," she says. "Totally unused."

"Pumpkin, he's a dickweed."

"Will you stop calling me pumpkin," she asks, annoyed.

"Listen, Cindy, if you had a choice to read *WWD* or . . ." I stop, unsure of what I was going to say. "Listen, is there anything going on tonight?" I ask. "Something not too . . . boisterous?"

"What do you want, Patrick?" she sighs.

"I just want peace, love, friendship, understanding," I say dispassionately.

"What-do-you-want?" she repeats.

"Why don't the two of you come with us?"

"We have other plans."

"Hamlin made the goddamn reservations," I cry, outraged.

"Well, *you guys* use them."

"Why don't you *come*?" I ask lasciviously. "Dump dickweed off at Juanita's or something."

"I think I'm passing on dinner," she says. "Apologize to 'the guys' for me."

"But we're going to Kaktus, uh, I mean Zeus Bar," I say, then, confused, add, "No, Kaktus."

"Are you guys really going *there*?" she asks.

"Why?"

"Conventional wisdom has it that it is no longer the 'in' place to dine," she says.

"But Hamlin made the fucking reservation!" I cry out.

"Did he make reservations *there*?" she asks, bemused.

"Centuries ago!" I shout.

"Listen," she says, "I'm getting dressed."

"I'm not at all happy about this," I say.

"Don't worry," she says, and then hangs up.

I get back on the other line.

"Bateman, I know this sounds like an impossibility," McDermott says. "But the void is actually widening."

"I am not into Mexican," Van Patten states.

"But wait, we're not having Mexican, are we?" I say. "Am I confused? Aren't we going to Zeus Bar?"

"No, moron," McDermott spits. "We couldn't get into Zeus Bar. Kaktus. Kaktus at nine."

"But I don't *want* Mexican," Van Patten says.

"But *you*, Van Patten, made the reservation," McDermott hollers.

"I don't either," I say suddenly. "Why Mexican?"

"It's not *Mexican* Mexican," McDermott says, exasperated. "It's something called nouvelle Mexicana, tapas or some other south of the border thing. Something like that. Hold on. My call waiting."

He clicks off, leaving Van Patten and myself on the line.

"Bateman," Van Patten sighs, "my euphoria is quickly subsiding."

"What are you talking about?" I'm actually trying to remember where I told Jeanette and Evelyn to meet us.

"Let's change the reservation," he suggests.

I think about it, then suspiciously ask, "Where to?"

"1969," he says, tempting me. "Hmmm? 1969?"

"I *would* like to go there," I admit.

"What should we do?" he asks.

I think about it. "Make a reservation. Quick."

"Okay. For three? Five? How many?"

"Five or six, I guess."

"Okay. Hold."

Just as he clicks off, McDermott gets back on.

"Where's Van Patten?" he asks.

"He . . . had to take a piss," I say.

"Why don't you want to go to Kaktus?"

"Because I'm gripped by an existential panic," I lie.

"*You* think that's a good enough reason," McDermott says. "*I* do not."

"Hello?" Van Patten says, clicking back on. "Bateman?"

"Well?" I ask. "McDermott's here too."

"Nope. No way, José."

"Shit."

"What's going on?" McDermott asks.

"Well, guys, do we want margaritas?" Van Patten asks. "Or no margaritas?"

"I could go for a margarita," McDermott says.

"Bateman?" Van Patten asks.

"I would like several bottles of beer, preferably *un*-Mexican," I say.

"Oh shit," McDermott says. "Call waiting. Hold on." He clicks off.

If I am not mistaken it is now eight-thirty.

An hour later. We're still debating. We have canceled the reservation at Kaktus and maybe someone has remade it. Confused, I actually cancel a nonexistent table at Zeus Bar. Jeanette has left her apartment and cannot be reached at home and I have no idea which restaurant she's going to, nor do I remember which one I

told Evelyn to meet us at. Van Patten, who has already had two
large shots of Absolut, asks about Detective Kimball and what we
talked about and all I really remember is something like how people
fall between cracks.

"Did *you* talk to him?" I ask.

"Yeah, yeah."

"What did he say happened to Owen?"

"Vanished. Just vanished. Poof," he says. I can hear him opening
a refrigerator. "No incident. Nothing. The authorities have nada."

"Yeah," I say. "I'm in heavy turmoil over it."

"Well, Owen was . . . I don't know," he says. I can hear a beer
being opened.

"What else did you tell him, Van Patten?" I ask.

"Oh the usual," he sighs. "That he wore yellow and maroon ties.
That he had lunch at '21.' That in reality he was not an arbitrageur—
which was what Thimble thought he was—but a merger-maker.
Only the usual." I can almost hear him shrug.

"What else?" I ask.

"Let's see. That he didn't wear suspenders. A belt man. That
he stopped doing cocaine, simpatico beer. *You* know, Bateman."

"He was a moron," I say. "And now he's in London."

"Christ," he mutters, "general competence *is* on the fucking
decline."

McDermott clicks back on. "Okay. *Now* where to?"

"What time is it?" Van Patten asks.

"Nine-thirty," both of us answer.

"Wait, what happened to 1969?" I ask Van Patten.

"What's this about 1969?" McDermott doesn't have a clue.

"I don't remember," I say.

"Closed. No reservations," Van Patten reminds me.

"Can we get back to 1500?" I ask.

"1500 is now *closed*," McDermott shouts. "The kitchen is *closed*.
The restaurant is *closed*. It's over. We *have* to go Kaktus."

Silence.

"Hello? Hello? Are you guys there?" he hollers, losing it.

"Bouncy as a beach ball," Van Patten says.

I laugh.

"If you guys think this is funny," McDermott warns.

"Oh yeah, what? What are you going to do?" I ask.

"Guys, it's just that I am apprehensive about failure in terms of securing a table before, like, well, midnight."

"Are you sure about 1500?" I ask. "That seems really bizarre."

"That suggestion is *moot!*" McDermott screams. "Why, you may ask? Because-they-are-*closed*! Because-they-are-closed-they-*have-stopped-taking-reservations*! Are-you-following-this?"

"Hey, no sweat, babe," Van Patten says coolly. "We'll go to Kaktus."

"We have a reservation there in ten, no, fifteen minutes ago," McDermott says.

"But I canceled them, I thought," I say, taking another Xanax.

"I remade them," McDermott says.

"You are indispensable," I tell him in monotone.

"I can be there by ten," McDermott says.

"By the time I stop at my automated teller, I can be there by ten-fifteen," Van Patten says slowly, counting the minutes.

"Does anyone have any idea that Jeanette and Evelyn are meeting us at Zeus Bar, where we do *not* have a reservation? Has this passed through anyone's mind?" I ask, doubting it.

"But Zeus Bar is closed and besides that we canceled a reservation we *didn't even have there*," McDermott says, trying to stay calm.

"But I think I told Jeanette and Evelyn to meet us there," I say, bringing my fingers up to my mouth, horrified by this possibility.

After a pause McDermott asks, "Do you want to get into trouble? Are you asking for it or something?"

"My call waiting," I say. "Oh my god. What time is it? My call waiting."

"It's gotta be one of the girls," Van Patten says gleefully.

"Hold on," I croak.

"Good luck," I hear Van Patten say before I click off.

"Hello?" I ask meekly. "You have reached the—"

"It's *me*," Evelyn shouts, the noise in the background almost drowning her out.

"Oh hi," I say casually. "What's going on?"

"Patrick, what are you doing at home?"

"Where *are* you?" I ask good-naturedly.

"I-am-at-Kaktus," she hisses.

"What are you doing *there*?" I ask.

"You said you'd meet me here, that-is-what," she says. "I confirmed your reservations."

"Oh god, I'm sorry," I say. "I forgot to tell you."

"Forgot-to-tell-me-*what*?"

"To tell you that we aren't"—I gulp—"going there." I close my eyes.

"Who-in-the-hell-is-Jeanette?" she hisses calmly.

"Well, aren't you guys having fun?" I ask, ignoring her question.

"No-we-are-not."

"Why not?" I ask. "We'll be there . . . soon."

"Because this whole thing feels, gee, I don't know . . . *inappro-priate*?" she screams.

"Listen, I'll call you right back." I'm about to pretend to take the number down.

"You won't be able to," Evelyn says, her voice tense and lowered.

"Why not? The phone strike's over," I joke, sort of.

"Because-Jeanette-is-behind-me-and-wants-to-use-it," Evelyn says.

I pause for a very long time.

"Pat-rick?"

"Evelyn. Let it slide. I'm leaving right now. We'll all be there shortly. I promise."

"Oh my god—"

I click back to the other line.

"Guys, guys, someone fucked up. I fucked up. You fucked up. I don't know," I say in a total panic.

"What's wrong?" one of them asks.

"Jeanette and Evelyn are at Kaktus," I say.

"Oh boy." Van Patten cracks up.

"You know, guys, it's not beyond my capacity to drive a lead pipe repeatedly into a girl's vagina," I tell Van Patten and Mc-Dermott, then add, after a silence I mistake for shock, finally on their parts an acute perception of my cruelty, "but compassionately."

"We all know about *your* lead pipe, Bateman," McDermott says. "Stop bragging."

"Is he like trying to tell us he has a big dick?" Van Patten asks Craig.

"Gee, I'm not sure," McDermott says. "Is that what you're trying to tell us, Bateman?"

I pause before answering. "It's . . . well, no, not exactly." My call waiting buzzes.

"Fine, I'm officially jealous," McDermott wisecracks. *"Now* where? Christ, what time is it?"

"It doesn't really matter. My mind has already gone numb." I'm so hungry now that I'm eating oat-bran cereal out of a box. My call waiting buzzes again.

"Maybe we can get some drugs."

"Call Hamlin."

"Jesus, you can't walk into a bathroom in this city without coming out with a gram, so don't worry."

"Anyone hear about Bell South's cellular deal?"

"Spuds McKenzie is on *The Patty Winters Show* tomorrow."

GIRL

On a Wednesday night another girl, who I meet at M.K. and I plan to torture and film. This one remains nameless to me and she sits on the couch in the living room of my apartment. A bottle of champagne, Cristal, half empty, sits on the glass table. I punch in tunes, numbers that light up the Wurlitzer. She finally asks, "What's that . . . smell in here?" and I answer, under my breath, "A dead . . . rat," and then I'm opening the windows, the sliding glass door that leads out to the terrace, even though it's a chilly night, mid-autumn, and she's dressed scantily, but she has another glass of the Cristal and it seems to warm her enough so that she is able to ask me what I do for a living. I tell her that I went to Harvard then started working on Wall Street, at Pierce & Pierce, after I graduated from business school there, and when she asks, either confused or jokingly, "What's that?" I swallow and with my back to her, straightening the new Onica, find the strength to force out, "A . . . shoe store." I did a line of cocaine I found in my medicine cabinet when we first came back to my place, and the Cristal takes the edge off it, but only slightly. *The Patty Winters Show* this morning was about a machine that lets people talk to the dead. This girl is wearing a wool barathea jacket and shirt, a silk georgette blouse, agate and ivory earrings by Stephen Dweck, a silk jacquard torsolette vest, all from . . . where? Charivari, I'm guessing.

In the bedroom she's naked and oiled and sucking my dick and I'm standing over her and then I'm slapping her in the face with it, grabbing her hair with my hand, calling her a "fucking whore bitch," and this turns her on even more and while lamely sucking my cock she starts fingering her clit and when she's asking me "Do you like this?" while licking at the balls, I'm answering "yup, yup" and breathing hard. Her breasts are high and full and firm, both nipples very stiff, and while she's choking on my cock while I'm fucking her mouth roughly with it, I reach down to squeeze them and then while I'm fucking her, after ramming a dildo up her ass and keeping it there with a strap, I'm scratching at her tits, until she warns me to stop. Earlier in the evening I was having dinner with Jeanette at a new Northern Italian restaurant near Central Park on the Upper East Side that was very expensive. Earlier in the evening I was wearing a suit tailored by Edward Sexton and thinking sadly about my family's house in Newport. Earlier in the night after dropping Jeanette off I stopped at M.K. for a fund-raiser that had something to do with Dan Quayle, who even *I* don't like. At M.K. the girl I'm fucking came on to me, hard, upstairs on a couch while I was waiting to play pool. "Oh god," she's saying. Excited, I slap her, then lightly punch her in the mouth, then kiss it, biting her lips. Fear, dread, confusion overwhelm her. The strap breaks and the dildo slides out of her ass while she tries to push me off. I roll away and pretend to let her escape and then, while she's gathering her clothes, muttering about what a "crazy fucking bastard" I am, I leap out at her, jackal-like, literally foaming at the mouth. She cries, apologizing, sobbing hysterically, begging for me not to hurt her, in tears, covering her breasts, now shamefully. But even her sobs fail to arouse me. I feel little gratification when I Mace her, less when I knock her head against the wall four or five times, until she loses consciousness, leaving a small stain, hair stuck to it. After she drops to the floor I head for the bathroom and cut another line of the mediocre coke I scored at Nell's or Au Bar the other night. I can hear a phone ringing, an answering machine picking up the call. I'm bent low, over a mirror, ignoring the message, not even bothering to screen it.

Later, predictably, she's tied to the floor, naked, on her back, both feet, both hands, tied to makeshift posts that are connected to boards which are weighted down with metal. The hands are shot full of nails and her legs are spread as wide as possible. A pillow props her ass up and cheese, Brie, has been smeared across her open cunt, some of it even pushed up into the vaginal cavity. She's barely gained consciousness and when she sees me, standing over her, naked, I can imagine that my virtual absence of humanity fills her with mind-bending horror. I've situated the body in front of the new Toshiba television set and in the VCR is an old tape and appearing on the screen is the last girl I filmed. I'm wearing a Joseph Abboud suit, a tie by Paul Stuart, shoes by J. Crew, a vest by someone Italian and I'm kneeling on the floor beside a corpse, eating the girl's brain, gobbling it down, spreading Grey Poupon over hunks of the pink, fleshy meat.

"Can you see?" I ask the girl not on the television set. "Can you see this? Are you watching?" I whisper.

I try using the power drill on her, forcing it into her mouth, but she's conscious enough, has strength, to close her teeth, clamping them down, and even though the drill goes through the teeth quickly, it fails to interest me and so I hold her head up, blood dribbling from her mouth, and make her watch the rest of the tape and while she's looking at the girl on the screen bleed from almost every possible orifice, I'm hoping she realizes that this would have happened to her no matter what. That she would have ended up lying here, on the floor in my apartment, hands nailed to posts, cheese and broken glass pushed up into her cunt, her head cracked and bleeding purple, no matter what other choice she might have made; that if she had gone to Nell's or Indochine or Mars or Au Bar instead of M.K., if she had simply not taken the cab with me to the Upper West Side, that this all would have happened anyway. *I would have found her.* This is the way the earth works. I decide not to bother with the camera tonight.

I'm trying to ease one of the hollow plastic tubes from the dismantled Habitrail system up into her vagina, forcing the vaginal lips around one end of it, and even with most of it greased with olive oil, it's not fitting in properly. During this, the jukebox plays Frankie Valli singing "The Worst That Could Happen" and I'm grimly lip-syncing to it, while pushing the Habitrail tube up into this bitch's cunt. I finally have to resort to pouring acid around the outside of the pussy so that the flesh can give way to the greased end of the Habitrail and soon enough it slides in, easily. "I hope this hurts you," I say.

The rat hurls itself against the glass cage as I move it from the kitchen into the living room. It refused to eat what was left of the other rat I had bought it to play with last week, that now lies dead, rotting in a corner of the cage. (For the last five days I've purposefully starved it.) I set the glass cage down next to the girl and maybe because of the scent of the cheese the rat seems to go insane, first running in circles, mewling, then trying to heave its body, weak with hunger, over the side of the cage. The rat doesn't need any prodding and the bent coat hanger I was going to use remains untouched by my side and with the girl still conscious, the thing moves effortlessly on newfound energy, racing up the tube until half of its body disappears, and then after a minute—its rat body shaking while it feeds—all of it vanishes, except for the tail, and I yank the Habitrail tube out of the girl, trapping the rodent. Soon even the tail disappears. The noises the girl is making are, for the most part, incomprehensible.

I can already tell that it's going to be a characteristically useless, senseless death, but then I'm used to the horror. It seems distilled, even now it fails to upset or bother me. I'm not mourning, and to prove it to myself, after a minute or two of watching the rat move under her lower belly, making sure the girl is still conscious, shaking her head in pain, her eyes wide with terror and confusion, I use a chain saw and in a matter of seconds cut the girl in two with it. The whirring teeth go through skin and muscle and sinew and bone so fast that she stays alive long enough to watch me pull her legs away from her body—her actual *thighs*, what's left of her mutilated vagina—and hold them up in front of me, spouting blood, like trophies almost. Her eyes stay open for a minute, desperate and unfocused, then close, and finally, before she dies, I force a knife uselessly up her nose until it slides out of the flesh on her forehead, and then I hack the bone off her chin. She has only half a mouth left and I fuck it once, then twice, three times in all. Not caring whether she's still breathing or not I gouge her eyes out, finally using my fingers. The rat emerges headfirst—somehow it turned itself around inside the cavity—and it's stained with purple blood (I also notice where the chain saw took off about half of its tail) and I feed it extra Brie until I feel I have to stomp it to death, which I do. Later the girl's femur and left jawbone lie in the oven, baking, and tufts of pubic hair fill a Steuben crystal ashtray, and when I light them they burn very quickly.

AT ANOTHER NEW RESTAURANT

For a limited period of time I'm capable of being halfway cheerful and outgoing, so I accept Evelyn's invitation to dinner during the first week of November at Luke, a new superchic nouvelle Chinese restaurant that also serves, oddly enough, Creole cuisine. We have a good table (I reserved under Wintergreen's name—the simplest of triumphs) and I feel anchored, calm, even with Evelyn sitting across from me prattling on about a very large Fabergé egg she thought she saw at the Pierre, rolling around the lobby of its own accord or something like that. The office Halloween party was at the Royalton last week and I went as a mass murderer, complete with a sign painted on my back that read MASS MUR-DERER (which was decidedly lighter than the sandwich board I had constructed earlier that day that read DRILLER KILLER), and beneath those two words I had written in blood *Yep, that's me* and the suit was also covered with blood, some of it fake, most of it real. In one fist I clenched a hank of Victoria Bell's hair, and pinned next to my boutonniere (a small white rose) was a finger bone I'd boiled the flesh off of. As elaborate as my costume was, Craig McDermott still managed to win first place in the competition. He came as Ivan Boesky, which I thought was unfair since a lot of people thought I'd gone as Michael Milken last year. *The Patty Winters Show* this morning was about Home Abortion Kits.

The first five minutes after being seated are fine, then the drink I ordered touches the table and I instinctively reach for it, but I find myself cringing every time Evelyn opens her mouth. I notice that Saul Steinberg is eating here tonight, but refuse to mention this to Evelyn.

"A toast?" I suggest.

"Oh? To what?" she murmurs uninterestedly, craning her neck, looking around the stark, dimly lit, very white room.

"Freedom?" I ask tiredly.

But she's not listening, because some English guy wearing a three-button wool houndstooth suit, a tattersall wool vest, a spread-collar oxford shirt, suede shoes and a silk tie, all by Garrick Anderson, whom Evelyn pointed out once after we'd had a fight at Au Bar and called "gorgeous," and whom I had called "a dwarf," walks over to our table, openly flirting with her, and it pisses me off to think that she feels I'm jealous about this guy but I eventually get the last laugh when he asks if she still has the job at "that art gallery on First Avenue" and Evelyn clearly stressed, her face falling, answers no, corrects him, and after a few awkward words he moves on. She sniffs, opens her menu, immediately starts on about something else without looking at me.

"What are all these T-shirts I've been seeing?" she asks. "All over the city? Have you seen them? Silkience Equals Death? Are people having problems with their conditioners or something? Am I missing something? What were we talking about?"

"No, that's absolutely wrong. It's *Science* Equals Death." I sigh, close my eyes. "Jesus, Evelyn, only you could confuse *that* and a hair product." I have no idea what the hell I'm saying but I nod, waving at someone at the bar, an older man, his face covered in shadow, someone I only half know, actually, but he manages to raise his champagne glass my way and smile back, which is a relief.

"Who's that?" I hear Evelyn asking.

"He's a friend of mine," I say.

"I don't recognize him," she says. "P & P?"

"Forget it," I sigh.

"Who *is* it, Patrick?" she asks, more interested in my reluctance than in an actual name.

"Why?" I ask back.

"Who is it?" she asks. "Tell me."

"A friend of mine," I say, teeth gritted.

"Who, Patrick?" she asks, then, squinting, "Wasn't he at my Christmas party?"

"No, he was not," I say, my hands drumming the tabletop.

"Isn't it ... Michael J. Fox?" she asks, still squinting. "The actor?"

"Hardly," I say, then, fed up, "Oh for Christ sakes, his name is George Levanter and no, he didn't star in *The Secret of My Success.*"

"Oh how interesting." Already Evelyn is back poring over the menu. "Now, what were we talking about?"

Trying to remember, I ask, "Conditioners? Or some *kind* of conditioner?" I sigh. "I don't know. You were talking to the dwarf."

"Ian is *not* a midget, Patrick," she says.

"He is unusually *short*, Evelyn," I counter. "Are you sure *he* wasn't at your Christmas party"—and then, my voice lowered—"serving hors d'oeuvres?"

"You cannot keep referring to Ian as a dwarf," she says, smoothing her napkin over her lap. "I will not stand for it," she whispers, not looking at me.

I can't restrain myself from snickering.

"It isn't funny, Patrick," she says.

"*You* cut the conversation short," I point out.

"Did you expect me to be flattered?" she spits out bitterly.

"Listen, baby, I'm just trying to make that encounter seem as legitimate as possible, so don't, uh, you know, screw it up for yourself."

"Just stop it," she says, ignoring me. "Oh look, it's Robert Farrell." After waving to him, she discreetly points him out to me and sure enough, Bob Farrell, whom everyone likes, is sitting on the north side of the room at a window table, which secretly drives me mad. "He's very good-looking," Evelyn confides admiringly, only because she's noticed me contemplating the twenty-year-old hardbody he's sitting with, and to make sure I've registered this she teasingly chirps, "Hope I'm not making you jealous."

"He's handsome," I admit. "Stupid-looking but handsome."

"Don't be nasty. He's very handsome," she says and then suggests, "Why don't you get your hair styled that way?"

Before this comment I was an automaton, only vaguely paying

attention to Evelyn, but now I'm panicked, and I ask, "What's wrong with my hair?" In a matter of seconds my rage quadruples. "What the hell is wrong with my hair?" I touch it lightly.

"Nothing," she says, noticing how upset I've gotten. "Just a suggestion," and then, really noticing how flushed I've become, "Your hair looks really . . . really great." She tries to smile but only succeeds in looking worried.

A sip—half a glass—of the J&B calms me enough to say, looking over at Farrell, "Actually, I'm horrified by his paunch."

Evelyn studies Farrell too. "Oh, he doesn't have a paunch."

"That's definitely a paunch," I say. "Look at it."

"That's just the way he's sitting," she says, exasperated. "Oh you're—"

"It's a *paunch*, Evelyn," I stress.

"Oh you're crazy." She waves me off. "A lunatic."

"Evelyn, the man is *barely* thirty."

"So what? Everyone's not into weight lifting like you," she says, annoyed, looking back at the menus.

"I do not 'weight lift,'" I sigh.

"Oh go over and sock him in the nose, then, you big bully," she says, brushing me off. "I really don't care."

"Don't tempt me," I warn her, then looking back at Farrell I mutter, "What a creep."

"Oh my god, Patrick. You have no right to be so embittered," Evelyn says angrily, still staring into her menu. "Your animosity is grounded on nothing. There must be something really the matter with you."

"Look at his suit," I point out, unable to help myself. "Look at what he's wearing."

"Oh so *what*, Patrick." She turns a page, finds it has nothing on it and turns back to the page she was previously studying.

"Hasn't it occurred to him that his suit might inspire *loathing*?" I ask.

"Patrick you are being a *lunatic*," she says, shaking her head, now looking over the wine list.

"Goddamnit, Evelyn. What do you mean, *being*?" I say. "I fucking *am* one."

"Must you be so militant about it?" she asks.

"I don't know," I shrug.

"Anyway, I was going to tell you what happened to Melania and Taylor and . . ." She notices something and in the same sentence adds, sighing, ". . . stop looking at my chest, Patrick. Look at *me, not* my chest. Now anyway, Taylor Grassgreen and Melania were . . . You know Melania, she went to Sweet Briar. Her father owns all those banks in Dallas? And Taylor went to Cornell. Anyway, they were supposed to meet at the Cornell Club and then they had a reservation at Mondrian at seven and he was wearing . . ." She stops, retraces. "No. Le Cygne. They were going to Le Cygne and Taylor was . . ." She stops again. "Oh god, it *was* Mondrian. Mondrian at seven and he was wearing a Piero Dimitri suit. Melania had been shopping. I think she'd been to Bergdorf's, though I'm not positive—but anyway, oh yes . . . it *was* Bergdorf's because she was wearing the scarf at the office the other day, so anyway, she hadn't been to her aerobics class for something like two days and they were mugged on one of—"

"Waiter?" I call to someone passing by. "Another drink? J&B?" I point to the glass, upset that I phrased it as a question rather than a command.

"Don't you want to find out what happened?" Evelyn asks, displeased.

"With bated breath," I sigh, totally uninterested. "I can hardly wait."

"Anyway, the most amusing thing happened," she starts.

I am absorbing what you are saying to me, I'm thinking. I notice her lack of carnality and for the first time it taunts me. Before, it was what attracted me to Evelyn. Now its absence upsets me, seems sinister, fills me with a nameless dread. At our last session—yesterday, in fact—the psychiatrist I've been seeing for the past two months asked, "What method of contraception do you and Evelyn use?" and I sighed before answering, my eyes fixed out the window on a skyscraper, then at the painting above the Turchin glass coffee table, a giant visual reproduction of a graphic equalizer by another artist, not Onica. "Her job." When he asked about her preferred sexual act, I told him, completely serious, "Foreclosure." Dimly aware that if it weren't for the people in the restaurant I would take the jade chopsticks sitting on the table and push them deep into Evelyn's eyes and snap them in two, I nod, pretending to listen, but I've already phased out and I don't do the chopsticks thing. Instead I order a bottle of the Chassagne Montrachet.

"Isn't that amusing?" Evelyn asks.

Casually laughing along with her, the sounds coming out of my mouth loaded with scorn, I admit, "Riotous." I say it suddenly, blankly. My gaze traces the line of women at the bar. Are there any I'd like to fuck? Probably. The long-legged hardbody sipping a kir on the last stool? Evelyn is agonizing between the mâché raisin and gumbo *salade* or the gratinized beet, hazelnut, baby greens and endive salad and I suddenly feel like I've been pumped full of clonopin, which is an anticonvulsive, but it wasn't doing any good.

"Christ, twenty dollars for a fucking egg roll?" I mutter, studying the menu.

"It's a moo shu custard, lightly grilled," she says.

"It's a fucking egg roll," I protest.

To which Evelyn replies, "You're *so* cultivated, Patrick."

"No." I shrug. "Just reasonable."

"I'm desperate for some Beluga," she says. "Honey?"

"No," I say.

"Why not?" she asks, pouting.

"Because I don't want anything out of a can or that's Iranian," I sigh.

She sniffs haughtily and looks back at the menu. "The moo foo jambalaya is really first-rate," I hear her say.

The minutes tick by. We order. The meal arrives. Typically, the plate is massive, white porcelain; two pieces of blackened yellowtail sashimi with ginger lie in the middle, surrounded by tiny dots of wasabi, which is circled by a minuscule amount of hijiki, and on top of the plate sits one lone baby prawn; another one, even smaller, lies curled on the bottom, which confuses me since I thought this was primarily a Chinese restaurant. I stare at the plate for a long time and when I ask for some water, our waiter reappears with a pepper shaker instead and insists on hanging around our table, constantly asking us at five-minute intervals if we'd like "some pepper, perhaps?" or "more pepper?" and once the fool moves over to another booth, whose occupants, I can see out of the corner of my eye, both cover their plates with their hands, I wave the maître d' over and ask him, "Could you please tell the waiter with the pepper shaker to stop hovering over our table? We don't want pepper. We haven't ordered anything that *needs* pepper. No *pepper*. Tell him to get lost."

"Of course. My apologizes." The maître d' humbly bows.

Embarrassed, Evelyn asks, "Must you be so overly po*lite*?"

I put down my fork and shut my eyes. "Why are you constantly undermining my stability?"

She breathes in. "Let's just have a conversation. Not an interrogation. Okay?"

"About *what*?" I snarl.

"Listen," she says. "The Young Republican bash at the Pla . . ." She stops herself as if remembering something, then continues, "at the *Trump* Plaza is next Thursday." I want to tell her I can't make it, hoping to god she has other plans, even though two weeks ago, drunk and coked up at Mortimer's or Au Bar, I *invited* her, for Christ sakes. "Are we going?"

After a pause, "I guess," I say glumly.

For dessert I've arranged something special. At a power break-fast at the "21" Club this morning with Craig McDermott, Alex Baxter and Charles Kennedy, I stole a urinal cake from the men's room when the attendant wasn't looking. At home I covered it with a cheap chocolate syrup, froze it, then placed it in an empty Godiva box, tying a silk bow around it, and now, in Luke, when I excuse myself to the rest room, I make my way instead to the kitchen, after I've stopped at the coatcheck to retrieve the package, and I ask our waiter to present this to the table "in the box" and to tell the lady seated there that Mr. Bateman called up earlier to order this especially for her. I even tell him, while opening the box, to put a flower on it, whatever, hand him a fifty. He brings it over once a suitable amount of time has elapsed, after our plates have been removed, and I'm impressed by what a big deal he makes over it; he's even placed a silver dome over the box and Evelyn coos with delight when he lifts it off, saying "Voi-ra," and she makes a move for the spoon he's laid next to her water glass (that I make sure is empty) and, turning to me, Evelyn says, "Patrick, that's *so* sweet," and I nod to the waiter, smiling, and wave him away when he tries to place a spoon on my side of the table.

"Aren't you having any?" Evelyn asks, concerned. She hovers over the chocolate-dipped urinal cake anxiously, poised. "I *adore* Godiva."

"I'm not hungry," I say. "Dinner was . . . filling."

She leans down, smelling the brown oval, and, catching a scent of something (probably disinfectant), asks me, now dismayed, "Are you . . . sure?"

"No, darling," I say. "I want you to eat it. There's not a lot there."

She takes the first bite, chewing dutifully, immediately and obviously disgusted, then swallows. She shudders, then makes a grimace but tries to smile as she takes another tentative bite.

"How is it?" I ask, then urging, "Eat it. It's not poisoned or anything."

Her face, twisted with displeasure, manages to blanch again as if she were gagging.

"What?" I ask, grinning. "What is it?"

"It's so . . ." Her face is now one long agonized grimace mask and, shuddering, she coughs. ". . . minty." But she tries to smile appreciatively, which becomes an impossibility. She reaches for my glass of water, and gulps it down, desperate to rid her mouth of the taste. Then, noticing how worried I look, she tries to smile, this time apologetically. "It's just"—she shudders again—"it's just . . . so *minty*."

To me she looks like a big black ant—a big black ant in an original Christian Lacroix—eating a urinal cake and I almost start laughing, but I also want to keep her at ease. I don't want her to get second thoughts about finishing the urinal cake. But she can't eat any more and with only two bites taken, pretending to be full, she pushes the tainted plate away, and at this moment I start feeling strange. Even though I marveled at her eating that thing, it also makes me sad and suddenly I'm reminded that no matter how satisfying it was to see Evelyn eating something I, and countless others, had pissed on, in the end the displeasure it caused her was at *my* expense—it's an anticlimax, a futile excuse to put up with her for three hours. My jaw begins to clench, relax, clench, relax, involuntarily. There is music playing somewhere but I can't hear it. Evelyn asks the waiter, hoarsely, if perhaps he could get her some Life Savers from the Korean deli around the block.

Then, very simply, dinner reaches its crisis point, when Evelyn says, "I want a firm commitment."

The evening has already deteriorated considerably so this comment doesn't ruin anything or leave me unprepared, but the unreasonableness of our situation is choking me and I push my water glass back toward Evelyn and ask the waiter to remove the half-eaten urinal cake. My endurance for tonight is shot the second the melting dessert is taken away. For the first time I notice that she has been eyeing me for the last two years not with adoration but with something closer to greed. Someone finally brings her a water glass along with a bottle of Evian I didn't hear her order.

"I think, Evelyn, that . . ." I start, stall, start again. ". . . that we've lost touch."

"Why? What's wrong?" She's waving to a couple—Lawrence Montgomery and Geena Webster, I think—and from across the room Geena (?) holds up her hand, which has a bracelet on it. Evelyn nods approvingly.

"My . . . my *need* to engage in . . . homicidal behavior on a massive scale cannot be, um, corrected," I tell her, measuring each word carefully. "But I . . . have no other way to express my blocked . . . needs." I'm surprised at how emotional this admission makes me, and it wears me down; I feel light-headed. As usual, Evelyn misses the essence of what I'm saying, and I wonder how long it will take to finally rid myself of her.

"We need to talk," I say quietly.

She puts her empty water glass down and stares at me. "Patrick," she begins. "If you're going to start in again on why I should have breast implants, I'm *leaving*," she warns.

I consider this, then, "It's over, Evelyn. It's all over."

"Touchy, touchy," she says, motioning to the waiter for more water.

"I'm serious," I say quietly. "It is fucking over. Us. This is no joke."

She looks back at me and I think that maybe *someone* is actually comprehending what I'm trying to get through to them, but then she says, "Let's just avoid the issue, all right? I'm sorry I said anything. Now, are we having coffee?" Again she waves the waiter over.

"I'll have a decaf espresso," Evelyn says. "Patrick?"

"Port," I sigh. "Any kind of port."

"Would you like to see—" the waiter begins.

"Just the most expensive port," I cut him off. "And oh yeah, a dry beer."

"My, my," Evelyn murmurs after the waiter leaves.

"Are you still seeing your shrink?" I ask.

"Pat*rick*," she warns. "*Who?*"

"Sorry," I sigh. "Your *doctor*."

"No." She opens her handbag, looking for something.

"Why not?" I ask, concerned.

"I told you why," she says dismissively.

"But I don't remember," I say, mimicking her.

"At the end of a session he asked me if I could get him plus three into Nell's that night." She checks her mouth, the lips, in the mirror of the compact. "Why do you ask?"

"Because I think you need to see someone," I begin, hesitantly, honestly. "I think you are emotionally unstable."

"*You* have a poster of Oliver North in your apartment and you're calling *me* unstable?" she asks, searching for something else in the handbag.

"No. *You* are, Evelyn," I say.

"Exaggerating. You're exaggerating," she says, rifling through the bag, not looking at me.

I sigh, but then begin gravely, "I'm not going to push the issue, but—"

"How uncharacteristic of you, Patrick," she says.

"Evelyn. This has got to end," I sigh, talking to my napkin. "I'm twenty-seven. I don't want to be weighed down with a commitment."

"Honey?" she asks.

"Don't call me that," I snap.

"What? Honey?" she asks.

"Yes," I snap again.

"What do you *want* me to call you?" she asks, indignantly. "CEO?" She stifles a giggle.

"Oh Christ."

"No, really Patrick. What do you want me to call you?"

King, I'm thinking. King, Evelyn. I want you to call me King.

But I don't say this. "Evelyn. I don't want you to call me anything. I don't think we should see each other anymore."

"But your friends are my friends. My friends are your friends. I don't think it would work," she says, and, staring at a spot above my mouth, "You have a tiny fleck on the top of your lip. Use your napkin."

Exasperated, I brush the fleck away. "Listen, I know that your friends are my friends and vice versa. I've thought about that." After a pause I say, breathing in, "You can have them."

Finally she looks at me, confused, and murmurs, "You're really serious, aren't you?"

"Yes," I say. "I am."

"But . . . what about us? What about the past?" she asks blankly.

"The past isn't real. It's just a dream," I say. "Don't mention the past."

She narrows her eyes with suspicion. "Do you have something against me, Patrick?" And then the hardness in her face changes instantaneously to expectation, maybe hope.

"Evelyn," I sigh. "I'm sorry. You're just . . . not terribly important . . . to me."

Without missing a beat she demands, "Well, *who* is? Who do you think *is*, Patrick? Who do you *want*?" After an angry pause she asks, "Cher?"

"Cher?" I ask back, confused. "*Cher?* What are you talking about? Oh forget it. I want it over. I need sex on a regular basis. I need to be distracted."

In a matter of seconds she becomes frantic, barely able to contain the rising hysteria that's surging through her body. I'm not enjoying it as much as I thought I would. "But what about the past? Our *past*?" she asks again, uselessly.

"Don't *mention* it," I tell her, leaning in.

"Why *not*?"

"Because we never really shared one," I say, keeping my voice from rising.

She calms herself down and, ignoring me, opening her handbag again, mutters, "Pathological. Your behavior is pathological."

"What does *that* mean?" I ask, offended.

"Abhorrent. You're pathological." She finds a Laura Ashley pillbox and unsnaps it.

"Pathological *what*?" I ask, trying to smile.

"Forget it." She takes a pill that I don't recognize and uses my water to swallow it.

"*I'm* pathological? *You're* telling *me* that *I'm* pathological?" I ask.

"We look at the world differently, Patrick." She sniffs.

"Thank god," I say viciously.

"You're inhuman," she says, trying, I think, not to cry.

"I'm"—I stall, attempting to defend myself—"in touch with . . . humanity."

"No, no, no." She shakes her head.

"I know my behavior is . . . erratic sometimes," I say, fumbling.

Suddenly, desperately, she takes my hand from across the table, pulling it closer to her. "What do you want me to do? What is it you want?"

"Oh Evelyn," I groan, pulling my hand away, shocked that I've finally gotten through to her.

She's crying. "What do you want me to do, Patrick? Tell me. Please," she begs.

"You should . . . oh god, I don't know. Wear erotic underwear?" I say, guessing. "Oh Jesus, Evelyn. I don't know. Nothing. You can't do anything."

"Please, what can I do?" she sobs quietly.

"Smile less often? Know more about cars? Say my name with less regularity? Is this what you want to hear?" I ask. "It won't change anything. You don't even drink beer," I mutter.

"But you don't drink beer either."

"That doesn't matter. Besides, I just ordered one. So there."

"Oh Patrick."

"If you really want to do something for me, you can stop making a scene right now," I say, looking uncomfortably around the room.

"Waiter?" she asks, as soon as he sets down the decaf espresso, the port and the dry beer. "I'll have a . . . I'll have a . . . a what?" She looks over at me tearfully, confused and panicked. "A Corona? Is that what you drink, Patrick? A Corona?"

"Oh my god. Give it up. Please, just excuse her," I tell the waiter, then, as soon as he walks away. "Yes. A Corona. But we're in a fucking Chinese-Cajun bistro so—"

"Oh god, Patrick," she sobs, blowing her nose into the handkerchief I've tossed her. "You're so lousy. You're . . . inhuman."

"No, I'm . . ." I stall again.

"You . . . are not . . ." She stops, wiping her face, unable to finish.

"I'm not what?" I ask, waiting, interested.

"You are not"—she sniffs, looks down, her shoulders heaving—"all there. You"—she chokes—"don't add up."

"I do too," I say indignantly, defending myself. "I do too add up."

"You're a ghoul," she sobs.

"No, no," I say, confused, watching her. "*You're* the ghoul."

"Oh god," she moans, causing the table next to ours to look over, then away. "I can't believe this."

"I'm leaving now," I say soothingly. "I've assessed the situation and I'm going."

"Don't," she says, trying to grab my hand. "Don't go."

"I'm leaving, Evelyn."

"Where are you going?" Suddenly she looks remarkably composed. She's been careful not to let the tears, which actually I've just noticed are very few, affect her makeup. "Tell me, Patrick, where are you going?"

I've placed a cigar on the table. She's too upset to even comment. "I'm just leaving," I say simply.

"But *where*?" she asks, more tears welling up. "Where are you going?"

Everyone in the restaurant within a particular aural distance seems to be looking the other way.

"Where are you going?" she asks again.

I make no comment, lost in my own private maze, thinking about other things: warrants, stock offerings, ESOPs, LBOs, IPOs, finances, refinances, debentures, converts, proxy statements, 8-Ks, 10-Qs, zero coupons, PiKs, GNPs, the IMF, hot executive gadgets, billionaires, Kenkichi Nakajima, infinity, Infinity, how fast a luxury car should go, bailouts, junk bonds, whether to cancel my subscription to *The Economist*, the Christmas Eve when I was fourteen and had raped one of our maids, Inclusivity, envying someone's life, whether someone could survive a fractured skull, waiting in airports, stifling a scream, credit cards and someone's passport and a book of matches from La Côte Basque splattered with blood, surface surface surface, a Rolls is a Rolls is a Rolls. To Evelyn our relationship is yellow and blue, but to me it's a gray place, most of it blacked out, bombed, footage from the film in my head is endless shots of stone and any language heard is utterly foreign, the sound flickering away over new images: blood pouring from automated tellers, women giving birth through their assholes, embryos frozen or scrambled (which is it?), nuclear warheads, billions of dollars, the total destruction of the world, someone gets beaten up, someone else dies, sometimes bloodlessly, more often mostly by rifle shot, assassinations, comas, life played out as a sitcom, a blank canvas that reconfigures itself into a soap opera. It's an isolation ward that serves only to expose my own severely impaired capacity to feel. I am at its center, out of season, and no one ever asks me for any identification. I suddenly imagine Evelyn's skeleton, twisted and crumbling, and this fills me with glee. It takes a long time to answer her question—*Where are you going?*—but after a sip of the port, then the dry beer, rousing myself, I tell her, at the same time wondering: If I were an actual automaton what difference would there really be?

"Libya," and then, after a significant pause, "Pago Pago. I meant to say Pago Pago," and then I add, "Because of your outburst I'm not paying for this meal."

TRIES TO COOK AND EAT GIRL

Dawn. Sometime in November. Unable to sleep, writhing on my futon, still in a suit, my head feeling like someone has lit a bonfire on it, in it, a constant searing pain that keeps both eyes open, utterly helpless. There are no drugs, no food, no liquor that can appease the forcefulness of this greedy pain; all my muscles are stiff, all my nerves burning, on fire. I'm taking Sominex by the hour since I've run out of Dalmane, but nothing really helps and soon even the box of Sominex is empty. Things are lying in the corner of my bedroom: a pair of girls' shoes from Edward Susan Bennis Allen, a hand with the thumb and forefinger missing, the new issue of *Vanity Fair* splashed with someone's blood, a cummerbund drenched with gore, and from the kitchen wafting into the bedroom is the fresh smell of blood cooking, and when I stumble out of bed into the living room, the walls are breathing, the stench of decay smothers everything. I light a cigar, hoping the smoke will mask at least some of it.

Her breasts have been chopped off and they look blue and deflated, the nipples a disconcerting shade of brown. Surrounded by dried black blood, they lie, rather delicately, on a china plate I bought at the Pottery Barn on top of the Wurlitzer jukebox in the corner, though I don't remember doing this. I have also shaved all the skin and most of the muscle off her face so that it resembles a skull with a long, flowing mane of blond hair falling from it, which is connected to a full, cold corpse; its eyes are open, the actual eyeballs hanging out of their sockets by their stalks. Most of her chest is indistinguishable from her neck, which looks like ground-up meat, her stomach resembles the eggplant and goat cheese lassagna at Il Marlibro or some other kind of dog food, the dominant colors red and white and brown. A few of her intestines are smeared across one wall and others are mashed up into balls that lie strewn across the glass-top coffee table like long blue snakes, mutant worms. The patches of skin left on her body are blue-gray, the color of tinfoil. Her vagina has discharged a brownish syrupy fluid that smells like a sick animal, as if that rat had been forced back up in there, had been digested or something.

I spent the next fifteen minutes beside myself, pulling out a bluish rope of intestine, most of it still connected to the body, and shoving it into my mouth, choking on it, and it feels moist in my mouth and it's filled with some kind of paste which smells bad. After an hour of digging, I detach her spinal cord and decide to Federal Express the thing without cleaning it, wrapped in tissue, under a different name, to Leona Helmsley. I want to drink this girl's blood as if it were champagne and I plunge my face deep into what's left of her stomach, scratching my chomping jaw on a broken rib. The huge new television set is on in one of the rooms, first blaring out *The Patty Winters Show*, whose topic today is Human Dairies, then a game show, *Wheel of Fortune*, and the applause coming from the studio audience sounds like static each time a new letter is turned. I'm loosening the tie I'm still wearing with a blood-soaked hand, breathing in deeply. This is my reality. Everything outside of this is like some movie I once saw.

In the kitchen I try to make meat loaf out of the girl but it becomes too frustrating a task and instead I spend the afternoon smearing her meat all over the walls, chewing on strips of skin I ripped from her body, then I rest by watching a tape of last week's new CBS sitcom, *Murphy Brown*. After that and a large glass of J&B I'm back in the kitchen. The head in the microwave is now completely black and hairless and I place it in a tin pot on the stove in an attempt to boil any remaining flesh I forgot to shave off. Heaving the rest of her body into a garbage bag—my muscles, slathered with Ben-Gay, easily handling the dead weight—I decide to use whatever is left of her for a sausage of some kind.

A Richard Marx CD plays on the stereo, a bag from Zabar's loaded with sourdough onion bagels and spices sits on the kitchen table while I grind bone and fat and flesh into patties, and though it does sporadically penetrate how unacceptable some of what I'm doing actually is, I just remind myself that this thing, this girl, this meat, is nothing, is shit, and along with a Xanax (which I am now taking half-hourly) this thought momentarily calms me and then I'm humming, humming the theme to a show I watched often as a child—*The Jetsons*? *The Banana Splits*? *Scooby Doo*? *Sigmund and the Sea Monsters*? I'm remembering the song, the melody, even the key it was sung in, but not the show. Was it *Lidsville*? Was it *H. R. Pufnstuf*? These questions are punctuated by other questions, as diverse as "Will I ever do time?" and "Did this girl have a trusting heart?" The smell of meat and blood clouds up the condo until I don't notice it anymore. And later my macabre joy sours and I'm weeping for myself, unable to find solace in any of this, crying out, sobbing "I just want to be loved," cursing the earth and everything I have been taught: principles, distinctions, choices, morals, compromises, knowledge, unity, prayer—all of it was wrong, without any final purpose. All it came down to was: die or adapt. I imagine my own vacant face, the disembodied voice coming from its mouth: *These are terrible times*. Maggots already writhe across the human sausage, the drool pouring from my lips dribbles over them, and still I can't tell if I'm cooking any of this correctly, because I'm crying too hard and I have never really cooked anything before.

TAKING AN UZI TO THE GYM

On a moonless night, in the starkness of the locker room at Xclusive, after working out for two hours, I'm feeling good. The gun in my locker is an Uzi which cost me seven hundred dollars and though I am also carrying a Ruger Mini ($469) in my Bottega Veneta briefcase and it's favored by most hunters, I still don't like the way it looks; there's something more manly about an Uzi, something dramatic about it that gets me excited, and sitting here, Walkman on my head, in a pair of two-hundred-dollar black Lycra bicycle shorts, a Valium just beginning to take effect, I stare into the darkness of the locker, tempted. The rape and subsequent murder last night of an NYU student behind the Gristede's on University Place, near her dorm, however inappropriate the timing, no matter how uncharacteristic the lapse, was highly satisfying and though I'm unprepared by my change of heart, I'm in a reflective mood and I place the gun, which is a symbol of order to me, back in the locker, to be used at another time. I have videotapes to return, money to be taken out of an automated teller, a dinner reservation at 150 Wooster that was difficult to get.

CHASE, MANHATTAN

Tuesday night, at Bouley, in No Man's Land, a fairly unremarkable marathon dinner, even after I tell the table, "Listen, guys, my life is a living hell," they utterly ignore me, the group assembled (Richard Perry, Edward Lampert, John Constable, Craig McDermott, Jim Kramer, Lucas Tanner) continuing to argue about allocating assets, which stocks look best for the upcoming decade, hardbodies, real estate, gold, why long-term bonds are too risky now, the spread collar, portfolios, how to use power effectively, new ways to exercise, Stolichnaya Cristall, how best to impress very important people, eternal vigilance, life at its best, here in Bouley I cannot seem to control myself, here in a room that contains a whole host of victims, lately I can't help noticing them everywhere— in business meetings, nightclubs, restaurants, in passing taxis and in elevators, on line at automated tellers and on porno tapes, in David's Cookies and on CNN, everywhere, all of them having one thing in common: they are *prey*, and during dinner I almost become unglued, plummeting into a state of near vertigo that forces me to excuse myself before dessert, at which point I use the rest room, do a line of cocaine, pick up my Giorgio Armani wool overcoat and the .357 magnum barely concealed within it from the coatcheck, strap on a holster and then I'm outside, but on *The Patty Winters Show* this morning there was an interview with a man who set his daughter on fire while she was giving birth, at dinner we all had shark . . .

. . . in Tribeca it's misty out, sky on the verge of rain, the restaurants down here empty, after midnight the streets remote, unreal, the only sign of human life someone playing a saxophone on the corner of Duane Street, in the doorway of what used to be DuPlex, which is now an abandoned bistro that closed last month, a young guy, bearded, white beret, playing a very beautiful but clichéd saxophone solo, at his feet an open umbrella with a dollar, damp, and some change in it, unable to resist I move up to him, listening to the music, something from *Les Misérables*, he acknowledges my presence, nods, and while he closes his eyes—lifting the instrument up, leaning his head back during what I guess he thinks is a passionate moment—in one fluid motion I take the .357 magnum out of its holster and, not wanting to arouse anyone in the vicinity, I screw a silencer onto the gun, a cold autumn wind rushes up the street, engulfing us, and when the victim opens his eyes, spotting the gun, he stops playing, the tip of the saxophone still in his mouth, I pause too, then nod for him to go on, and, tentatively, he does, then I raise the gun to his face and in midnote pull the trigger, but the silencer doesn't work and in the same instant a huge crimson ring appears behind his head the booming sound of the gunshot deafens me, stunned, his eyes still alive, he falls to his knees, then onto his saxophone, I pop the clip and replace it with a full one, then something bad happens . . .

. . . because while doing this I've failed to notice the squad car that was traveling behind me—doing what? god only knows, handing out parking tickets?—and after the noise the magnum makes echoes, fades, the siren of the squad car pierces the night, out of nowhere, sending my heart into palpitations, I start walking away from the trembling body, slowly, casually at first, as if innocent, then I break into a run, full-fledged, the cop car screeching after me, over a loudspeaker a cop shouts uselessly, "halt stop halt put down your weapon," ignoring them I make a left on Broadway, heading down toward City Hall Park, ducking into an alleyway, the squad car follows but only makes it halfway as the alley narrows, a spray of the blue sparks flying up before it gets stuck and I run out the end of the alley as fast as I can onto Church Street, where I flag down a cab, hop in the front seat and scream at its driver, a young Iranian guy completely taken by surprise, to "get the hell out of here fast—no drive," I'm waving the gun at him, in his face, but he panics, cries out in mangled English "don't shoot me please don't kill me," holding his hands up, I mutter "oh shit" and scream "drive" but he's terrified, "oh don't shoot me man don't shoot," I impatiently mutter "fuck yourself" and, raising the gun to his face, pull the trigger, the bullet splatters his head open, cracks it in half like a dark red watermelon against the windshield, and I reach over him, open the door, push the corpse out, slam the door, start driving . . .

. . . in an adrenaline rush causing panting, I can only get a few blocks, partly because of panic, mostly because of the blood, brains, chunks of head covering the windshield, and I barely avoid a collision with another cab on Franklin—is it?—and Greenwich, veering the taxi sharply to the right, swerving into the side of a parked limousine, then I shift into reverse, screech down the street, turn on the windshield wipers, realizing too late that the blood sprayed across the glass is on the *inside*, attempt to wipe it away with a gloved hand, and racing blindly down Greenwich I lose control entirely, the cab swerves into a Korean deli, next to a karaoke restaurant called Lotus Blossom I've been to with Japanese clients, the cab rolling over fruit stands, smashing through a wall of glass, the body of a cashier thudding across the hood, Patrick tries to put the cab in reverse but nothing happens, he staggers out of

the cab, leaning against it, a nerve-racking silence follows, "nice
going, Bateman," he mutters, limping out of the store, the body on
the hood moaning in agony, Patrick with no idea where the cop
running toward him across the street has come from, he's yelling
something into his walkie-talkie, thinking Patrick is stunned, but
Patrick surprises him by lunging out before the cop can get to his
gun and he knocks him over onto the sidewalk . . .

    . . . where people from the Lotus Blossom are now standing,
staring dumbly at the wreckage, no one helping the cop as the two
men lie struggling on the sidewalk, the cop wheezing from exertion
on top of Patrick, trying to wrestle the magnum from his grasp, but
Patrick feels infected, like gasoline is coursing through his veins
instead of blood, it gets windier, the temperature drops, it starts
raining, but softly they roll into the street, Patrick keeps thinking
there should be music, he forces a demonic leer, his heart thumping, and manages quite easily to bring the gun up to the cop's face,
two pairs of hands holding it but Patrick's finger pulls the trigger,
the bullet blowing a crease in the top of the officer's skull yet failing
to kill him, but lowering his aim with the aid of the loosening grip
of the officer's fingers Patrick shoots him in the face, the bullet's
exit casting a lingering pinkish mist while some of the people on the
sidewalk scream, do nothing, hide, run back into the restaurant, as
the cop car Patrick thought he evaded in the alley careens toward
the deli, red lights flashing, screeching to a halt right when Patrick
trips over the curb, collapsing onto the sidewalk, at the same time
reloading the magnum, hiding behind the corner, the terror he
thought had passed engulfing him again, thinking: I have no idea
what I've done to increase my chances of getting caught, I shot a
saxophonist? a *saxophonist*? who was probably a *mime* too? for *that*
I get *this*? and in the near distance he can hear other cars coming,
lost in the maze of streets, the cops now, right here, don't bother
with warnings anymore, they just start shooting and he returns their
gunfire from his belly, getting a glimpse of both cops behind the
open doors of the squad car, guns flashing like in a movie and this
makes Patrick realize he's involved in an actual gunfight of sorts,
that he's trying to dodge bullets, that the dream threatens to break,
is gone, that he's not aiming carefully, just obliviously returning
gunfire, lying there, when a stray bullet, sixth in a new round, hits
the gas tank of the police car, the headlights dim before it bursts

apart, sending a fireball billowing up into the darkness, the bulb of
a streetlamp above it exploding unexpectedly in a burst of yellow-
green sparks, flames washing over the bodies of the policemen both
living and dead, shattering all the windows of Lotus Blossom,
Patrick's ears ringing . . .

. . . while running toward Wall Street, still in Tribeca, he stays
away from where the streetlamps shine the brightest, notices that
the entire block he's lurching down is gentrified, then he dashes
past a row of Porsches, tries to open each one and sets a string of
car alarm sirens off, the car he would like to steal is a black Range
Rover with permanent four-wheel drive, an aircraft-grade aluminum
body on a boxed steel chassis and a fuel-injected V-8 engine, but he
can't find one, and though this disappoints him he's also intoxicated
by the whirlwind of confusion, by the city itself, the rain falling from
an ice-cold sky but still warm enough in the city, on the ground, for
fog to drift through the passageways the skyscrapers create in
Battery Park, in Wall Street, wherever, most of them a kaleidoscopic
blur, and now he's jumping over an embankment, *somersaulting*
over it, then he's running like crazy, running full tilt, his brain
locked into the physical exertion of utter, sheer panic, helter-skelter,
now he thinks a car is following him down a deserted highway, now
he feels the night accepts him, from somewhere else a shot is heard
but doesn't really register because Patrick's mind is out of sync,
forgetting his destination, until like a mirage his office building,
where Pierce & Pierce is located, comes into view, the lights in it
going off, floor by floor, as if a darkness is rising through it, running
another hundred yards, two hundred yards, ducking into the stairs,
below, where? his senses blocked for the first time with fear and
bewilderment, and dumbstruck with confusion he rushes into the
lobby of what he thinks is his building, but no, something seems
wrong, what is it? *you moved* (the move itself was a nightmare even
though Patrick has a better office now, the new Barney's and Godiva
stores adjacent to the lobby ease the strain) and he's gotten the
buildings mixed up, it's only at the elevator . . .

. . . doors, both of which are locked, where he notices the huge
Julian Schnabel in the lobby and he realizes *wrong fucking building*
and he whirls around, making a mad scramble for the revolving
doors, but the night watchman who tried to get Patrick's attention
before now waves him in, as he's about to bolt out of the lobby,

"Burning the midnight oil, Mr. Smith? You forgot to sign in," and frustrated, Patrick shoots at him while spinning once, twice through the glass doors which thrust him back into the lobby of god only knows where as the bullet catches the watchman in the throat, knocking him backward, leaving a spray of blood hanging momentarily in midair before drizzling down on the watchman's contorted, twisted face, and the black janitor Patrick has just noticed has been watching the scene from a corner of the lobby, mop in hand, bucket by his feet, drops the mops, raises his hands, and Patrick shoots him right between the eyes, a stream of blood covers his face, the back of his head explodes in a spray, behind him the bullet knocks out a chunk of marble, the force of the blast slams him against the wall, Patrick dashing across the street toward the light of his new office, when he walks in . . .

. . . nodding toward Gus, *our night watchman*, signing in, heading up in the elevator, higher, toward the darkness of his floor, calm is eventually restored, safe in the anonymity of my new office, able with shaking hands to pick up the cordless phone, looking through my Rolodex, exhausted, eyes falling upon Harold Carnes' number, dialing the seven digits slowly, breathing deeply, evenly, I decide to make public what has been, until now, my private dementia, but Harold isn't in, business, London, I leave a message, admitting everything, leaving nothing out, thirty, forty, a hundred murders, and while I'm on the phone with Harold's machine a helicopter with a searchlight appears, flying low over the river, lightning cracks the sky open in jagged bolts behind it, heading toward the building I was last at descending to land on the building's roof across from this one, the bottom of the building surrounded already by police cars, two ambulances, and a SWAT team leaps out of the helicopter, a half-dozen armed men disappear into the entrance on the deck of the roof, flares are lined up what seems like everywhere, and I'm watching all of this with the phone in my hand, crouched by my desk, sobbing though I don't know why, into Harold's machine, "I left her in a parking lot . . . near a Dunkin' Donuts . . . somewhere around midtown . . ." and finally, after ten minutes of this, I sign off by concluding, "Uh, I'm a pretty sick guy," then hang up, but I call back and after an interminable beep, proving my message was indeed recorded, I leave another: "Listen, it's Bateman again, and if you get back tomorrow, I may show up at

Da Umberto's tonight so, you know, keep your eyes open," and the sun, a planet on fire, gradually rises over Manhattan, another sunrise, and soon the night turns into day so fast it's like some kind of optical illusion . . .

HUEY LEWIS AND THE NEWS

Huey Lewis and the News burst out of San Francisco onto the national music scene at the beginning of the decade, with their self-titled rock-pop album released by Chrysalis, though they really didn't come into their own, commercially or artistically, until their 1983 smash, *Sports*. Though their roots were visible (blues, Memphis soul, country) on *Huey Lewis and the News* they seemed a little too willing to cash in on the late seventies/early eighties taste for New Wave, and the album—though it's still a smashing debut—seems a little too stark, too punk. Examples of this being the drumming on the first single, "Some of My Lies Are True (Sooner or Later)," and the fake handclaps on "Don't Make Me Do It" as well as the organ on "Taking a Walk." Even though it was a little bit strained, their peppy boy-wants-girl lyrics and the energy with which Lewis, as a lead singer, instilled all the songs were refreshing. Having a great lead guitarist like Chris Hayes (who also shares vocals) doesn't hurt either. Hayes' solos are as original and unrehearsed as any in rock. Yet the keyboardist, Sean Hopper, seemed too intent on playing the organ a little too mechanically (though his piano playing on the second half of the album gets better) and Bill Gibson's drumming was too muted to have much impact. The songwriting also didn't mature until much later, though many of the catchy songs had hints of longing and regret and dread ("Stop Trying" is just one example).

Though the boys hail from San Francisco and they share some similarities with their Southern California counterparts, the Beach Boys (gorgeous harmonies, sophisticated vocalizing, beautiful melodies—they even posed with a surfboard on the cover of the debut album), they also carried with them some of the bleakness and

nihilism of the (thankfully now forgotten) "punk rock" scene of Los
Angeles at the time. Talk about your Angry Young Man!—listen to
Huey on "Who Cares," "Stop Trying," "Don't Even Tell Me That
You Love Me," "Trouble in Paradise" (the titles say it all). Huey hits
his notes like an embittered survivor and the band often sounds as
angry as performers like the Clash or Billy Joel or Blondie. No one
should forget that we have Elvis Costello to thank for discovering
Huey in the first place. Huey played harmonica on Costello's second
record, the thin, vapid *My Aim Was You*. Lewis has some of
Costello's supposed bitterness, though Huey has a more bitter,
cynical sense of humor. Elvis might think that intellectual wordplay
is as important as having a good time and having one's cynicism
tempered by good spirits, but I wonder what he thinks about Lewis
selling so many more records than he?

Things looked up for Huey and the boys on the second album,
1982's *Picture This*, which yielded two semihits, "Workin' for a
Livin'" and "Do You Believe in Love," and the fact that this
coincided with the advent of video (there was one made for both
songs) undoubtedly helped sales. The sound, though still tinged
with New Wave trappings, seemed more roots-rock than the previous album, which might have something to do with the fact that
Bob Clearmountain mixed the record or that Huey Lewis and the
News took over the production reins. Their songwriting grew more
sophisticated and the group wasn't afraid to quietly explore other
genres—notably reggae ("Tell Her a Little Lie") and ballads ("Hope
You Love Me Like You Say" and "Is It Me?"). But for all its power-
pop glory, the sound and the band seem, gratefully, less rebellious,
less angry on this record (though the blue-collar bitterness of
"Workin' for a Livin'" seems like an outtake from the earlier album).
They seem more concerned with personal relationships—four of
the album's ten songs have the word "love" in their title—rather
than strutting around as young nihilists, and the mellow good-times
feel of the record is a surprising, infectious change.

The band is playing better than it last did and the Tower of
Power horns give the record a more open, warmer sound. The
album hits its peak with the back-to-back one-two punch of "Workin' for a Livin'" and "Do You Believe in Love," which is the best
song on the album and is essentially about the singer asking a girl
he's met while *"looking for someone to meet"* if she *"believes in*

love." The fact that the song never resolves the question (we never find out what the girl says) gives it an added complexity that wasn't apparent on the group's debut. Also on "Do You Believe in Love" is a terrific sax solo by Johnny Colla (the guy gives Clarence Clemons a run for his money), who, like Chris Hayes on lead guitar and Sean Hopper on keyboards, has by now become an invaluable asset to the band (the sax solo on the ballad "Is It Me?" is even stronger). Huey's voice sounds more searching, less raspy, yet plaintive, especially on "The Only One", which is a touching song about what happens to our mentors and where they end up (Bill Gibson's drumming is especially vital to this track). Though the album should have ended on that powerful note, it ends instead with "Buzz Buzz Buzz," a throwaway blues number that doesn't make much sense compared to what preceded it, but in its own jokey way it amuses and the Tower of Power horns are in excellent form.

There are no such mistakes made on the band's third album and flawless masterpiece, *Sports* (Chrysalis). Every song has the potential to be a huge hit and most of them were. It made the band rock 'n' roll icons. Gone totally is the bad-boy image, and a new frat-guy sweetness takes over (they even have the chance to say "ass" in one song and choose to bleep it instead). The whole album has a clear, crisp sound and a new sheen of consummate professionalism that gives the songs on the album a big boost. And the wacky, original videos made to sell the record ("Heart and Soul," "The Heart of Rock 'n' Roll," "If This Is It," "Bad Is Bad," "I Want a New Drug") made them superstars on MTV.

Produced by the band, *Sports* opens with what will probably become their signature song, "The Heart of Rock 'n' Roll," a loving ode to rock 'n' roll all over the United States. It's followed by "Heart and Soul," their first big single, which is a trademark Lewis song (though it's written by outsiders Michael Chapman and Nicky Chinn) and the tune that firmly and forever established them as the premier rock band in the country for the 1980s. If the lyrics aren't quite up to par with other songs, most of them are more than serviceable and the whole thing is a jaunty enterprise about what a mistake one-night stands are (a message the earlier, rowdier Huey would never have made). "Bad Is Bad," written solely by Lewis, is the bluesiest song the band had recorded up to this point and Mario Cipollina's bass playing gets to shine on it, but it's really Huey's harmonica solos that give it an edge. "I Want a New Drug," with its killer guitar riff (courtesy of Chris Hayes), is the album's center-piece—not only is it the greatest antidrug song ever written, it's also a personal statement about how the band has grown up, shucked off their bad-boy image and learned to become more adult. Hayes' solo on it is incredible and the drum machine used, but not credited, gives not only "I Want a New Drug" but most of the album a more consistent backbeat than any of the previous albums—even though Bill Gibson is still a welcome presence.

The rest of the album whizzes by flawlessly—side two opens with their most searing statement yet: "Walking on a Thin Line," and no one, not even Bruce Springsteen, has written as devastatingly about the plight of the Vietnam vet in modern society. This song, though written by outsiders, shows a social awareness that was new to the band and proved to anyone who ever doubted it that the band, apart from its blues background, had a heart. And again in "Finally Found a Home" the band proclaims its newfound sophisti-cation with this paean to growing up. And though at the same time it's about shedding their rebel image, it's also about how they "found themselves" in the passion and energy of rock 'n' roll. In fact the song works on so many levels it's almost too complex for the album to carry, though it never loses its beat and it still has Sean Hopper's ringing keyboards, which make it danceable. "If This Is It" is the album's one ballad, but it's not downbeat. It's a plea for a lover to tell another lover if they want to carry on with the relationship, and the way Huey sings it (arguably the most superb vocal on the album), it becomes instilled with hope. Again, this song—as with the rest of the album—isn't about chasing or longing after girls, it's about dealing with relationships. "Crack Me Up" is the album's only hint at a throwback to the band's New Wave days and it's minor but amusing, though its antidrinking, antidrug, pro-growing-up statement isn't.

And as a lovely ending to an altogether remarkable album, the band does a version of "Honky Tonk Blues" (another song written by someone not in the band, named Hank Williams), and even though it's a very different type of song, you can feel its presence throughout the rest of the album. For all its professional sheen, the album has the integrity of honky-tonk blues. (Aside: During this period Huey also recorded two songs for the movie *Back to the*

Future, which both went Number One, "The Power of Love" and "Back in Time," delightful extras, not footnotes, in what has been shaping up into a legendary career.) What to say to *Sports* dissenters in the long run? Nine million people can't be wrong.

Fore! (Chrysalis: 1986) is essentially a continuation of the *Sports* album but with an even more professional sheen. This is the record where the guys don't need to prove they've grown up and that they've accepted rock 'n' roll, because in the three-year transition between *Sports* and *Fore!* they already *had*. (In fact three of them are wearing suits on the cover of the record.) It opens with a blaze of fire, "Jacob's Ladder," which is essentially a song about struggle and overcoming compromise, a fitting reminder of what Huey and the News represents, and with the exception of "Hip to Be Square" it's the best song on the album (though it wasn't written by anyone in the band). This is followed by the sweetly good-natured "Stuck with You," a lightweight paean to relationships and marriage. In fact most of the love songs on the album are about sustained relationships, unlike the early albums, where the concerns were about either lusting after girls and not getting them or getting burned in the process. On *Fore!* the songs are about guys who are in control (who have the girls) and now have to deal with them. This new dimension in the News gives the record an added oomph and they seem more content and satisfied, less urgent, and this makes for their most pleasingly crafted record to date. But also for every "Doing It All for My Baby" (a delightful ode about monogamy and satisfaction) there's a barn-burning blues scorcher number like "Whole Lotta Lovin'," and side one (or, on the CD, song number five) ends with the masterpiece "Hip to Be Square" (which, ironically, is accompanied by the band's only bad video), the key song on *Fore!*, which is a rollicking ode to conformity that's so catchy most people probably don't even listen to the lines, but with Chris Hayes blasting guitar and the terrific keyboard playing—who cares? And it's not just about the pleasures of conformity and the importance of trends—it's also a personal statement about the band itself, though of what I'm not quite sure.

If the second part of *Fore!* doesn't have the intensity of the first, there are some real gems that are actually quite complicated. "I Know What I Like" is a song that Huey would never have sung six years back—a blunt declaration of independence—while the carefully placed "I Never Walk Alone," which follows, actually complements the song and explains it in broader terms (it also has a great organ solo and except for "Hip to Be Square" has Huey's strongest vocals). "Forest for the Trees" is an upbeat antisuicide tract, and though its title might seem like a cliché, Huey and the band have a way of energizing clichés and making them originals wholly their own. The nifty a cappella "Naturally" evokes an innocent time while showcasting the band's vocal harmonies (if you didn't know better you'd think it was the Beach Boys coming out of your CD player), and even if it's essentially a throwaway, a trifle of sorts, the album ends on a majestic note with "Simple as That," a blue-collar ballad that sounds not a note of resignation but one of hope, and its complex message (it wasn't written by anyone in the band) of survival leads the way to their next album, *Small World*, where they take on global issues. *Fore!* might not be the masterpiece *Sports* is (what could be?), but in its own way it's just as satisfying and the mellower, gentler Huey of '86 is just as happening.

Small World (Chrysalis: 1988) is the most ambitious, artistically satisfying record yet produced by Huey Lewis and the News. The Angry Young Man has definitely been replaced by a smoothly professional musician and even though Huey has only really mastered one instrument (the harmonica), its majestic Dylanesque sounds give *Small World* a grandeur few artists have reached. It's an obvious transition and their first album that tries to make thematic sense—in fact Huey takes on one of the biggest subjects of all: the importance of global communication. It's no wonder four out of the album's ten songs have the word "world" in their titles and that for the first time there's not only one but *three* instrumentals.

The CD gets off to a rousing start with the Lewis/Hayes-penned "Small World (Part One)," which, along with its message of harmony, has a blistering solo by Hayes at its center. In "Old Antone's" one can catch the zydeco influences that the band has picked up on touring around the country, and it gives it a Cajun flavor that is utterly unique. Bruce Hornsby plays the accordion wonderfully and the lyrics give you a sense of a true Bayou spirit. Again, on the hit single "Perfect World," the Tower of Power horns are used to extraordinary effect. It's also the best cut on the album (written by Alex Call, who isn't in the band) and it ties up all the album's themes—about accepting the imperfections of this world but still learning to *"keep on dreamin' of livin' in a perfect world."* Though the song is fast-paced pop it's still moving in terms of its intentions and the band plays splendidly on it. Oddly this is followed by two instrumentals: the eerie African-influenced reggae dance track "Bobo Tempo" and the second part of "Small World." But just because these tunes are wordless doesn't mean the global message of communication is lost, and they don't seem like filler or padding because of the implications of their thematic reprise; the band gets to show off its improvisational skills as well.

Side two opens smashingly with "Walking with the Kid," the first Huey song to acknowledge the responsibilities of fatherhood. His voice sounds mature and even though we, as listeners, don't find out until the last line that "the kid" (who we assume is a buddy) is actually his son, the maturity in Huey's voice tips us off and it's hard to believe that the man who once sang "Heart and Soul" and "Some of My Lies Are True" is singing *this*. The album's big ballad, "World to Me," is a dreamy pearl of a song and though it's about sticking together in a relationship, it also makes allusions to China and Alaska and Tennessee, carrying on the album's "Small World" theme—and the band sounds really good on it. "Better Be True" is also a bit of a ballad, but it's not a dreamy pearl and its lyrics aren't really about sticking together in a relationship nor does it make allusions to China or Alaska and the band sounds really good on it.

"Give Me the Keys (And I'll Drive You Crazy)" is a good-times blues rocker about (what else?) driving around, incorporating the album's theme in a much more playful way than previous songs on the album did, and though lyrically it might seem impoverished, it's still a sign that the new "serious" Lewis—that Huey the artist— hasn't totally lost his frisky sense of humor. The album ends with "Slammin'," which has no words and it's just a lot of horns that quite frankly, if you turn it up really loud, can give you a fucking big headache and maybe even make you feel a little sick, though it might sound different on an album or on a cassette though I wouldn't know anything about that. Anyway it set off something wicked in me that lasted for days. And you cannot dance to it very well.

It took something like a hundred people to put *Small World* together (counting all the extra musicians, drum technicians, accountants, lawyers—who are all thanked), but this actually adds to the CD's theme of community and it doesn't clutter the record—it makes it a more joyous experience. With this CD and the four previous ones behind it, Huey Lewis and the News prove that if this really *is* a small world, then these guys are the *best* American band of the 1980s on this or any other continent—and it has with it Huey Lewis, a vocalist, musician and writer who just can't be topped.

IN BED WITH COURTNEY

I'm in Courtney's bed. Luis is in Atlanta. Courtney shivers, presses against me, relaxes. I roll off her onto my back, landing on something hard and covered with fur. I reach under myself to find a stuffed black cat with blue jewels for eyes that I think I spotted at F.A.O. Schwarz when I was doing some early Christmas shopping. I'm at a loss as to what to say, so I stammer, "Tiffany lamps . . . are making a comeback." I can barely see her face in the darkness but hear the sigh, painful and low, the sound of a prescription bottle snapping open, her body shifting in the bed. I drop the cat on the floor, get up, take a shower. On *The Patty Winters Show* this morning the topic was Beautiful Teenage Lesbians, which I found so erotic I had to stay home, miss a meeting, jerk off twice. Aimless, I spent an inordinate amount of the day at Sotheby's, bored and confused. Last night, dinner with Jeanette at Deck Chairs, she seemed tired and ordered little. We split a pizza that cost ninety dollars. After toweling my hair dry I put on a Ralph Lauren robe and walk back into the bedroom, start to dress. Courtney is smoking a cigarette, watching *Late Night with David Letterman*, the sound turned down low.

"Will you call me before Thanksgiving?" she asks.

"Maybe." I button up the front of my shirt, wondering why I even came here in the first place.

"What are you doing?" she asks, speaking slowly.

My response is predictably cool. "Dinner at the River Café. Afterwards Au Bar, maybe."

"That's nice," she murmurs.

"You and . . . Luis?" I ask.

"We were supposed to have dinner at Tad and Maura's," she sighs. "But I don't think we're going to anymore."

"Why not?" I slip on my vest, black cashmere from Polo, thinking: I am really interested.

"Oh you know how Luis is about the Japanese," she starts, her eyes already glazed over.

When she fails to continue I ask, annoyed, "You're making sense. Go on."

"Luis refused to play Trivial Pursuit at Tad and Maura's last Sunday because they have an Akita." She takes a drag off her cigarette.

"So, like . . ." I pause. "What happened?"

"We played at my place."

"I never knew you smoked," I say.

She smiles sadly but in a dumb way. "You never noticed."

"Okay, I admit I'm embarrassed, but just a little." I move over to the Marlian mirror that hangs above a Sottsass teakwood desk to make sure the knot in my Armani paisley tie isn't crooked.

"Listen, Patrick," she says, with effort. "Can we talk?"

"You look marvelous." I sigh, turning my head, offering an airkiss. "There's nothing to say. You're going to marry Luis. Next week, no less."

"Isn't that special?" she asks sarcastically, but not in a frustrated way.

"Read my lips," I say, turning back to the mirror. "You look marvelous."

"Patrick?"

"Yes, Courtney?"

"If I don't see you before Thanksgiving . . ." She stops, confused. "Have a nice one?"

I look at her for a moment before replying, tonelessly, "You too."

She picks up the stuffed black cat, strokes its head. I step out the door into the hallway, heading down it toward the kitchen.

"Patrick?" she calls softly from her bedroom.
I stop but don't turn around. "Yes?"
"Nothing."

SMITH & WOLLENSKY

I'm with Craig McDermott in Harry's on Hanover. He's smoking a cigar, drinking a Stoli Cristall martini, asking me what the
rules are for wearing a pocket square. I'm drinking the same thing,
answering him. We're waiting for Harold Carnes, who just got back
from London on Tuesday, and he's half an hour late. I'm nervous,
impatient, and when I tell McDermott that we should have invited
Todd or at least Hamlin, who was sure to have cocaine, he shrugs
and says that maybe we'll be able to find Carnes at Delmonico's.
But we don't find Carnes at Delmonico's so we head uptown to
Smith and Wollensky for an eight o'clock reservation that one of us
made. McDermott is wearing a six-button double-breasted wool suit
by Cerruti 1881, a tattersall cotton shirt by Louis, Boston, a silk
tie by Dunhill. I'm wearing a six-button double-breasted wool suit
by Ermenegildo Zegna, a striped cotton shirt by Luciano Barbera,
a silk tie by Armani, suede wing-tips by Ralph Lauren, socks by
E. G. Smith. Men Who've Been Raped by Women was the topic on
The Patty Winters Show this morning. Sitting in a booth at Smith
and Wollensky, which is strangely empty, I'm on Valium, drinking a
good glass of red wine, wondering absently about that cousin of
mine at St. Alban's in Washington who recently raped a girl, biting
her earlobes off, getting a sick thrill not ordering the hash browns,
how my brother and I once rode horses together, played tennis—
this is burning from my memory but McDermott eclipses these
thoughts when he notices I haven't ordered the hash browns after
dinner has arrived.

"What is this? You can't eat at Smith and Wollensky without
ordering the hash browns," he complains.

I avoid his eyes and touch the cigar I'm saving in my jacket
pocket.

"Jesus, Bateman, you're a raving lunatic. Been at P & P too long," he mutters. "No fucking hash browns."

I don't say anything. How can I tell McDermott that this is a very disjointed time of my life and that I notice the walls have been painted a bright, almost painful white and under the glare of the fluorescent lights they seem to pulse and glow. Frank Sinatra is somewhere, singing "Witchcraft." I'm staring at the walls, listening to the words, suddenly thirsty, but our waiter is taking orders from a very large table of exclusively Japanese businessmen, and someone who I think is either George MacGowan or Taylor Preston, in the booth behind this one, wearing something by Polo, is eyeing me suspiciously and McDermott is still staring at my steak with this stunned look on his face and one of the Japanese businessmen is holding an abacus, another one is trying to pronounce the word "teriyaki," another is mouthing, then singing, the words to the song, and the table laughs, an odd, not completely foreign sound, as he lifts up a pair of chopsticks, shaking his head confidently, imitating Sinatra. His mouth opens, what comes out of it is: *"that sry comehitle stale . . . that clazy witchclaft . . ."*

SOMETHING ON TELEVISION

While getting dressed to meet Jeanette for a new British musical that opened on Broadway last week and then dinner at Progress, the new Malcolm Forbes restaurant on the Upper East Side, I watch a tape of this morning's *Patty Winters Show*, which is split into two parts. The first section is a feature on the lead singer of the rock band Guns N' Roses, Axl Rose, whom Patty quoted as telling an interviewer, "When I get stressed I get violent and take it out on myself. I've pulled razor blades on myself but then realized that having a scar is more detrimental than not having a stereo . . . I'd rather kick my stereo in than go punch somebody in the face. When I get mad or upset or emotional, sometimes I'll walk over and play my piano." Part two consists of Patty reading letters that Ted Bundy, the mass murderer, had written to his fiancée during

one of his many trials. "'Dear Carole,'" she reads, while an unfairly
bloated head shot of Bundy, just weeks away from execution, flashes
across the screen, "'please do not sit in the same row in court with
Janet. When I look over toward you there she sits contemplating
me with her mad eyes like a deranged seagull studying a clam . . . I
can feel her spreading hot sauce on me already . . .'"

I wait for something to happen. I sit in my bedroom for close
to an hour. Nothing does. I get up, do the rest of the coke—a
minuscule amount—that's in my closet left over from a late Saturday
at M.K. or Au Bar, stop at Orso for a drink before meeting Jeanette,
who I called earlier, mentioning that I had two tickets to this
particular musical and she didn't say anything except "I'll go" and I
told her to meet me in front of the theater at ten to eight and she
hung up. I tell myself while I'm sitting alone at the bar in Orso that
I was going to call one of the numbers that flashed on the bottom
of the screen, but then I realize that I didn't know what to say and
I remember ten of the words Patty read: *I can feel her spreading
hot sauce on me already.*

I remember these words again for some reason while Jeanette
and I are sitting in Progress after the musical and it's late, the
restaurant is crowded. We order something called eagle carpaccio,
mesquite-grilled mahi-mahi, endive with chèvre and chocolate-
covered almonds, this weird kind of gazpacho with raw chicken in
it, dry beer. Right now there really is nothing edible on my plate,
what there is tastes like plaster. Jeanette is wearing a wool smoking
jacket, a silk chiffon shawl with one sleeve, wool tuxedo pants, all
Armani, antique gold and diamond earrings, stockings from Givenchy, grosgrain flats. She keeps sighing and threatens to light a
cigarette even though we're seated in the nonsmoking section of
the restaurant. Jeanette's behavior deeply unsettles me, causes black
thoughts to form and expand in my head. She's been drinking
champagne kirs but has already had too many and when she orders
her sixth I suggest that maybe she's had enough. She looks at me
and says, "I am cold and thirsty and I will order what I fucking
want."

I say, "Then have an Evian or San Pellegrino for Christ sakes."

SANDSTONE

My mother and I are sitting in her private room at Sandstone, where she is now a permanent resident. Heavily sedated, she has her sunglasses on and keeps touching her hair and I keep looking at my hands, pretty sure that they're shaking. She tries to smile when she asks what I want for Christmas. I'm not surprised at how much effort it takes to raise my head and look at her. I'm wearing a two-button wool gabardine suit with notched lapels by Gian Marco Venturi, cap-toed leather lace-ups by Armani, tie by Polo, socks I'm not sure where from. It's nearing the middle of April.

"Nothing," I say, smiling reassuringly.

There's a pause. I break it by asking, "What do you want?"

She says nothing for a long time and I look back at my hands, at dried blood, probably from a girl named Suki, beneath the thumbnail. My mother licks her lips tiredly, and says, "I don't know. I just want to have a nice Christmas."

I don't say anything. I've spent the last hour studying my hair in the mirror I've insisted the hospital keep in my mother's room.

"You look unhappy," she says suddenly.

"I'm not," I tell her with a brief sigh.

"You look unhappy," she says, more quietly this time. She touches her hair, stark blinding white, again.

"Well, you do too," I say slowly, hoping that she won't say anything else.

She doesn't say anything else. I'm sitting in a chair by the window, and through the bars the lawn outside darkens, a cloud passes over the sun, soon the lawn turns green again. She sits on her bed in a nightgown from Bergdorf's and slippers by Norma Kamali that I bought her for Christmas last year.

"How was the party?" she asks.

"Okay," I say, guessing.

"How many people were there?"

"Forty. Five hundred." I shrug. "I'm not sure."

She licks her lips again, touches her hair once more. "What time did you leave?"

"I don't remember," I answer after a long pause.

"One? Two?" she asks.

"It must have been one," I say, almost cutting her off.

"Oh." She pauses again, straightens her sunglasses, black Ray-Bans I bought her from Bloomingdale's that cost two hundred dollars.

"It wasn't very good," I say uselessly, looking at her.

"Why?" she asks, curious.

"It just wasn't," I say, looking back at my hand, the specks of blood under the nail on my thumb, the photograph of my father, when he was a much younger man, on my mother's bedside table, next to a photograph of Sean and me when we were both teenagers, wearing tuxedos, neither one of us smiling. In the photograph of my father he's wearing a six-button double-breasted black sport coat, a white spread-collar cotton shirt, a tie, pocket square, shoes, all by Brooks Brothers. He's standing next to one of the topiary animals a long time ago at his father's estate in Connecticut and there's something the matter with his eyes.

THE BEST CITY FOR BUSINESS

And on a rainy Tuesday morning, after working out at Xclusive, I stop by Paul Owen's apartment on the Upper East Side. One hundred and sixty-one days have passed since I spent the night in it with the two escort girls. There has been no word of bodies discovered in any of the city's four newspapers or on the local news; no hints of even a rumor floating around. I've gone so far as to ask people—dates, business acquaintances—over dinners, in the halls of Pierce & Pierce, if anyone has heard about two mutilated prostitutes found in Paul Owen's apartment. But like in some movie, no one has heard anything, has any idea of what I'm talking about. There are other things to worry over: the shocking amount of laxative and speed that the cocaine in Manhattan is now being cut

with, Asia in the 1990s, the virtual impossibility of landing an eight
o'clock reservation at PR, the new Tony McManus restaurant on
Liberty Island, crack. So what I'm assuming is that, essentially, like,
no bodies have been found. For all I know, Kimball has moved to
London too.

The building looks different to me as I step out of the taxi,
though I can't figure out why. I still have the keys I stole from
Owen the night I killed him and I take them out, now, to open the
lobby door but they don't work, won't fit properly. Instead, a
uniformed doorman who wasn't here six months ago opens it for
me, excusing himself for taking so long. I stand there in the rain,
confused, until he ushers me in, merrily asking, with a thick Irish
accent, "Well, are you coming in or staying out—you're getting
soaked." I move into the lobby, my umbrella held under one arm,
tucking the surgical mask I brought with me to deal with the smell
back into my pocket. I'm holding a Walkman, debating what to say,
how to phrase it.

"Well, now what can I do for you sir?" he asks.

I stall—a long, awkward pause—before saying, simply, "Four-
teen-A."

He looks me over carefully before checking his book, then
beams, marking something down. "Ah, of course. Mrs. Wolfe is up
there right now."

"Mrs. . . . Wolfe?" Weakly, I smile.

"Yes. She's the real estate agent," he says, looking at me. "You
do have an appointment, don't you?"

The elevator operator, also a new addition, stares at the floor as
the two of us rise up into the building. I'm trying to retrace my
steps on that night, during that whole week, uselessly knowing I
have never been back to this apartment after murdering the two
girls. *How much is Owen's apartment worth?* is a question that
keeps forcing its way into my mind until finally it just rests there,
throbbing. *The Patty Winters Show* this morning was about people
with half their brains removed. My chest feels like ice.

The elevator doors open. I step out, cautiously, watching behind
me as they close, then I'm moving down the hallway toward Owen's
apartment. I can hear voices inside. I lean against the wall, sighing,
keys in my hand, knowing already the locks have been changed. As
I wonder what I should do, trembling, staring at my loafers, which

are black and by A. Testoni, the door to the apartment opens, startling me out of a momentary flash of self-pity. A middle-aged real estate broker walks out, offers a smile, asks, checking her book, "Are you my eleven o'clock?"

"No," I say.

She says, "Excuse me" and, making her way down the hall, looks back at me, once, with a strange expression on her face, before disappearing around the corner. I'm staring into the apartment. A couple in their late twenties stand, conferring with each other, in the middle of the living room. She's wearing a wool jacket, a silk blouse, wool flannel slacks, Armani, vermeil earrings, gloves, holding a bottle of Evian water. He has on a tweed sport jacket, cashmere sweater vest, cotton chambray shirt, tie, Paul Stuart, Agnes B. cotton trench coat draped over arm. Behind them, the apartment looks spotless. New venetian blinds, the cowhide paneling is gone; however, the furniture, the mural, the glass coffee table, Thonet chairs, black leather couch, all seem intact; the large-screen television set had been moved into the living room and it's been turned on, the volume low, a commercial where a stain walks off a jacket and addresses the camera is on now, but it doesn't make me forget what I did to Christie's breasts, to one of the girls' heads, the nose missing, both ears bitten off, how you could see her teeth through where I had ripped the flesh from her jaws and both cheeks, the torrents of gore and the blood that washed over the apartment, the stench of the dead, my own confused warning that I had drawn in—

"Can I help you?" the real estate agent, Mrs. Wolfe I'm guessing, intrudes. She has a very angular thin face, the nose is large, distressingly *real*-looking, heavily lipsticked mouth, white-blue eyes. She's wearing a wool bouclé jacket, washed-silk blouse, shoes, earrings, a bracelet, from where? I don't know. Maybe she's younger than forty.

I'm still leaning against the wall, staring at the couple, who move back into the bedroom, leaving the main room empty. I'm just noticing that bouquets in glass vases, dozens of them, fill the apartment everywhere, and I can smell them from where I'm standing in the hall. Mrs. Wolfe glances behind her to see what I'm staring at, then back to me. "I'm looking for . . . Doesn't Paul Owen live here?"

A long pause before she answers. "No. He doesn't."

Another long pause. "Are you, like . . . sure?" I ask, before feebly adding, "I don't . . . understand."

She realizes something that causes the muscles in her face to tighten. Her eyes narrow but don't close. She's noticed the surgical mask I'm gripping in a damp fist and she breathes in, sharply, refusing to look away. I am definitely not feeling right about any of this. On the TV, in a commercial, a man holds up a piece of toast and tells his wife, "Hey, you're right . . . this margarine really *does* taste better than shit." The wife smiles.

"You saw the ad in the *Times*?" she asks.

"No . . . I mean yes. Yes, I did. In the *Times*," I falter, gathering a pocket of strength, the smell from the roses thick, masking something revolting. "But . . . doesn't Paul Owen . . . still *own* this?" I ask, as forcibly as possible.

There's a long pause before she admits, "There was no ad in the *Times*."

We stare at each other endlessly. I'm convinced she senses I'm about to say something. I've seen this look on someone's face before. Was it in a club? A victim's expression? Had it appeared on a movie screen recently? Or had I seen it in the mirror? It takes what seems like an hour before I can speak again. "But that's . . . his"—I stop, my heart skips, resumes beating—"furniture." I drop my umbrella, then lean down quickly to retrieve it.

"I think you should go," she says.

"I think . . . I want to know what happened." I feel sick, my chest and back covered with sweat, drenched, it seems, instantaneously.

"Don't make any trouble," she says.

All frontiers, if there had ever been any, seem suddenly detachable and have been removed, a feeling that others are creating my fate will not leave me for the rest of the day. This . . . is . . . not . . . a . . . game, I want to shout, but I can't catch my breath though I don't think she can tell. I turn my face away. I need rest. I don't know what to say. Confused, I reach out for a moment to touch Mrs. Wolfe's arm, to steady myself, but I stop it in midair, move it to my chest instead, but I can't feel it, not even when I loosen my tie; it rests there, trembling, and I can't make it stop. I'm blushing, speechless.

"I suggest you go," she says.

We stand there in the hallway facing each other.

"Don't make any trouble," she says again, quietly.

I stand there a few seconds longer before finally backing away, holding up my hands, a gesture of assurance.

"Don't come back," she says.

"I won't," I say. "Don't worry."

The couple appears in the doorway. Mrs. Wolfe watches me until I'm at the elevator door, pressing the button for the attendant. In the elevator, the smell of the roses is overpowering.

WORKING OUT

Free weights and Nautilus equipment relieve stress. My body responds to the workout accordingly. Shirtless, I scrutinize my image in the mirror above the sinks in the locker room at Xclusive. My arm muscles burn, my stomach is as taut as possible, my chest steel, pectorals granite hard, my eyes white as ice. In my locker in the locker room at Xclusive lie three vaginas I recently sliced out of various women I've attacked in the past week. Two are washed off, one isn't. There's a barrette clipped to one of them, a blue ribbon from Hermès tied around my favorite.

END OF THE 1980S

The smell of blood works its way into my dreams, which are, for the most part, terrible: on an ocean liner that catches fire, witnessing volcanic eruptions in Hawaii, the violent deaths of most of the inside traders at Salomon, James Robinson doing something bad to me, finding myself back at boarding school, then at Harvard, the dead walk among the living. The dreams are an endless reel of car wrecks and disaster footage, electric chairs and grisly suicides, syringes and mutilated pinup girls, flying saucers, marble jacuzzis, pink peppercorns. When I wake up in a cold sweat I have to turn on the wide-screen television to block out the construction sounds that continue throughout the day, rising up from somewhere. A month ago was the anniversary of Elvis Presley's death. Football games flash by, the sound turned off. I can hear the answering machine click once, its volume lowered, then twice. All summer long Madonna cries out to us, *"life is a mystery, everyone must stand alone . . ."*

When I'm moving down Broadway to meet Jean, my secretary, for brunch, in front of Tower Records a college student with a clipboard asks me to name the saddest song I know. I tell him, without pausing, "You Can't Always Get What You Want" by the Beatles. Then he asks me to name the happiest song I know, and I say "Brilliant Disguise" by Bruce Springsteen. He nods, makes a note, and I move on, past Lincoln Center. An accident has happened. An ambulance is parked at the curb. A pile of intestines lies on the sidewalk in a pool of blood. I buy a very hard apple at a Korean deli which I eat on my way to meet Jean who, right now, stands at the Sixty-seventh Street entrance to Central Park on a cool, sunny day in September. When we look up at the clouds she sees an island, a puppy dog, Alaska, a tulip. I see, but don't tell her, a Gucci money clip, an ax, a woman cut in two, a large puffy white puddle of blood that spreads across the sky, dripping over the city, onto Manhattan.

We stop at an outdoor café, Nowheres, on the Upper West Side, debating which movie to see, if there are any museum exhibits we should attend, maybe just a walk, she suggests the zoo, I'm nodding mindlessly. Jean is looking good, like she's been working out, and she's wearing a gilt lamé jacket and velvet shorts by Matsuda. I'm imagining myself on television, in a commercial for a new product—wine cooler? tanning lotion? sugarless gum?—and I'm moving in jump-cut, walking along a beach, the film is black-and-white, purposefully scratched, eerie vague pop music from the mid-1960s accompanies the footage, it echoes, sounds as if it's coming from a calliope. Now I'm looking into the camera, now I'm holding up the product—a new mousse? tennis shoes?—now my hair is windblown then it's day then night then day again and then it's night.

"I'll have an iced decaf au lait," Jean tells the waiter.

"I'll have a decapitated coffee also," I say absently, before
catching myself. "I mean . . . de*caff*einated." I glance over at Jean,
worried, but she just smiles emptily at me. A Sunday *Times* sits on
the table between us. We discuss plans for dinner tonight, maybe.
Someone who looks like Taylor Preston walks by, waves at me.
I lower my Ray-Bans, wave back. Someone on a bike pedals past. I
ask a busboy for water. A waiter arrives instead and after that a dish
containing two scoops of sorbet, cilantro-lemon and vodka-lime, are
brought to the table that I didn't hear Jean order.

"Want a bite?" she asks.

"I'm on a diet," I say. "But thank you."

"You don't need to lose any weight," she says, genuinely
surprised. "You're kidding, right? You look great. Very fit."

"You can always be thinner," I mumble, staring at the traffic in
the street, distracted by something—what? I don't know. "Look . . .
better."

"Well, maybe we shouldn't go out to dinner," she says, concerned. "I don't want to ruin your . . . willpower."

"No. It's all right," I say. "I'm not . . . very good at controlling it
anyway."

"Patrick, seriously. I'll do whatever you want," she says. "If you
don't want to go to dinner, we won't. I mean—"

"It's okay," I stress. Something snaps. "You shouldn't fawn over
him . . ." I pause before correcting myself. "I mean . . . *me*. Okay?"

"I just what to know what you want to do," she says.

"To live happily ever after, right?" I say sarcastically. "That's
what *I* want." I stare at her hard, for maybe half a minute, before
turning away. This quiets her. After a while she orders a beer. It's
hot out on the street.

"Come on, smile," she urges sometime later. "You have no
reason to be sad."

"I know," I sigh, relenting. "But it's . . . tough to smile. These
days. At least *I* find it hard to. I'm not used to it, I guess. I don't
know."

"That's . . . why people need each other," she says gently, trying
to make eye contact while spooning the not inexpensive sorbet into
her mouth.

"Some don't." I clear my throat self-consciously. "Or, well, people compensate ... They adjust ..." After a long pause, "People can get accustomed to anything, right?" I ask. "Habit does things to people."

Another long pause. Confused, she says, "I don't know. I guess ... but one still has to maintain ... a ratio of more good things than ... bad in this world," she says, adding, "I mean, right?" She looks puzzled, as if she finds it strange that this sentence has come out of her mouth. A blast of music from a passing cab, Madonna again, *"life is a mystery, everyone must stand alone ..."* Startled by the laughter at the table next to ours, I cock my head and hear someone admit, "Sometimes what you wear to the office makes all the difference," and then Jean says something and I ask her to repeat it.

"Haven't you ever wanted to make someone happy?" she asks.

"What?" I ask, trying to pay attention to her. "Jean?"

Shyly, she repeats herself. "Haven't you ever wanted to make someone happy?"

I stare at her, a cold, distant wave of fright washes over me, dousing something. I clear my throat again and, trying to speak with great purposefulness, tell her, "I was at Sugar Reef the other night ... that Caribbean place on the Lower East Side ... you know it—"

"Who were you with?" she interrupts.

Jeanette. "Evan McGlinn."

"Oh." She nods, silently relieved, believing me.

"Anyway ..." I sigh, continuing, "I saw some guy in the men's room ... a total ... Wall Street guy ... wearing a one-button viscose, wool and nylon suit by ... Luciano Soprani ... a cotton shirt by ... Gitman Brothers ... a silk tie by Ermenegildo Zegna and, I mean, I recognized the guy, a broker, named Eldridge ... I've seen him at Harry's and Au Bar and DuPlex and Alex Goes to Camp ... all the places, but ... when I went in after him, I saw ... he was writing ... something on the wall above the ... urinal he was standing at." I pause, take a swallow of her beer. "When he saw me come in ... he stopped writing ... put away the Mont Blanc pen ... he zipped up his pants ... said Hello, Henderson to me ... checked his hair in the mirror, coughed ... like he was nervous or ... something and ... left the room." I pause again, another swallow. "Anyway ... I went over to use the ... urinal and ... I leaned over . . . to read what he . . . wrote." Shuddering, I slowly wipe my forehead with a napkin.

"Which was?" Jean asks cautiously.

I close my eyes, three words fall from my mouth, these lips: "'Kill . . . All . . . Yuppies.'"

She doesn't say anything.

To break the uncomfortable silence that follows, I mention all I can come up with, which is, "Did you know that Ted Bundy's first dog, a collie, was named Lassie?" Pause. "Had you heard this?"

Jean looks at her dish as if it's confusing her, then back up at me. "Who's . . . Ted Bundy?"

"Forget it," I sigh.

"Listen, Patrick. We need to talk about something," she says. "Or at least *I* need to talk about something."

. . . where there was nature and earth, life and water, I saw a desert landscape that was unending, resembling some sort of crater, so devoid of reason and light and spirit that the mind could not grasp it on any sort of conscious level and if you came close the mind would reel backward, unable to take it in. It was a vision so clear and real and vital to me that in its purity it was almost abstract. This was what I could understand, this was how I lived my life, what I constructed my movement around, how I dealt with the tangible. This was the geography around which my reality revolved: it did not occur to me, *ever*, that people were good or that a man was capable of change or that the world could be a better place through one's taking pleasure in a feeling or look or a gesture, or receiving another person's love or kindness. Nothing was affirmative, the term "generosity of spirit" applied to nothing, was a cliché, was some kind of bad joke. Sex is mathematics. Individuality no longer an issue. What does intelligence signify? Define reason. Desire— meaningless. Intellect is not a cure. Justice is dead. Fear, recrimination, innocence, sympathy, guilt, waste, failure, grief, were things, emotions, that no one really felt anymore. Reflection is useless, the world is senseless. Evil is its only permanence. God is not alive. Love cannot be trusted. Surface, surface, surface was all that anyone found meaning in . . . this was civilization as I saw it, colossal and jagged . . .

". . . and I don't remember who it was you were talking to . . . it doesn't matter. What does is that you were very forceful, yet . . .

very sweet and, I guess, I knew then that . . ." She places her spoon down, but I'm not watching her. I'm looking out at the taxis moving up Broadway, yet they can't stop things from unraveling, because Jean says the following: "A lot of people seem to have . . ." She stops, continues hesitantly, "lost touch with life and I don't want to be among them." After the waiter clears her dish, she adds, "I don't want to get . . . bruised."

I think I'm nodding.

"I've learned what it's like to be alone and . . . I think I'm in love with you." She says this last part quickly, forcing it out.

Almost superstitiously, I turn toward her, sipping an Evian water, then, without thinking, say, smiling, "I love someone else."

As if this film had speeded up she laughs immediately, looks quickly away, down, embarrassed. "I'm, well, sorry . . . gosh."

"But . . ." I add quietly, "you shouldn't be . . . afraid."

She looks back up at me, swollen with hope.

"Something can be done about it," I say. Then, not knowing why I'd said that, I modify the statement, telling her straight on, "Maybe something can't. I don't know. I've thrown away a lot of time to be with you, so it's not like I don't care."

She nods mutely.

"You should never mistake affection for . . . passion," I warn her. "It can be . . . not good. It can . . . get you into, well, trouble."

She not saying anything and I can suddenly sense her sadness, flat and calm, like a daydream. "What are you trying to say?" she asks lamely, blushing.

"Nothing. I'm just . . . letting you know that . . . appearances can be deceiving."

She stares at the *Times* stacked in heavy folds on the table. A breeze barely causes it to flutter. "Why . . . are you telling me this?"

Tactfully, almost touching her hand but stopping myself, I tell her, "I just want to avoid any future misconnections." A hardbody walks by. I notice her, then look back at Jean. "Oh come on, don't look that way. You have nothing to be ashamed of."

"I'm not," she says, trying to act casual. "I just want to know if you're disappointed in me for admitting this."

How could she ever understand that there isn't any way I could be disappointed since I no longer find anything worth looking forward to?

"You don't know much about me, do you?" I ask teasingly.

"I know enough," she says, her initial response, but then she shakes her head. "Oh let's just drop this. I made a mistake. I'm sorry." In the next instant she changes her mind. "I want to know more," she says, gravely.

I consider this before asking, "Are you sure?"

"Patrick," she says breathlessly, "I know my life would be . . . much emptier without you . . . in it."

I consider this too, nodding thoughtfully.

"And I just can't . . ." She stops, frustrated. "I can't pretend these feelings don't exist, can I?"

"Shhh . . ."

. . . there is an idea of a Patrick Bateman, some kind of abstraction, but there is no real me, only an entity, something illusory, and though I can hide my cold gaze and you can shake my hand and feel flesh gripping yours and maybe you can even sense our lifestyles are probably comparable: *I simply am not there*. It is hard for me to make sense on any given level. Myself is fabricated, an aberration. I am a noncontingent human being. My personality is sketchy and unformed, my heartlessness goes deep and is persistent. My conscience, my pity, my hopes disappeared a long time ago (probably at Harvard) if they ever did exist. There are no more barriers to cross. All I have in common with the uncontrollable and the insane, the vicious and the evil, all the mayhem I have caused and my utter indifference toward it, I have now surpassed. I still, though, hold on to one single bleak truth: no one is safe, nothing is redeemed. Yet I am blameless. Each model of human behavior must be assumed to have some validity. Is evil something you are? Or is it something you do? My pain is constant and sharp and I do not hope for a better world for anyone. In fact I want my pain to be inflicted on others. I want no one to escape. But even after admitting this—and I have, countless times, in just about every act I've committed—and coming face-to-face with these truths, there is no catharsis. I gain no deeper knowledge about myself, no new understanding can be extracted from my telling. There has been no reason for me to tell you any of this. This confession has meant *nothing* . . .

I'm asking Jean, "How many people in this world are like me?"

She pauses, carefully answers, "I don't . . . think anyone?" She's guessing.

"Let me rephrase the ques— Wait, how does my hair look?" I ask, interrupting myself.

"Uh, fine."

"Okay. Let me rephrase the question." I take a sip of her dry beer. "Okay. *Why* do you like me?" I ask.

She asks back, "*Why?*"

"Yes," I say. "Why."

"Well . . ." A drop of beer has fallen onto my Polo shirt. She hands me her napkin. A practical gesture that touches me. "You're . . . concerned with others," she says tentatively. "That's a very rare thing in what"—she stops again—"is a . . . I guess, a hedonistic world. This is . . . Patrick, you're embarrassing me." She shakes her head, closing her eyes.

"Go on," I urge. "Please. I want to know."

"You're sweet." She rolls her eyes up. "Sweetness is . . . sexy . . . I don't know. But so is . . . *mystery*." Silence. "And I think . . . mystery . . . you're mysterious." Silence, followed by a sigh. "And you're . . . considerate." She realizes something, no longer scared, stares at me straight on. "And I think shy men are romantic."

"How many people in this world are like me?" I ask again. "Do I really appear like that?"

"Patrick," she says. "I wouldn't lie."

"No, of course you wouldn't . . . but I think that . . ." My turn to sigh, contemplatively. "I think . . . you know how they say no two snowflakes are ever alike?"

She nods.

"Well, I don't think that's true. I think a lot of snowflakes are alike . . . and I think a lot of people are alike too."

She nods again, though I can tell she's very confused.

"Appearances *can* be deceiving," I admit carefully.

"No," she says, shaking her head, sure of herself for the first time. "I don't think they are deceiving. They're not."

"Sometimes, Jean," I explain, "the lines separating appearance—what you see—and reality—what you don't—become, well, blurred."

"That's not true," she insists. "That's simply not true."

"Really?" I ask, smiling.

"I didn't use to think so," she says. "Maybe ten years ago I didn't. But I do now."

"What do you mean?" I ask, interested. "You *used* to?"

. . . a flood of reality. I get an odd feeling that this is a crucial moment in my life and I'm startled by the suddenness of what I guess passes for an epiphany. There is nothing of value I can offer her. For the first time I see Jean as uninhibited; she seems stronger, less controllable, wanting to take me into a new and unfamiliar land—the dreaded uncertainty of a totally different world. I sense she wants to rearrange my life in a significant way—her eyes tell me this and though I see truth in them, I also know that one day, sometime very soon, she too will be locked in the rhythm of my insanity. All I have to do is keep silent about this and not bring it up—yet she weakens me, it's almost as if *she's* making the decision about who I am, and in my own stubborn, willful way I can admit to feeling a pang, something tightening inside, and before I can stop it I find myself almost dazzled and moved that I might have the capacity to accept, though not return, her love. I wonder if even now, right here in Nowheres, she can see the darkening clouds behind my eyes lifting. And though the coldness I have always felt leaves me, the numbness doesn't and probably never will. This relationship will probably lead to nothing . . . this didn't change anything. I imaging her smelling clean, like tea . . .

"Patrick . . . talk to me . . . don't be so upset," she is saying.

"I think it's . . . time for me to . . . take a good look . . . at the world I've created," I choke, tearfully, finding myself admitting to her, "I came upon . . . a half gram of cocaine . . . in my armoire last . . . night." I'm squeezing my hands together, forming one large fist, all knuckles white.

"What did you do with it?" she asks.

I place one hand on the table. She takes it.

"I threw it away. I threw it all away. I wanted to *do* it," I gasp, "but I threw it away."

She squeezes my hand tightly. "Patrick?" she asks, moving her hand up until it's gripping my elbow. When I find the strength to look back at her, it strikes me how useless, boring, physically beautiful she really is, and the question *Why not end up with her?* floats into my line of vision. An answer: she has a better body than most other girls I know. Another one: everyone is interchangeable anyway. One more: it doesn't really matter. She sits before me, sullen but hopeful, characterless, about to dissolve into tears. I squeeze her hand back, moved, no, touched by her ignorance of evil. She has one more test to pass.

"Do you own a briefcase?" I ask her, swallowing.

"No," she says. "I don't."

"Evelyn carries a briefcase," I mention.

"She does . . .?" Jean asks.

"And what about a Filofax?"

"A small one," she admits.

"Designer?" I ask suspiciously.

"No."

I sigh, then take her hand, small and hard, in mine.

. . . and in the southern deserts of Sudan the heat rises in airless waves, thousands upon thousands of men, women, children, roam throughout the vast bushland, desperately seeking food. Ravaged and starving, leaving a trail of dead, emaciated bodies, they eat weeds and leaves and . . . lily pads, stumbling from village to village, dying slowly, inexorably; a gray morning in the miserable desert, grit flies through the air, a child with a face like a black moon lies in the sand, scratching at his throat, cones of dust rising, flying across the land like whirling tops, no one can see the sun, the child is covered with sand, almost dead, eyes unblinking, grateful (stop and imagine for an instant a world where someone is grateful for something) none of the haggard pay attention as they file by, dazed and in pain (no—there *is* one who pays attention, who notices the boy's agony and smiles, as if holding a secret), the boy opens and closes his cracked, chapped mouth soundlessly, there is a school bus in the distance somewhere and somewhere else, above that, in space, a spirit rises, a door opens, it asks *"Why?"*—a home for the dead, an infinity, it hangs in a void, time limps by, love and sadness rush through the boy . . .

"Okay."

I am dimly aware of a phone ringing somewhere. In the café on Columbus, countless numbers, hundreds of people, maybe thousands, have walked by our table during my silence. "Patrick," Jean says. Someone with a baby stroller stops at the corner and purchases a Dove Bar. The baby stares at Jean and me. We stare back. It's really weird and I'm experiencing a spontaneous kind of internal sensation, I feel I'm moving toward as well as away from something, and anything is possible.

ASPEN

It is four days before Christmas, at two in the afternoon. I'm sitting in the back of a pitch-black limousine parked in front of a nondescript brownstone off Fifth Avenue trying to read an article about Donald Trump in the new issue of *Fame* magazine. Jeanette wants me to come in with her but I say "Forget it." She has a black eye from last night since I had to coerce her over dinner at Il Marlibro to even consider doing this; then, after a more forceful discussion at my apartment, she consented. Jeanette's dilemma lies outside my definition of guilt, and I had told her, truthfully, over dinner that it was very hard for me to express concern for her that I don't feel. During the entire drive from my place on the Upper West Side, she's been sobbing. The only clear, identifiable emotion coming from her is desperation and maybe longing, and though I successfully ignore her for most of the ride I finally have to tell her, "Listen, I've already taken two Xanax this morning so, uh, you're incapable of, like, upsetting me." Now, as she stumbles out of the limo onto the frozen pavement, I mumble, "It's for the best," and, offering consolation, "Don't take it so seriously." The driver, whose name I've forgotten, leads her into the brownstone and she gives a last, regretful look back. I sigh and wave her off. She's still wearing, from last night, a leopard-print cotton balmacaan coat with wool challis lining over a wool crepe shirtless dress by Bill Blass. Bigfoot was interviewed on *The Patty Winters Show* this morning and to my shock I found him surprisingly articulate and charming. The glass I'm drinking Absolut vodka from is Finnish. I'm very sun-tanned compared to Jeanette.

The driver comes out of the building, gives me thumbs-up, carefully pulls the limousine away from the curb and begins the trek to JFK airport, where my flight to Aspen leaves in ninety minutes. When I get back, in January, Jeanette will be out of the country. I relight a cigar, search for an ashtray. There's a church on the corner of this street. Who cares? This is, I think, the fifth child I've had aborted, the third I haven't aborted myself (a useless statistic, I admit). The wind outside the limousine is brisk and cold and the rain hits the darkened windows in rhythmic waves, mimicking Jeanette's probable weeping in the operating room, dizzy from the anesthesia, thinking about a memory from her past, a moment where the world was perfect. I resist the impulse to start cackling hysterically.

At the airport I instruct the chauffeur to stop by F.A.O. Schwarz before picking Jeanette up and purchase the following: a doll, a rattle, a teething ring, a white Gund polar bear, and have them sitting in the backseat for her, unwrapped. Jeanette should be okay—she has her whole life in front of her (that is, if she doesn't run into me). Besides, this girl's favorite movie is *Pretty in Pink* and she thinks Sting is cool, so what is happening to her is, like, not totally undeserved and one shouldn't feel bad for her. This is no time for the innocent.

VALENTINE'S DAY

Tuesday morning and I'm standing by my desk in the living room on the phone with my lawyer, alternately keeping my eye on *The Patty Winters Show* and the maid as she waxes the floor, wipes blood smears off the walls, throws away gore-soaked newspapers without a word. Faintly it hits me that she too is lost in a world of shit, completely drowning in it, and this somehow sets off my remembering that the piano tuner will be stopping by this afternoon and that I should leave a note with the doorman to let him in. Not that the Yamaha has ever been played; it's just that one of the girls fell against it and some strings (which I used later) were pulled out, snapped or something. Into the phone I'm saying, "I need more tax breaks." Patty Winters is on the TV screen asking a child, eight or nine, "But isn't that just another term for an orgy?" The timer buzzes on the microwave. I'm heating up a soufflé.

There's no use in denying it: this has been a bad week. I've started drinking my own urine. I laugh spontaneously at nothing. Sometimes I sleep under my futon. I'm flossing my teeth constantly until my gums are aching and my mouth tastes like blood. Before dinner last night at 1500 with Reed Goodrich and Jason Rust I was almost caught at a Federal Express in Times Square trying to send the mother of one of the girls I killed last week what might be a dried-up, brown heart. And to Evelyn I successfully Federal Expressed, through the office, a small box of flies along with a note, typed by Jean, saying that I never, *ever* wanted to see her face again and, though she doesn't really need one, to go on a fucking diet. But there are also things that the average person would think are nice that I've done to celebrate the holiday, items I've bought Jean and had delivered to her apartment this morning: Castellini cotton napkins from Bendel's, a wicker chair from Jenny B. Goode, a taffeta table throw from Barney's, a vintage chain-mail-vent purse and a vintage sterling silver dresser set from Macy's, a white pine whatnot from Conran's, an Edwardian nine-carat-gold "gate" bracelet from Bergdorf's and hundreds upon hundreds of pink and white roses.

The office. Lyrics to Madonna songs keep intruding, bursting into my head, announcing themselves in tiring, familiar ways, and I stare into space, my eyes lazily lit up while I try to forget about the day looming before me, but then a phrase that fills me with a nameless dread keeps interrupting the Madonna songs—*isolated farmhouse* constantly returns to me, over and over. Someone I've been avoiding for the last year, a nerd from *Fortune* who wants to write an article about me, calls again this morning and I end up calling the reporter back to arrange an interview. Craig McDermott is having some kind of fax frenzy and won't take any of my phone calls, preferring to communicate by fax only. The *Post* this morning says the remains of three bodies that disappeared aboard a yacht last March have been recovered, frozen in ice, hacked up and bloated, in the East River; some maniac is going around the city poisoning one-liter bottles of Evian water, seventeen dead already; talk of zombies, the public mood, increasing randomness, vast chasms of misunderstanding.

And, for the sake of form, Tim Price resurfaces, or at least I'm pretty sure he does. While I'm at my desk simultaneously crossing out the days in my calendar that have already passed and reading a new bestseller about office management called *Why It Works to Be a Jerk*, Jean buzzes in, announcing that Tim Price wants to talk, and fearfully I say, "Send him . . . in." Price strolls into the office wearing a wool suit by Canali Milano, a cotton shirt by Ike Behar, a silk tie by Bill Blass, cap-toed leather lace-ups from Brooks Brothers. I'm pretending to be on the phone. He sits down, across from me, on the other side of the Palazzetti glass-top desk. There's a smudge on his forehead or at least that's what I think I see. Aside from that he looks remarkably fit. Our conversation probably resembles something like this but is actually briefer.

"Price," I say, shaking his hand. "Where have you been?"

"Oh, just making the rounds." He smiles. "But hey, I'm back."

"Far out." I shrug, confused. "How was . . . it?"

"It was . . . surprising." He shrugs too. "It was . . . depressing."

"I thought I saw you in Aspen," I murmur.

"Hey, how are you, Bateman?" he asks.

"I'm okay," I tell him, swallowing. "Just . . . existing."

"And Evelyn?" he asks. "How is she?"

"Well, we broke up." I smile.

"That's too bad." He takes this in, remembers something. "Courtney?"

"She married Luis."

"Grassgreen?"

"No. Carruthers."

He takes this in too. "Do you have her number?"

While writing it down for him, I mention, "You've been gone, like, forever, Tim. What's the story?" I ask, again noticing the smudge on his forehead, though I get the feeling that if I asked someone else if it was truly there, he (or she) would just say no.

He stands up, takes the card. "I've been back. You just probably missed me. Lost track. Because of the move." He pauses, teasingly. "I'm working for Robinson. Right-hand man, you know?"

"Almond?" I ask, offering one, a futile effort on my part to mask my dismay at his smugness.

He pats my back, says, "You're a madman, Bateman. An animal. A total animal."

"I can't disagree." I laugh weakly, walking him to the door. As he leaves I'm wondering and not wondering what happens in the world of Tim Price, which is really the world of most of us: big ideas, guy stuff, boy meets the world, boy gets it.

BUM ON FIFTH

I'm coming back from Central Park where, near the children's zoo, close to the spot I murdered the McCaffrey boy, I fed portions of Ursula's brain to passing dogs. Walking down Fifth Avenue around four o'clock in the afternoon, everyone on the street looks sad, the air is full of decay, bodies lie on the cold pavement, miles of it, some are moving, most are not. History is sinking and only a very few seem dimly aware that things are getting bad. Airplanes fly low across the city, crossing in front of the sun. Winds shoot up Fifth, then funnel down Fifty-seventh Street. Flocks of pigeons rise in slow motion and burst up against the sky. The smell of burning chestnuts mixes with carbon monoxide fumes. I notice the skyline has changed only recently. I look up, admiringly, at Trump Tower, tall, proudly gleaming in the late afternoon sunlight. In front of it two smart-ass nigger teenagers are ripping off tourists at three-card monte and I have to fight the impulse to blow them away.

A bum I blinded one spring sits cross-legged on a ratty blanket near the corner of Fifty-fifth Street. Moving closer I see the beggar's scarred face and then the sign he's holding beneath it, which reads VIETNAM VET BLINDED IN VIETNAM. PLEASE HELP ME. WE ARE HUNGRY AND HOMELESS. We? Then I notice the dog, who is already eyeing me suspiciously and, as I approach its master, gets up, growling, and when I'm standing over the bum, it finally barks, wagging its tail frantically. I kneel down, threateningly raise a hand at it. The dog back off, its paws askew.

I've pulled out my wallet, pretending to drop a dollar into his empty coffee can, but then realize: Why bother pretending? No one's watching anyway, definitely not *him*. I retract the dollar, leaning in. He senses my presence and stops shaking the can. The sunglasses he wears don't even begin to cover the wounds I inflicted. His nose is so junked up I can't imagine a person breathing through it.

"You never were in Vietnam," I whisper in his ear.

After a silence, during which he pisses in his pants, the dog whimpering, he croaks, "Please . . . don't hurt me."

"Why would I waste my time?" I mutter, disgusted.

I move away from the bum, noticing, instead, a little girl smoking a cigarette, begging for change outside Trump Tower. "Shoo," I say. She says "Shoo" back. On *The Patty Winters Show* this morning a Cheerio sat in a very small chair and was interviewed for close to an hour. Later this afternoon, a woman wearing a silver fox and mink coat has her face slashed in front of the Stanhope by an enraged fur activist. But now, still staring at the sightless bum from across the street, I buy a Dove Bar, a coconut one, in which I find part of a bone.

NEW CLUB

Thursday night I run into Harold Carnes at a party for a new club called World's End that opens in a space where Petty's used to be on the Upper East Side. I'm with Nina Goodrich and Jean in a booth and Harold's standing at the bar drinking champagne. I'm drunk enough to finally confront him about the message I left on his machine. Excused from the booth, I make my way to the other side of the bar, realizing that I need a martini to fortify myself before discussing this with Carnes (it has been a *very* unstable week for me—I found myself sobbing during an episode of *Alf* on Monday). Nervously, I approach. Harold is wearing a wool suit by Gieves & Hawkes, a silk twill tie, cotton shirt, shoes by Paul Stuart; he looks heavier than I remember. "Face it," he's telling Truman Drake, "the Japanese will own most of this country by the end of the '90s."

Relieved that Harold is, as usual, still dispensing valuable and *new* information, with the addition of a faint but unmistakable trace of, god forbid, an English accent, I find myself brazen enough to blurt out, "Shut up, Carnes, they will *not*." I down the martini, Stoli, while Carnes, looking quite taken aback, stricken almost, turns around to face me, and his bloated head breaks out into an uncertain smile. Someone behind us is saying, "But look what happened to Gekko . . ."

Truman Drake pats Harold on the back and asks me, "Is there one suspender width that's more, well, appropriate than others?" Irritably I push him into the crowd and he disappears.

"So Harold," I say, "did you get my message?"

Carnes seems confused at first and, while lighting a cigarette, finally laughs. "Jesus, Davis. Yes, that was hi*lar*ious. That *was* you, was it?"

"Yes, naturally." I'm blinking, muttering to myself, really, waving his cigarette smoke away from my face.

"Bateman killing Owen and the escort girl?" He keeps chuckling. "Oh that's bloody marvelous. Really key, as they say at the Groucho Club. Really key." Then looking dismayed, he adds, "It was a rather long message, no?"

I'm smiling idiotically and then I say, "But what exactly do you mean, Harold?" Secretly thinking to myself that this fat bastard couldn't possibly have gotten into the fucking Groucho Club, and even if he had, to admit it in such a fashion obliterates the fact that his entrance was accepted.

"Why, the message you left." Carnes is already looking around the club, waving to various people and bimbos. "By the way, Davis, how is Cynthia?" He accepts a glass of champagne from a passing waiter. "You're still seeing her, right?"

"But wait, Harold. What-do-you-mean?" I repeat emphatically.

He's already bored, neither concerned nor listening, and excusing himself, says, "Nothing. Good to see you. Oh my, is that Edward Towers?"

I crane my neck to look, then turn back to Harold. "No," I say. "Carnes? *Wait*."

"Davis," he sighs, as if patiently trying to explain something to a child. "I am not one to bad-mouth anyone, your joke *was* amusing. But come on, man, you had one fatal flaw: Bateman's such a bloody ass-kisser, such a brown-nosing goody-goody, that I couldn't fully appreciate it. Otherwise it was amusing. Now let's have lunch, or we'll have dinner at 150 Wooster or something with McDermott or Preston. A real raver." He tries to move on.

"Ray-vah? Ray-vah? Did you say *ray-vah*, Carnes?" I'm wide-eyed, feeling wired even though I haven't done any drugs. "What are you *talking* about? Bateman is *what*?"

"Oh good god, man. Why else would Evelyn Richards dump him? You know, really. He could barely *pick up* an escort girl, let alone . . . what was it you said he did to her?" Harold is still looking distractedly around the club and he waves to another couple, raising his champagne glass. "Oh yes, 'chop her up.'" He starts laughing again, though this time it sounds polite. "Now if you'll excuse me, I must really."

"Wait. Stop," I shout, looking up into Carnes' face, making sure he's listening. "You don't seem to understand. You're not really comprehending any of this. *I* killed him. *I* did it, Carnes. *I* chopped Owen's fucking head off. *I* tortured dozens of girls. That whole message I left on your machine was *true*." I'm drained, not appearing calm, wondering why this doesn't feel like a blessing to me.

"Excuse me," he says, trying to ignore my outburst. "I really *must* be going."

"No!" I shout. "Now, Carnes. Listen to me. Listen very, very carefully. I-killed-Paul-Owen-and-I-liked-it. I can't make myself any clearer." My stress causes me to choke on the words.

"But that's simply not possible," he says, brushing me off. "And I'm not finding this amusing anymore."

"It never was supposed to be!" I bellow, and then, "Why isn't it possible?"

"It's just not," he says, eyeing me worriedly.

"Why not?" I shout again over the music, though there's really no need to, adding "You stupid bastard."

He stares at me as if we are both underwater and shouts back, very clearly over the din of the club, "Because . . . I had . . . dinner . . . with Paul Owen . . . twice . . . in London . . . *just ten days ago*."

After we stare at each other for what seems like a minute, I finally have the nerve to say something back to him but my voice lacks any authority and I'm not sure if I believe myself when I tell him, simply, "No, you . . . didn't." But it comes out a question, not a statement.

"Now, Donaldson," Carnes says, removing my hand from his arm. "If you'll excuse me."

"Oh you're excused," I sneer. Then I make my way back to our booth where John Edmonton and Peter Beavers are now sitting and I numb myself with a Halcion before taking Jean home, back to my place. Jean is wearing something by Oscar de la Renta. Nina Goodrich was wearing a sequined dress by Matsuda and refused to give me her number, even though Jean was in the women's room downstairs.

TAXI DRIVER

Another broken scene in what passes for my life occurs on Wednesday, seemingly pointing to someone's fault, though whose I can't be sure. Stuck in gridlock in a cab heading downtown toward Wall Street after a power breakfast at the Regency with Peter Russell, who used to be my dealer before he got a real job, and Eddie Lambert. Russell was wearing a two-button wool sport coat by Redaelli, a cotton shirt by Hackert, a silk tie by Richel, pleated wool trousers by Krizia Uomo and leather Cole-Haan shoes. *The Patty Winters Show* this morning was about girls in the fourth grade who trade sex for crack and I almost canceled with Lambert and Russell to catch it. Russell ordered for me while I was in the lobby on the phone. It was, unfortunately, a high-fat, high-sodium breakfast and before I could comprehend what was happening, plates of herbed waffles with ham in Madeira cream sauce, grilled sausages and sour cream coffee cake were set at our table and I had to ask the waiter for a pot of decaf herbal tea, a plate of sliced mango with blueberries and a bottle of Evian. In the early morning light that poured through the windows at the Regency I watched as our waiter shaved black truffles gracefully over Lambert's steaming eggs. Overcome, I broke down and demanded to have the black truffles shaved over my mango slices. Nothing much happened during the breakfast. I had to make another phone call, and when I returned to our table I noticed that a mango slice was missing, but I didn't accuse anyone. I had other things on my mind: how to help America's schools, the trust gap, desk sets, a new era of possibilities and what's in it for me, getting tickets to see Sting in *The Threepenny Opera*, which just opened on Broadway, how to take more and remember less . . .

In the cab I'm wearing a double-breasted cashmere and wool overcoat by Studio 000.1 from Ferré, a wool suit with pleated trousers by DeRigueur from Schoeneman, a silk tie by Givenchy Gentleman, socks by Interwoven, shoes by Armani, reading the *Wall Street Journal* with my Ray-Ban sunglasses on and listening to a Walkman with a Bix Beiderbecke tape playing in it. I put down the *Journal*, pick up the *Post*, just to check Page Six. At the light on Seventh and Thirty-fourth, in the cab next to this one sits, I think, Kevin Gladwin, wearing a suit by Ralph Lauren. I lower my sunglasses. Kevin looks up from the new issue of *Money* magazine and spots me looking over at him in a curious way before his cab moves forward in the traffic. The cab I'm in suddenly breaks free of the gridlock and turns right on Twenty-seventh, taking the West Side Highway down to Wall Street. I put the paper down, concentrate on the music and the weather, how unseasonably cool it is, and I'm just beginning to notice the way the cabdriver looks at me in the rearview mirror. A suspicious, hungry expression keeps changing the features on his face—a mass of clogged pores, ingrown hairs. I sigh, expecting this, ignoring him. Open the hood of a car and it will tell you something about the people who designed it, is just one of many phrases I'm tortured by.

But the driver knocks on the plexiglass divider, motions to me. While taking the Walkman off I notice he's locked all the doors—I see the locks lower in a flash, hear the hollow clicking noise, the moment I turn the volume off. The cab is speeding faster than it should down the highway, in the far right lane. "Yes?" I ask irritably. "What?"

"Hey, don't I know you?" he asks in a thick, barely penetratable accent that could easily be either New Jersey or Mediterranean.

"No." I start putting the Walkman back on.

"You look familiar," he says. "What's your name?"

"No I don't. You don't either," I say, then, an afterthought, "Chris Hagen."

"Come on." He's smiling like there's something wrong. "I know who you are."

376   Bret Easton Ellis

"I'm in a movie. I'm an actor," I tell him. "A model."

"Nah, that's not it," he says grimly.

"Well"—I lean over, checking his name—"Abdullah, do you have a membership at M.K.?"

He doesn't answer. I reopen the *Post* to a photo of the mayor dressed as a pineapple, then close it again and rewind the tape in my Walkman. I start counting to myself—one, two, three, four—my eyes focus in on the meter. Why didn't I carry a gun with me this morning? Because I didn't think I had to. The only weapon on me is a used knife from last night.

"No," he says again. "I've seen your face somewhere."

Finally, exasperated, I ask, trying to appear casual, "You have? *Really?* Interesting. Just watch the road, Abdullah."

There's a long, scary pause while he stares at me in the rearview mirror and the grim smile fades. His face is blank. He says, "I know. Man, I know who you are," and he's nodding, his mouth drawn tight. The radio that was tuned in to the news is shut off.

Buildings pass by in a gray-red blur, the cab passes other cabs, the sky changes color from blue to purple to black back to blue. At another light—a red one he races straight through—we pass, on the other side of the West Side Highway, a new D'Agostino's on the corner where Mars used to be and it moves me to tears, almost, because it's something that's identifiable and I get as nostalgic for the market (even though it's not one I will ever shop at) as I have about anything and I almost interrupt the driver, tell him to pull over, have him let me out, let him keep the change from a ten—no, a twenty— but I can't move because he's driving too fast and something intervenes, something unthinkable and ludicrous, and I hear him say it, maybe. "You're the guy who kill Solly." His face is locked into a determined grimace. As with everything else, the following happens very quickly, though it feels like an endurance test.

I swallow, lower my sunglasses and tell him to slow down before asking, "Who, may I ask, is Sally?"

"Man, your face is on a wanted poster downtown," he says, unflinching.

"I think I would like to stop here," I manage to croak out.

"You're the guy, right?" He's looking at me like I'm some kind of viper.

Another cab, its light on, empty, cruises past ours, going at least eighty. I'm not saying anything, just shaking my head. "I am going to take"—I swallow, trembling, open my leather datebook, pull out a Mont Blanc pen from my Bottega Veneta briefcase—"your license number down . . ."

"You kill Solly," he says, definitely recognizing me from some-where, cutting another denial on my part by growling, "You son-of-a-bitch."

Near the docks downtown he swerves off the highway and races the cab toward the end of a deserted parking area and it hits me somewhere, now, this moment, when he drives into and then over a dilapidated, rust-covered aluminum fence, heading toward water, that all I have to do is put the Walkman on, blot out the sound of the cabdriver, but my hands are twisted into paralyzed fists that I can't unclench, held captive in the cab as it hurtles toward a destination only the cabdriver, who is obviously deranged, knows. The windows are rolled down partially and I can feel the cool morning air drying the mousse on my scalp. I feel naked, suddenly tiny. My mouth tastes metallic, then it gets worse. My vision: a winter road. But I'm left with one comforting thought: I am rich—millions are not.

"You've, like, incorrectly identified me," I'm saying.

He stops the cab and turns around toward the backseat. He's holding a gun, the make of which I don't recognize. I'm staring at him, my quizzical expression changing into something else.

"The watch. The Rolex," he says simply.

I listen, silent, squirming in my seat.

He repeats, "The *watch*."

"Is this some kind of prank?" I ask.

"Get out," he spits. "Get the fuck out of the car."

I stare past the driver's head, out the windshield, at gulls flying low over the dark, wavy water, and opening the door I step out of the cab, cautiously, no sudden moves. It's a cold day. My breath steams, wind picks it up, swirls it around.

"The watch, you scumbag," he says, leaning out the window, the gun aimed at my head.

"Listen, I don't know what you think you're doing or what you're exactly trying to accomplish or what it is you *think* you're going to be able to do. I've never been fingerprinted, I have alibis—"

"Shut up," Abdullah growls, cutting me off. "Just shut your fucking mouth."

"I am innocent," I shout with utter conviction.

"The watch." He cocks the gun.

I unhook the Rolex and, sliding it off my wrist, hand it to him.

"Wallet." He motions with his gun. "Just the cash."

Helplessly I take out my new gazelleskin wallet and quickly, my fingers freezing, numb, hand him the cash, which amounts to only three hundred dollars since I didn't have time to stop at an automated teller before the power breakfast. Solly, I'm guessing, was the cabdriver I killed during the chase scene last fall, even though that guy was Armenian. I suppose I could have killed another one and I am just not recalling this particular incident.

"What are you going to do?" I ask. "Isn't there a reward of some kind?"

"No. No reward," he mutters, shuffling the bills with one hand, the gun, still pointed at me, in the other.

"How do you know I'm not going to call you in and get your license revoked?" I ask, handing over a knife I just found in my pocket that looks as if it was dipped into a bowl of blood and hair.

"Because you're guilty," he says, and then, "Get that away from me," waving the gun at the stained knife.

"Like *you* know," I mutter angrily.

"The sunglasses." He points again with the gun.

"How do you know I'm guilty?" I can't believe I'm asking this patiently.

"Look what you're doing, asshole," he says. "The sunglasses."

"These are expensive," I protest, then sigh, realizing the mistake. "I mean cheap. They're very cheap. Just . . . Isn't the money enough?"

"The sunglasses. Give them now," he grunts.

I take the Wayfarers off and hand them to him. Maybe I really did kill a Solly, though I'm positive that any cabdrivers I've killed lately were *not* American. I probably did. There probably *is* a wanted poster of me at . . . where, the taxi—the place where all the taxis congregate? What's it called? The driver tries the sunglasses on, looks at himself in the rearview mirror and then takes them off. He folds the glasses and puts them in his jacket pocket.

"You're a dead man." I smile grimly at him.

"And you're a yuppie scumbag," he says.

"You're a dead man, Abdullah," I repeat, no joke. "Count on it."

"Yeah? And you're a yuppie scumbag. Which is worse?"

He starts the cab up and pulls away from me.

While walking back to the highway I stop, choke back a sob, my throat tightens. "I just want to . . ." Facing the skyline, through all the baby talk, I murmur, "keep the game going." As I stand, frozen in position, an old woman emerges behind a *Threepenny Opera* poster at a deserted bus stop and she's homeless and begging, hobbling over, her face covered with sores that look like bugs, holding out a shaking red hand. "Oh will you please go away?" I sigh. She tells me to get a haircut.

AT HARRY'S

On a Friday evening, a group of us have left the office early, finding ourselves at Harry's. Group consists of Tim Price, Craig McDermott, myself, Preston Goodrich, who is currently dating a total hardbody named, I think, Plum—no last name, just Plum, an actress/model, which I have a feeling we all think is pretty hip. We're having a debate over where to make reservations for dinner: Flamingo East, Oyster Bar, 220, Counterlife, Michael's, SpagoEast, Le Cirque. Robert Farrell is here too, the Lotus Quotrek, a portable stock-quotation device, in front of him on the table, and he's pushing buttons while the latest commodities flash by. What are people wearing? McDermott has on a cashmere sport coat, wool trousers, a silk tie, Hermès. Farrell is wearing a cashmere vest, leather shoes, wool cavalry twill trousers, Garrick Anderson. I'm wearing a wool suit by Armani, shoes by Allen-Edmonds, pocket square by Brooks Brothers. Someone else has on a suit tailored by Anderson and Sheppard. Someone who looks like Todd Lauder, and may in fact be, gives thumbs-up from across the room, etc., etc.

Questions are routinely thrown my way, among them: Are the

rules for wearing a pocket square the same as for a white dinner jacket? Is there any difference at all between boat shoes and Top-Siders? My futon has already flattened out and it's uncomfortable to sleep on—what can I do? How does one judge the quality of compact discs before buying them? What tie knot is less bulky than a Windsor? How can one maintain a sweater's elasticity? Any tips on buying a shearling coat? I am, of course, thinking about other things, asking myself my own questions: Am I a fitness junkie? Man vs. Conformity? Can I get a date with Cindy Crawford? Does being a Libra signify anything and if so, can you prove it? Today I was obsessed with the idea of faxing Sarah's blood I drained from her vagina over to her office in the mergers division at Chase Manhattan, and I didn't work out this morning because I'd made a necklace from the bones of some girl's vertebrae and wanted to stay home and wear it around my neck while I masturbated in the white marble tub in my bathroom, grunting and moaning like some kind of animal. Then I watched a movie about five lesbians and ten vibrators. Favorite group: Talking Heads. Drinks: J&B or Absolut on the rocks. TV show: *Late Night with David Letterman*. Soda: Diet Pepsi. Water: Evian. Sport: Baseball.

The conversation follows its own rolling accord—no real structure or topic or internal logic or feeling; except, of course, for its own hidden, conspiratorial one. Just words, and like in a movie, but one that has been transcribed improperly, most of it overlaps. I'm having a sort of hard time paying attention because my automated teller has started *speaking* to me, sometimes actually leaving weird messages on the screen, in green lettering, like "Cause a Terrible Scene at Sotheby's" or "Kill the President" or "Feed Me a Stray Cat," and I was freaked out by the park bench that followed me for six blocks last Monday evening and it too spoke to me. Disintegration—I'm taking it in stride. Yet the only question I can muster up at first and add to the conversation is a worried "I'm not going anywhere if we don't have a reservation someplace, so do we have a reservation someplace or not?" I notice that we're all drinking dry beers. Am I the only one who notices this? I'm also wearing mock-tortoiseshell glasses that are nonprescription.

On the TV screen in Harry's is *The Patty Winters Show*, which is now on in the afternoon and is up against Geraldo Rivera, Phil

Donahue and Oprah Winfrey. Today's topic is Does Economic Success Equal Happiness? The answer, in Harry's this afternoon, is a roar of resounding "Definitely," followed by much hooting, the guys all cheering together in a friendly way. On the screen now are scenes from President Bush's inauguration early this year, then a speech from former President Reagan, while Patty delivers a hard-to-hear commentary. Soon a tiresome debate forms over whether he's lying or not, even though we don't, can't, hear the words. The first and really only one to complain is Price, who, though I think he's bothered by something else, uses this opportunity to vent his frustration, looks inappropriately stunned, asks, "How can he lie like that? How can he pull that *shit*?"

"Oh Christ," I moan. "*What* shit? Now where do we have reservations at? I mean I'm not really hungry but I would like to have reservations somewhere. How about 220?" An afterthought: "McDermott, how did that rate in the new Zagat's?"

"No way," Farrell complains before Craig can answer. "The coke I scored there last time was cut with so much laxative I actually had to take a shit in M.K."

"Yeah, yeah, life sucks and then you die."

"Low point of the night," Farrell mutters.

"Weren't you with Kyria the last time you were there?" Goodrich asks. "Wasn't *that* the low point?"

"She caught me on call waiting. What could I do?" Farrell shrugs. "I apologize."

"Caught him on call waiting." McDermott nudges me, dubious.

"Shut up, McDermott," Farrell says, snapping Craig's suspenders. "Date a beggar."

"You forgot something, Farrell," Preston mentions. "McDermott *is* a beggar."

"How's Courtney?" Farrell asks Craig, leering.

"Just say no." Someone laughs.

Price looks away from the television screen, then at Craig, and he tries to hide his displeasure by asking me, waving at the TV, "I don't believe it. He looks so . . . *normal*. He seems so . . . out of it. So . . . *un*dangerous."

"Bimbo, bimbo," someone says. "Bypass, bypass."

"He *is* totally harmless, you geek. *Was* totally harmless. Just like *you* are totally harmless. But he *did* do all that shit and *you* have failed to get us into 150, so, you know, what can I say?" McDermott shrugs.

"I just don't get how someone, *anyone*, can appear that way yet be involved in such total shit," Price says, ignoring Craig, averting his eyes from Farrell. He takes out a cigar and studies it sadly. To me it still looks like there's a smudge on Price's forehead.

"Because Nancy was right behind him?" Farrell guesses, looking up from the Quotrek. "Because Nancy did it?"

"How can you be so fucking, I don't know, *cool* about it?" Price, to whom something really eerie had obviously happened, sounds genuinely perplexed. Rumor has it that he was in rehab.

"Some guys are just born cool, I guess." Farrell smiles, shrugging.

I'm laughing at this answer since Farrell is so *obviously* uncool, and Price shoots me a reprimanding look, says, "And Bateman— what are *you* so fucking zany about?"

I shrug too. "I'm just a happy camper." And I add, remembering, *quoting*, my brother: "Rocking and a rolling."

"*Be* all that you can *be*," someone adds.

"Oh brother." Price won't let it die. "Look," he starts, trying for a rational appraisal of the situation. "He presents himself as a harmless old codger. But inside . . ." He stops. My interest picks up, flickers briefly. "But inside . . ." Price can't finish the sentence, can't add the last two words he needs: *doesn't matter*. I'm both disappointed and relieved for him.

"Inside? Yes, inside?" Craig asks, bored. "Believe it or not, we're actually listening to you. Go on."

"Bateman," Price says, relenting slightly. "Come on. What do you think?"

I look up, smile, don't say anything. From somewhere—the TV?—the national anthem plays. Why? I don't know. Before a commercial, maybe. Tomorrow, on *The Patty Winters Show*, Doormen from Nell's: Where Are They Now? I sigh, shrug, whatever.

"That's, uh, a pretty good answer," Price says, then adds, "You're a real nut."

"That is the most valuable piece of information I've heard since"—I look at my new gold Rolex that insurance paid for—

"McDermott suggested we all drink dry beers. Christ, I want a Scotch."

McDermott looks up with an exaggerated grin and purrs, "Bud. Long neck. Beautiful."

"Very civilized." Goodrich nods.

Superstylish English guy Nigel Morrison stops by our table and he's wearing a flower in the lapel of his Paul Smith jacket. But he can't stay long since he has to meet *other* British friends, Ian and Lucy, at Delmonico's. Seconds after he walks away, I hear someone sneer, "Nigel. A pâté animal."

Someone else: "Did you know that cavemen got more fiber than we do?"

"Who's handling the Fisher account?"

"Screw that. What about the Shepard thing? The Shepard account?"

"Is that David Monrowe? What a burnout."

"Oh brother."

"For Christ sakes."

". . . lean and mean . . ."

"What's in it for me?"

"The Shepard *play* or the Shepard account?"

"Rich people with cheap stereos."

"No, girls who *can* hold their liquor."

". . . total lightweight . . ."

"Need a light? Nice matches."

"What's in it for me?"

"yup yup yup yup yup yup . . ."

I think it's me who says, "I have to return some videotapes."

Someone has already taken out a Minolta cellular phone and called for a car, and then, when I'm not really listening, watching instead someone who looks remarkably like Marcus Halberstam paying a check, someone asks, simply, not in relation to anything, "*Why?*" and though I'm very proud that I have cold blood and that I can keep my nerve and do what I'm supposed to do, I catch something, then realize it: *Why?* and automatically answering, out of the blue, for no reason, just opening my mouth, words coming out, summarizing for the idiots: "Well, though I know I should have done *that* instead of not doing it, I'm twenty-seven for Christ sakes and this is, uh, how life presents itself in a bar or in a club in New York, maybe *anywhere*, at the end of the century and how people, you know, *me*, behave, and this is what being *Pat*rick means to me, I guess, so, well, yup, uh . . ." and this is followed by a sigh, then a slight shrug and another sigh, and above one of the doors covered by red velvet drapes in Harry's is a sign and on the sign in letters that match the drapes' color are the words THIS IS NOT AN EXIT.

picador.com

blog
videos
interviews
extracts